90

DEC 1 4 1981

Thayer
    Three women at the waters'
edge

25¢ fine charged
for cards missing
from book pocket

THREE WOMEN
AT THE
WATERS' EDGE

Also by Nancy Thayer

STEPPING

Nancy Thayer

THREE WOMEN AT THE WATERS' EDGE

DOUBLEDAY & COMPANY, INC.
GARDEN CITY, NEW YORK
1981

Lyrics from "If You Remember Me," by Carole Bayer Sager and Marvin Hamlisch Copyright © 1979 by Chappell & Co., Inc., Red Bullet Music, Unichappell Music, Inc., and Begonia Melodies, Inc. Red Bullet Music Administered by Chappell & Co., Inc. Begonia Melodies Administered by Unichappell Music, Inc., throughout the world.
International Copyright Secured
All Rights Reserved
Used by permission.

ISBN: 0-385-17299-0
Library of Congress Catalog Card Number 80-2879
Copyright © 1981 by Nancy Thayer
All Rights Reserved
PRINTED IN THE UNITED STATES OF AMERICA
FIRST EDITION

This book is for my mother *Jane*,
my sister *Martha*, and for *Jean*,
Robb, *Dina*, *Vicki*, *Merry*, *Jill*,
Katherine, and *Miriam*

There is a ship, and it sails the sea,
It's loaded deep, as deep can be.
But not as deep as the love I'm in:
I know not how I sink or swim.

                    Traditional folk song

THREE WOMEN
AT THE
WATERS' EDGE

ONE

◄‹‹◊‹‹◊‹‹◊‹‹◊‹‹◊‹‹◊‹‹◊‹‹◊‹‹◊‹‹◊‹‹◊►

Daisy read what her mother, Margaret Wallace, had written:

"Dearest Daisy,

"I am happier than I have ever been in my life. Oh, darling, of course I was very happy—ecstatic—when you were born, and when Dale was born, but that was such a tired, hot, muddled happiness. This happiness is an energetic sort, completely selfish, clear and pure. If you could see me, how I look now, and my house, this dear house with its windows full of ocean, you would understand. You *should* see me now, my goodness, you should—

"There, darling, I've just written you a check. I'm sure it will be sufficient to cover air fare from Chicago to Vancouver. You really should see Vancouver, you know, and you should get away from your babies and Paul for a while; it would do you good. Just for a few days. Perhaps, if you fly coach instead of first class, my check will cover a baby-sitter's costs, so Paul can't complain about a thing, not a thing. Would you come out? Oh, how I want to share this all with you! There is nothing like it in the world. I feel reborn. I wish I could tell you, *show* you, how happy I am. I am so glad to be divorced and free; and I am so much in love with my new life here in Vancouver. Yes—that's just it —being here is like falling in love, you know that feeling one has that at last, *at last, here it is,* what you have been tending toward all your life, and it is all okay, everything is okay, your entire past life is justified, because it was all leading you to this place. And you can rest. You can rest, and even die, because it has been given to you, it has not been withheld, this total, complete, and completing joy. Bitterness goes away; envy, even desire goes away—except the desire for one more day of this, and then again, one more day. But bitterness falls away, and all the petty unpleasant emotions that used to prickle at one's life, and you are pleasant to everyone, smiling at everyone, because you are here, it has been given to you, you have found it, you are content. Yes, like falling in love, those first dazed and grateful days."

Daisy put her mother's letter down. She couldn't bear to read any more of it right at this moment: *falling in love, dazed and grateful days.* How could her mother *write* such stuff? What did her mother know about falling in love? Falling in love, falling in love—a *pox* on falling in love, and a pox on those who did it. All illusion, falling in love, an illusion which brought a momentary and false joy to two people—and trouble and pain to everyone else.

Paul too said he had fallen in love, and now look how he was, not pleasant, not smiling, not content. No. He was cranky and mean and depressed and confused. She was terrified that Paul would leave her.

Daisy sat up in bed suddenly, meaning to go off to get herself a drink, a scotch and water, a light one. But the movement of pulling herself up into a sitting position made her head spin. She lay back down. She shouldn't drink during the daytime, anyway, especially not now, when she was three months pregnant. It was two o'clock; her rest time. Danny, four years old, was at nursery school until three; Jenny, her two-year-old daughter, was taking a nap in her small pink-and-white bedroom. Daisy had perhaps an hour to lie with her feet up, indulging herself in the luxury of silence. Then Jenny would awake and Danny would come home and they would need walks and snacks and a referee for fights and dinner and bath and a story.

And Paul would be home, roughhousing on the floor with the children, eating his dinner like a cowed slave, never meeting Daisy's eyes. He would pace restlessly about the house, and finally, he would burst out of the house with a desperate, transparent excuse: "I have to mail a letter," "I'm out of shaving cream," "I want to buy a copy of *Newsweek*." He would escape to some pay phone, Daisy knew, to call Monica. He would come home sometimes calmer, sometimes not; sometimes he would go into the bathroom, and run water, and sit on the toilet and cry. She had opened the bathroom door once, not knowing he was in there, thinking that Danny had left the water running. And there he was, Paul, her husband, sitting fully clothed on the toilet, head in his hands, crying with love for another woman. He had flinched when she opened the door, exposing him so suddenly; he had flinched and looked up at her, his blue eyes blazing through his tears, his look so like Danny's when he knew he was being caught at something which deserved a spanking. Guilt, regret, defiance. Damn. Falling in love.

It seemed the baby moved. Daisy put her hand on her slightly rounded stomach, longing to feel that first definite kick. Such subtle joy, a baby inside. She pulled the blue afghan up around her, and her mother's letter, which she had put down on top of it, slid off the bed to the floor.

It was strange how happy Daisy could feel, now with the

world shattering all about her, when she was here, quiet and warm in bed, alone with her third gentle quiet child, so subdued and tantalizing there inside her. It was a true sensual pleasure just to put her feet up. She could feel a release of pressure at the back of her knees, and a firm hard resting where her calves and buttocks touched the bed. Her feet seemed to flow like a river, to glow like fire. Her shoulders and arms cramped and uncramped and the long stretch of her back touching the bed seemed to be the most real thing in her life. Relief. Support of those parts of the body which had been all day long supporting others, other bodies, other things. Sometimes Daisy put a heating pad underneath her on the bed, and the warmth spread into her flesh like soft butter on toast, and how could she not be happy? It was almost an ecstasy, it almost made the rest of the day worthwhile, when this one hour was so delicious.

But she was tired. She was always so tired.

She was not only tired, she was also fat, and she was absorbed by her children, and she was happy. She liked living the life her children demanded, centered around the bedroom and kitchen and playroom where the TV was. Now it was late September, and the weekdays were graced with a loose and lazily pleasurable routine. Daisy would lie in bed as long as she could in the morning—Paul would get up early, too early, at six-thirty, and he wanted only black coffee for breakfast, which she could make the night before and plug into the timer on the stove. He would shower, shave, dress, drink the coffee and leave for work while Daisy still lay sunk in her special early-morning dreams. Daisy would lie in bed as long as she could until the children finally woke her up. Never wanting to leave the warm ease of her bed, the small hot home she had made there under the blankets, she could often entice Danny and Jenny into the bed with her, where she would cuddle them and tell them fairy tales, or play games with them, pulling the sheet and blankets up over their heads, pretending to be caterpillars in a cocoon, or bears in a cave. It was dim and stuffy and hot and crowded under the sheets, close and satisfying. Finally everyone would get bored, though, and they would throw back the covers and leave the bed for the rest of the world. The bed when they left it would look like a shattered boat, abandoned on the bright rocks of day-time, wrecked and unappealing.

Still in her long wide Lanz nightgown, as old and com-fortable as her skin, Daisy would send Danny and Jenny in to watch TV while she fixed breakfast. She made enor-mous sweet first meals: pancakes with maple syrup and butter, or hot oatmeal with butter and brown sugar, or eggs and toast with butter and thick layers of raspberry jam. Daisy drank more milk than Danny and Jenny, more juice, too; after all, she was pregnant. She usually left the plates and glasses on the breakfast table, so that she could watch "Captain Kangaroo" with the children.

The children loved Captain Kangaroo, but Daisy loved him even more than they did. She would sink into an armchair with a cup of sweet and creamy coffee steaming in her hands, and Danny and Jenny would spread out on the floor or on the old grimy child-worn sofa, and they would spend another perfectly contented hour together. They were all heartbroken if they somehow missed the singing introduction to the show. It was the best part; it made them all happy; it made Daisy irrationally happy, and gay as if at a wonderful party, and full of love for the entire world, to see and hear the introduction to "Captain Kangaroo." "Good morning, Captain!" everyone sang. She loved seeing all the actors and celebrities as they said their idiosyncratic and cheerful good mornings, and she loved best the last of the introduction: always, something you could count on, Captain Kangaroo himself, wishing his au-dience a good morning. He wore bangs, and he never had a cold or bags under his eyes. She loved him. There was something of Santa Claus about him—plump face, red coat, love of children, magic winks, sexlessness. He was diverting and clever and familiar and kind. He was unique and reassuring: he did not ask for involvement as so many of the other children's shows did, he didn't throw in any sappy psychology to help you like yourself more, he wasn't a goody-goody. He was really like an elf or a gnome; it was impossible to believe that he would ever die; yet somehow fitting that he should grow old. He was not a part of the real world. He was special. Daisy could not believe, grown-up as she was, that there was not in fact a man who was named Captain Kangaroo; that an actor ever took off the red coat and left the pink house and walked the mortal city streets.

"Parents, spend a little time with your children today," Captain Kangaroo would always say sometime during the show. It was his only request, and it seemed a reasonable one, and it showed that he knew, he knew, that the grown-ups were watching.

"You're right, Captain, I will," Daisy would think. She would stack the dishes in the dishwasher while a commercial or "Dancing Bear" was on, sometimes stopping in the midst of her work to run back to the playroom when Danny cried, "Mommy, Mommy, 'Uncle Backwards' is on!" After giving the kitchen table an irresolute swipe, she would begin the hardest part of the day: taking the children out for fresh air. In warm weather it was a lovely thing to do, but now in the fall it seemed a backbreaking task. Jenny was too little to get herself dressed in her cumbersome sweater or coat, and even Danny needed help, with boots, mittens, hat, muffler. When the weather was warm, they went down the hill to the beach to play in the sand or to see what new things had happened to the long curved shore of the lake. But when the brisk autumn breeze came sweeping up off the lake they had to stay close to the house. Danny would ride his bike on the driveway and Daisy would push Jenny on the swing or help her steer her little plastic pedal cart, or they would all play running games. Finally someone, usually Jenny, would complain of the cold. They would go back into the house and play with modeling clay, or paint, or build with plastic building bricks, or play house, or something, something. There were no children in the neighborhood around them—one of the disadvantages of owning a large expensive home in an older area—so Daisy felt it her duty to entertain the children. Usually she could get them to play nicely with each other or by themselves for fifteen minutes here and there so that she could do the laundry, vacuum, dust, clean out the re- frigerator, start a cake, anything that could be begun and not instantly finished. Finally she would fix lunch, and an- other mother would come by and honk in the driveway and Danny would go off to preschool, and Daisy would put Jenny down for her nap. Jenny was a good child, reliable; she always slept for at least two hours. For the first hour Daisy would do housework. Laundry, folding clothes and putting them away, ironing. Once a week, sweeping and scrubbing and waxing the large kitchen floor. Wiping sticky fingerprints off the high chair, the table, the counters, the cupboard doors in the kitchen. Cleaning the toilets and bathtubs and bathroom walls, cleaning the bathroom sink where Paul's mustache trimmings lay like small blond bugs, and the soap dish was soggy and streaked from the children. It was a large house; they had wanted a large house; they had been delighted to find this house, on the lake, huge and rambling, with lots of angles and land- ings and elaborate woodwork. But they could afford only the mortgage on the large, interesting house, and had no money left over to pay for a woman to help dust the interesting, elaborate woodwork or to shine the leaded glass. Daisy did this while Jenny slept.

She often felt that if she had to fill out a form which asked for her occupation, she would put down: Mover. For that was what much of her work consisted of—moving: moving dusty socks and underwear from under beds where the small cotton articles hid like shy white mice, moving them from under the beds into the laundry chute, then into the appropriate laundry pile, then into the washing machine, into the dryer, onto the table to be folded, and finally back upstairs to the proper drawer, where they would lie obediently until someone else would take them out and wear them and take them off, dropping them somewhere else: perhaps under the sofa in the TV room. She moved dishes and pots and pans to the table and stove and back to the sink and down to the dishwasher and up to their shelves and back to the table and stove again. She moved infinite numbers of miniscule objects: blue plastic barrettes shaped like bows or ducks, tiny orange sticks belonging to the Tinkertoy set or even smaller white plastic squares with bumps on the bottom belonging to the Lego building set, pens, books, papers, paperclips, fingernail clippers, broken Crayolas, cufflinks, old crumpled Klee-nexes, ugly hard forgotten pieces of cookie, diapers, doll socks, screwdrivers, pennies, petrified pieces of old bubble gum, telephone books, newspapers, magazines, mail, small smeary tubes of ChapStick, bottles of cough medicine and sticky spoons, the Scotch tape holder, rubber bands, twist ties, bits of string, Matchbox cars, doll aprons, shoelaces, puzzle pieces, bills, business cards. She moved things from wherever they didn't belong to where they did. She moved groceries from their store shelves into the car, out of the car onto the kitchen counters, into their proper storage places, out again to be cooked or sliced and eaten, and some of it into the garbage disposer, and some of it, bones and eggshells, into trash sacks and out into the trash barrels, and down the driveway to the edge of the curb. She swept the back hall and steps to the basement where the laundry room was. She swept under the kitchen table. They had a cat and loved her; she shed fine white hairs everywhere; these gathered into clumps on the bottom of the broom or stuck to the broken halves of jelly beans which Daisy dug out from under the sofa cushions. Sometimes, if the job was a big one, such as cleaning the stove and cleaning off the burners and lining the little pans with aluminum foil, or baking her own bread or a cake or pie for a dinner party they were having over the weekend, sometimes then Daisy worked all afternoon, and did not take her rest. But because her physician had told her that she *had* to rest, she *needed* to rest, that because she was pregnant and had two small children, she must think of rest as a medicine and take it regularly, because of the backing of that particular outside authority, she usually did spend the last hour of Jenny's naptime resting.

As she was resting now.

It was not a hard or difficult life. She did not dislike it. It made her happy because she had decided to let it make her happy for a while; it would not have suited her permanently, but temporarily it was fine. She was capable of doing it all with good humor and even grace, even though sometimes while she rested she cried with exhaustion. Each day the simple lovely pleasure of lifting Jenny, damp and clinging, from her crib, made Daisy's shoulders and back ache and cramp, as if this simple act which she loved were for her dumb body a sort of torture.

At three-fifteen, the other mother would drop Danny off; he would come running into the house to hand her a splotchy bright painting or some crafted item made from straws or dried beans. Sometimes, if necessary, Daisy took them then to get groceries, or new rain boots, or vacuum cleaner bags or dry cleaning, or a birthday card or gift; there was always an errand to do. Sometimes, once or twice a week, Daisy took them to a friend's house, and she would sit with the other mother and drink coffee or diet soda and laugh, while the children played. Tuesdays she took them to Storytime at the library. Around four-thirty or five, she would come home and put the children in front of the television, and she would fix dinner, and give the children baths and read them stories and finally, with a heroic attempt to be nice about it all, she would put them to bed. Most nights she carried it off pleasantly enough, but some nights, when Jenny asked for more water, more water, and Danny whined, "But I'm not tired, I don't want to go to bed yet, you don't love me, why won't you read me another story, scratch my back," sometimes then she shouted at the children. The tears came easily. If Paul were home, he might come up and look at her in amazement, as if she had gone mad and were doing something insane in front of the children, and he would talk to Danny in an adult and calm and reasonable voice, the voice of a *good* parent. Then Daisy would slink off into the bathroom, to soak in a tub of bath water so hot that she came out with parched and reddened skin.

Saturdays Danny did not have school, and she took the children with her to get the bulk of the week's groceries. Perhaps there was a birthday party then, or an afternoon children's movie, or a trip to the zoo or museum, or a visit to a friend. Sundays there was church, and Paul would be home so she did not clean house; then they tried to do something together as a family. Sundays were usually long and unsuccessful days.

It was a good enough life for a while, especially if you could indulge yourself as Daisy did in chocolates with cherry or marshmallow centers, and novels with heroines who had no husbands, no children, usually not even a house that required dusting. There were other, sensual pleasures: holding and handling the children, even changing Jenny's diaper, and bending down to bite her fat thigh; drinking coffee with a friend; lying down in a warm bed in a quiet room.

It was not, however, a very romantic life. Daisy knew she had grown unappealing, especially to Paul. Her body had changed; even if she saw it as temporary, certainly it was a grotesque change. And her cheerful energetic morning self was something Paul rarely saw—he was usually gone then, and so saw her mostly in the dragging, ragged evenings when she cursed and whined with fatigue. She did not want Paul in bed with her much anymore; the more sensual pleasure was in not touching anyone, in lying perfectly still, tending to no one else's needs—this was now more satisfying than the pleasure of stroking skin, fitting Paul's body to hers. She saw what she was doing and could understand, finally, why Paul would want to have an affair, play around with someone else for a while. She was betraying him a bit, but it was for the children; it was, therefore, okay if he betrayed her a bit, for a sexy young girl.

But to fall in love with the girl, to pine and weep over her, to want to leave his wife and children so that he could live with her, to make it seem that all of Daisy's past and present life was without meaning—that was unforgivable, an inordinate betrayal. It was a violation of the flexible laws of their love. It was a wound, a tear, in the fabric of their lives. It was monumentally unfair.

The best way Daisy could think to handle it was to ignore it, to pretend it wasn't there. For the past few weeks, she had simply gone on ignoring it, she had been living in a false world. She knew it was a false world, she knew she was purposefully avoiding unchangeable, unbearable facts. She thought of the story by Isak Dinesen in *Winter's Tales* where Peter and Rosa, two young lovers, are swept away from the mainland into the sea on a great sheet of ice. That was what was happening to her, except that unlike faithful Peter, Paul had jumped off, had made it safely to shore, in fact had given the crucial push to the ice sheet that set it off on its way toward doom; and there she was, Daisy, stranded on a sheet of ice, unlike Rosa, without a lover; instead with her two small and completely dependent children. Dinesen's tale had ended beautifully, in a bursting, a sinking, of true love and passion: the two lovers drowned in each other's arms. The story ended, saying, "The current was strong; they were swept down, in each other's arms, in a few seconds." But Daisy had only the children to hold in her arms, and she certainly didn't want all of them to be swept down into a cold lonely sea. Dear God, who could face a future like that? It didn't bear thinking of. So, she did not think of it.

She did not think of it, she would not talk of it. Paul paced, he stormed from the house, he did not make love to her or touch her, he sat in the bathroom and cried. She could see sometimes in his eyes that he wanted to kill her, or at least to shake her and shake her until she agreed to at least listen, and talk, and be reasonable, and say yes, all right, I'll give you a divorce. Sometimes when she sat in a hot bathtub late at night, sipping tea from a blue plastic cup (so that if she dropped it in the tub it could not break into tiny shards of glass that could cut her or the children's feet), sometimes she thought about it this way: What kind of man would leave a woman who has borne two of his children and is about to bear a third? What kind of man would leave his family? A bad man, that's what kind. And Paul was basically a good man, and wanted to be a good man. So by denying his insane pleas, by refusing to even hear them, she was protecting him from changing from a good man to a bad one. Later he would even thank her.

But even as she thought it, as she was pulling her

weighty body out of the bathtub, she knew that she was wrong. Thoughts like that, which soothed her and made her feel secure, evaporated like the steam that clouded the bathroom mirror.

And today, resting in bed, under her blue afghan with her mother's letter lying unread on the carpet beside the bed, Daisy was frightened. Through the comfort came the fear. She could not lie still, she twisted this way and that in bed, and the covers pulled away, and she kept getting cold.

Paul was taking her out to dinner tonight. He had arranged for the babysitter all by himself, something he had never done before. The dinner was entirely his idea. He had said, "Daisy, I've arranged for Barbara to come over tonight. I'm taking you out to dinner. Can you be ready at seven?" For one wild moment, Daisy had burned with hope. He was taking her out to dinner, he wanted to start all over again, he loved her after all!

"Why, yes," she said, smiling at him. "What a good idea!" She thought: her red maternity dress, she would wear that, it always made her look sexy because it had a plunging neckline that flattered her large breasts, and her tummy wouldn't show at all: the sight of her in the dress, the red silky fabric against her white skin, flashed before her eyes. So she did not right away read the message in Paul's eyes, in the taut lines of his face.

"Okay, then," he said, and went out the front door.

It had been seven forty-five in the morning; Daisy had just gotten out of bed and was moving around slowly in her shapeless warm old robe. Her hair was mussed, of course, she had been sleeping; she had not washed her face yet or brushed her teeth, because she had been awakened by Jenny, who had soiled her diaper and needed changing. Daisy had slowly gone down the stairs, holding Jenny in her arms for the pleasure of it, smooching Jenny's soft sleep-warmed skin. She stopped at the bottom of the stairs and awkwardly bent to put Jenny down; it was just beginning to be difficult for her to bend gracefully at the waist. Straightening up, she saw Paul standing there, by the front door, hand on the doorknob, looking at her with realistic eyes. He looked wonderful: clean, fresh, shaven, well dressed, young, firm, proud. His expensive aftershave spangled the air between them. She was aware, too, of what she looked like: something the children were comfortable with, a warm, loving sloven of a woman, as lazy and plump as pillows.

And he had said he was taking her out to dinner, and she had smiled, her body startled awake with hope, and he had looked at her, and left, and by the time he had gone out the door the vision of herself in her red maternity dress had vanished and she could tell by the way the door closed so firmly in Paul's retreating hand that the end of the day was something she should fear.

What could she do about it? She really did not know. Even if she got out of bed and got a sitter and went to a beauty shop and had her hair done and her face made up and her nails manicured, that still would not change things. It was possible that nothing could change things; it had all been going on too long. Paul had loved her six years ago when they were married, she was sure of that. And she had loved him.

They had met in Chicago, where she was finishing her B.A. degree and wondering what on earth to do next with her life, and he was finishing his M.A. degree in business administration. It had been at a huge drunken party where they both had other dates that they first saw each other, and although they spoke to each other only briefly, the meeting had been so intense that the next day Paul had called her, and taken her out for pizza that night, and they had slept with each other immediately, knowing each other only twenty-four hours: it had been like that. Chemistry.

Now when Daisy looked back at it all, she sometimes thought that it had all been evolutionary, that Danny and Jenny and this new evolving child were the cause of her passion for Paul, and his passion for her, rather than the effect. They had wanted to be born, these children, or nature had wanted them born, and so Daisy and Paul had come together, each of them a tiny helpless stick of steel jumping together at a magnet's pull. How else could it be explained? They did not know each other very well, and had different values, but in the face of their sexual passion, that hardly mattered. And Paul had been impressed with Daisy because she was tall and had what he considered a "classy" look, and he had been even more impressed because her father was a physician, a wealthy, important burgher of a physician. Paul's own family was poor and insignificant. Daisy had simply thought that what had happened was the way of the world, was fate. She had wondered what to do with her life, having no strong desires or goals of her own, and here was Paul, coming along almost predictably; she had known she would get married sometime.

The party they had met at had been in the spring. By August they had married and rented an apartment; Paul had finished his master's degree and had been given a very good executive job at a large manufacturing company in Milwaukee. Daisy's parents gave them a large check, because Paul and Daisy had wanted money instead of a large, expensive wedding. They had not really had a honeymoon at all, but hadn't minded. They felt that they were on their way somewhere, and would not have enjoyed a pause. Daisy found a good secretarial position, and on weekends learned how to make cassoulet, beef Wellington, crepes, Doboschtorte, strong highballs, and champagne punch; they had many successful parties that were a completely different sort of enterprise than the beer-and-wine parties at the university. Paul was looked upon with great favor by his company, and he should have been, because he worked so very hard, into the nights, on the weekends, on holidays. He loved it. They saved a lot of money. Paul wanted to be wealthy and stable; Daisy wanted whatever Paul wanted. Many nights during those first two years they had been simply too tired to make love, but when they did it was with their usual greedy and generous passion. And so of course, after a while, in spite of calendars and devices, Daisy got pregnant.

She had thought that was a natural, inevitable part of their fate. Paul had disagreed. Their first real fights began.

It was possible that their marriage had begun to end then, with Danny the size of a freckle inside Daisy, and Daisy sitting on their living-room sofa wearing lavender eye shadow and a see-through blouse, because she was making it an occasion to tell Paul, and Paul doing something Daisy had before seen only as a word in a book: blenching. He shrank away, he went white, he looked sick, he looked scared. Daisy's beef Stroganoff sat unstirred in the kitchen, unnoticed, growing dry and cold.

"I'm not ready for children yet," Paul had said. "I don't want the responsibility. I don't want the expense."

Daisy had argued that if she had the baby now (while she was young and healthy), she could go back to work seriously, permanently, in only five years, when the child was in school, but if they put it off, it would interrupt whatever job or career she had for herself, so it would be more economical in the long run to have the baby now and get it over with. And, she argued, stressing this point, if they had a baby, Paul's employers would feel that he was a more settled and respectable person, a family man, with real responsibilities; they would probably give him a raise, they would feel they could trust him. Being a father would make him look stable, solid. Besides, Daisy added, a baby would not cost all that much, would not change their lives all that much. She could probably even continue working part time. Daisy was secretly surprised at her ingenuity at coming up with so many reasons for protecting what was still only a gathering of molecules.

After Danny was born, she could not remember how Paul had not wanted him; if asked, she would have said in all honesty that Paul had wanted the baby, too, right from the start. And she had been right about Paul's employers; they were pleased by his fatherhood, they did advance his position, they did give him a raise. In the first two years of Danny's life, Daisy was so wrapped up with the child that Paul had time and energy to work even harder, and so he was given better positions, more raises, he was a golden boy. When Daisy found out she was pregnant with Jenny—an act she had committed without really consulting Paul, but she felt sure Paul wouldn't want Danny to be an only child—they had bought a house.

The house was a large, aging Tudor full of drafts and gracious lines. Its best point was that it was "on the lake," which Paul thought would impress people, and which Daisy thought would make her eternally happy. Going through the empty, echoing house together with the real estate agent, Daisy had looked past the weathered wooden windowsills out at the expansive sheen of blue lake. It seemed so large, so endless, more like an ocean; Lake Michigan was, after all, 80 miles across and 300 miles long. And the back of the land sloped gently down to a small sandy beach. It would be heaven, Daisy thought, for the children.

They could not really afford the house. It cost too much money. But it was so imposing, with its steep slate roof and weighty oak front door, so solid, that Paul felt it suited him, and after that no other houses seemed appealing. They borrowed a little money from Daisy's parents, and used up all their savings toward a down payment, and took

out a large mortgage. They didn't have a penny left over
for repairs or decorating; they scarcely had enough to eat.
So Daisy spent six months working on the house: stripping
old, peeling paint off the woodwork, painting, hanging
wallpaper, sewing curtains and drapes, even hammering
loose doorframes back to security, screwing brass door-
knobs on tightly. She did not work as a secretary anymore,
she brought no money in, but she did work like crazy in
the house. Whenever she wasn't cooking or taking care of
Danny, she was working on the house. She didn't nap, she
didn't read books or magazines, she didn't sit and chat
with friends. If they wanted to see her, they had to come to
the house, and sit on the floor with a scarf on their heads
to keep sawdust or paint out of their hair, and talk to her
as she worked.

Daisy thought at the time, and it was probably true, that
Paul did not appreciate the work she did. He would go off
in the morning, and make money, and come back in the
evening; and perhaps an entire double casement window,
with its strips of wood separating the diamond-shaped
panes, would have been perfectly, painstakingly painted.
Because he never did any of the painting, he did not understand what an achievement that was. He usually said something appropriately complimentary, but he felt that of
course Daisy was only doing her job as wife. He was doing
his job, she was doing hers. When most of the work was
done on the house, they threw a large party—Daisy wore
her sexy red maternity dress—and invited all their friends
and acquaintances from Paul's company. The purpose of
the party was not purely exhibitory. It really was a party, a
fete, a celebration. Paul felt he had finally achieved stability, as represented by the house; stability, respectability, a
kind of worthiness. It was symbolic, for him, the house; a
goal, a milestone, a marker in his life. Of course, because it
was that for him, a marker, he could pass it by once he had

attained it, he could leave it behind. While for Daisy the house was not a symbol. For Daisy it was real, a home, a place to live in and keep and know; it was a shelter of large and graceful rooms which would be part of her and her children's lives.

After Daisy gave birth to Jenny, and Paul got another raise, and they were able to breathe a little easier, they could have babysitters in, go to movies, have dinner parties more often, because now they could afford suitable food. So when the house was finally finished, more or less, Paul wanted Daisy to go back to work. But Daisy didn't want to. She wanted to stay home and take care of her beautiful new house, she wanted to stay home and take care of her beautiful new children. The idea of leaving the house and dropping Danny and Jenny off with some strange person while she sat in a gray office and typed seemed totally unappealing. So she argued: the cost of transportation and child care would take up the greater part of her salary. Again she was ingenious; she added that if she went out to work she would have to buy new, appropriate clothes; *that*, alone, would use up the first few months' gain. Since Danny's birth, she had stopped buying good clothes, which among other things required a good figure, and had gone about quite happily in jeans and large soft old shirts that had once been Paul's. Paul, on the other hand, because he had to appear well dressed, spent a great deal of money on clothes, and had become almost vain. In any cast, he certainly loved clothes, loved adorning himself; and it was even possible that he liked looking better than Daisy. He agreed with Daisy, finally: she should stay home and take care of the children, at least for a while longer. And he realized that the elegant dinners she prepared for his colleagues took up a great deal of time, and planning and work. So Daisy did stay home, and she kept the house clean and attractive, and planted graceful flower gardens.

She looked stunning at their parties (if a bit plump), and sloppy the rest of the time, with little bits of gnawed food stuck on the back of her shirts where Jenny had spit past the diaper or towel, and brown crusts which could have been dirt or mucus on her jeans, just at child height. In spite of her happiness, she was often tired, and grew to treasure the hours between eight and ten in the evening as her private time to relax, alone, to watch TV, or to soak in a hot tub with a good novel. And before long, she was accidentally pregnant again, and pleased about it.

That was when they had another fight. Paul wanted Daisy to have an abortion. Already they were facing the costs of preschool for Danny, and the doctor bills were incredible, and the mortgage consumed Paul's salary, and they could not afford another child. He wanted Daisy to have an abortion. Daisy wanted the baby. She screamed that it was her baby, her body, she would not kill her child, she would not have her body violated. And because the baby was in her body, she won: Paul could not, after all, drag her off by her hair to an abortionist. But he told her he hated her; he told her he would hate the new child. She told him that she didn't care: already she loved the new baby more than she loved Paul.

They had stared at each other then, amazed to have shouted out such things, things they had not as yet even whispered to themselves.

Paul had left the room and the house; of course he could, he did not have to remain to take care of the children. Daisy had fixed herself a drink, and cried, and called a friend, and with the help of the drink and the friend had cheered up; decided that all married couples have such fights when faced with such decisions. It was like giving birth; you had to go through a period of pain and tribulation in order to have a new life. She fixed a good dinner for them that night, and tried to be pleasant to Paul when he returned. She thought that nothing had really changed. But she was wrong. Everything had.

So now here she was, alone in bed in the afternoon, full of fear. She was not a stupid or shallow woman. She had simply made two mistakes that she knew of: doing what she wanted to do, and misjudging another person. Most people make those mistakes more than once in the course of their lives. She knew that it was not Paul she loved, not any longer; it was *being married* she loved. The thought of not having a *daddy* in the home filled her with a primitive desperation. What could she do, what could she do! Her children needed a father. She felt she was doing all she reasonably could: she had said to Paul, often, during the fights that sprang up between them if they were alone together for any length of time, that he could have his lover, he could go places with another woman, he could sleep with her all he wanted, and she wouldn't make a fuss—as long as he remained Daisy's husband, and their children's father. Other women, she had said, would have wanted him to give up the girl, but she was not asking that of him. She was being as generous and open-minded as she could. *Think of your employers*, she had said, *what would they think if you left your wife and three babies to go off with a young woman like Monica? Think about that.* What can I do? she had even asked, what can I do to make you happy within our marriage, what else can I do? Tell me and I'll try.

She had seen Monica, several times. The girl was a reporter for a local paper with a liberal, almost socialistic bent. Her family was wealthy; Monica wore horn-rimmed glasses and chewed gum and was interested in social welfare. Paul, who was just learning that a wealthy liberal is usually more classy than a wealthy conservative, thought Monica very classy indeed. And it was true: she was thin while Daisy was fat, and chic and breezy while Daisy was

slack and slow, and quick to impressive righteous indigna-
tion while Daisy was quick to yawn or laugh. There could
be no doubt that she was better in bed than Daisy was;
Daisy didn't care much about that anymore. Monica's conversation was surely better, too. And it was even probably
true that she loved Paul much more than Daisy did. One
of the times Daisy had seen Monica, Daisy had been coming out of a jeweler's; she had just bought a silver comb
and brush for a friend's new baby. She had left her own
children with a babysitter that afternoon, but still had
them on her mind: she wanted to stop by a department
store and buy Danny some new socks and Jenny some
more rubber pants, and she would surprise her children
with a new toy: a turtle they had been wanting, that
chimed when you pulled its string. Well, she had come out
of the jeweler's, feeling happy, with the new baby present
in its white-and-silver wrapping filling her hands, and the
thought of the children's faces when they saw the turtle
filling her thoughts, and there, right across the street, she
saw Paul and Monica come out of a restaurant.

Monica was wearing sexy high boots—Daisy felt she
would have tripped and fallen and probably killed herself
wearing such boots—and a long floppy brown sweater that
on Daisy would have sloped and clung. Her hips looked
smaller than Daisy's nonpregnant waist. Daisy stood absolutely still on the pavement, staring at the girl; Paul didn't
interest her, she knew what he looked like. It was this girl
who fascinated Daisy. And she saw the girl smile at something Paul said to her, and reach up in an impetuous
rush to kiss Paul's mouth, right there in public. She looked
like such a happy girl, so happy to be there with that man,
so obviously in love, it made people watching smile to see.
Even Daisy smiled. She recognized the sweet rush of adora-
tion that had to be expressed by touching; but in her case,

she realized, she now always reached down, not up—down to the short squirmy bodies of her son and daughter.

Paul and Monica walked off, arm in arm, oblivious of Daisy's stunned observation, and Daisy watched them go, thinking how happy the two people were, and how she would not want Paul to not have that. Who would want to take such a thing away from anyone, it was so rare. She thought that if she could generously, honestly want that for Paul, why couldn't he also want happiness for her?

But the trouble was, Daisy thought, that Paul didn't care what Daisy wanted anymore; he had gone past that. He had come to regard Daisy as the enemy; he wanted to escape her, or to obliterate her.

And he did not love the children, either, they both knew that. Well, he had never been around them much, had seldom held them, and it's hard to love something one doesn't know. Daisy had wanted Paul to be there at Danny's birth, she had begged him to take part in the natural childbirth classes and in the delivery. But Paul had thrown up in the delivery room; it was not the sight of Daisy's pain that nauseated him, but the shock of blood and excrement oozing from between her long slim legs. When Jenny was born, Daisy asked one of her best woman friends to come hold her hand and count and coach her, while Paul went to the friend's husband's house to drink; Danny stayed with a sitter. So, Daisy thought, she wouldn't miss him, then, when the new child was born.

But DAMN HIM! How could he leave his family, how could he leave a child he hadn't even seen? Was he mad? Was he insane? Hardhearted? He had had some tenderness in him once. Didn't his overwhelming love for Monica leave anything for his own family?

Daisy twisted again, and the afghan fell off onto the floor. She shivered, and wiped her tears onto the pillowcase. It was almost three o'clock, she ought to get up, she ought to do something. She wished she could call her mother and ask her what to do, but recently her mother had changed so dramatically that Daisy was not sure of her response, and she couldn't face a new weird mother on top of everything else. So Daisy could only sigh and get up. She smoothed the bed, picked up the afghan, gathered together the sheets of her mother's letter, and laid them on the bedside table. She heard her friend's car in the driveway, and looked out the window at her son running up the walk to the door, and was filled with a wonderful love. She could not believe it—that little boy, so full of grace, was something she had made in her body. She smiled with anticipation at how she would hug him when he came in the door, at how she would see him smile.

"Let's not talk about anything serious," Paul had said that night as he helped Daisy get into her chair at the restaurant. "Let's just enjoy our meal, and have our talk over coffee."

Daisy blithely agreed, although, looking back at it, she saw that she should have guessed by those very words what was coming. But it's hard not to have hope at even the most difficult times. And then, would anything have been gained if she had let herself worry throughout the meal? It was such an excellent meal. She hadn't been to such a fine restaurant in months, why should she have spoiled the occasion? It would not have changed a thing.

So she ate crusty French onion soup, and duck, sweet with cherries and wine, and a sharp salad full of oily smooth avocados and a creamy mocha dessert.

"Why not have an Irish coffee?" Paul asked Daisy, and she agreed, already blurry and agreeable from all the wine.

Paul seemed to have been pacing himself: as the Irish coffee was set on the table, he began to talk. He put his elbows on the table, and clasped his coffee cup in both hands, and did not attempt to be subtle.

"I've had a good offer from a firm based in Los Angeles," he said. "It's a good position, with a chance for advancement. I could make a lot of money."

Daisy thought: No. I don't want to move. I don't want to leave my house, the lake.

"I want to take the job," Paul said, without waiting for Daisy to speak. "I want to take the job, and I want to marry Monica. I've talked to a lawyer. There's a new divorce law in Wisconsin. All I have to do is claim irretrievable breakdown of our marriage, and the divorce is granted. There's not a thing you can do about it. I'm going to get a divorce. If you'll be decent about it, I'll be as generous as I can with money, and I'll be nice to the children. But if you fight me over this, if you get nasty, I'll be nasty right back. I'll be a bastard about money, and I'll be a bastard to the children. I won't come to see them, I won't remember their birthdays, I'll hit them."

Daisy stared at her husband. Her entire body curled backward from him, sick with distaste. "My God," she said.

"I'm desperate," Paul said.

"You are contemptible," Daisy said.

"So are you," Paul replied.

"My father was right about you," Daisy said then, in a whisper of amazement, talking more to herself than to Paul.

"What do you mean?" Paul said. "What did your father say?" It was one of his most vulnerable points; he idolized Daisy's father, and wanted to be liked by him.

Daisy smiled, confident of her father's protection. "I don't dare tell you," she said. "You might accuse me of not being decent to you, you might walk in the house and hit Danny."

To her surprise, tears came into Paul's eyes and his voice went mushy. "Daisy, please," he said. "I told you I'm desperate. I'm trying to play the heavy, anything, to make you let me go. I don't want to hit the children."

"Why can't you stay married to me, remain a father to your children, and have your sweetie on the side?" Daisy asked. Something had happened; the worst moment was over; she began to sip her Irish coffee.

"Because I don't love you. I can't bear to look at you. You used to be beautiful; now you're not. You don't interest me. There's just nothing there for me. I don't enjoy life with you. I am not interested in anything you're interested in. When I was sitting at that parent-teacher meeting for Danny's preschool, I thought I'd get sick or start tearing my hair, and you were so happy, making suggestions, really caring. The life you want is just not the life I want. I want to live with Monica; I want to eat elegant meals every night without children whining and interrupting, I want to be free to go out on the spur of the moment or to lie in bed screwing all Sunday morning, or to sleep all night long without some kid wailing. I want to be selfish."

"So what will you do if Monica gets pregnant?" Daisy said. "She's young. Accidents happen. Will you leave her then, too?"

"I'm going to get a vasectomy," Paul said. "And Monica's getting her tubes tied. There is no way we will have children in our lives. Although she's perfectly willing to be agreeable to Danny and Jenny and the new baby whenever they come to visit," he added.

Daisy stared at him over the rim of her glass. How completely Paul had planned his new life. Monica was even willing to be *agreeable* to the children! An urge moved through Daisy: covertly she looked about the table, searching for something hot and peppery, or oily and sharp with onions, to throw in Paul's face. But the table had been cleared, had even been brushed clean of crumbs. There was only the expanse of white linen, and the water glasses, and Paul's cup, and her own Irish coffee, which tasted too good to be thrown away. It occurred to Daisy that there was not very much left she could do about the situation. It occurred to her that Paul had become the sort of person she did not like, would not even have wanted to know. And perhaps she had gotten what she wanted from him, the lovely children, the good house. She did not need to keep him around, as he was, as a father; his genes might be okay, because he was tall and good-looking, but perhaps it would be best if his influence ended right there.

"Well," Paul said impatiently. "Well?"

Yet she did not want to admit this. She did not want to give in too easily. She was afraid, of vague things she could not even name. She felt that now she still somehow had the upper hand, and she was not willing to relinquish it, not when she was so unsure of the rules of the game, of the game itself. She hesitated. She stared at Paul, seeing a handsome man just past thirty, who had a neatly trimmed mustache riding a voluptuous mouth, and eyes as hard as— as what? His heart?

"You bastard," she said calmly. "You bastard."

To her awe and consternation, Paul burst into tears, right there in the restaurant. "Oh, *Jesus*, Daisy, *come on*," he said. "Why are you doing this? You don't love me anymore. You haven't loved me for a long time. You haven't wanted me to touch you for *years*. You've detested me because I've scrambled to make money, because I haven't gotten rich in the offhanded, altruistic, quiet way your father has. Yet you've been quick enough to want all the things that take money: the house, Montessori for the children. Somewhere along the way you stopped seeing *me*; the only time I please you is when I'm doing something with or for the children. How in the world can you want me to live with you? Can't you be generous? Can't you be kind? You have so much—you love the children, and they love you. Won't you let me go off somewhere so I can be loved, too?"

At the end of this speech, Paul did an incredible thing: he blew his nose in the restaurant's white linen napkin. It made Daisy laugh, and she sat there, knowing she felt silly because she was slightly drunk, and aware that she could say something snide and cutting now. But Paul's head was bent as he blew his nose and wiped his tears on the napkin, and across his white forehead a speckling of red appeared: the same nervous rash that broke out on Danny and Jenny's foreheads when they were sad and upset. So because for a moment he was vulnerable, and reminded her of a child, and reminded her that he could feel enough pain to cry in public and that she was, as she was with her children, the only person in the world who could stop the tears and end the pain, because of all that, the child's rash on the grown man's forehead, Daisy said, "Okay, Paul." She reached across the table and stroked his forehead lightly with her long fingers. Her pain would come later, she knew, when no one was there to stroke her. "Okay, Paul," she repeated. "Okay. It's all right. Okay."

Later that night, much later, Daisy lay alone in bed again, propped up on pillows, drinking brandy from a large snifter, feeling extremely drunk and somehow queenly. With a gesture of her hand, she could dispense favors. "And to you, I grant complete freedom." She was enormous in her majesty. The brandy in her hand looked like liquid gold. Paul was sleeping in the guest room, so Daisy had the entire double bed to herself, and she sat right in the middle of it with the blue satin comforter spread out over her knees and the rest of the bed like a realm. The house was very quiet; it was after twelve. At the restaurant, Paul had quickly calmed down and begun to discuss the concrete details of their divorce: how soon he could get it, whom he would use as a lawyer, whom she would use as a lawyer, that he would move out of the house and to Monica's as soon as possible.

"I think I need another drink," Daisy had said.

Insulated by the liquor, another Irish coffee, and then another, she said very little and nodded her head to everything Paul said. I may never see this man naked again, she was thinking inanely, I may never again see this man's penis. I know the shape of his chest, where his birthmarks are, I know about the peculiar toenail on the little toe of his left foot. All these are things I will never see again. Not that I've seen all that much of them recently, his body is not one I've held very much in the past few years. Take your weird toenail and go, Paul, who cares, who cares. I'm too drunk to care.

"Daisy," Paul said, "are you listening?"

She was beginning to be overcome by a great drunken weariness. "I'm listening, Paul," she said. "I'm hearing every word you're saying." But by the time they were ready to leave she was thinking: who is this stranger, why is he telling me all these things, what does it matter to me?

So they rode home in silence. Daisy's head fell back against the headrest and she dozed as Paul drove. They walked into the house, said ordinary normal words to the babysitter—it really was curious how normal they could act in front of such an audience, a fourteen-year-old girl—and Paul drove the babysitter home. He was a very long time doing it; Daisy suspected in a dull way that he had stopped somewhere to call Monica, to tell her that the evening had been a success.

When he returned, he came into the bedroom, took his pajamas from the drawer, and said, "I'll sleep in the guest room tonight."

"Oh," said Daisy, who had brushed her teeth and

washed her face and was beginning to wake up. This announcement seemed to bother her greatly, in an obscure way, and because she felt she was on the verge of feeling, she hurried downstairs in the dark and poured herself a water glass full of brandy. She drank some of it right away, in great burning swallows, then said out loud to herself, "What am I doing standing down here drinking in the dark?" She went back upstairs. The children were sleeping beautifully in their rooms; Paul had gone into the guest room and shut the door tightly.

"Oh, well," Daisy said to the door, and drank some more.

She went to the bedroom—her bedroom now—and put two pillows in the very middle of the bed, and settled down against them. She sat and drank for a while, staring at the blue comforter and the walls, and feeling rather powerful, because she was the only person in the house who was awake, and also rather sovereign, which in her mind at that moment meant large and stately, and alone. She felt very important somehow, but couldn't understand why; she supposed it was the alcohol. Looking about the room, she saw her mother's letter lying still largely unread on the bedside table. She picked it up, and began to read, drinking in gulps as she did. She finished the eight ounces of brandy before she finished the letter, and fell asleep sitting up, with the bedside light on, and the sticky brandy glass lying on its side on the blue comforter, and her mother's letter loosely fallen from her hand.

Margaret Wallace had written: "Each morning I awaken to the dazzling bright splendor of sunlight on water, and I lie in bed watching the long, serious, slender freighters glide past, and I try to think of the proper names for all the different blues I see dancing in the water. (Robin's egg, indigo, sapphire, mauve.) I stretch in my wide bed, on my cool blue sheets, and don't want to rise, and then think, I don't have to! And sometimes I cry for joy, for the beauty and luxuriousness of my life.

"At night it is the same. I cannot bear to go to sleep, I sit up in my old blue chair (I found a cotton batik spread in a shop in Dundarave, a spread covered with wide wild stripes of rainbow, and threw it over the chair, so it does not look the same, it is new, as I am). And I stare and stare out the window at the water, at the dark. Sometimes the moon spreads itself across the water in uneven, uneasy strips; it is always shimmering, changing, curving into new forms, as if lying very lightly and restlessly on the surface of the water, which otherwise would absorb it, drink it, cause it to vanish, unlike the reliable certain earth which only refuses and reflects. Sometimes there is no moon, but still the show of dancing lights as the cars cross over and back on the Lion's Gate Bridge, over and back, and then the lights of the houses and the city flash and tease, and even very late at night I can see lights somewhere. I do not feel alone, I feel sufficiently accompanied, and I wonder if across the harbor, on the eastern shore, another woman is sitting with a glass of brandy in her hand, staring at the water, smiling back at me. Pandora often comes into the room at night— she likes to go about then, you know—and she often comes into my bedroom and leaps up onto my bed, just out of touching distance, and our eyes meet for a moment. I do not need to speak to her; our eyes meet, that is enough, and then she sits and watches the night with me and is elegant and understanding enough to refuse to break our happy silence with a sound. A most companionable cat.

"What is it I am in love with, I wonder sometimes: is it Vancouver, this blue and silver city, that glitters and shines and spangles, yet is real, or is it this house, my house, or is it my life, my wonderful brave new freedom, or is it me, what I have become? Everything gives me such enormous pleasure: looking at myself in the mirror, in my loose and gay new clothes; walking through the rooms of my house, which respond to me as flowers do, silently but generously, almost giving off perfumes; walking the streets of this city, seeing the wet streets glisten with rain. It's as if I am living inside a rainbow, and everything is shimmering and iridescent and fine— Do you remember, the summer we all were in Paris, seeing the movie *Peau d'Ane*, with Catherine Deneuve? Do you remember that she asked for a gown the color of the sky, and magically, she was given that gown, a whole piece of fabric which she wore, which was the most pale and glorious of blues, with real clouds floating on it? Remember the horses the knights and soldiers rode in the movie, the horses that were really red, really blue? My life is like that now, my real life is like that, like a dress made from the sky, like a blue horse, like a princess's hair so fine and bright it seems spun from gold.

"This morning, for breakfast—actually, it was almost lunch, it was a little after eleven when I finally rose—this morning for breakfast, I had fresh strawberries and a glass of champagne. I ate the strawberries and drank the champagne from the platinum-rimmed crystal etched with leaves which my grandmother had given me, and which your father and I used only for our most formal and pompous dinners. I wiped my hands on a linen napkin of dove gray brightened by swooping dark-blue birds and huge pink flowers. You have not seen these napkins, they are new. I wrote in my journal, I dressed, I went out to the beach and walked, I pulled my skirts up like a peasant or a queen and stepped about in the waves. The water was very cold; fall is coming. I sat for a while leaning up against a driftwood log, letting sand fall through my fingers onto my bare toes, or rubbing a smooth rock between my third finger and thumb. People passed by—people are always strolling along the beach, poking about in the sand, walking just on the edge of the water—and some of them smiled at me and said hello, and one elderly woman said to me, 'You look so perfect sitting there in that blue dress, you look as if you have just swum up from the sea, as if you are a mermaid who has just now come up to live on the land.' She was probably just a dotty old lady, but I can't remember when anyone has said anything that pleased me more. I think she *knew* about me, that old woman, like a witch knows, I think she sensed that I had been through a change as dramatic as that of a mermaid coming to live on the land. Although in my case, I feel more like a mermaid who finally found the sea, that is, I feel I have found my real element, found my *home*. I *belong* here. And how I love it, that the old woman spoke to me that way. Can you imagine anyone in Liberty, Iowa, saying such a thing? I can't imagine them *thinking* it in the first place, let alone speaking so intimately to a stranger. Liberty, Iowa. My God. Now *there* is irony for you.

"The only thing that can depress me now is the thought of how many years I lived there, mindlessly doing all the right things, the things that the wife of Harry Wallace, G.P., should do. Remember Arnold Baker, the minister the First Methodist Church had for just about a month before he went crazy and they took him away to the state mental asylum? He said to me, at the welcoming tea Gladys Fletcher had: 'Harry Wallace, G.P., eh? I guess that means he's a general practitioner. And that must mean you have to be *Mrs.* Harry Wallace, G.P., but in your case the G.P. has to stand for Good and Proper.' I could only stand there with my mouth hanging open, feeling both vaguely insulted and terribly threatened—this was years ago, when you and Dale were small and I still thought that being good and proper in Liberty, Iowa, was the only way possible to live. I've often thought about Reverend Baker since then. I wonder if he is still in an asylum. I wonder whether he might have changed my life if he had stayed a few more weeks in Liberty, if he had kept chipping at me that way. Now I think he should not be in an asylum at all; on the contrary, he should be paid money to go around to small towns all across the United States to say unsettling things to good and proper housewives.

"I fret sometimes because I am so old. Forty-eight years old. I don't have that much time left, and I hate myself for having wasted it, living out all that time like a thoughtless automaton, in Liberty, Iowa. If only Arnold Baker had stayed around longer, been sharper with me, would I have come to my senses sooner? Would I have left sooner? But then I think, no, you girls did have a good and happy childhood in Liberty, and that is important. It would not have suited either one of your personalities to be brought up away from your father. No, my time was not wasted, because it resulted in the serenity and completion of you two girls. And now I have made the change, when it can't harm either of you, and I have made it on my own, without anyone haggling me into it, which is worth some kind of point on some kind of scale of values, and I *am* here.

"*I am here.* I am here, an independent woman, a free woman, a woman who owes nothing to anyone, I am here in Vancouver, the most beautiful city in the world, in a small pure house that is mine and only mine. I have no plans. Perhaps I'll start taking courses to finish my B.A. degree, you know I had only one year of college, and then I married your father and had my babies right away. We women did that sort of thing in my day, you know, and I suppose some women still do, but not as many, thank God, not as many. I don't regret it, I won't waste my time on regrets. Really it doesn't even matter to me that I don't have a degree, it's just that everyone expects me to have one. I try to explain that I'm a *reader*, and always have been, that I have read not just the gothic romances that are written to help housewives make it through a bleak winter with sick children—although Lord knows I've read those, too, and love them still. I won't be snobbish. There is something quite satisfying about a good gothic romance. Do you ever read them?

"What was my point? Oh, that I'm a reader, that I read everything: fiction, biographies, history, philosophy, science, anthropology, and so on. I've read Plato, I've read Voltaire, I've read Walker Percy. Why should I go take courses at a university? Well, though, perhaps I would like it—next year—it might be a pleasant thing to do then. And there is a university here I love, it's called Simon Fraser, after the explorer, and it's a new university, new and liberal. It's built at the summit of a mountain, and the architecture is stunning, quite modern and yet classical, so clean, so pure. I like going there very much. I often go out to use the library—Miriam is on the faculty there, you know, and she checks out books for me. And I like sitting in Miriam's office, talking with her and looking out her wide glass window at the sky. Quite often it is all clouds, the sky, because the university is so very far up the mountain, and as one descends the road back down to Vancouver, one goes back down under the clouds. It is Olympian, Simon Fraser. Yes, I think I might take courses there next year. Next year. I don't want to be rushed, there is no need to hurry. I'll only be a year older next year, and Simon Fraser is the sort of place where I can feel comfortable, even if I am twenty years older than the other students.

"Dear Daisy, what a long letter I've written you! I am sure that your two children have not let you read it all in one sitting. You must think I've rambled on and on, but this is the first letter I've written you since I divorced your father, and I feel like such a new person, I wanted to somehow introduce myself to you. Please use the check, please fly out and spend some time with me. There is so much I want to show you, so much I want to talk about! I hope you are not worrying about your father. Please don't worry about him. Just think how it is for him: the minute I sat down on the plane all the women in Liberty showed up at his front door with chicken casseroles and chocolate cakes. He will be in heaven. He won't spend an evening alone. And he is bound to marry again, very soon, I'm sure, he is so terribly eligible. Who wouldn't want to be Mrs. Harry Wallace, G.P., wealthy and stable, the first citizeness of Liberty, Iowa? Mark my words, your father will be married again very soon. He is a man who likes being taken care of, and Liberty is full of women who like taking care.

"But I will stop before I begin to sound snide or bitter. All I meant to do was to cheer you up, to free you from any worrisome thoughts. Your father is undoubtedly fine, and I am, as I said before, happier than I have ever been in my life. I am happy, and I am free, and I am new. Doesn't this intrigue you? Wouldn't you like to meet me, see my house, see me? I think you would be surprised. Please let me know. Please fly out soon. I would love to see you, Daisy, my flower. Give all my love to Paul and the children. I hope all is well with you—I know how you must be too busy to write, I remember those days very well.

Love, love, love, Mother"

TWO

❦❦❦❦❦❦❦❦❦❦❦❦❦

Rocheport, Maine, is twenty miles south of Portland on the Atlantic Ocean. The town itself is set inland a few miles, away from the whims of the sea, but there is a long stretch of public beach that is officially part of the town. It took Dale Wallace fifteen minutes to get from the Rocheport high school, where she taught, to the edge of the Rocheport public beach. She parked her car—a dark-blue Volkswagen Beetle with a gray convertible top—with an abrupt screeching thump, and looked out the window at the beach, and laughed out loud. It was all right if she acted strange, laughed and talked to herself, for most of the houses that ran along the street, facing the ocean, were summer houses, and it was October now, and no one was around to see. It wouldn't have mattered if people had been around, though, it wouldn't have mattered at all. Dale laughed, and tore off her clogs and fuzzy green knee socks, and rolled up her Levi's, and jumped out of the car barefoot.

The tide was out. The white smooth sand of the beach stretched up and down the coast, far out into the ocean.

Dale ran out onto the sand, yelping with shock as her bare feet touched down on the firm cold. She ran for the water, the tantalizing edge of ocean that frothed far out, and when she reached it, she turned and ran along the edge of the water, playing games with the little waves, seeing how close she could get, how long she could stay, before the water surprised her and surged up high, chilling her feet and ankles with an unconcerned painful cold.

Dale ran and ran. The sun was low and the water was silver, the sand was silver, the sky was silver: the world was silver. It was a fluid jewel. And she was the fire at its heart. She ran and ran. She skipped, she laughed with her head thrown back, she splashed on the edge of the gentle surf till her jeans were wet. She could not stop running. She ran until she reached the rocks at the northern end of the beach, then she turned around and ran back the other way. The ocean reached for, then crested and exploded on, her slender ankles, on her firm smooth legs. Dale put her arms out straight and began spinning around in circles, around and around and around, until she was so dizzy and out of breath she had to stop, bent over, double, hands braced on her knees, laughing and gasping, catching her breath so she could run again. She ran, she ran. She was in love.

The man she was in love with, Hank Kennedy, might have been surprised to know of Dale's love. Dale and Hank had seen each other only twice in their lives. Yet Dale felt sure that at last it had happened: she was in love. She was twenty-four years old and had almost decided that it was *never* going to happen to her. Of course there had been high school boy friends back in Iowa, and lovers—meaning men she had slept with—during college and her two-year sojourn in Europe. But she had never *loved* them, not one of them. She had never felt giddy at the sight of any of them, even though some of them had been quite good-looking. She had never felt that astonishing thump that happened inside her chest the first time she saw Hank, and again the second time, a thump so physically real that it was as if her heart had suddenly come alive, had jumped up with a delirious furious force, had thudded wildly about like a wild live creature inside her skin. The first time it had happened Dale had stood quite still, smiling inanely, happily amazed at the sensation. So this was what they were writing about, all those poets, all the songwriters, so this was what everyone had been trying to tell her about. My God, it was so *sweet*.

It had happened in the cafeteria of the high school one Thursday evening last month, in September, when she and other teachers had come from all over the region to discuss what new programs to implement with the federal grant the region had just received. Dale was a new teacher in the area; it was her first year and she was full of energy and enthusiasm. She taught biology and French to juniors and seniors at the high school, but she had come to the meeting to ask for funds to start a good regional film series. There was no movie theater in Rocheport and the closest one was twenty minutes away in Portland, and she loved movies; she didn't want to face a long cold winter without them. Of course she thought the series would benefit the students and community as well. She had entered the cafeteria just at six-thirty, the time the meeting was scheduled to begin, and looked about the large room for someone she knew to sit with, and her eyes had caught on the figure of a dark-haired man standing across the room, leaning with both arms on a long narrow table, talking earnestly to a group of teachers. Her eyes had caught on his figure; her heart had leaped. She had not been able to take her eyes off him, she had stood there, foolishly entranced, unable to stop smiling, lost in the ferocious workings of her heart. She had never been so happy in her life.

"Oh, there you are," Carol Mellon said to her, coming in

laden with notebooks and papers. "Let's go sit down. What's the matter? You look strange. Are you sick?"

"No, no," Dale had said. "I'm fine, just fine. Where do you want to sit?" And so she had managed to follow Carol across the room, to settle at a table with amiable colleagues; she had managed to appear natural.

But she couldn't take her eyes off the man. He was about her age, she thought, probably a few years older, twenty-seven or twenty-eight. He was perhaps only a few inches taller than she was: Dale was five seven, and guessed that he was around five ten or five eleven. Of course she couldn't judge too accurately from so far away, but they would fit together quite nicely, she thought, and went warm throughout her body, and smiled, and could not get her breath.

"Are you all right? Are you all right?" Carol kept saying to her, buzzing at her like a mosquito.

His body was beautifully proportioned. He looked solid and lean and strong and powerful; he had to be some kind of athlete. His hair was dark brown, and slightly wavy; she could not tell what color his eyes were. But his eyebrows were exquisitely arched, and his cheekbones high. His movements were those of a man of greatly controlled energy.

"Listen, did you get into my Preludin?" Carol asked. Carol was two years older than Dale. They had met at Williams when Dale was a freshman and Carol a junior, and had become close friends. It was Carol who had encouraged Dale to come back from Europe, to settle down to "real life," to take the teaching position in Rocheport. She had even arranged for Dale to move into her apartment for the first year, until she got used to the long winters and the quietness of the small town. Carol was a good, smart, efficient woman who managed both to withstand all foolishness and to be generous and warm. She had short brown hair, rimless glasses, spreading hips. She was teaching history in the high school, but it was obvious that her talents were administrative, and because she was from the region and was so tactful yet so sharp, people were already saying that she would be the next principal of the high school when Loren Hansen, who was in his late fifties, retired.

Dale did not know that Carol had any Preludin; she couldn't imagine why Carol would ever need them. But the question caught her attention. She forced herself to take her eyes off the man across the room, to bring them to Carol's face. "No," she said, "of course I didn't. To be honest with you, I'm just—well, that man over there. He's really so— Who is he? Do you know him?" She had to look back at him, to be sure he was real, that he hadn't vanished. "Is he a teacher? Where does he teach? Is he married?"

Carol looked over at the man, who by now had sat down at the table with some other teachers. He was talking and smiling, totally at ease. He rubbed his ear.

"That's Hank Kennedy," Carol said. "He teaches up at Shelton Academy for Boys in Portland. I think he comes down to our school to teach a course in history on Tuesdays and Thursdays. Is it history? I can't remember. He isn't from this area originally, I think he was always a summer resident, came up from Boston or somewhere with his family. Then he took a job up here and he bought himself a little farm. I don't think he's married, but I really don't know that much about him. Would you like me to introduce you to him later?"

"Oh, God, *no*," Dale said, horrified. "I just wondered who he was, that's all. There aren't that many attractive men wandering around here this time of year, as you know."

"I know," Carol said. "Believe me, I know." But her

voice did not carry any emotional weight; she was firmly engaged to her childhood boy friend, who was in Massachusetts finishing up his D.V.M. He was smart and capable and calm like Carol, and no one doubted that eventually they would marry and be pillars of the community.

The meeting had started and carried forth into the September night—it was raining out, and everyone was eager to accomplish as much as possible on this damp evening so that other, crisper fall evenings could be free. People talked, put forth proposals, made suggestions, made objections. Even Dale talked, discussing the idea for a film series, reading figures she had found, answering questions. She was pleased that so many people thought her idea a good one, and they voted unanimously that she should work up a definite schedule with realistic cost figures, and they asked her if she wouldn't be the chairman of the committee, since it was her idea. Several people volunteered to be on her committee, to assist her, but Hank Kennedy was not one of them. Throughout the evening, Dale was very aware of herself, especially when she was standing up in front of the group, talking. She could not keep herself from doing sexually suggestive things: tilting her head to one side as she spoke, so that her long light-brown hair fell silkily about her shoulder, like a light cloak; slowly licking her lips (she hoped people would think she was nervous); leaning forward, hands on the table—as he had been doing when she first saw him—so that her high large breasts were emphasized against her sweater. She was dismayed at herself, but could not control her body; she might as well have been a peafowl in heat. But because of her excitement she did speak eloquently for the film series, and so she refused to feel guilty about what she felt was her almost wanton display.

So she was devastated when at eleven-thirty the meeting ended, and Hank Kennedy went out the door without a backward glance at her. The room closed in, was suddenly a bleak gray cafeteria with stale cigarette smoke circling up toward the fluorescent lights and all the metal and plastic chairs in disarray. Carol was busy gathering up her papers and folders, and was so thoroughly involved with the meeting that she had completely forgotten Dale's interest in the man.

"Come on," she said. "We've got to teach tomorrow. Let's go home and get some sleep. God, these meetings. They should pay us extra for them."

"Umm," Dale said, and followed Carol out the door.

Somehow she had gotten through that night, and then through several long weeks with no sign of Hank Kennedy. She was too cautious to ask Carol about him again; she knew Carol, knew what Carol would do—she would insist that she introduce Dale to Hank, or she would carelessly mention to another teacher, "If you ever run into Hank Kennedy, tell him Dale Wallace would like to get to know him." Dale decided there was nothing she could do about it but to forget him, and after three weeks, it seemed that forgetting him would be easy. She had seen him only for a few hours across a large cafeteria, after all; she was beginning to lose the outlines of his body in her mind's eye. Still the feeling, the glorious rush of thudding joy, remained. She could remember it easily; it was the first thing she thought of when she awoke in the morning. And she dreamed about Hank almost every night. He was always approaching her in her dreams, always coming toward her, looking right at her, smiling, and she would moan and sigh with excited anticipation. But that was all that happened in her dreams; he never managed to get close to her; he never touched her.

And then today, when she had been walking down the hall to the principal's office with her attendance sheets, not even thinking of him, not really thinking of anything except that she was tired and ought to go to the laundromat that evening, just then as she was about to go into the principal's office, the door opened, and Hank Kennedy walked out. In fact he almost walked into her. He was busy talking to another teacher, had pushed the door open with one hand, but was looking back over his shoulder, saying something that was making the secretaries laugh, and he nearly walked right into Dale, who was just moving to open the door to walk in.

"Oh, excuse me," Hank said, and stopped so suddenly that the man behind him smashed into his back. He looked at Dale, who had gone into a state of semi-shock at having him materialize so suddenly before her. "Hi," he said, almost as an afterthought.

"I—I was just going in," Dale said weakly, almost inaudibly.

"Well, I was just going out." Hank smiled, and stepped back to hold the door for her.

For a moment Dale could not move; she was frozen with delight—there he really was! Hank Kennedy: lean, powerful, dark, fine. He was wearing jeans, Frye boots, a plaid button-down shirt, a pullover sweater. His dark-brown hair was parted on the left side, and some of it fell over his forehead. His mouth was finely chiseled and long and exquisite. His eyes were green and long-lashed, thick-lashed; Dale's heart leaped and spun.

"Thank you," she said at last, and walked into the office, and Hank and the other man walked out. Dale could not bring herself to close the office door; she stood there dumbly staring, holding the door open, watching as the two men walked down the hall. She could not force herself to stop staring at him; she was too hungry for the sight of him. And she liked so well the sensation of desire which ran through her body so fiercely it bordered on alarm; she felt totally focused on the moment, on the reality of his presence. She did not want the moment to end.

Hank continued to walk down the hall, and then, casually, he stopped talking to the other man, and looked over his shoulder, and looked right at Dale. Their eyes met. For a moment Dale thought he would surely leave the man and come back down the hall to her—she wanted that so much. But he only looked at her, and then the other man said something to him, and Hank smiled and turned away and went around the corner, out of sight.

There was nothing more she could do. She handed in her attendance sheets and chatted with the secretaries automatically, then returned to her classroom to do the necessary things that the end of the day required. Finally she was through, she was free. She walked with great control to her Beetle convertible, and drove immediately to the ocean, and tore off her shoes and socks, and ran. She ran and ran. She ran for joy, she ran for love. She ran wildly at the edge of the surf because Hank Kennedy's eyes were green.

She ran, thinking how drab the rest of her life seemed in comparison to this moment, how the rest of her life had not prepared her for this. She was full of such joy, such energy, such elation, simply because one man lived on this earth and had stopped for a few moments to meet her stare. And he would call her now, she was sure of it. If she had learned nothing else during her two years in Europe, she had learned how to say, merely by the way she held her body and her mouth, by the way she held her eyes: *I am interested in you*, or *leave me alone*. Of course in the high school office, her brain had short-circuited, and she had done nothing intentionally, but everything in her body had been tingling, moving outward toward him, and surely, oh, surely he could read those signs. And she was not unattractive, she had learned that, too. She had grown up thinking

that her older sister Daisy was the beauty of the family and
that she, Dale, was the brain, mainly because Daisy had
blond hair and blue eyes, while Dale had light-brown hair
and hazel eyes. But in college, and in Europe, she had discovered first to her delight and later to her disdain that she
had something that attracted many men: large breasts.
During her last six months in Europe she had gotten so
tired of it all, of the fuss men made over her breasts, that
she had gone to a surgeon in Paris to see about having her
breasts reduced. But the cost was prohibitive, and the surgeon, a woman, had warned her against it. "You wait," she
had said, "you're young, you're not married. You wait."
Dale had bought looser and looser sweaters and shirts, and
that had become a sort of style for her: jeans, high boots,
loose sweaters or shirts, loose dresses. Her one vanity now
was her hair, which was a rich, soft brown with auburn
lights, and which she had let grow during the past two
years so that it now reached below her waist. She could not
quite sit on it, but in another six months she would be able
to. Her hair was beautiful, and she liked the feeling of it
sweeping protectively across her back like a cloak, or pulled
straight back and tied with a striped ribbon into a single
luxurious fall. So she had that, her hair, and she had her
large breasts, and the bones of her face were good—no, she
was not unattractive. She was attractive. Attractive. Would
she attract him, would Hank Kennedy have been attracted
to her by those few minutes in the high school office? She
thought so, she hoped so, she hoped so desperately. Because underneath the free flow of joy which now surged
about inside her, a thin line of tension was running, the
tension of desire.

The sun went down finally, and as it did the lumines-
cence went out of things. The sky, the water, the sand,
went from silver to gray. It was really quite cold on the
beach. Dale's feet and ankles had gone numb. Still she

kept moving along the line of the water, not running now, but walking, hugging herself for warmth. The tide was beginning to come in, and it gradually pushed her closer and closer into the shore, up toward the solid world where there were houses and cars and people and telephones. Dale did not want to leave the edge of the ocean, she did not want to leave her pure wild sense of ecstasy—she did not want to face the rest of her life wondering if she would ever see the man again, wondering if he would ever call. *He had to call.* She willed it. If he did not call, if she did not see him again, her life would seem as bleak and cold and gray as the world did right now, and she could not bear that. Better to walk and walk, savoring the last shivers of joy and desire; while she walked on the beach she still had it all, there was still hope.

But when her teeth began to chatter, she knew she had to go home. As she sat down inside her car, she realized how weak she was, how tired. She could not stop shaking, she was so cold. She managed to pull her socks on, but her wooden clogs felt too heavy to pick up, to attach to her feet. She drove home with the car heater on full blast, her sock-covered foot occasionally slipping off the gas pedal. It was quite dark by the time she arrived at the colonial house where she and Carol shared the large second-floor apartment. Carol was home, and had all the lights on, and apparently had fixed dinner, even though it was Dale's night to do it. The apartment smelled of the good thick beef stew that Carol loved to make. Dale yearned for its warmth and substance.

"My God, where have you been?" Carol said, springing up out of a chair when she saw Dale walk in. "You look like a drowned cat."

"I've been walking by the beach," Dale said. "It was so beautiful, so fantastic, I can't describe it. But I've gotten so cold. I can't stop shivering."

"Get in the bathtub right away, get in the hottest water you can stand. Hurry up, take those clothes off, they're soaked. Walking on the beach at this time of year? You're crazy. What's gotten into you? Look at your hair, it's marvelous the way it goes all curly and fuzzy when it's damp. Go on, get in the tub, I'll bring you—what? What should I bring you, what would be good for you? What do we have in the way of liquor? Here. How about a nice stiff scotch? That's as close to brandy as we can get. What in the world were you doing out there on the beach anyway?"

Dale went into the bathroom and started the water into the tub. She poured in a great dollop of bath oil. She piled her hair on top of her head and held it there with two wooden prongs, then peeled her wet jeans and sweater off her body; the jeans were almost iced. Her skin had gone very white, and she was covered with gooseflesh. The hot water on her cold skin was painful, a sort of shocking burn, but she forced herself into the tub, down into the hot foamy depths, so that only her head was above the water. She could hear Carol going on and on in the other room, and she smiled to herself. Carol was the most perfect person to live with at times like these, because she excelled in taking charge, taking care. Carol would make a fine mother, Dale thought, Carol should have ten children. Carol made taking care of people an art. In fact, Carol reminded Dale of her mother—at least of her mother as she remembered her. Dale hadn't seen her mother since the divorce, since her mother had undergone her mysterious and unexplainable transformation; she could not believe her mother had changed as much as her father wrote she had. Dale could not imagine her mother being any way other than she had been the twenty-four years Dale had known her: warm, generous, kind, thoughtful, always ready to help.

"Here," Carol said, coming into the bathroom. "A nice neat scotch. No ice, no water. Have a sip. You need it."

She handed the glass to Dale and then put the lid of the toilet seat down and sat down on it, crossed her legs, and looked at Dale affectionately. "Feel better? At least your teeth have stopped chattering."

"God, Carol, I'm sorry about dinner," Dale said. "I forgot it was my turn to cook tonight." She sipped the scotch. It burned. She could feel it burning all the way down through her chest and into her stomach.

"Oh, heavens, don't worry about that," Carol said. "I was in the mood to make a beef stew anyway. Smells good, doesn't it? I made enough so we won't have to cook tomorrow night, we can just warm it up. Oh, by the way, Hank Kennedy phoned. He called twice, once when I just got home and then about fifteen minutes ago."

"He *did*?" Dale tried her best to sound casual, and she was astounded that she did not drop the glass of scotch into the tub. "Did he say why he was calling?"

"No, he just said he wanted to talk to you. I told him you would be home any minute. He said he'd call you back. Hey, the scotch is working. Your color is returning, you're beginning to look human again. Shall I go put dinner on the table or would you like to soak some more?"

"Yes, I'd like to soak a few minutes more," Dale said. "I want to get thoroughly warmed up. Even my bones got cold out there. That beef stew smells better than anything I've ever smelled before in my life. I'm so hungry, I can't tell you how hungry I am."

"Well, you should be, after running around on the beach at the end of October," Carol said sensibly, and rose, and left the bathroom. "Call me when you're getting out, and I'll dish up the stew."

Dale sipped more of the scotch, and reached out to set the glass on the bath mat, her arm dripping water and suds onto the floor. Then she sank back into the heat of the water and pressed both hands against her heart, and thought: she would lie in the tub until she was completely warm, and then she would put on her warmest nightgown and robe and slippers, and then she would eat the beef stew, and drink a glass of red wine, and then she would help Carol with the dishes, and then she would grade papers, and eat a crisp pear and drink coffee. And when would Hank Kennedy call: when she was tying the sash of her robe? Or biting into the sweet white flesh of the pear?

He called just as Dale had finished grading all the papers, when she had almost given up hope. When the phone rang, she nearly screamed. "I'll get it," she said to Carol.

His voice was very low, very male. "Dale Wallace?" he said. "This is Hank Kennedy. I'm not sure you know who I am—"

"I know who you are," Dale said evenly. *I know who you are: I'm in love with you.*

"Well, then," he said, "I was wondering— I'd like to see you sometime."

"Yes," Dale said. "I'd like that, too." Was she being too obvious, too forward? She didn't care.

"When?" he asked. "I mean, when would be good for you?"

Tonight, she yearned to say, *now*. But instead she put it in his charge: "Well, almost any time is fine. When would be good for you?"

"Well—perhaps tomorrow? After school? I could pick you up and we could go have dinner together. There are several nice restaurants around—"

"That would be fine," Dale said. "That would be really fine."

"I'll pick you up in front of the high school tomorrow. What is a good time?"

"Five," she said. "Five would be good. I can get everything cleaned up and in order by then."

"All right," he said. "I'll see you then."

"Yes. See you then," Dale said, and hung up. She turned to Carol and smiled. "That was Hank Kennedy," she said calmly.

"Well, good," Carol said, smiling back at her. "And just think what we'll save on the electric bill. All we'll have to do is set our appliances next to you and they'll run full speed."

"Carol," Dale said in drawn-out syllables, pleadingly. She wanted every ounce of Carol's attention and understanding and good warm humor, because it was true: Dale was radiant, she was electric. She was shaking. She could not imagine how she could sleep, and so she sat with Carol and talked about her years in Europe, and her college days, and her high school days, until Carol finally said, "I'm sorry, Dale, but I've got to get some sleep. And you should, too."

So Dale dutifully climbed into bed to sleep. But it seemed to her that she spent the entire night lying on her back, smiling up at the ceiling with anticipation and great delight, never closing her eyes.

They had dinner at a small seafood restaurant in Ogunguit. As the day had drawn on toward five o'clock, Dale had come to be more and more apprehensive, afraid that when she finally was close to Hank Kennedy, something would be wrong: he would have bad teeth, bad breath, or he would be dull or silly, or have some enormous imperfection that would ruin everything. So as the evening went on, she became more and more giddy with relief, because he was not imperfect, he was perfect: he was beautiful, and intelligent, and in control. Her heart thumped up when she first saw him, and for the rest of the evening she was in a frenzy, wanting to touch him, wanting to touch him. She wanted it all right away, she wanted to squeeze across the bench seat of the cab of his red pickup truck to press her thigh against his, she wanted to reach across the table at the restaurant to touch his hand. Yet his words were of vital interest to her, too.

At the beginning of the evening they talked about the obvious things: his job, her job, what they thought of various administrators, Carol and her position in the community, the bleakness of the Maine coast in the winter, the beauty of the Maine coast the rest of the year. It seemed to Dale that she agreed with Hank about everything, that everything he said was just and true. Finally, when they had finished their excellent meal and were sitting over coffee and cognac, their talk became more personal.

"You're from Iowa?" Hank said. "How in the world did you end up here?"

"Because of Carol," Dale said. "We met at Williams, and became close friends. The summer of my freshman year, instead of going home, I came up to stay with Carol and her family. And of course I got hooked. I worked as a waitress at the Blue Barn Inn in Rocheport, and that left me every afternoon free—they served only breakfast and dinner. So I spent my whole summer on the beach, or poking about the town, and I fell in love with it. Well, then I went to Europe for two years, but last spring Carol wrote me that they needed a teacher here, someone who could handle both biology and French, and so I came. You can see it's all because of Carol. She brought me here that summer, and then she found me the job. But she knew how much I loved the area, especially the ocean. It's funny, you know, how *at home* I feel here. I think I should miss Iowa, the rolling hills, the countryside, the sky, but I don't. Or I *do*, but it's all right, because of the ocean. It's very— I don't know how to say how I feel about the ocean, the water. I spend a lot of time there."

"I know," Hank said. "That's partly why I'm here, too. My family lives in Arlington, right outside of Boston, and they would have liked me to stay there. We used to spend every summer up here when I was growing up—for fifteen years we had a summer house right on the ocean. In fact, we still own it, but since my brother and I are gone, my parents don't spend as much time up here as they used to. So we still own it, but they usually rent it out for most of the summer. They thought I was crazy to want to live here permanently, and sometimes—in February, for example—I think they're right."

"But you have a farm, don't you?" Dale asked, and even as she spoke she sensed Hank drawing back into himself.

"Yes," he said. "I do. That's another reason they think I'm crazy. But it's what I wanted to do, and I'm satisfied. How did you end up majoring in biology and in French?"

The sudden switch back from him to her as a topic of conversation startled Dale, and she felt discontented for a moment, somehow cheated. Why wouldn't he talk to her about his farm? But he was leaning toward her again, and he looked interested in what she would say.

"I only have a minor in French," Dale said. "But I picked up a lot in Europe over the past two years. So it's good enough for high school students. My major was biology. Actually, all my life I thought I would become a doctor. My father is a physician, a general practitioner in Iowa, and he's sort of a god back there. Everyone loves him. And they should, he's really tremendous, he's devoted his entire life to the town. Well, I always thought my older sister Daisy would grow up to be my mother—a pretty, organized, generous wife and mother. And I thought I would grow up to be my father. A wise and beloved physician. Well"— Dale smiled at herself then; she had come to the point in her life where she could smile about it now, where it did not hurt to say it—"I tried taking premed my freshman year in college, and I did just horribly. I'm still not sure why, because I always got straight A's in biology and physics and chemistry in high school. I can't tell you what a surprise it was to me to find the courses so difficult and the competition so tough. And the ones who were doing well in the courses were real grinds, they had no other life except their studies. So I decided at the end of my freshman year to become a biology major. I was told I could get good jobs with it, jobs in labs and so on. But I can't tell you how devastated I was at the end of my freshman year. I had gotten C's in all my science courses, and I had slaved to get those. Oh, God, I still can scarcely bear to think of it. I felt like such a failure. That's one of the reasons I was so glad to come to Rocheport that summer with Carol. I didn't think I could bear to go back to Iowa, to face my father with my defeat. He had wanted me to be a physician, too, though he never pushed it. That was the worst year of my life—I think that might have been the worst thing that ever happened to me, realizing that I wasn't going to make my childhood fantasy into a reality. I felt sort of dazed for the next few years, for the rest of my college career. I mean I made A's in many courses, but I discounted that, it didn't matter. I still felt like a failure. That's partly why I went to Europe; I just couldn't seem to get started in life. It wasn't that I really wanted to *be a doctor*. It was more that I suddenly was faced with the fact that the rest of my life was not going to be as easy and perfect as my childhood had been."

Suddenly she wanted to *be* there, in her childhood, to take Hank by the hand and lead him around through her happy life in Iowa, as through some sort of far-off and fabulous land. She wanted to show him Liberty, a large and gentle village set among rolling hills, where it seemed all during her childhood that her father and mother were the king and queen, and she and her sister Daisy the princesses. It had been such a storybook town; all her days had been as easy as waking up in her pink-and-white-flowered room. The town's population was only about 4500 and most of the people were farmers, or else they worked at the feed mill or sold trucks and tractors and farm equipment, or repaired trucks and tractors and farm equipment. And there were the teachers, of course, who taught in the consolidated public schools, and the keepers of the various necessary shops: the drugstore, which had a soda fountain and small coffee shop—everyone wandered in on Sunday mornings after church to get the Sunday papers and to gossip; the post office; the grocery store; the general store which sold everything from hard candy to women's girdles; the hardware store.

"My God," Hank said, "it sounds like Mr. Rogers' Neighborhood."

Dale laughed. "It was," she said. "It was."

She went on, she told him everything, it all flooded back through her and out toward him. Liberty was the county seat, and so the town was quite pretty, symmetrical, four blocks squared around a courtyard, with a graystone courthouse solidly standing on the north side, like a serious castle blocking the rest of the town from the worst winter winds. In the middle of the courtyard was a brass statue dedicated to the valiant dead of the two world wars; small boys climbed on the statue to sit on the cannons. And there was a small fountain, which children played in in the summer, and flower gardens, and sidewalks and a few trees —one towering evergreen which was always decorated for Christmas every December—and even a bandstand, with a striped octagonal roof and seven wide steps and railings. And the high school band gave concerts there on the Fourth of July. There were three churches: the Catholic, the Baptist, and the Methodist. Her parents had gone to the Methodist church, and for a long while Dale's mother had been president of the ladies' auxiliary. There was only one bar in town, in the American Legion building that stood on one corner. That was the only building in all of Liberty that Dale had never been in. Now, looking back at it as an adult, Dale could see that there was not much going on in Liberty: there was no movie theater, although there was a small library in a tiny yellow frame house, and in Dale's teenage years they had begun to show old black-and-white children's films on Saturday afternoons. But Dale had had a marvelously busy life as a child: there was Brownies, and then Girl Scouts; and Sunday school, and then Methodist Youth Fellowship; and band when she was smaller—she had played the flute for a while, but not all that well—and cheerleading and French Club and Student Council and high school plays when she was older.

And their house—their wonderful, wonderful house. It was only a block back from the main square. It was enormous, post-Victorian, brick, with wooden porches and stained-glass windows and a large flat yard. Her mother grew vegetables in the back yard and flowers in the front. Dale and Daisy roller-skated to school together. Each of the girls had separate rooms—Daisy's of course had been yellow and white, with daisies on the wallpaper; Dale's had been pink and white, with roses. Dale could close her eyes and see the sun slanting in her window on a summer morning, striking the white bookcase where her books and figurines and stuffed animals sat, turning the white into an indescribable color; it was not a color, it was a light, a brilliance, at once calm and motionless and yet somehow vividly alive. And the kitchen, which smelled of hot chocolate or cherry pie or her mother's homemade grape jam, and her father's study, the forbidden room, where he kept his accounts and sometimes had private talks with distraught patients, and her parents' bedroom, huge and mysterious, with her mother's books piled everywhere, and the bathroom, with its white octagonal tiles.

On Sunday afternoons, every Sunday afternoon of her life, it seemed, Dale's father would walk with her and Daisy across the street and around the town square to the drugstore. In good weather they made the most of the walk, going around several blocks to look at the flowers in bloom in the spring or the colors of the maples in the fall; in the winter they hurried, bundled against the wind, eager for the refuge of the overheated store. Inside, Dr. Wallace would treat his daughters to cocoa or lemonade, and he would have a cup of Ovaltine, and they would all sit chatting with Mr. Pendergast, the druggist, and with whoever else came in. And then Dr. Wallace would buy his daughters a treat—paper dolls in the early years, and then comic books or *Mad* magazine in their early teens, and finally *Seventeen* as they grew older. That was his weekly treat for them. He liked to give them something pleasant to do on Sunday evenings when he and his wife went to the church socials or to dinner with friends. Every Sunday afternoon of their young lives, Dale and Daisy had been treated to this pleasure, the king taking his daughters for a stroll. They would still be wearing their best dresses, which they had worn to church. They would have eaten a large Sunday dinner after church, then helped their mother clean up the kitchen. Then they would go for the walk with their father, while their mother lay stretched out on her bed, reading, sucking white peppermint Lifesavers from a blue wrapper. This was the day when Dale and Daisy were complimented; always some old lady who hadn't seen them for a while would declare over how tall and pretty they had grown; or they would run into the Catholic priest, who would praise Dale for winning the local essay contest; or someone, someone they vaguely knew, but who knew—and who worshiped, this was the important point, who *wor-shiped*—their father, would say hello, tell them what nice dresses they were wearing, tell them what fine girls they were getting to be. Dr. Wallace would stand smiling casually at them, as if their achievements and all the praise were totally deserved, and had nothing to do with him.

Dale hadn't wanted to leave. She had wanted to go to the state university that was only a thirty-minute drive away. But her mother had been ferocious in her insistence that Dale go back East to college. "You've got to get out of here," she had said over and over again to Dale, and when Dale asked her why, she would only say, "You've got to see more of life, you've got to get a wider view." Her father had wanted her to attend the state university, but had acquiesced in the face of his wife's vehement wishes. His wife usually did not oppose him, seldom asked for things to be her way.

Dale often thought now that if she had gone to the state university she would have been able to make it into medical school, she would have been able to become a physician. She would have been able to go back to Liberty as a general practitioner, to work with her father. Sometimes the thought of her loss made her waste weeks in a hopeless bog of despair.

"What did your sister do?" Hank asked.

"Daisy? Well, she went to college at Northwestern," Dale said. "She was four years older than I, and never made such good grades in school—I'm not saying she wasn't as smart as I was, because she was, she just wasn't as *interested*. She wasn't planning all her life to be a doctor. Anyway, Mother made her get out of Liberty, too, but she didn't make her go so far away. Actually, I don't think Daisy got accepted anywhere back East. Well, she did what we all knew she'd do, what she'd always wanted to do, she married at twenty-two, and had a baby two years later, and a baby two years after that, and another baby is on the way now. She lives in Milwaukee. They have a house right on Lake Michigan. Daisy writes that it's great, the house. I've never seen it. I really should visit them sometime . . ."

"Are you close to your sister?" Hank asked.

"Close? I don't know. We were when we were little, of course, but we haven't seen each other for three years now. And we lead such different lives. But we write each other about once a month. She has beautiful children. Enchanted children. I don't know. I should go visit her, it would be fun."

"Do you ever go back to Liberty?"

"Well, the last time I was back was just after I graduated from college. It looked good to me, Liberty. It looked pretty much the same. It's a boring sort of place, I know, just a dumb little farm town, but I still love it. I wouldn't mind living out my life there, or someplace like it. It has its charms. But then the ocean—this coast—this place—now I feel *home* here, I feel that I would go berserk if I couldn't get to the ocean every day. It's become something I need. So I'll probably end up settling here, if I can." Dale went quiet then, thinking of her situation: the apartment she shared with Carol, which she would have to give up when Carol married; her job in the high school, which gave her security for the three years of her contract, but no longer; would she get tenure? She couldn't know yet.

And now this man sitting across from her, listening to her intently. Where was he to fit in her life? All through the evening she had been talking rapidly, earnestly, her desire to touch him channeled into her words, her words, could she somehow touch him with her words? He was sitting there so calmly, watching her, listening: how did he feel now after she had revealed so much of herself to him? Did he like her? Did he want to touch her in return?

An apologetic waitress came to say that it was closing time, and Dale and Hank left the warmth of the restaurant for the chill of Hank's red pickup truck. Dale admired the way Hank took care of the bill; in Europe she had usually paid for her own meals, and quite often had paid for the man's meal, too, since many of the men she had struck up relationships with had had less money than she. As she climbed into the truck, she began to say something pleasantly grateful to Hank about the meal; she almost said that she would like to have him to dinner at her apartment sometime. But she was afraid that that would make her seem too eager to see him again, and too coyly domestic. The very action of getting into the small enclosed space of the dark cab, where he could hear her slightest breath, made her feel self-conscious. It made her lose the easiness she had felt with him inside the warm, bright restaurant where other people walked and talked and ate; it made the lust she had held back all evening in that reasonable room come surging to the front of her thoughts and gestures. Hank got into the cab behind the steering wheel. His jacket was rough suede, his hand was large and hairy; she was aware of the solidity of his right thigh as he pushed on the accelerator. Her mouth went suddenly dry. The evening was almost over. She felt panicked. And he was saying nothing. She sat in silence, loosely hugging herself, leaning slightly against the door.

"The heater will be warmed up in a minute," Hank said.

"It's getting cold," Dale replied.

"Well, it's late October. We'll have some more warm days, but summer is definitely over."

Then they rode in silence. By the time they reached Dale's apartment she was nearly in tears of desperation. Should she invite him up? It was after eleven; they both had to teach the next day. Should she invite him to dinner? Should she—what? What could she possibly do? The bold of coming around the front of the truck to open her door and help her out; another thing the men she had known in Europe seldom did. He took her hand as she jumped down from the truck, but then he let go of it immediately. They walked in silence toward the large colonial house. The lights were on in the front room; Carol was either still up or had left them on for her. And there they were then, standing down by Dale's front door in the dark.

"It was a very good dinner," Dale said. "Thank you again. I—I'd like to invite you to dinner at my apartment sometime. I—there are some things I can cook fairly well."

"That would be nice," Hank said. He was staring down at her so seriously that for a moment Dale thought that he might be feeling the same panic she felt. But then he said, "I had a nice evening. Let's do it again sometime."

And she said "Yes," and he smiled and walked off, back to the truck.

Dale went inside the house and shut the big old door and stood blankly staring at the stairs she had to climb to her second-floor apartment. She did not want to climb them, she did not want to go one step farther from her contact with him. But she heard the truck pull away and go off down the road, and then the night was empty of sounds. She went blindly storming up the stairs then, and by the time she was inside her apartment she was sobbing with frustration.

Carol was sitting in an overstuffed chair, wearing a quilted peach-colored robe, reading. "Did you have a nice time?" she asked.

"Jesus Christ!" Dale sobbed. "He didn't even kiss me good night! He didn't even *touch* me!"

"Oh, dear," Carol said, coming over to Dale and putting her arms around her. "Don't let it upset you so, Dale. Hank Kennedy is the quiet type. You're the first woman I've heard of him dating since he moved up here."

casual woman who had lived inside her skin for two years
in France had deserted her now. She would truly die before
she would say now, as she had said so often in the past two
years to so many men: "Would you like to kiss me?" Or
even, "Would you like to go to bed with me?" Now she realized how smug she had been in Europe, how safe and invulnerable she had been, how *cowardly*: and all along she
had thought of herself as a bold woman with daring sexual
habits and strong sexual needs. In Europe she had been in
love with no one, and so she had been vulnerable to no
one. The men she had slept with had not touched her.
They did not hurt her; they could not have hurt her. If
they had turned down her proposal—and no one ever did,
but if they had—she would have only shrugged. And when
they made love to her, they had not touched her; she realized that now. And now here she was, nearly ill with despair because the evening was over and she did not know
how to carry on from there, what to say, what to do. They
were both adults, for heaven's sake; surely she could say to
him, "Wouldn't you like to kiss me?" Or even, "Would
you like to spend the night with me?" And he would not
be appalled. But she was afraid he would refuse her. His
face, when she glanced over at him, was stern and set. Was
he already thinking of the next day, of a test he had to
give? Suddenly she hated him. Why wasn't he bristling out
toward her as she was toward him? Didn't he find her attractive?

When they stopped in front of Dale's apartment, she
said, "Would you like to come up for some coffee?" It hurt
her throat to speak.

"I'd better not," Hank said. "I've got some grading to do
tonight. As a matter of fact, I've got some chores to do,
too. I'll walk you to the door," he said.

He got out of the truck, and Dale sat there blindly, hot
with desire and pain, while Hank performed the courtly act

4

"He's probably gay," Dale said. "That would be just my luck."

Carol laughed. "He's not gay. There are plenty of girls around here who knew him when he came up in the summer with his family who could attest to that. Calm down, for heaven's sake. You've got to teach tomorrow. Would you like me to make you some warm milk?"

"*Warm milk?*" Dale burst out laughing. "*Warm milk?* The last person who offered to fix me warm milk was my mother. Oh, Carol, you're sweet, but I'm afraid I've gone past the warm milk stage, even if I am acting like a moony adolescent. No, I'll have a stiff scotch and go to bed."

And again it seemed that she did not sleep all night. For a long while she lay in bed, remembering the evening, listening for the phone to ring. Perhaps he would call her to say that he wanted to see her right away, he would come back and pick her up now, or that he wanted to see her the next evening. But the phone did not ring. Dale had to content herself with trying to remember the outlines of his hands, the exact green of his eyes, and the few intimate things he had mentioned about his life.

He did not call her the next day. He did not call her for a week. Dale was frantic, then alternately manic and listless. She thought of calling him, of asking him for dinner, but somehow could not do it. She began to think she would never see him again. She kept away from the beach; she worked industriously on her lesson plans, planning far into the year, making intricate, detailed charts and sheets.

And finally, eight days after their dinner together, he called. There was a movie on in Portland the next evening. He would pick her up at six.

The next evening was a Saturday; there was no school the next day, no reason to return to the apartment early. For their dinner together, Dale had worn her loosest of shirts, wanting to appear casual and altogether uninter-

ested in sex; she did not want to appear to be coming on
too strong. Now, for the movie, she wore her tightest
sweater. She did not care how she appeared; she was interested only in a reaction. She wore a sweater, tight jeans; she
wore lipstick and eye shadow and perfume. Then, at the
last moment, afraid of seeming too obvious, she desperately put her long thick hair into two braids, hoping that
would make her look innocent, would counteract everything else.

At the movie they did not touch, except briefly, when he
helped her with her coat. After the movie, Dale invited
him to her apartment for coffee and dessert. She did not
tell him that Carol was spending the weekend at her parents' home twenty miles away. It was wonderful hearing
Hank's heavy male step as he came up the stairs to the
apartment behind Dale. It was wonderful having him
stand so near, so real, as she unlocked the apartment door.

Inside the apartment she put on music, made the coffee,
served the cake. Hank sat on a chair in the kitchen, watching her. He talked about one of his problem students and
the administration of his school. The boy wanted to wear a
red cap all the time in school; the administration considered this deviant behavior but could not find any specific
restrictions in their books against constantly wearing a cap.
Dale sat sipping her coffee, not even pretending to eat her
cake, listening to Hank talk about the boy. She had hoped
that this second time with him she would feel less lustful;
but she desired him even more. His skin. It was so firm, so
smooth. She wondered if he had hair on his chest, on his
back. His thighs. She could not keep from looking at his
thighs, so substantial in the blue denim. His hands. They
were rough hands for a teacher, but she supposed that was
because he had animals, ran a farm. His hands were clean,
his nails were blunt and square and even; but his hands
seemed rough, and she wanted to feel their abrasiveness

against her skin. She could not respond intelligently to what he was saying. She could not keep interested in his words. Perhaps she seemed bored; he set his coffee cup down on the table and rose.

"I should be going," he said.

Dale rose, too. She thought she would cry. She could not help herself, she finally said the words she had said so often before, but this time she said them almost inaudibly, and to her helpless horror, her eyes filled with tears as she spoke: "Don't you want to kiss me?"

Hank stood there a moment, on one side of the kitchen table, looking at her so seriously Dale thought she would faint. Then he said, "My God," and crossed around to where Dale stood. He took her into his arms. She was stunned to feel that he was shaking. "My God," he said again. "Dale." And he bent his face to hers. He kissed her then, intently, firmly. He held her against him, his left hand on her head as he kissed her mouth, her eyes, her neck; his right hand resolutely pressing her body against his. And she understood why he had been so reluctant to kiss her; his feeling about her was not frivolous; he wanted her, too. And once he had begun making love to her there was no halfway point where they could stop.

His chest and his flat belly were hairy; his back was not. His skin had an olive cast, and his body was marked by different stripes of tan: his arms and neck were still the darkest from working on the farm; the area around his crotch and buttocks was paler than the rest, indicating the shape of his swimming trunks. His thighs were long and lean and as hard as iron, and covered with wonderful thick black hair like fur. Dale rubbed her face in his thighs, murmuring. The first time he entered her she did not come, she could not concentrate, she wanted too much to feel everything at once: his hands, his penis, his legs, his mouth.

And he came almost immediately, burrowing his head into her neck as he did. She watched him, she could not help looking at him, watching him, although she supposed it was not fair; when she saw him grimace, when she heard him moan, she felt pierced by an emotion she had never felt before, and she held on to him tightly, as if otherwise he might die. "Too quick," he said, "I'm sorry," but she kissed him and would not let him speak, and when he rolled on his back she sat up, naked, to study him. She looked and looked at his body, and ran her hands everywhere. He lay watching her. He touched her breasts, her belly. He undid her braids. Her hair fell about her shoulders. He became hard again, and he pushed her back down on the bed and entered her. He lasted for a long time this time, and this time Dale came to him. She cried aloud when she did, and Hank held on to her firmly and protectively as she helplessly surged through waves of fear, revelation, rapture; and at last was washed aground on the shores of the deepest peace.

They lay in each other's arms talking. Dale got up to get them a glass of water, and they sipped it, studying each other's faces and bodies, and then they curled against each other and slept. They awoke in the night and made love. They slept again. In the morning they made love again, smugly, taking their fond and easeful time at it; then Dale made breakfast, walking around naked, feeling comfortable and satisfied in her body. Finally Hank said he had to go to his farm to feed his animals, and he asked Dale to come with him. He told her he wanted to show her his farm, that he wanted her to spend the day with him there. And Dale understood then that some sort of contract had been made between them, for this man she had fallen in love with did not do anything lightly. She was nearly ill with the richness of what she had found.

They dressed sensibly and rode out to his farm in the truck; this time she sat close to him as he drove, with her hand on his thigh. He warned her that she would be disappointed in his farm, and at first she was. The house was not much of a house. It was perhaps eighty years old, and had gone uncared for for too long a time. The front porch had warped and broken boards. The outside of the house needed painting badly, and the gutters needed repairing, as did the roof. Behind the house, however, stood two large barns and several smaller outbuildings, and these had clearly been recently repaired and painted red, and they had new green roofs. Inside the house it was, to Dale's relief, clean, bright, and solid. There were two floors, but Hank lived entirely on the first floor in four large rooms: kitchen, bedroom, study, living room. The living room was actually an extension of the study; the walls were lined with books, and next to the old easy chair that was clearly Hank's chair was a pile of journals, magazines, books, and newspapers. Hank walked through the house with Dale, pointing out how he had done this and that to bring the house back into shape: he had repaired all the rotted wooden windowsills; stripped the floors of their layers of grimy paint and sanded the original pine and filled the cracks and covered it all with a shield of polyurethane; put up storm windows; put a woodburning stove in the kitchen and one in the study; given all the walls a coat of eggshell white. The bedroom, he added, would be the dining room if and when he ever finished work on the upstairs, if and when he would ever need a dining room. As it was he took all his meals in the kitchen. The kitchen was large and bright and clean; Hank had put in new linoleum, but left the large old slate sink. He had a refrigerator and a gas stove, but admitted that from time to time he cooked on the wood stove and had even tried baking bread. Dale walked around the house, loving it, hungry to explore every crack and plane of it, because it was owned by Hank. The furniture was old but good, castoffs from Hank's family. The house was comfortable enough, but lacked the grace that wallpaper or curtains or plants would have added. It was a comfortable, unpretentious place, with high ceilings and large long windows and beautiful wooden floors. Dale slowly ran her hand along the arm of the chair Hank usually sat in. She wanted to be that chair, to embrace him, provide him comfort and support, feel his bones and flesh sinking into her.

He did the chores while he showed her the barns. He had had the farm only a year, and clearly his work had all gone into the barns. They were clean and well maintained. In one smaller outbuilding Hank had chickens: seventeen of them, five of them banties. In a bigger barn he had his green John Deere tractor and his tools; his workroom was clearly one of his delights: hammers, nails, wrenches, saws, bolts, ropes, chains, barrels, cans, lanterns, wire, wire cutters—everything was in a correct place. In the third barn were the cows and Hank's horse. He seemed very pleased that Dale knew the cows were Herefords, beef cattle; and that the horse was a quarterhorse gelding. The large red-and-white cows were all milling around together in one large stall of the barn. There were eight of them, and they mooed at Hank and purposely bumped into him with their large rumps as they filed out the open door into the corral and then on out into the pasture. He slapped them lovingly in return. Dale could see how he felt about them; could see why he would not want to expose himself and his animals to an unsympathetic eye. He led the horse out into the field and stood scratching him, talking to him, giving him bits of corn, but finally the horse grew tired of the affection and tossed his head and trotted away. It was a cold brisk morning, but a sunny one. Dale and Hank walked around the pasture, and the edges of their boots grew dark from the heavy dew.

Hank owned only forty acres, but he had first option on an adjoining one hundred and fifty acres, which to his relief the owner was not yet ready to sell. He had made no profits from the farm yet; it absorbed every bit of his salary from teaching, and all of the money that his grandfather had willed him was in the equity. He discovered that it even cost more to feed the hens than it would have to buy eggs at a grocery store; but he liked the chickens, he liked the fresh eggs. He told Dale he would scramble her some for lunch. The pasture was wide and long and at one end was a large stand of trees. Not enough trees to be called a woods, but large enough and old enough so that Hank could get most of his firewood from it. That was another thing, he confessed, that pleased him greatly: felling an old tree, cutting it into the right lengths, stacking it in the trailer and pulling it in behind the tractor, then stacking it outside the house on the back porch, within easy reach of the kitchen. The wood stand was pleasantly varied: he got hard maple, birch, elm, oak, from it. And a man he knew down the road let him take all the applewood he wanted out of the orchard, provided the tree was dead or dying. The old farmer didn't have a fireplace or a stove and didn't need the wood, and he liked the orchard cleaned up. And Hank liked the smell of applewood in the winter; it sweetened the house.

The fences around Hank's property were barbed wire and in perfect condition. Not a strand sagged or was loose from the posts. They walked back through the barns, which were fragrant with the bales of new hay that Hank had been piling in for the winter. Dale sat on a bale and watched Hank clean the cows' stall, pitching the manure into a large stall in an opposite corner and putting fresh straw down. She felt enormous pleasure at the way his hands were sturdy and competent on the pitchfork, in the way his arm and back muscles flexed as he worked. She wanted to take a bite out of him.

For about an hour Hank worked. Dale sat with her elbows dug into her knees and her chin dug into her hands, watching. She felt quiet and content there in the barn with Hank, surrounded by the strong barn walls whose beams crossed and joined each other in intricate notched patterns, providing beauty, providing strength.

"You like it here, don't you?" Hank said, when he had finished.

"Of course," Dale said, "why do you seem so surprised?"

Hank shrugged. "Well, sometimes women don't like manure, or they worry about mice and things."

"Oh, no," Dale said, "that didn't even occur to me. I really do like it here." Then she had to hide her face, for she felt so proud of herself, so smug, to have pleased him with her ease.

Later he scrambled eggs for her in his kitchen, and lit the wood stove. It gave off an agreeable radiant warmth. He served her hot coffee and eggs and toast with honey from a beekeeper down the road, and they talked.

"My parents think I'm crazy," Hank said, and did not laugh. "They think this place is a waste of money, and that my entire life is now a waste of time. They wanted me to be a lawyer instead of a history teacher. And they wanted me to follow in my father's and brother's footsteps. A nice town house, a nice marriage, silver wedding presents, a respectable and useful life which everyone would know was respectable and useful because it would be reported in the proper sections of the proper papers. They were truly horrified when I told them that I was going to move here, take the academy job, and try to run a farm. God. Poor mother. First the divorce, and then this. I don't think—"

"Divorce?" Dale said. She could not breathe.

"Yes," Hank said. He had his back to her as he put more

wood into the stove, but turned to look at her directly when he spoke. "I'm divorced."

"You mean you were married?" Dale asked. What did this mean to her, why did it hurt her so?

He slammed the black cast-iron lid down onto the stove, and laughed. "Yes," he said gently. "In order to get divorced, you have to be married."

"Oh," Dale said, and went dumb. She had a thousand questions to ask, and yet was not sure of her right to ask even one.

"I was married only about two years," Hank said. He came back and sat down at the kitchen table with her. He talked into his coffee cup, suddenly weary, suddenly speaking as if by rote. "My ex-wife's name was—is—Elaine, and she was—is—very pretty, very sweet, very nice. She came from the right family. My parents approved of her; she was the kind of girl they thought I should marry. She was tall and slim, and she went to Wellesley, and she liked cities and galleries and people and fashions. We had a large formal wedding; the whole marriage was really just a justification for the wedding. It was grand. The rest of the marriage was not so grand. And she was brought up to believe—as I was—that happiness is a rather vulgar goal, and moderation is admirable, and the way to live one's life is to do what everyone else does, with a balance of flair to keep you interesting, and of restraint to keep you decorous. I don't want to speak ill of her. I don't hate her; I didn't love her. I caused her a great deal of—pain is too strong a word. A great deal of bother. I caused her a great deal of bother by marrying her only as a form of experiment, as a test to see if I could go ahead and live the life my parents wanted me to live. It didn't take me long to realize the whole package was disagreeable to me: law school; winter vacations at Elaine's parents' home in Sea Island; engraved stationery; propriety; moderate, continual success in work.

Oh, God. Poor thing that she married me and never sensed the doubt, the traitor in me. Well, she's married again, to a New York City banker, and she's happy, and I'm glad. And I'm here, doing what I chose to do, and I'm happy, and I won't impose my life-style on anyone else ever. I like teaching, I like this farm. I like a simple, private life. I don't mind being alone." He stopped then and looked up at Dale. "I'm sorry. I've talked too much."

"You haven't," she protested. "You haven't at all! I'm just stunned." She felt awkward, and wanted to let him know it was all okay—the marriage, the divorce, the farm, everything about him. "My parents just recently divorced," she told him. "They were married thirty years. I still can't believe they're divorced. I've got to go visit them. I'm afraid my mother's gone senile or crazy or something. She's apparently had a complete character change."

"Thirty years," Hank said. "God, that's a long time to be married. Although my parents have been married at least that long—they must be going on *forty* years. It boggles the mind, doesn't it?" He smiled.

"Tell me more about your parents," Dale said.

"I will," Hank replied. "But later. Now the sun has come out and I want to go out for a walk with you. I'll tell you all about my parents later. Don't get excited, though; it's not a very fascinating tale. Come on."

He pulled her to her feet and led her out the back kitchen door. "This way," he said, and outside he seemed different: freer, younger. "There's a path through the woods over there, that leads to some enormous old gray rocks, with a cave in one of them. It's not my property, but I know the owner—I have the option on his land—and he doesn't care if I walk there. I want to show it to you; it's great. Are you warm enough?"

Dale laughed. Was she warm enough? She was on fire inside her sweater and leather jacket; she was incandescent with delight. He was going to show her rocks and caves; he was going to tell her about his parents. He had slept with her, he had fed her, he had talked to her, he was holding her hand. The late October day was crisp and cold and golden. Leaves crunched beneath their feet, birds called. As they climbed the side of a hill they could look down on the cattle standing in the far end of the pasture, dumb with the pleasure of warm sun on their backs. Dale felt expansive with a warming contentment; she thought she felt the pleasure of the cows, the satisfaction of the singing birds, the solid complacency of the earth beneath her feet. When she looked at Hank, she could not keep from smiling, and he smiled in the same way at her. Everyone in the world was surely allotted one day of joy, she thought, and that day had finally arrived for her. She relished it, she did not care what it cost, it was so sweet, so fine, it was worth anything. Occasionally Hank stopped walking, and took Dale in his arms and kissed her face, her breasts, her neck, and then stood awhile, simply holding her close to him, as if perhaps he too felt the miraculousness of the day, of what had been given to them. They walked through the woods, holding hands, or stood against a tree, embracing each other, wondering over and over again at what they felt: a total, complete, completing joy, as enormous and consuming and splendid as an ocean full of flames.

THREE

The seventh day in November in Vancouver, the rain came down in sheets, as it had for three previous days. Rain dripped and drizzled down the masts of unused sailboats tossing in harbors, down and off branches and needles of pines and hawthorn trees, from holes in gutters into pools and rivulets in the grass. There was little light from the sky because the sun was hidden by such dense rainladen clouds. Children developed runny noses and distraught mothers took them out anyway, to the Stanley Park aquarium to watch the turtles glide through enormous green, dimly lit tanks, or simply to the drugstores where they strolled up and down buying colored soap they didn't need—anything that would allow them to stay awhile longer in a large busy bright place where they could ignore the rain. Businessmen were drenched crossing the parking lots from their cars to their offices, and the sodden cuffs of their trousers flapped forlornly against their ankles, and water dripped off their hats or ears and ran down their backs, ruining the feel of their freshly ironed shirts. Headlights shone on cars and lamps shone from houses during the day; people began to feel claustrophobic. Winter was setting in, day and night were becoming the same, the rain was monotonous, steady, insistent.

Margaret Wallace lay in bed for most of the four rainy days. She got out of bed now and then and exercised to music, or wrote in her journal, or took long baths, or ate, but mostly she stayed in bed, reading. She read three books: a brittle, sharp, well-written feminist novel; a collection of essays on the nature of man; and a new rich romantic mystery. Occasionally she felt one pang of regret—that she had vowed to give up chocolates, because eating them made her fat and made her face look bloated. And she loved chocolates so, especially when she was reading mysteries. But she ate a stalk of celery instead, which she had cut up into many small, elegant, bite-sized pieces. And at the end of the four days, when she was dressing to go out, she stepped on the scales to find that she had not gained a pound in spite of her days of lying about. So it all balanced out: she had to give up chocolates, but she had gained a precise and keen beauty of features and body because of it.

She did not mind the rain; she enjoyed it. She liked being cozy and self-sufficient and isolated inside her small house. She made fires; she made tea. She did not look out at the ocean often, because she could not see the ocean, though it was only one hundred yards from where she stood. She could see only gray sheets of rain. It didn't bother her. She dozed off in the middle of the day, she read in the middle of the night; it was all the same to her. She almost begrudged the interruption of her days by the evening she had planned with her friend Miriam, and Miriam's husband Gordon. But she roused herself: the program was a good one, the orchestra would be doing Vivaldi, and Holst, and Brahms. And afterward she was going to a cocktail party with Miriam and Gordon, and there would be lots of people there she hadn't met. It would be a good evening, and the next day she could sleep late and read again all day in bed.

Margaret put on slim black trousers that felt like silk, and a persimmon-colored blouse, very long and loose and flowing. She put on eye shadow, eye liner, rouge, lipstick, with a steady, subtle hand. Her dark-brown hair, still growing out, was an awkward length now, just below her ears. She swept one side of it back and held it with a black comb: there. She looked really quite good. Elegant, assured. She took up a warm dark-blue shawl for her wrap, and at the last moment grabbed up an umbrella before walking out the door to the car where Miriam and Gordon sat waiting for her with smiles. No one in Liberty, Iowa, would have recognized her, and she was completely, and deliciously, her true self.

The seventh day in November in Rocheport was a cool drab day, windy and bleak. Hank picked Dale up after school and drove her to his farm, as he had every night for the past two weeks. Tonight they had a lot to tell each other: the information Dale had received in the mail about the film series, and the trip Hank wanted to chaperone to Boston, and every detail of the day they had spent apart. As they talked, they rapidly chopped vegetables: tomatoes, lettuce, onions. And cheese. They were making tacos. While Dale stirred the meat and sauce, Hank made margaritas, and Dale's mouth watered to see the drinks, the rims of the glasses cold and thick with salt. They sat across the wooden kitchen table from each other, eating hungrily, scooping up any extra filling off their plates with greedy fingers. Their fingers and mouths became greasy and stained. "God, this is *good!*" they kept saying to each other, and were too gluttonous to say much else.

The first week they had come home and gone to bed immediately, then eaten. This second week they reversed the pattern and ate first. After they finished every scrap and chip of taco, they wiped their hands and mouths briefly, then hurried, laughing, carrying their margaritas with them into the chilly bedroom. They stripped off their clothes and crawled into bed, laughing and gasping in the cold sheets. After they made love they cleaned up the kitchen, and ate red raspberries, and listened to music, and read. Hank eventually drove Dale back to her apartment, for propriety's sake, and she washed her hair and bathed and fell into bed exhausted, sated, feeling fat and full with food and love.

It did not rain in Milwaukee on the seventh day of November, but there was a dramatic change in the weather; a windstorm from the east. Daisy woke to the sound of waves thudding against the breaker rocks below their house. The sky was teal-blue, ominous, strangely darker than the lake, and the lake itself pitched and tossed dramatically. Daisy was distracted; she was fascinated by the windstorm on the lake and longed to stand and watch the whitecaps grow and explode against the rocks. But Jenny was fussy and clingy, and breakfast had to be made. And then Paul moved out of the house.

He had told Daisy he would be leaving, that he was moving into Monica's apartment to live until they could move to California. He had been going through the house for several days, gathering up books, record albums, papers, clothes, personal belongings, and sticking them into cardboard boxes he'd brought from the grocery store. On this day, he had satisfied himself that he had packed up everything that he wanted, and he began to carry it all out to his car, hurrying, anxious about it, afraid that it would begin to rain and ruin his possessions. Daisy kept out of Paul's way—she did not like the way he looked at her, or avoided looking at her, when she was in the same room—and she al-

ternated between tending to the children's needs and staring out the window at the lake. She couldn't *think*: she was
possessed by a demonic uneasiness, but she couldn't think,
she couldn't get her mind to work. Her head kept filling up
with absurd memories: of the first night she had spent with
Paul, locked in his arms, her bare legs twisted with his, of
their cozy smug meals together the first two years of their
marriage when they would compare their working days and
drink wine and talk about money, of the day she and Jenny
came home from the hospital: she had sat in the back seat
holding both her jealous two-year-old son and her tiny four-
day-old daughter, and Paul had sat in the front seat, driving the car, and Daisy had been so perfectly content, thinking that now they were a family, rich and full, and Paul
was at the front of their little group, steering their lives
through the world, controlling them, protecting them, because they all belonged together. She had thought it would
not end, that it would go on and on. She had assumed that
her new life would be like her old life in Liberty; she had
assumed that the life of this new family with her as the
mother and Paul as the father would progress with the
same gentle, orderly, harmonious, sensible unfolding that
her life with her parents and Dale had done. She felt that
they had become a unit, Daisy, Paul, Danny, Jenny, a real,
interlocked, fused unit—as if they were a table, and each
person were a leg. With Paul leaving, it was as if a leg of
the table were being lopped off, and the rest of them all
toppled over, smashed to the floor, and were suddenly without function or value. It hurt to think about it. It did not
make sense. It did not seem real. She expected any moment that she would wake up from this unbelievable situation, or that Paul would laugh and say, "Oh, Daisy, I can't
leave you and the children!" She had not told her mother
or her sister or any of her friends about the divorce, because she wanted to believe that Paul would suddenly an-

nounce that he had made a mistake, that he did not want to leave, and life would continue as it had before.

But now Paul was really leaving. Yet she could not see this clearly; she could not somehow receive the full impact of Paul's act. She was distraught, befuddled. She kept giving her head little shakes, as if to clear it, but it did not clear.

She was up in Jenny's bedroom, changing Jenny's diaper, when she heard Paul call up the stairs, "Well, then, I guess that's all. I'll be going now. I'll call you soon."

Jenny's bottom was gleaming red—she had diarrhea, and was screaming with rage. "What?" Daisy had yelled over Jenny's screams, wondering if Jenny was sick. "Just a minute, Paul."

But when she had finished smearing on the Vaseline and taping on a fresh paper diaper, when she had picked Jenny up in her arms and pressed her against her shoulder, soothing her, when she finally got out into the hall with Jenny whimpering against her, Paul had gone. The front door was shut.

Daisy stood at the top of the stairs, looking down at the closed front door. Automatically she continued to rub Jenny's back. "This is all a mistake," she said aloud. Then, more clearly, she said, "Paul? This is all wrong. This is all a mistake."

No one answered. Daisy hurried down the stairs and got to the front window in time to see Paul's small red Mustang turn the corner and pass from view. Jenny dug her face into Daisy's shoulder, streaking Daisy's robe with tears and mucus. Daisy carried Jenny into the family room and set her on the sofa. It was just after ten o'clock in the morning. Danny had put a Walt Disney ABC record on his little yellow plastic record player, and shrill children were singing a song about numbers. Danny was building a spaceship out of Legos. Jenny slid off the sofa and headed for her dolls. Daisy sank onto the sofa and stared. Except for the children's record—"nine-ten, you're a big fat hen!"—the house seemed quiet and bare. Daisy looked at her hands. They were shaking. She sat watching her children play, and they played happily, ignoring her, and she sat shaking. She got up, hoping that movement would help. She went into the kitchen to make herself a cup of tea. It all seemed so ordinary: the white teakettle with flowers on its side, the white flowered mug, the sight and sound of steam, the commonness of the dirty breakfast dishes and crumbs of toast on the counter. She was still herself, fat and pregnant, wearing her same old fuzzy green robe. But her life had changed completely, and there was nothing she could do to stop it, there was nothing she could do to improve things. She could only pour her tea and pick up the soggy striped dishcloth to wipe the counter clean of crumbs.

She was afraid. Something enormous and drastic had happened to her, and she was afraid, and she did not know what to do. She was vividly aware of the presence of danger in her life, yet there was nothing specific and available for her to do. Her mind raced with fears: How could she raise Danny without a man around? Would her children be psychologically damaged forever without a father in the house? Who would take care of them if she were to fall ill? Indeed, who would take care of them when the new baby was born? How could she possibly find any thread of meaning in life, when the pattern of her life had been so recklessly ripped apart? If she told her friends, what would they do? Would they pity her, yet see her as a woman who had suddenly lost her worth? How could she plan her life? She felt as an astronaut might if his lifeline to the space capsule were suddenly severed and he were falling helplessly through a void.

All day the wind howled, and Daisy wandered the house,

nursing her vague but powerful fears, not quite calling a friend, afraid that might unleash a torrent of emotions she was not yet ready to handle. She felt so alone. When Danny came home from preschool, Daisy could stand it no longer, she had to *move*, to get out of the house. She dressed the children in warm clothes and took them down to the lakeshore. The waves were crashing quite splendidly over the breaker rocks. She knelt with her children just a few yards back from the water, watching with glorious dread as each enormous wave rolled in toward the shore, gathering strength as it came, finally smashing against the rocks with such force that the rocks thudded under the impact. Great sprays of water from the thwarted waves burst up over the breaker rocks and showered down on Daisy and the children. They all shrieked. It was spectacular, intoxicating, it called up something wild in their blood to see the wave approach, approach—knowing there was no way they could stop it or dim its force—to see it approach, approach, swell, swell, and *hit*. It was as if the water were alive, an embodiment perhaps of an angry giant, that came battering and battering against the rocks, trying to reach the people, and each time was tricked and tripped, magically shattering into cold harmless rain. Each time a wave surged and smashed against the rocks, the children jumped up and down and clapped their hands and screamed for joy. Daisy let them scream; she could scarcely hear them above the noise of the wind and the water. She clapped her hands and screamed with them; and screamed again and again.

Finally she brought them back up to the house. They were all drenched and shivering. She immediately put Danny and Jenny into a tub of hot steamy water, then dried them and put them in warm clothes. She served them hot chocolate and chicken noodle soup and lots of cinnamon toast. As Daisy ate the sweet toast, the anxiety which had been gnawing at her all day eased, and instead she was filled with a great exhaustion. She watched television with the children, read them stories, and finally got them into bed. Then she sat in front of the television set, staring for three hours without changing the channel; it didn't matter what she saw, anything was diversion enough. Finally she dragged herself upstairs at eleven-thirty. She fell into bed, too exhausted to think or worry, and quickly fell asleep.

A few hours later Jenny's cries woke her. Daisy pulled herself up from her heavy sleep and went into Jenny's room. The little girl was trying to say something, but she could only emit dry, barking sobs. She had croup. She could scarcely breathe.

This had happened before, with Danny, and Daisy automatically and calmly grabbed Jenny up and took her into the bathroom and sat holding her on the edge of the tub while the shower ran full blast, filling the room with steam. Jenny's breathing improved, and she fell back to sleep, but Daisy remained awake with worry: there was still a wheeze in her daughter's breath that disturbed her. She filled a vaporizer and set it in Jenny's room. She propped Jenny up on pillows and watched her, and finally, unable to sleep in her own room, took her pillow and blanket and slept on the floor in Jenny's room, where she could hear her in the night.

The rest of the night passed quietly, but at six in the morning, Jenny awoke crying and breathing again with an eerie honking catch. Daisy felt her forehead: she had a temperature, and her eyes were dull. Oh, God, Daisy thought, oh, God, what had she done, how foolish she had been to take her little girl out into bad weather. She called the doctor, sent Danny to preschool, and the entire afternoon was organized around Jenny: getting her dressed and to the clinic, sitting in the waiting room for an eternity while Jenny sat on her lap, pale and passive, struggling for each breath. The physician saw Jenny finally, and said that she had a serious bronchial infection and an inflamed throat.

"I don't like to hospitalize such young children," he told her, "when a breathing problem is involved. The anxiety of being in a strange place often counteracts the good a hospital can do. Besides, you can catch things in hospitals; it's full of sick people." He attempted levity, but it was lost on Daisy, who was achingly tired. He became businesslike again: "So she can go home with you, but you've got to be vigilant. You've got to keep Jenny quiet. You've got to keep her in a room full of moisture—use two vaporizers if you have them, and be sure they keep going. The next twenty-four hours are crucial. You'll need to watch her constantly. I'll give you a prescription for the bronchial infection, but it will be a few hours before the penicillin really helps. She'll be okay if she gets through the next twenty-four hours; that's up to you."

As she listened to the doctor, Daisy felt all her unfocused fears disappear: she could no longer worry generally about something as insubstantial as the future; she was sick with terror because her child was so suddenly, desperately ill; and she was overwhelmed with responsibility. She wrapped Jenny in blankets and drove to the drugstore, then walked up and down the aisles holding Jenny in her arms as she waited for the pharmacist to fill the prescription for the antibiotic and expectorant. Jenny snuffled and fussed and wriggled in Daisy's arms, poking at Daisy's swollen belly with her elbows and knees. Damn it, Daisy thought, why didn't they have chairs in the pharmacy so that sick people or mothers with sick children could sit down? And why was the pharmacist taking so long, how could he be so nonchalant, back up behind the high counter—she hated that high counter, it made her feel that the pharmacists were setting themselves up like gods, dispensing the lifesaving medicine at their own pleasure. She could hear the male pharmacist chattering away, laughing and joking with his female colleague, and she wanted to stamp her feet and scream: "Stop it! Hurry up and give me that medicine! How can you do this? My child needs that medicine inside her now!" But when the pharmacist finally announced that the medicine was ready, Daisy took the white sack with meek gratitude, and hurried out the door.

In the parking lot she discovered that her car was almost completely shut in, blocked on both sides by cars which had been parked at close and awkward angles to her own. She settled Jenny in the back seat and forced her own bulgy body behind the steering wheel, and began to maneuver her car out of its trap, furiously turning the wheel this way and that. She had to twist her body around to see if she was going to scrape the station wagon next to her; she grew sweaty inside her coat from the effort. Jenny began to cough and cry and the sack of medicine rolled off the seat with an ominous thump. Daisy stopped the car and searched around on the floor for the medicine, mashing her cumbersome stomach against the seat as she did. But the medicine bottle had not broken. She returned her attention to the task of squeezing her car out into free space, and as she did she saw two old men leaning against the wall of the pharmacy, watching her with smug, superior, critical eyes. Their scrutiny made her so nervous that she turned the wheel the wrong way, and all at once felt that it was all hopeless: she would never get the car out. She saw the watching men laugh and mutter, and frantic with anger at the entire situation, she rolled down her window and stuck her head out to yell at them:

"Just shut up! Just shut up, damn it! Who do you think you are to criticize the way I drive! *I* didn't park my car wrong, the idiots on both sides of me did! How dare you stand there, damn you, making fun of me! I've got a sick child here, I've got a sick *child!* You two should be ashamed of yourselves! Don't you have anything better to do than to stand around laughing at someone with a sick child!"

The men looked at Daisy with such total amazement that it occurred to her that perhaps they hadn't been criticizing her after all. Burning with embarrassment and effort, she frantically edged her car up and back, and finally released herself from her parking space. She drove home in tears, wondering just how in the world she was going to cope with it all.

But once in her house she calmed down, grateful to be on her own ground, to be getting on with it, to be performing the necessary tasks. Danny returned from preschool, and she put both children in the family room, with Jenny drained and unmoving on the sofa. She gave Jenny her medicine, then filled the vaporizer and lugged it into the family room. She covered Jenny with blankets; she told Danny that Jenny was very sick and that he would have to be very good and quiet. She sat for a while holding Danny on her lap for their mutual comfort, for his warmth, and at the same time she stroked Jenny's hand or back. When Danny grew bored with television, she sat on the floor next to the sofa and did puzzles with him. She fixed Danny dinner and gave Jenny a bottle of apple juice and made herself a pot of tea. She watched Jenny, watched Jenny. Jenny lay staring at nothing, laboring for breath. It hurt Daisy to watch her daughter struggle for breath; it hurt not to be able to help.

Night came early, and as the windows grew blind with darkness, Daisy felt suddenly abandoned by the world, isolated. The wind stopped blowing and it began to rain, and as she hurried about the house, changing into her nightgown and robe, setting up a vaporizer in Jenny's bedroom, the sound of the rain beating against the house made her feel besieged. Finally she carried Jenny up to bed, and gave her more medicine and settled her in, grateful that the room had grown thick and warm with steam. She helped Danny get ready for bed, and was touched by his willingness to be good; yet when he fell into his deep healthy sleep, she felt forlorn. She returned to Jenny's room to pull down the shades; she closed the curtains to hide the cold of the night. She closed the bedroom door to keep the steam in the bedroom, but felt uneasy as she did, because then she felt shut off from Danny; she hoped she would hear him if he called her in the night.

Jenny was not asleep; she lay in her bed, her eyes barely open, seeming to concentrate seriously on each breath. Daisy sat on the bed next to her.

"Would you like me to read you a book or sing you a lullaby?" Daisy asked. But Jenny did not answer. Daisy could only sit, watching her daughter, watching the small chest under the fuzzy pajamas rise and fall. She wanted to *do* something, anything, and there was nothing she could do. It had been less painful, less tortuous, Daisy thought, when she had been giving birth to Jenny; then she had been able to labor for her child's life. But now she was impotent. It was not fair, not fair—what could Daisy possibly have with which to bribe Fate that would be equal to her daughter's life? At least, she thought, there was the knowledge of the antibiotics working inside Jenny's body, a real and definite force.

Outside the rain came down steadily, sounding like a persistent, gentle thunder. The room grew more and more moist from the vaporizer, and Jenny's fine hair grew damp and curled around her head. Daisy stroked her daughter's face awhile, then stopped, not knowing if her touch soothed or bothered. She thought she heard a noise: she looked up to see tiny drops of water dripping down the

vinyl window shades. A minute movement caught her eye
and she turned to see a yellow felt chicken losing its head.
It was a sweet little chicken that Daisy had made for an
Easter present for Jenny last spring. She had spent several
nights after the children were in bed, cutting animals out
of different colors of felt and pasting them together on a
long bright green felt strip. The bodies and heads of the
chickens were yellow, the feet orange, the wings and eyes
black. Jenny had squealed with delight at the present on
Easter morning—Danny had loved his felt bunnies—and
Daisy had finally had to hang the chickens up high in
Jenny's bedroom where she could see them but not touch,
not pull them apart with her eager love. Now the paste was
coming loose from the moisture in the air. With infinite
patience, as if part of a chic and subtle joke, the chicken's
head slowly, teasingly, tilted downward, downward, downward, and then fell free. It made no sound as it landed on
the rug. Daisy watched, near tears, and saw that the wing of
the next chicken was also beginning to droop.

"Oh, God," Daisy said, "everything's falling apart."

But when she looked back at Jenny, she saw that her
eyes were closed. She touched her face—it was all right;
Jenny had simply fallen asleep. Daisy hurried down the
stairs to fix herself more tea, then sat at the end of her
daughter's bed, sipping the hot sweetened drink, watching
Jenny, waiting.

At ten-thirty, she woke Jenny to give her the spoonful of
pink antibiotic, the spoonful of yellow expectorant. Jenny
fussed a little at being awakened, and Daisy soothed her,
held her, and within minutes Jenny was asleep again. How
pleased Daisy felt to see her daughter's simple sleep; it
made her nearly cry with relief. The next twenty-four hours
were crucial; the doctor had said so. Daisy determined to
stay on guard.

But as the hours passed and Jenny continued to sleep

peacefully, Daisy became aware of the discomforts of her own body. Slowly she eased herself off the bed and onto the floor. She arranged her nest of pillows and blankets so that she could recline against them yet still be high enough to watch Jenny. Though the room was full of moisture, Daisy's eyes felt dry and harsh with the strain of watching. A very slight sound in the room made Daisy jump: another chicken's head had fallen onto the floor, within inches of Daisy's fingers. Oh, God, Daisy thought in her exhaustion, let all the chickens come apart, just let Jenny live. The vaporizer hissed steadily. It seemed almost a living creature, an obliging friend. She pulled a blanket about her and the warmth seemed so friendly that tears sprang to her eyes. She was so tired. She thought she would close her eyes for just a moment, to relieve the burning sensation under the lids. She could still hear, still listen to Jenny's breathing. It was so steady now, in and out, in and out, and the rasping sound was gone . . . It was after two in the morning. Daisy slept.

At five in the morning Jenny screamed. "MOMMY!"

Daisy leaped up instantly, fighting out through clouds of sleep as thick as pillows to get to her daughter. Jenny's breathing had gone insane: HONK. Pop. HONK. "MOMMY!" Jenny screamed again.

"I'm here, I'm here!" Daisy called to her daughter and stumbled to the bed and grabbed her up in her arms. Her eyes cleared, her brain cleared, everything became painfully, achingly clear: the vaporizer had stopped. The room had grown dry. Jenny was sobbing, and a honking sound tore from her breast. Immediately after each breath, the honking sound came, followed by a strange palpable pop, the tiniest of trap doors snapping shut over her lungs.

"Mommy! Mommy!" Jenny screamed, yet she hit at Daisy, fighting her off. She was awake and terrified by the fact that she could not breathe. Her eyes were as bright and frightened as a wild animal caught in a trap.

"It's all right, it's all right," Daisy said, and grabbed her flailing daughter and ran into the bathroom with her. Jenny screamed and hit and kicked, and Daisy felt the blows in her stomach, a quick surge of fear for the new baby, and then the thought—no, let the new baby die, let this child live, let me make the trade! She nearly fell into the bathroom, nearly threw Jenny onto the floor, then shut the door behind them. She turned on the hot-water faucet full blast, closed the drain, pulled up the shower lever, yanked the shower curtain about the tub with such a force that the metal rings jangled. Then she grabbed up Jenny again and sat with her on the edge of the bathtub, inside the clinging shower curtain.

"It's okay, Jenny, it's okay," she said, absurdly sweet and gentle, trying to calm her frantic daughter. "It's okay, darling, it's okay."

Jenny had stopped screaming, but her sobbing was almost uncontrollable and her breathing had gone wild and wheezy, each breath followed by the hideous, damnable honk and pop.

"It's all right, Jenny, it's okay, darling, Mommy's here, I'll take care of you, see the steam coming, it will make it all better, it will make it all right. See, there it comes, see that funny misty stuff rising, that's steam, like in your vaporizer, it will rise and make your breathing better, you mustn't cry." Daisy babbled. She rubbed at her daughter's back, she stroked her face. She had to make her daughter stop crying, she had to make her calm down, Jenny was nearly choking and her breath was coming in ragged uneven jags. "Calm down, Jenny, Mommy's here, it will be all right, you mustn't cry—JENNY STOP IT STOP THAT CRYING NOW OR I WILL SPANK YOU! STOP IT!!"

To her horror Daisy heard herself yelling at her daughter, saw her own hands give her daughter a sudden desperate shake. Oh dear God, Daisy thought, and despair plunged deep within her, what kind of a mother can I be to scream at my child at a time like this?

But incredibly, her anger had worked. Shocked at the sudden change from the lulling babble to the furious shout, Jenny had choked off a sob and turned to stare at her mother with wide eyes. Her lower lip quivered petulantly, but her breathing regained some evenness.

"That's better, Jenny. For heaven's sake, you'll wake up Danny," Daisy heard herself say in her bossy mama tone of voice, one that Jenny was so familiar with. Obediently, Jenny calmed even more, her chest quivering with repressed sobs. "Settle down," Daisy repeated. "Stop squirming." Jenny was barely moving at all, but seemed to be reassured by Daisy's irritated voice. She relaxed. And the steam rose and rose, while the hot water thundered into the tub, roaring like a flood.

Daisy sat there holding Jenny, not thinking, full of agony, hypnotized by Jenny's honking breaths and the force of the water, bursting downward from the shower nozzle, bubbling about, filling the air with lifesaving steam. She looked at her daughter who was now leaning weakly against her and saw a green streak of mucus run down her nose to her mouth. Jenny didn't seem to be aware of it, but Daisy could scarcely stand the sight; she held her daughter against her with one hand and felt around in the pocket of her robe with the other for a Kleenex. She was so awkward with her swollen tummy that she nearly fell into the steaming tub, but she recovered, and pulled out a Kleenex, used but still usable. She wiped Jenny's nose, and kissed the top of her head. As she kissed her, Jenny began to cough, a painful violent cough that shook her entire body. Daisy's heart exploded within her; she was mad with fear, afraid that Jenny was dying. Jenny choked; her face went scarlet; she gagged and retched; and then she vomited. She leaned forward, retching, and the vomit, thick with mucus, shot into the hot water in the bathtub.

"Mommy!" Jenny screamed.

"That's *good*, Jenny, that's good, it's helping you," Daisy said, but she was sobbing now, too, and clutching Jenny almost helplessly. "That's *good*, it's *all right*," Daisy called out. Jenny screamed again in fear; her body shuddered; she vomited again. Daisy held Jenny by the shoulders, tears streaming down her face; and Jenny vomited again, and again.

And then it stopped. Jenny fell back against Daisy's breasts, panting. The honking noise had gone away.

Daisy held Jenny firmly with one arm, and with the other reached out and grabbed a towel from the rack and wiped Jenny's mouth and chin. Then she managed to reach the sink, to fill Jenny's plastic Mickey Mouse cup with cool water. She put it to Jenny's lips.

"Drink this, Jenny love, it will make your mouth feel better," she said. Jenny sipped at it obediently, then pushed it away. Her face was white with exhaustion. But she was breathing almost evenly, and the honking noise had stopped.

"Mommy," Jenny said after long moments, "I'm tired."

Daisy turned off the hot-water tap; the water was growing cooler, but the room was still steamy.

"We'll get you back to bed soon," Daisy said, softly stroking her daughter. "Just a few minutes more. See how the steam is helping? Don't you feel better?"

In answer, Jenny closed her eyes. Her body sagged heavily against Daisy. She breathed noisily, laboriously, but evenly, and the honking noise had stopped.

"Jenny," Daisy said, "I want you to sit right here on this soft bath mat. I'm going to go fill the vaporizer again. You wait here." She arranged her daughter's limp exhausted body against the bathtub, inside the shower curtain, her head against the white porcelain of the tub, close to the steam. Then she went out of the bathroom and got the vaporizer and filled it. She ran down into the family room and got the vaporizer she had had going that evening while they watched television, and filled that and got it going in the bedroom, too. She put an extra teaspoon of baking soda in to make the steam come faster. When she plugged it in, it nearly exploded with steam, and sputtered so much that she had to put a towel under it. But the room quickly became dense with warm moisture again, and Daisy brought Jenny back to bed. She gave her more medicine. She propped her against pillows, covered her with blankets, and sat staring, as Jenny fell helplessly into sleep. Her breathing was almost normal. It continued evenly, in and out, with no trace of the honking or rasping noise.

Daisy began to shake. Now fear and the lack of sleep hit her in the head and stomach; she hurried from the bedroom down the hall to the bath. The air of the hall was startlingly cooler and drier than the bedroom and bathroom; she felt as though she were hurrying through an icy tunnel. In the bathroom she leaned on the sink, wanting to retch, but nothing happened. Her stomach churned, she shook, but she could manage no relief.

"Oh, *Paul*," Daisy cried. "Oh, *someone*. Please help me." But there was nothing, only silence and the feel of cold porcelain on her hands.

Finally she straightened and took a sip of cold water. That seemed to help. She went into Danny's bedroom and saw him sleeping easily, and she tucked his covers about him, and that helped, too. She went back down the hall to sit with Jenny.

Jenny was totally asleep, pale and small, breathing quietly and evenly. Daisy sat on the edge of her bed, watching. She sagged with exhaustion, but still could not feel sure enough of Jenny's breathing to truly relax. Light was beginning to glimmer around the edges of the window shades; morning had come. Daisy thought of Paul, lying asleep in bed with his lover, thought of the breakfast they would have together, graceful and serene. For a moment she longed to call him, just to share the worry, to say, "Jenny is so sick, and I can't bear it alone." But she knew calling him would not help, and would only irritate him. He would think Daisy was inventing it or exaggerating it simply to call him. They—Paul and Monica—would think she was a harpy, a spurned woman turned bitter and vexatious. No, she would not bother Paul; and what could he do anyway? He could come over and stare at Jenny, now asleep, but then he would go off to work, he had never lost a day's work before because of a sick child, so he certainly wouldn't now. No, he would not be of any help.

But Daisy longed for someone. She wanted to be held, comforted, praised for getting Jenny through the night. She wanted someone to say, "I'll watch Jenny for a while; you go on to bed and get some sleep." But who could do it? No one. Her mother, her sister, were miles away. Her friends all had families of their own, and could not come over; Daisy would not ask it of them. Also she somehow felt that it was necessary that she, Daisy, be the one there at her daughter's side, as if only through Daisy's diligence and concern could Jenny's life be saved. Looking down at her daughter, sleeping so innocently and easily now, Daisy felt at once achingly tired and profoundly glad. She had taken Jenny through the dark night and brought her out alive to a new day. She felt Jenny's forehead: the fever had gone. Instinctively she knew that although there had been steam and antibiotics, it had been the power of her spirit, of her love, which was the real vital force that saved Jenny, that had fought back the spirit of Death from the room.

She remembered her own mother's constant generous care during the times she or Dale or their father was ill; she remembered the feel of a cool hand on her forehead, the feel of someone strong and good standing next to her bed, guarding her, willing health back into her body. Now it was her turn to tend to her children, and she did not begrudge the need or the work. It seemed almost an honor to be able to do it, as if invited to join an ancient ritual of magic. So she was glad. But she was so tired. And so alone.

Daisy sat on her daughter's bed, watching her, until seven-thirty, when she heard Danny stirring in his room. She woke Jenny to give her more medicine, and Jenny took it, still more than half asleep, and fell back against her pillow. Her breathing seemed almost normal. Daisy went out into the hall to see Danny. She cuddled with him in his bed for a moment, almost overcome with the need to let go of her consciousness and to sleep, then she managed to get up, to help him dress, to fix him breakfast. She was not hungry, nothing appealed to her; she drank black coffee, hoping it would keep her awake.

At eight o'clock she turned on the television, and there was Captain Kangaroo in his red coat at a marina with performing dolphins. Daisy stared, entranced. She was amazed to realize that the whole world was out there: Captain Kangaroo, obliging dolphins, laughing children, cameramen. All around the world women were fixing breakfast, children were worrying about tests in school, old people were putting in false teeth, dogs were whining to be let out on the lawn; all over the world people were awake, walking, eating, driving cars, listening to radios, gargling, slamming doors and calling goodbye. It was marvelous, marvelous, and overwhelming to consider.

Yes, Daisy thought, watching a gray dolphin jump and titter, all that is out there, and yet sick children were out there, too, with mothers and fathers riveted to the bedside, sick with fear and hope, with the entire marvelous world shrunk to the size of one closed and steamy room.

"Danny," she said, "I've got to go check on Jenny awhile. You'll have to be a very good, quiet boy today. Jenny is very sick, she was sick all night, and I'm very tired. I'll tell you what, you can watch television all morning today."

"Any program I want?" Danny asked.

"Anything," Daisy said. She turned and went back up the stairs to Jenny's room. Jenny was sleeping peacefully.

The day went on. Daisy drank coffee and gave Jenny medicine and managed to get her to drink a bottle of apple juice. Danny went to preschool, came home again. Jenny felt good enough in the late afternoon to sit down in the family room and watch cartoons. Daisy moved about like an automaton with a few blown fuses, doing this and that, the necessary things. She did not change out of her robe and gown all day. She called no one; isolation crowded around herself and her house like a mist.

By six in the evening, she could hardly move, she was so tired, so deathly tired. Jenny had revived, was breathing easily, had good color, and wanted to move around, but Daisy would not let her. She longed and longed for the bedtime hour to come. She felt constantly nauseated; it hurt to walk, to talk, to smile. Finally she got the children into bed, finally they fell asleep. Daisy fed the cat and washed up the dishes from Danny's dinner and made a brief attempt to tidy the family room, but soon gave up. She was too tired, too tired. At nine o'clock she checked both children, then curled up in her nest on Jenny's floor, with both vaporizers hissing away, and fell into a deep sleep.

Danny woke her at midnight, crying. He was vomiting. Daisy pulled herself up off the floor with weak arms, and after glancing quickly at Jenny—she was breathing normally

—rushed out to help Danny. She carried him to the bathroom (how *heavy* he was) and he threw up on her robe as she did. He threw up on the bath mat and finally into the toilet. He cried as he vomited. Daisy felt his head; he was warm, but not terribly hot. She stripped off her smelly robe and Danny's sticky pajamas, dressed her son in clean pajamas, ran down to the kitchen to get him a glass of 7-Up, carried him into the bedroom and sat him on the floor while she changed his sheets and cleaned up the mess on the carpet, got Danny back into bed with a towel spread over his pillows and another over his sheets and blankets. He whined nastily when she wanted to put a thermometer in his mouth, he said he felt just fine, he just wanted to go back to sleep. Daisy felt his forehead, then left him alone. She went into her bedroom and dug out an old robe that would not close over her stomach but which still kept her arms and back warm. She checked Danny again, piled the smelly clothes into one heap in the bathroom, then stumbled down the stairs to get the pink antibiotic medicine for Jenny out of the refrigerator. She climbed the stairs, gave her sleepy daughter the medicine, then shuffled back down the stairs to put the medicine away. Climbing the stairs again, she nearly cried with fatigue. She filled the vaporizers, then fell into her nest in Jenny's room and slept.

Two hours later, Danny cried and threw up again. Daisy helped him again, gave him 7-Up again, changed his sheets again, and put him back to sleep. She found herself sobbing and cursing Paul as she stacked more sticky sheets in the pile; she found herself horrified at the amount of washing she suddenly had to do, when all she wanted to do was sleep. She checked Jenny again, then crawled into her own bed, desperately hoping no one would wake up till noon. But Danny woke her again at six, vomiting again, weakly this time. Daisy carried, soothed, cleaned, finally got him back asleep, and went back to bed.

The children woke up at eight, as if it had been a normal night. Danny was cranky and tired, and he had blue rings under his eyes, but Jenny had apparently recovered. She was full of movement and noise; she bumped and jumped against Daisy until Daisy felt seasick watching her. By now Daisy was nearly ill with the need for sleep; she blundered down the stairs and filled two bowls full of dry sweet cereal and put the children in front of "Captain Kangaroo" and told them to stay quiet until it was over. Then she went back to her bed and passed out for one sweet lost hour. At nine the phone rang, waking her.

"Daisy? This is Karen. I'm afraid I won't be able to drive Danny to school today. Andrea is really sick with a stomach flu."

"Oh, no!" Daisy said, stunned at the sound of a friendly voice. "Oh, Karen. Danny is sick, too. He was up all night."

"Well, get ready for a busy week," Karen said cheerfully. "This stuff is very contagious. You'll get it, Jenny will get it, Paul will get it, if you have a dog or cat, they'll get it."

"Oh, God," Daisy said, and began to cry weakly. "Karen, Jenny's sick with bronchitis. I can't let her get this stomach flu."

"Well, if Danny's got it, you can't do anything about it," Karen said. "Don't worry too much, it doesn't last too long, it's just a forty-eight-hour thing. You can take care of the kids, and then Paul can take care of you, and then you can take care of Paul. Hey, are you crying?"

"Oh, Karen," Daisy wailed. "I'm so tired. I haven't slept for three nights. And Paul's gone, he's left, he's living with another woman."

After a long pause, Karen said, "Oh, Daisy. My God. I don't know what to say. I'm so sorry. What on earth is Paul thinking of? What's the matter? Is he having his midlife crisis?"

Daisy burst out laughing, wiping tears from her face as she did. "Oh, Karen, Paul hasn't even reached midlife yet, how could he be having his midlife crisis? He's too young for a midlife crisis. This is not a crisis for him, it's romance and freedom and falling in love. It's divorce. I just hope Danny managed to bring the flu bug into the house before Paul left, I'd like his new sweetie to hear him when he throws up."

"Well, Daisy, what can I do? How can I help? I can't even come over today because of this flu thing."

"I know, I know. It's all right. Listen, maybe I'll call you later. It will help just to know you're there. I've got to go check on the kids now, I stuck them downstairs with cereal and 'Captain Kangaroo,' and I think I forgot to give Jenny her medicine this morning. Don't worry, I'll be okay. I'll call you later."

Daisy hung up the phone, crawled out of bed, and went downstairs. She felt dizzy from three nights of interrupted sleep, but otherwise rather cheerful, simply to know she could count on talking to Karen later. The family room was a mess. Jenny hadn't wanted her cereal, and had accidentally knocked her bowl on the floor, and little round sugar-coated balls of corn were lying everywhere. But both children were sitting placidly, hollow-eyed, against the sofa, staring at "Romper Room." Daisy crawled about on the floor picking up the cereal. She gave Jenny her medicine and held her and forced her to drink more 7-Up. She trudged up the stairs, picked the soiled laundry up in her arms, and trudged down to the laundry room to begin washing the clothes. By the time she got back upstairs, Danny was crying again, and throwing up pathetic amounts of clear liquid. She cleaned up Danny and the mess on the family room rug, and wrapped him in a blanket, and read him stories until he fell asleep in her arms.

The doorbell rang. Daisy looked at her watch; it was ten-thirty. She was reluctant to answer the door, knowing how she must look on this bright morning in her too-small rumpled robe and nightgown, with her hair sticking out every which way. But she still put Danny down on the sofa and went to answer the door.

A prim, neatly-suited woman in her sixties stood there smiling, a large black notebook in her hand.

"Mrs. Mitchell?" she said. "I'm Corinne Wentworth. I'm with Hamilton, Hamilton and Dunne Realty. I'm sorry if I've caught you at a bad time, but I was in the neighborhood and thought you wouldn't mind if I looked through the house."

"Why? What about the house?" Daisy felt numb.

"Well, to get information for our listing sheets and our clients, of course," Corinne Wentworth said brightly. "I'm sure you'll have no trouble selling this house; everyone wants to live on the lake."

"This house isn't for sale," Daisy said.

The woman stared at her. "Why, yes it is," she said. "Yes, indeed it is. Mr. Mitchell talked with us just this morning."

"*This house is not for sale,*" Daisy said, and she began to shake. "This house is not for sale now, and it never will be. It's none of Mr. Mitchell's business. I live in this house, and so do my children, both of whom are sick, and no one is going to come in this house and bother me and my children, now or ever."

"Well, I'm terribly sorry, I'm sure," Corinne Wentworth said, not backing off an inch. "But Mr. Mitchell spoke with me personally this morning, and he assured me—"

"THIS HOUSE IS NOT FOR SALE!" Daisy screamed. "If you try to come in this house I will kill you! Mr. Mitchell is a liar and there is no way this house can be for sale! The deed is in my name as well as Mr. Mitchell's and my father gave me money for the down payment, and the house is not for sale and never will be, and if you ever bother me again I'll call the police and have you arrested for harassment. Now get off my property!" Daisy slammed the door in the woman's face, and turned the night lock firmly.

She ran to the family room: Danny was asleep and Jenny was staring docilely at a game show. The sunlight streaming in the window seemed unreasonably and harshly sane. Daisy went into the kitchen and dialed Paul's office. When he answered she had to dig her fingernails into her shoulder to force herself not to scream at him. She was not crazy, she reminded herself, *he* was: crazy and wicked.

"Paul," she said. "I've just sent away a woman who seems to think this house is for sale and that you told her so."

"Daisy," Paul began.

"Before you go on," Daisy said, her voice shaking but resolute, "let me tell you that Jenny nearly died two nights ago, and everyone is sick now. Jenny has bronchitis and Danny has stomach flu. You are not going to kick us out of this house, not now, not ever."

"Daisy," Paul said, "I'm sorry to hear the children are sick. And I'm sorry Mrs. Wentworth bothered you. She shouldn't have come over there this morning. She was rushing things. I mentioned that I was going to put the house on the market, and she just got overeager, I guess."

"You are not going to put the house on the market," Daisy said.

"Daisy, I don't want to argue with you while everyone's sick. You shouldn't have to discuss this now. Why don't we talk about it another time, when you feel better?"

"You are not going to put this house on the market. You are not going to sell this house."

"Daisy, I need the money. I can't possibly keep up the

mortgage payments, and I need the money from the equity."

"Most of the equity is money my father lent us," Daisy said coldly.

"Twenty thousand of it is," Paul replied. "The other twenty thousand is ours. Half yours, half mine. If you can figure out some way to pay your father back his twenty thousand, and some way to give me my ten thousand, and some way to keep up the God-awful mortgage payments and fuel bills, then you can keep the house. But otherwise you've got to sell the house, and that's that."

"This is our *home*," Daisy whispered desperately.

"It's too big for you," Paul said. "One woman and two little children don't need such a big house."

"We needed a big house when you were living with us, and all you ever did was sleep here," Daisy said. "And let me remind you that it's going to be one woman and *three* little children. Paul, I've been as nice to you about all this as I could. But if you try to take the house away from me, you're in for a lot of trouble."

"Daisy, I don't want to fight with you. You've got to be reasonable. It will end up in court anyway, and no judge will let you keep such a big house, no judge will expect me to make such payments. My God, if I make the house payments, I won't have anything left to pay you child support and to live on myself."

"You can't sell this house," Daisy repeated stubbornly.

"Daisy, you're tired. You're distraught. I won't sell the house now. We'll wait. I'm sorry that woman bothered you. Just wait, and we'll talk about it again. Maybe early next week."

Daisy hung up and walked away. She wandered the house in a stupor, staring at the dark oak woodwork she had oiled and polished, at the casement windows she had painted, at the ten-foot-high walls she had papered. She tried to think through the blur of fatigue that was waving inside her. The house. She realized that she had not done much reasonable thinking in the past few weeks, that she had gone around like a sleepwalker, or an accident victim in shock, not openly acknowledging the results, the irreversible changes in her life. Paul was leaving. Paul had left. He wasn't coming back. She didn't really *want* him back. And she leaned against the winding oak staircase and cried gently, to think that she felt more pain at losing a house than at losing her husband. It made her feel guilty to realize that. And yet it was somehow obscene that she should have to lose both, that Paul should take away from her all security, all help with the children, and now their home. She was so tired that it was like being possessed by a demon, or like being drugged, her body was pulling against her, trying to sink down to any flat surface where it could collapse. But she stumbled back into the kitchen and dialed Paul's office again.

"Paul," she said when he answered, "I am going to go to Vancouver next week to see my mother. Don't get upset, it won't cost you a cent. Mother is paying for the ticket. All you have to do is come stay with the children."

"Oh, Daisy, don't be foolish," Paul said. "I can't stay with the children—"

She interrupted him. Her voice was cold and immensely sane. "Of course you can," she said. "In a few months you are going to live in California, leaving me to take care of three children for the rest of their lives. All I'm making you do is take care of two children for one week. It won't kill you. Danny's in preschool every afternoon. I can give you names and phone numbers for lots of sitters. All you have to do is give them dinner, and spend the night here with them, and give them breakfast and get them dressed. That's not much. And you can ask Monica to help. If you're living with her, if she's got the fun of you, well she surely won't mind being *agreeable* to the children as you said she would."

"Daisy," Paul began. "This is absurd. I can't—"

"Paul," Daisy said, "next Monday I'm flying to Vancouver, and I'm leaving this house with two children, *your* children, in it. You have to be responsible for your children for one week in your life, and it won't kill you. If you don't come take care of the children, they'll just have to sit alone in the house for a week and starve to death or electrocute themselves, and it will all be on *your* head, because I'm going to Vancouver. Think of it financially, Paul. While I'm there I'm going to see if I can get some money from Mother so I can keep the house. Think of it that way."

"All right, all right," Paul said, his voice dark with irritation. "All right. But you line up the sitters for me for next week, will you? Someone to take care of the kids in the day. I'll take care of them at night, but I've got to work in the day, you know."

Daisy hung up the phone again, and then, before the momentum could leave her, called a travel agency to have them make reservations for her to fly to Vancouver. She called babysitters and arranged for them to come. Later when she called Karen she would ask her to check in on the children. And suddenly it was all done, it was all arranged. If she had stopped to consider it before doing it, she would have thought it impossible, to leave her two small children for a week. She had never left them for more than five hours at a time before.

She went back into the family room. Now both children had sagged into sleep, lying sprawled on the sofa, snoringly content. It made Daisy nearly retch to see the family room; every toy and book and crayon and doll had been taken out of its proper place and scattered across the floor during the past few days. Little violet and orange and red and black and green circles of flat plastic from Danny's Winnie-the-

Pooh game were scattered across the carpet like large confetti; puzzle pieces had been stacked like towers; all the dolls had been undressed and their clothes unzipped, unbuttoned, unfolded, and flung into different corners of the room; a pile of soiled towels spilled over next to the sofa. On television a clean housewife with a polka-dot scarf on her head was holding a mop in one hand and kissing her husband with what would have been taken as insane glee in a normal household. Daisy crossed the room and turned the television off. She sat down on the floor of the family room and began to sort the puzzle pieces out: Little Red Riding Hood in one pile; the Owl Family in another; the dump truck in another; and so on. She lost interest in it after a while, and after checking on the children again, went up the stairs to the bathroom to brush her teeth.

She was surprised at how old and bleak and haggard she looked. Her skin was gray. Her hair was stringy and matted. Her lips were chapped. Her eyelids drooped. She looked fifty years old, and she was only twenty-nine. The thought of the next few days ahead of her, home with sick children and no diversions except those involved in cleaning up the house, made her shudder. She couldn't in good conscience ask a babysitter to come to the house to relieve her for a few hours, not when Danny's stomach flu was so contagious. She would simply have to muddle through, survive the next few days by herself. Alone. Survive until she could leave on Monday, see her mother.

It occurred to her then that this was the way it would be from now on. Forever. Except that there would soon be another baby to take care of. Then she might have three sick children on her hands at one time; she might as well plan on that happening at least once.

It was really funny. How had it worked out this way, that she was to have three children and no house, and Paul was to have a new young wife? The whole thing was enough to make her howl with fury and resentment at the man she had married, at her plight. When she had been growing up, when she had married, she had never once thought of herself as becoming a bitter woman, a woman burdened with despair. And even now she did not want to be that way. Yet so many things were weighing her down—all the immediate, concrete things, Danny and Jenny's sickness, the loss of her house; and even worse, a great weight of nameless fear. Suddenly she felt lonely and rejected and unloved and unlovable and ugly. She wanted to hurt Paul and Monica, yet hated herself for that desire. She felt helplessly, heavily full of grief. She was afraid of the future, and too exhausted to do more than survive her present. And she could feel rage building up inside her just as surely as the whitecaps grew as they approached the shore of the lake. She wanted to collapse onto the bathroom floor in a fit of tears and raving.

But she could not, not yet. She had to see to the children, she had to watch over them. When she got to her mother's house, she would let her guard down and really rant, really cry; she would hold herself in until then. She was not sure of the direction her life was going, but she knew she wanted to safeguard her little charges: her son, her daughter, and this new baby which now kicked and kicked inside her, as if reacting to the turbulence of her heart.

She smiled down at her stomach, and said, "Hello, Baby." She took off her robe and nightgown and began to take a hot shower, caressing her stomach a long time, as if to get reacquainted with the new baby, to apologize for not thinking of it much in the past few days. She washed her hair, rubbed moisturizing lotion on her face, put on fresh clothes and perfume. She made plans for the day, the tiny fragile plans women with sick children make for themselves, like rewards they would give themselves for simply going on: she would call Karen, and she would call her two other close women friends. And tonight she would call her mother to tell her she was coming out to visit next week. And she would even call Dale; she hadn't spoken with Dale for a long time. She would ask a babysitter to come over tomorrow so that she could sleep if the children were up again in the night, or so she could get out of the house for a while; surely by tomorrow Danny's sickness would not be contagious. She would make chocolate chip cookies today, even though Danny and Jenny were probably too sick to eat them; she could put them in the cookie jar for next week—and eat most of the uncooked dough herself. Chocolate chip cookie dough was one of the best things in her life. She would pick up the family room and do laundry, but let the rest of the house go—let Paul clean it if it bothered him. At three o'clock she'd have a glass of Chablis. She would play with the children and take care of them, but while they were watching television—and they could watch a lot of television today, because they were sick—she would read a new romantic paperback. She would make it through this day and the next and the next until she could get to her mother, until she could reach a place where she could be a child again, and receive a child's portion of consolation and care.

Daisy went back down the stairs and into the kitchen to begin making the cookies. She loved creaming the sweet brown sugar and the soft butter together, she loved the alcoholic aroma of vanilla, she loved the richness of the chocolate chips. She began to feel almost happy, exhilarated with fatigue. She went into the family room, sucking on a great spoon of dough, and stood there, swaying, watching her sweet sleeping children: listening to them breathe.

FOUR

Daisy couldn't help but laugh. She was thinking of the little bags of surprises she had given to her children that morning, so that in their eagerness to look at their loot they wouldn't cry to see their mother leave. She had given them some candy, some Little Golden Books, and some cheap dime-store toys, including, for each of them, a yellow and red plastic harmonica. The children loved harmonicas and played them ceaselessly when they had them; Daisy usually threw them away as soon as one entered the house, because the noise was wildly unnerving even to the most doting of mothers. Jenny usually contented herself with walking around the house simply inhaling and exhaling over and over again at one certain note, making a sound exactly like that of a French police car siren. But Danny attempted to play real songs on his harmonica, and was inventive and tireless. Neither he nor Jenny seemed bothered by the fact that their music was dissonant, loud, and painful—just as children didn't seem to be driven mad by other children's shrieking, wailing, or sniveling—and they could stay in the same room together playing harmonica duets until Daisy's head ached and she found herself tense with inexplicable rage. Well, she hoped that the children would like their presents, and that they would play their harmonica duets for their father when he returned home from work that evening, and when he awoke first thing in the morning. It was a trivial sort of treachery, giving the children harmonicas when she left, but it was the best she could do in the situation, and it gave her a real satisfaction; it made her laugh.

It was two-thirty in the afternoon, and Daisy was almost at the end of her four-hour flight from Chicago to Vancouver. She had truly enjoyed the flight. As the plane lifted off the ground with its almost unimaginable speed and ease, she had suddenly felt set free—released, relieved. Danny and Jenny were both over their illnesses, and Daisy was exhausted from the constant pressure and worry. Now she was wearing fresh, clean clothes and she was sitting alone with an entire coach-class airplane seat to herself. It was real luxury—no sweet but wriggling child could climb up on her now to accidentally kick her in her big belly with a careless knee or to spill a drink or wipe sticky hands on her pretty dress. For the first time in four years she was completely alone, with only her own needs to tend to—and she was traveling toward her mother, who would give her the help and advice she so desperately needed. It was lovely. There were reliable babysitters in the house with the children now, and they would be there every day, and Daisy's friends Karen and Jane had promised to drop in every day to check on things. Paul would be with the children at night. Daisy had an entire week of freedom to look forward to. She would rest, relax, and tell her mother about the mess her life was in, and get a good full helping of love and support to carry back with her to face the frightening future.

The future. Daisy had been too totally involved with the

real struggle of getting through each day to think of the future, but as the plane ascended into the sky and gently lev-
eled off, she tried to gather together her thoughts to plan.
She settled back in her seat and folded her hands on her
belly and thought how the very plane that was carrying her
seemed both a metaphor and a sign. Rising so gracefully
from the pull of earth, it seemed to say: look, I am
weighted, too, and tied to the world, I am burdened with
life, and yet for a while I can set myself free. And though
that escape took power, perhaps it was the power of imagination that was the most important of all. So Daisy
wanted to use her powers of imagination, she wanted to
summon up her courage and intelligence to think of the future, to plan.

There would be Danny and Jenny, and there would be
the new baby. That was always first. And Paul would be
gone; she would be alone. It was hard to go much further
than that; it was so different from anything she had ever
planned on. At some point Daisy knew she would have to
break down and cry for herself, to mourn and wail over all
that she had lost—and sometimes it seemed that she had
lost the meaning of her life. If Paul did not want her and
his children, who would? She had been too busy caring for
the children to grieve for what she had lost, but that grief
was there, building up inside her, as real and heavy a
weight as the baby she carried. Perhaps, Daisy hoped, when
she was with her mother she would be able to let go, let
down, collapse and cry. She hadn't yet told her mother
about the coming divorce; she wanted to tell her face to
face. She wanted to fall into her mother's comforting arms
and cry; she wanted her mother to take away the pain. In
fact she did not want to turn to face the pain until her
mother was there to help her. When she had married Paul,
she had thought she was a grown-up, that she would not
need her mother again. But for the past few weeks she

had been dreaming of her mother, of her mother's tender
warmth and ample soothing love, and it was the kindest
thing in Daisy's life that the plane was carrying her toward
that.

So—the future. It might also mean moving out of
their home, the graceful welcoming house that Daisy had
painted and oiled and polished and made her own. Now it
was early November. She had persuaded Paul to let them
stay in the house through Christmas at least; she had tried
to persuade him to let them stay in the house until the end
of March when the new baby would be born. But Paul had
pressed her; he needed the money, and the real-estate
agents were pressing him, wanting to show their house to
clients who were eager to find a large house on the lake.
Also, Paul had said, and actually he had been right, it
would be much easier for Daisy to go ahead and move before the baby came. Afterward she would be so tired. If she
moved out in January, that would give her two months to
get herself and the children settled in a new home before
the baby disrupted their lives. Daisy had acquiesced, more
out of a sense of unreality than of accord. And Paul,
relieved by what he took to be her reasonableness, offered
to show the house in the evenings while he was living there
—two or three people were almost ready to buy the house
simply from seeing it from the street—so that Daisy
wouldn't be bothered. He had even asked Mrs. Wentworth
to look for a pleasant little home in a good neighborhood
for Daisy and the children; he was trying to be helpful, he
said.

"You're in the wrong profession, Paul," Daisy had said
to him once over the phone. "You should be a used-car
dealer. You'd make a killing."

"What?" Paul had asked, an edge of fear in his voice.

"Never mind," Daisy had said. "Never mind." She had
known that nastiness would do no good, but the tempta-

tion was always so strong; she wanted to scratch at Paul, to cause him little wounds, because the one he was dealing her went so deep.

Of course she knew being nasty would not help. The only thing that would really change matters was money. Daisy sat in the plane, unable to think much further than that: that she needed comfort from her mother, and she wanted money from her mother, too. Oh, how Daisy hoped her mother would offer her some money, enough money so that Daisy could keep her house. She hoped her mother would just *give* her the money with the easy generosity with which she had once given Daisy bikes and party dresses and dolls. Yet she was not sure just how much available money her mother had, or what rights she as a grown child had to ask for such a large sum. Was she being too demanding, too greedy? How could she bring up the question if her mother did not immediately make the offer? And what would she do if her mother had really changed? Daisy had been taken aback a few days earlier when her mother had said on the phone, "Oh, I'm glad you're not planning to bring the children. I was afraid you would want to." What kind of grandmother was she who did not want to see her grandchildren? It was obvious from her letters that she had changed, and Daisy tried to prepare herself. Still, her mother was her *mother*, Daisy thought stubbornly. Her mother would have to help.

The no-smoking, fasten-seat-belt lights flashed on and Daisy looked out the window. The plane was descending through clouds, and Daisy could see little but mist and flat, gray land. This was beautiful Vancouver? Maybe her mother *had* gone mad. She took up her purse and combed her hair again and put on fresh lipstick. A few nights of good sleep had restored her face to its normal prettiness, and excitement made her eyes shine. The plane landed with a customary bump, and Daisy relaxed in her seat as it rushed to a stop, then headed in toward the gate. She let almost all the other travelers fill the aisle and leave before getting up herself; she wanted to do it all slowly, to savor every moment. She loved her mother, she had always loved and adored her mother, and a gentle joy was spreading through her now that the actual moment of being with her again was so close. She left the plane and impatiently went through the routine of claiming her luggage and going through customs. Finally she was able to pass through the glass doors and out to the waiting area. She looked about, smiling with anticipation.

But she could not find her mother. There was a crowd of people milling about, some waving, some grabbing other people out of the line of arriving passengers, but her mother was not in the crowd. Daisy glanced at her watch; the plane had been a few minutes late: her mother should be here, she had said that she would be. Daisy set her heavy suitcases on the floor and just stood there helplessly. It was not like her mother not to be on time. A few feet away a slender older woman, chic and stunning and vaguely familiar, smiled at Daisy. Daisy returned the smile politely, looked away, then looked back, stunned.

"Hello, darling," her mother said, and reached out to embrace her. She was wearing a long loose skirt of blue cotton and a long, lighter-blue cotton top; when she reached out for Daisy the full sleeves of the shirt fell as gracefully as angel's wings to her side. Margaret's hair was dark brown, and it fell smoothly about her face and neck; she was wearing violet eye shadow; silver earrings dangled from her pierced ears. She was beautiful. This woman was beautiful—and the mother Daisy had known had never been more than clean.

The mother Daisy had known. She had been, Daisy remembered, overweight; that was her most salient feature. Margaret had not been *obese*, which implied unacceptable amounts of flesh, but she had been acceptably fat. She had been large and round. She had had a big bowl of a tummy, and heavy thighs which never saw the sun, and sagging watermelon breasts, and chubby calves and arms. All that fat had been packaged into plain and shapeless but nevertheless costly and respectable dresses with cloth flowers at a white collar, or a brooch or bow at the neck. Margaret's hair had been very short and curly: every week she had had it done at the hairdresser's. And for as long as Daisy could remember, that short, curly, rather old-fashioned hair had been gray. Margaret had never worn makeup other than a plain pink lipstick which protected her lips from chapping. She had never worn jewelry except for her wedding ring and the respectable brooches. Her ears had certainly never been pierced as this woman's were! Daisy's mother had looked as a *mother* should look: dumpy, expensively dowdy, sexless. She had appeared completely ungiven to any questions of self-vanity—and therefore totally available for assisting the vanity of others.

But now she had completely changed. Now Margaret was slim, chic, well-dressed, lovely—it was as if a magician had waved a wand and transformed Margaret entirely. But if Daisy knew anything at all for sure, it was that magicians of that sort simply did not exist: Margaret had had to change herself, and that meant a vanity and self-discipline and strength of will that Daisy had not known her mother had. Daisy knew better than anything just what kind of effort it took to lose five pounds: and her mother had lost at least thirty. It was fascinating. It was really amazing. Daisy was intrigued. And her mother was a pleasure to look at.

"Mother," Daisy said, "I'm amazed. I'm overwhelmed. I can't believe my eyes. You look fabulous."

"Oh, thank you, dear," Margaret said. "You look wonderful, too—although you have gained a little weight."

"Mother," Daisy said. "For heaven's sake. I'm five months pregnant!"

"Well, that's obvious," Margaret said. "But you've also put on weight. You're much heavier than you were with Danny."

"Mother," Daisy said, "I think I have to sit down."

"Of course, darling," Margaret said. "Let's go on out to the car. It takes about an hour to drive into Vancouver and we can have a lovely talk on the way. There's so much I want to tell you."

"There's so much I want to tell *you*," Daisy said, but now her heart wasn't in it. As she picked up a suitcase and followed her mother out of the airport, she thought ruefully that this was not at all what she had planned on. She had planned on falling apart in the plump comforting arms of her mother; but her mother's arms were no longer plump—and Margaret did not seem comforting at all. In fact Daisy had felt as though Margaret had actually been appraising her, as if Daisy were a book Margaret might or might not consider reading. How her mother had changed! As Margaret walked along, a few feet in front of Daisy, carrying Daisy's largest suitcase with an easy grace, a good-looking man who was waiting for a porter to unload his luggage from a taxi studied Margaret and smiled at her in obvious admiration. And Margaret smiled back, easily, and went confidently on out to the parking lot, while Daisy followed, feeling as waddly and anonymous as a duck.

"Am I walking too fast for you, Daisy?" Margaret said, turning and waiting for Daisy to catch up. "I'm sorry, dear, I didn't mean to rush ahead." And she took Daisy's arm and hugged her to her. But Daisy responded warily; she had decided that her feelings were hurt. This wasn't fair! In fact she was jealous of her mother for the moment, because her mother looked so good and had had such a smile from that handsome man—and he had certainly been closer to Daisy's age than to Margaret's. As they walked through the parking lot, Margaret chatted about the people she wanted Daisy to meet, and Daisy thought how complicated this week was going to be. What she wanted was her mother's wholehearted concentration and assistance; and it was beginning to look as though it would be a task just to get Margaret's attention.

The car, sitting docilely on the flat cement of the parking lot, was another surprise. It was a small bright-blue Mercedes 280S convertible.

"Wow," Daisy said. "Mother, how much did this thing cost?"

"Not all that much more than those enormous station wagons I used to drive," Margaret said, expertly stashing the luggage behind the front seats and sliding into the car. "Besides, you know we've always had money, we just never felt wicked enough to spend it on luxuries. Furthermore," she added, grinning mischievously, "I bought it second-hand, from a friend, so it didn't cost what you might think."

Daisy settled her girth into the car and stared frankly at her mother as she maneuvered the car out of the lot, and down into the traffic of the highway. "This area is called Delta," Margaret was saying. "If you look carefully to your left, you can barely see the outline of the Coast Mountains in the distance. It will take about an hour to get into the heart of Vancouver, so you won't see anything spectacular for a while. There's mostly farmland around here, and peat bogs and such."

"Mother," Daisy interrupted her, "why did you change? How did you change so much? I just can't believe this is you."

Margaret was quiet for a while, then said, softly, "Oh, well, let's do go ahead and talk about it. Then when we get into Vancouver we'll be able to concentrate on the scenery.

All right." She went quiet and Daisy could see her face tensing as she gathered her thoughts. "I want to share my new life with you, but I don't like discussing any of the past; it makes me so irritable, thinking about the past. It's —it's just very hard. Nevertheless, you probably do deserve some sort of explanation. I must seem very different to you —I *am* different. The last time we were together for any length of time was when I came to help you when Jenny was born and Danny was just two. Then I was still a fat old matron. The perfect grandmother. Two years ago— well, it doesn't bear dwelling on, the past, the time I've wasted. There I was, old and fat and respectable, and I can tell you the exact moment my life changed. Do you remember Dee-Dee Lubbock, whose father was the minister at the Baptist church? Dee-Dee was just about Dale's age, in fact I think she was in Dale's class at school. I never got along with Dee-Dee's mother Wanda; I never could forgive her for naming a child Dee-Dee; also, I always thought Wanda was sententious. Or do I mean tendentious? Probably both. Oh, you remember Wanda, she was so mawkish. And I always had to serve on the same committees for bazaars with her; it nearly drove me mad. Anyway, Dee-Dee had come over to the house one day just after Christmas two years ago and sat about awkwardly, and then started whining and weeping and puling about the fact that she was in love with Roger Mills, and he wanted to marry her but he was a Catholic, and her parents would kill her before they'd let her marry a Catholic, and could I please offer her some advice, could I please help her out in some way. So I gave her some cookies and milk, and told her I'd talk to her parents about it—I mean for heaven's sake, Dee-Dee was already twenty-two, and a hulk of a girl, none too bright, and I thought her parents would jump for joy to have any man take her off their hands. So I sat there, listening to her go on and on, bored out of my mind—Dee-

Dee was relishing her little drama, but I was not, I wanted to go back upstairs to the mystery I'd been reading. So finally I got Dee-Dee headed toward the door, and suddenly she turned to me and hugged me a big hot hug, and she said—she said, oh, God, it hurts every time I say it. She told me that she just adored me, she just idolized me, that she was so glad I lived in that town. She said she always thought of me as Mrs. Santa Claus. *Mrs. Santa Claus.* Good God. Well, I thanked her for her compliments, and shoved her out the door and went upstairs to my room, and instead of getting back into bed and reading, I stood there and took a good look at myself in the mirror. And I *did* look like Mrs. Santa Claus: round, old, gray-haired, fat, jolly, repugnantly good. And I knew right then that I couldn't stand it any longer. I couldn't be Mrs. Santa Claus to the Dee-Dees of the world another minute of my life. I grabbed my purse and got in the station wagon and drove all the way to Iowa City and went right to the Elaine Powers Figure Salon."

"Mother!" Daisy gasped. "You *didn't!*"

"Yes," Margaret said, and she was beginning to smile a bit now. "I did. I thought I would die when those skinny young women came at me with the tape measure, but I wrote them a check for a twelve-week course, I gave them the full amount, just to keep myself from backing out. Then I went out and bought a leotard and tights, and I went to the library and checked out books on health and nutrition and beauty and diet and exercise, and I signed up at the university for the Monday night art-film series they were offering. And then, then—I just kept changing. Poor Harry. He came home that night and sat there eating his roast beef and mashed potatoes and peas and white rolls and butter, and I sat there eating celery, and he couldn't stand it. 'I can't enjoy my food if you aren't eating the same thing,' he told me. I told him that was silly. I told him I had decided I had to lose weight for the sake of my health. I told him that as a physician he should know how dangerous excess fat was. But he *hated* it that I was dieting, and every time I lost a pound, he hated it more. He hated it when I drove into Iowa City every day to the exercise salon, and he hated it when I went to the film course on Monday nights. I argued that I wasn't gone any more from the house than I usually was, except that now I was doing something for myself instead of attending school or church meetings, but he said that when I was at the church or school meetings I was still with him somehow, because I was with the community we lived in.

"We went on that way for about a year. I kept losing weight, slowly and steadily; I joined the YWCA in Iowa City and went in twice a week to swim. God, Daisy, do you realize I hadn't been swimming for about fifteen years? Well, I kept swimming and exercising and dieting, and one day I looked at myself and saw that I'd lost about thirty pounds and was beginning to look—different. And Sonja, the manager of the beauty salon, had gotten to like me. I mean I was a big help to her business, you can imagine, she told everyone how I'd looked before; she put my charts up on the wall to encourage everyone. She was really proud of me. In a year I lost thirty pounds and about thirty inches— ten off my waist, five off my bust, five off my hips, two off each thigh and arm. Well, Sonja suggested that I do something with my hair. That I have it set differently, that I *dye* it. I was shocked at first, but then I grew to like the idea, so I got the name of a good beautician from Sonja, and went to her. She suggested that I let my hair grow out, and she dyed it this color—this is the color it was originally, when I was younger—and she cut it this way, so that it would just fall loosely about my head, instead of standing up in those militant little gray springs I had worn all my life. And I sat there in the beauty shop, staring at this new woman in

the mirror, and I began to cry. I was frightened, I'll admit
it. That was my greatest feeling—fear. Mrs. Santa Claus
had been a boring role to play, but it certainly had been
safe! But with my new brown hair and my almost slender
body, I saw that I didn't have to play Mrs. Santa Claus
anymore, that I could start being myself, whoever that was.

"Oh, well, then I went home, and Harry was there, and
he was so upset when he saw my hair that he almost had a
heart attack. I'm not being frivolous when I say that. He
went purple in the face and had to lie down. I ran upstairs
and got a scarf and wrapped it around my head. For a long
while he had been trying to convince himself that I was
just going through a menopausal fit of weirdness, but that I
would eventually return to normal. When he saw my hair,
he knew I had really made some kind of definite change.
And when I saw his reaction, I realized that I would have
to make an even greater change in my life. I would have to
leave Harry, leave Liberty. And the thought made me absolutely giddy, drunk with relief, discovery, hope— Oh, what
a crazy night that was! Harry couldn't stop yelling and ar-
guing, and I couldn't stop smiling to myself. I can't explain
it, Daisy," Margaret said, and took her eyes off the road for
one long moment to stare at her daughter. "You know I
have always loved your father. But suddenly I knew I
couldn't live with him a minute longer. I couldn't stand
the way my life was for one more minute, and I knew that
Harry wouldn't want to change, *couldn't* change if he
wanted to. He was so completely happy in his life. So I
told him I wanted to take a little vacation out to Vancouver to visit Miriam—she was my closest friend all
through high school, and had married and moved out here,
and I don't know why I decided to come see her, it just
came over me. Perhaps it was the only place I had to go.
Harry hoped that the trip would do me good, would make
me come to my senses. Well, you know the rest. I flew out

here, stayed for two months, made a down payment on the house, flew back to talk things over with Harry and to gather up what few belongings I wanted to keep from my former life, and left."

"Poor Daddy," Daisy said. "He must have felt as though a tornado had struck."

"Yes," Margaret said. "He was very bitter. And toward the end I unfortunately became rather bitter in return. I was not very nice, I'll admit it. I said many things that possibly should have gone unsaid. But I was fighting for my life. I think that if there had been a snowstorm that day that Dee-Dee Lubbock called me Mrs. Santa Claus, or if the car had had a flat tire, or if something had stopped me from getting out of Liberty and into that exercise salon in Iowa City, I would have gotten your father's old army revolver down from the closet and put a bullet through my head."

"Oh, Mother," Daisy whispered, appalled. "Was your life really so bad?"

Margaret looked over at her daughter with unsympathetic eyes. "Daisy," she said, "*please* don't start crying. I cannot tell you how tired I am of having people cry around me. No wonder I was so fat and bloated, I was always absorbing all that extra moisture from the air. What you're asking me is not was my life really so bad, but was it so bad when you were home, when you and Dale were growing up, being my little girls. No, my life was not bad then. I was happy. I felt wanted and needed and secure, and you girls both gave me great joy. But you've been gone for over ten years, Daisy, and Dale's been gone for six. So don't feel sorry for yourself, don't try to make yourself into some kind of unloved child. I won't put up with that. I loved you, I loved you both, I loved being your mother. But I've changed, and although that doesn't affect the love I felt for you when you were little, it does affect our relationship now. I feel that for the first time in my life I'm living according to *my* principles, *my* values; and I'd like to show you what they are. It's too late for me to instill them in you, you're no longer an impressionable child. So you'll have to get to know me as an adult. I'd like to stop being your mother. I'd like to start being your friend."

"Well," Daisy said. "Damn."

"Damn?" Margaret asked. "Why damn?"

"Because if I ever needed a mother instead of a friend, it's now. Paul's left me. We're getting a divorce. He's fallen in love with another woman and he's moving to California with her." Daisy stared straight ahead at the road as she spoke, and she felt tense all over as she waited for her mother's reply.

"Oh, dear," Margaret said, and took her eyes off the road for one minute to study Daisy. "Why didn't you tell me before now? My goodness. Divorce. Well, Daisy, how do you feel about all that?"

Daisy could only laugh. "How do I *feel* about it? Well, I feel *terrible*, of course. I'm sad and I'm angry and I'm scared to death. I'm almost thirty years old and I'm overweight and I'm going to have three little children to take care of all by myself. And Paul wants me to sell the house so he can have half the equity, and I don't have anywhere to live, and I've got no one to take care of me—and I'm terrified. I'm absolutely terrified. I wanted my life to have meaning, to be all of a piece, I wanted to be part of a family—and now everything's just in a mess. I'm miserable."

"Well, now," Margaret said, "I'm not sure that's the right attitude to take—"

"Attitude!" Daisy said, and turned to face her mother. This really was too much, she thought, this was really all crazy!

But Margaret went right on talking. "Yes, attitude," she

said. "So much in life depends on how you look at it. Why, Daisy, you've got a whole new life ahead of you, a fresh start. You know I never did care much for Paul, and if I were you, why, I think I'd be celebrating right now. In fact, that's what we'll do: we'll get a good bottle of champagne and drink to your future."

"Oh, *Mother!*" Daisy cried. "How you've changed! I wanted to break down and cry and have you put your arms around me and say 'There, there,' I wanted you to—" But the thought of all she wanted made Daisy's eyes fill with tears and her throat close up. She leaned her head on the car window and for one long moment felt totally helpless and pathetic. She felt so sorry for herself. Rejected by her husband, and now rejected by her mother. It was too much. It wasn't fair. She wanted advice and consolation and sympathy and comfort and she wasn't getting any of it; she felt hurt, pitiful. She felt like a little child who walked all the way to the candy store only to find it closed. "Mother," she said, "really. I don't know what I'm going to do."

"Well, first of all," Margaret replied, and she patted Daisy's hand so briefly that it was almost more of an admonition than a caress, "dry your eyes and stop thinking about yourself. You'll have plenty of time to think about yourself. You've never seen Vancouver before, and it's the closest thing to heaven I can think of. Forget the divorce and all of that for a little while, and enjoy yourself. Look at the mountains. Aren't they wonderful? Have you ever seen anything so lovely? We're in downtown Vancouver right now; aren't those office buildings a marvelous contrast to the mountains? I'm going to drive you through Stanley Park before I take you home. In fact, I think we'll get out and have a little walk. The exercise would do you good. And the second thing you can do, Daisy, is to realize that what you're asking from me I just can't give anymore. I used to give out advice as freely as milk and cookies. People seemed to need it, dull people, they seemed to think that advice came in an edible package, and I tried to keep everyone fed. Well, I don't make cookies anymore, and I don't hand out advice. That does not mean that you can't learn something from me, while you're here; you are not a dull person, Daisy. You are a pretty bright young woman. And you're my daughter, and I love you. I wish you well. But giving cookies and consolation is a hard habit to break, and now that I've managed to do it, I won't start up again, not for anyone. Especially not for you. Especially not for you, Daisy, because you and Dale are the people I love most in the world. You've got to learn to stand on your own.

"Look, here we are, this is Stanley Park. One thousand acres of parkland between the city and the sea. There is Lost Lagoon on the left. We'll stop here, at Prospect Point; that will give you the best view of West Vancouver, and the mountains, and the harbor. Look, isn't that a marvelous totem pole? I've been fascinated by all the Indian lore and art that's a part of British Columbia. Somehow the Canadians have managed to incorporate a lot of the wealth of their Indian heritage into their modern world in a way we Americans have failed to do. There's an artist, Emily Carr, who does marvelous sweeping paintings, a bit like Georgia O'Keeffe, but really there's no comparison, and she includes so much of the feeling of Indians, the primitive people who lived on the land as if they were part of the land rather than owners of it; they've a good exhibition of Emily Carr's works at the public gallery; I'll take you there tomorrow. Shall we get out now, and walk a bit?"

Daisy stared at her mother for one long moment. She decided that Margaret was about as sensitive and receptive as a railroad train; but there was no fighting against that blunt direct force. There was nothing to do, it seemed, but be carried along. Margaret got out of the car, walked to a railing, and stood looking out over the ocean, seemingly oblivious of Daisy. Daisy sighed and rather reluctantly pulled herself out of the car to follow. Without the restraint of the car to frame the landscape in, all of Vancouver seemed to spring up around her, demanding in its really startling beauty. Daisy leaned against the car, stunned, suddenly taken out of herself. She looked about her, and her gaze was carried up and up. On her left were crested, majestic snow-capped mountains rising above the glittering ocean. On her right was a forest of evergreens, taller than any trees she had seen or dreamed, and beyond that, where the forest had been cut back to make way for the city, was the bright clean human lift of cement and glass and steel buildings. It made Daisy almost dizzy to look about her; she was used to more moderate land, to flat land or rolling hills, which signified moderation and orderliness and calm. This land spoke of luxuriant extremes, of bold-faced triumphant isolation. It really was *too much*, Daisy thought, the change in her mother, and now this overwhelmingly beautiful land which would not let her ignore it, which called up wild desires and longings, which made impossible things seem possible simply by its presence—after all, here it was, Vancouver, more beautiful than a dream of heaven. If it could exist, what could not? She understood why her mother had moved here.

"It is fantastic, Mother!" Daisy said, approaching Margaret and leaning on the railing next to her. She watched cars cross back and forth from West Vancouver to Stanley Park on the arching green span of Lion's Gate Bridge. Below, the ocean sparkled with freighters and tugboats. "I've never seen anything like it in my life. Words can't touch it."

Margaret smiled, pleased. "I know," she said. "Miriam had written to me for years, telling me I should come out for a vacation, and she had sent me an occasional snapshot, too. But I always resisted coming here. I was afraid, I think. And of course when I did come, well, I knew I had found my home. It's funny, isn't it, how I could have lived all my life in the middle of the continent, stuffing myself with bread in the middle of the breadbasket, only to discover at the advanced age of forty-eight that I felt truly at home in another country, another city, another world."

"Do you think you would have felt that way—that you had found your home—if you had come out to Vancouver ten years ago, or fifteen years ago, or even five?" Daisy asked.

"Well, Daisy," Margaret said. "I've asked myself that often. I don't know the answer. Well, I couldn't have come twenty years ago, when you girls were small; I could not have taken you away from the safety of your home and your father. Five years ago—I don't know. Perhaps. I think one has to be *ready* for major changes like this; the timing has to be right. It's perfectly possible that five years ago, or even three, I might have come out here, admired the place, and gone back to Liberty quite happily. But the important thing is that I came when I did, and that I'm here, now. And I'm so glad you're here, too; there's so much I want to show you. Oh, I don't know where to take you first; there's so much to see, so much to do."

Daisy watched her mother closely as she spoke, noticing how almost childish she was in her enthusiasm, so self-centered and lighthearted, as if she hadn't a care in the world. Well, maybe she hadn't, Daisy thought sulkily; she certainly didn't seem to care much about Daisy's problems. Only two years before, Margaret had come to Milwaukee to take care of everyone while Jenny was born. How warm and generous she had been then, and what restfulness there had been for Daisy, with her mother there to cook and clean and tend. Oh, how was it, Daisy thought, that she had to lose her mother at the same time she lost her husband? For she had to face up to it: she had, in a very real way, lost her mother. She wanted to snivel and pout, but clearly Margaret would not put up with that; clearly Margaret was just not very interested in Daisy's problems at all.

As if Margaret were reading her mind, she turned to Daisy. Still leaning gracefully against the railing, her entire posture casual and relaxed, she said sternly, "You know, Daisy, I've spent my entire life listening to other people's problems. Your situation isn't half as bad as you think it is, not half as bad as some I've heard. You're young; you'll be attractive again if you lose weight; you will have some kind of house; and you will have three beautiful children. And now you have the chance to have a vacation. I'm not going to help you solve your problems, but I will give you one week of real pleasure, if you'll only let me. Try to enjoy this week. Relax, look about you. Maybe you'll learn something. And please remember: you have a right to your agitation; but I have a right to my tranquillity."

"All right, Mother," Daisy said, conceding. What else could she say?

"Good," Margaret said. "Let's go home. I'm so eager to show you my house."

Daisy sat in the car again, listening to her mother tell how she had found her wonderful house, offering up necessary words of admiration at the landscape they drove through on their way into West Vancouver—and she did admire the landscape; it was amazingly beautiful. But for Daisy it was rather like being on the moon, or another planet, with a guide one is not quite sure is human, so far removed is she from human concerns.

Margaret's house was another shock for Daisy. The house in Liberty had been full of overstuffed chairs, thick carpets, harmonious clutter. Everything in it had been touchable, usable, anyone could sit anywhere; it had been a house for a family to live in. But Daisy wandered through Margaret's new home as if through a museum. In fact her first thought was that of course she could not have brought Danny and Jenny here; they would have gotten the glass coffee table sticky with fingerprints, and they might have toppled over the strange green soapstone Eskimo statue that sat next to the fireplace hearth. They might have touched the white walls, and left marks; they might have left fingerprints on the sliding glass doors that looked out over the ocean, they might have knocked over the tall Chinese vase full of dried autumn leaves and flowers. Daisy's second thought was that *she* was *glad* that her children weren't with her, because now she was free to look through her mother's house without any distractions. It was a beautiful home, Daisy could not deny it. It was breathtaking.

The front door opened to a small entrance hall which Margaret had separated from the living room by a stunning Chinese screen in a silk so purple as to be almost black, with cherry-and-yellow designs blossoming on it. Stepping past the screen, one saw, with a gasp—it did cause a gasp, it was so splendid—the stretch of highly polished dark wood floor out to a wall of glass looking onto the ocean. The other walls of the room were white; there was a white marble fireplace, and a vivid abstract in blues and oranges, which Daisy had never seen before, above the mantel. There was a small white rug, an elegant white sofa and chair, a wicker rocker with what appeared to be a shawl thrown over it, and the coffee table. At one end of the room was the dining area, so gleaming in chrome and glass that Daisy had to turn away, remembering the enormous oak table, the comforting oak buffet she had grown up with. The kitchen was clever and small; and there were only two other rooms: Margaret's bedroom, and the spare room where Daisy was staying.

Margaret's bedroom walls were white and the carpet was

thick and rich and white, but everything else in the room was bright with color: in the corner near the glass wall was the chair Margaret had written about, with the batik bedspread draped over it, so that it undulated in stripes of red, violet, blue, green, yellow, and orange; Margaret's bed, which to Daisy's surprise was queen-size (Daisy would ask why later, when she found the energy to do so) and covered with a thick rich quilt of random dark and light blues; the cherry armoire that had belonged to Margaret's mother, where both Harry and Margaret had once stored their clothes but which now only Margaret used; a small walnut lady's writing desk with papers lying on it, and pens, and journals in red and blue leather. And the one familiar sign that made Daisy feel her mother might not be completely lost to her—the antique cherry washstand, used as it always had been as a bedside table, layered with Margaret's books, magazines, newspapers, and reviews. The lamp of Daisy's childhood was there, too: it was an antique oil lamp which had been electrified long ago; its base was marble and brass, and the globe was crystal etched with flowers. Twelve crystal prisms hung from the brass rimming the globe; six ended in triangular points and were connected to a round prism at the top; the other six were shorter and squarer and connected to an emerald-cut prism at the top. Daisy stared at the lamp, stunned with memory: every night the family would know when Margaret was through reading, because when she reached her hand out to pull the brass chain that turned the light off, she of necessity hit the prisms and they would chime and tinkle in the most clear and lovely way. Just so, in the middle of the night, if Dale or Daisy were sick, or if the phone rang, someone calling for their father, everyone could hear the less restrained tinkling of the prisms as Margaret fumbled in the dark for the brass chain. A few times, when Daisy or Dale had been very very sick, Margaret had released one of the prisms from its tiny brass hook and let the child take it in her hand, to feel its cold ungiving surfaces, or to hold it up in the sunlight, to see the rainbows the sun made from its facets.

In the Liberty house, the crystal lamp had seemed inordinately sensual and extravagant; its mere presence there in their parents' solid room had always been a bit of a mystery. But now it seemed perfect in Margaret's new bedroom. Daisy was struck by a wave of understanding: oh, so *that* is how she really was all along, *that* is what she wanted.

"Your house is absolutely splendid, Mother," Daisy said, coming back into the living room. "I think it's the most wonderful house I've ever seen—except for mine. It's certainly *different* from mine."

"Well, *we're* different," Margaret said. "Here, I made you some herb tea. It's very good. Why don't you take it with you into the guest room and unpack and rest awhile. We're going out to dinner tonight at a wonderful restaurant down on the harbor. It's a Greek restaurant, a *real* Greek restaurant. It's run by Greeks and frequented by the Greek sailors when their freighters are in dock. The food is delicious, and the men do wonderful dances, and if the other Greeks like the dancing, they get up and join, or they throw glasses which smash to pieces on the floor. Then the men dance, some of them barefoot, around the glass. It's rather wild. Not like anything we ever had in Liberty, *that*'s for sure. And I've got some lovely friends joining us. I'm eager for you to meet them. So do take your tea and have a little rest; we'll be up late tonight."

Daisy shut the door in the small guest bedroom and dutifully unpacked, musing all the while about this new mother of hers, who enjoyed watching Greek sailors dance around broken glass. Then she lay down on the bed and stared at the walls. She wondered vaguely how Danny and Jenny were; Paul would be with them now. They would enjoy that, for they never had had much time alone with their father. And though he did not adore them, he would be kind. He was probably even taking them to McDonald's for dinner as a treat. Well, she would not worry about them; her mother was right. It would be a waste of energy to worry about them this week while they were in someone else's care. It was the rest of her life, the real life that she would go back to after this week, that she had to worry about.

On the wall opposite the bed hung a bright Chagall print. Chagall! Daisy thought; she had never known that her mother liked or even *knew* about Chagall. On the wall above the bed hung another print that must be one of the Emily Carrs her mother so admired. It was an almost surrealistic watercolor of one extremely tall, bare, and lonely tree stretching above mountains into a radiance of white. Daisy sat up to read the title: "Scorned of Timber, beloved of the sky." She lay back down again, studying the print. The tree seemed queer and proud, so tall and lonely, with its small triangle of green peaking at the top of its long, thin trunk. It seemed self-sufficient, as if in love with the sky, or something in the sky which ordinary people could not see. It reminded Daisy of her mother, who had grown thin and strange and proud and self-sufficient, and in a flash Daisy remembered another tree, a tree in a book which she had read over and over again to her children, *The Giving Tree*. That tree loved a child so much that it sacrificed everything for him, gave him everything: shade, apples, branches, its trunk, and finally, at last, because there was nothing else it could give, its wretched stump as a seat of solace for the unhappy person it loved. Daisy felt a wave of self-pity begin to rise within her: she was going to try to be the giving tree to her own children; why did she have to be faced at this point in her life with a mother who was like that solitary monster of Emily Carr's?

Then Margaret appeared at the door, first knocking, then entering, and she did not look like a solitary monster at all. She looked like a quite lovely and intelligent woman —an *interesting* woman, and one Daisy would like to know.

"It's time to get ready," she said. "Would you like a bath first? Let me look at the clothes you've brought; they aren't very pretty, are they? Though I know it's hard when you're pregnant. Still, we'll go to some boutiques in Gastown tomorrow and find some batik and Indian print dresses for you. They're very comfortable, flowing soft cotton, in brilliant colors. Well, we'd better hurry, we should be there in half an hour."

"Who are the friends who are joining us?" Daisy asked, pulling herself up to sit on the edge of the bed.

"Miriam and Gordon, of course," Margaret said. "They're dying to meet you; they've only seen pictures of you, but you know Miriam has been my friend since high school. And Anthony Brooks—he's a new and"—Margaret paused to smile—"special friend of mine."

Daisy understood by that smile that Anthony was Margaret's lover. Her mother had a lover! "Mother!" she said. "Oh, Mother." And she sat there on the bed for a moment, her hands on her large matronly belly, looking at her strange new mother, returning her smile.

At seven o'clock the next morning, while Daisy was still asleep, Margaret was sitting by the side of the indoor pool at the rec center. She was wearing a plain black maillot suit and had a black rubber swimming cap on her head and a large green towel draped over her shoulders. She was trying to work up the courage to enter the pool. Two other people were already swimming, doing slow sputtering backstrokes across the water. The lifeguard sat on a bench on the other side of the pool, yawning into his cardboard cup of coffee. There was open swimming now until eight-thirty,

when women's swimnastics would begin. Margaret stayed
for the swimnastics sometimes, sometimes not, depending
on her mood. She disliked the turquoise swimming pool,
which was Olympic size and overly chlorinated, she disliked the enormous high-ceilinged room that echoed and
amplified each sound. She disliked the occasional clots of
hairs that lay on the slick cold tiles, she disliked the diving
boards, the clocks, the temperature gauge which assured
her that it was 78 degrees in the room when she felt as
though it were 30. She disliked the violence of forcing herself into the water, she disliked the reluctance, the laziness,
the sluggishness of her limbs as she worked her way back
and forth, back and forth across the pool.

But she loved the sensation of finally climbing out of the
pool, her entire body vivid and tingling from exertion. She
loved the long hot shower, the feeling of bright cleanliness
she felt as she dried. She felt about swimming the way
Dorothy Parker felt about writing; she hated swimming,
but she loved having swum.

She had come to swimming too late in her life to think
of it as more than necessary physical exercise, a disciplined
attempt to keep her good health. As a child she had rarely
gone swimming, because she had been raised on a farm in
Iowa with her righteous grandparents and her mother and
her retired missionary aunt, and they had not believed that
young girls should swim. It actually hadn't even been
much of an issue though, because there was no pond or
swimming pool near enough to tempt Margaret. Later,
after she had married, she had come into contact with
swimming pools, but by that time she had two small children, and the pools seemed a place for them, not for her.
She had owned swimming suits and only worn them so
that she could go into the water with one of her children,
to hold them by the waist as they splashed about in the
shallow end. And later, when the girls could swim by them-

selves, Margaret had acquired all that flesh, and felt ugly in a swimming suit, ugly and somehow obscene. She had sat in a flowered beach robe, wearing sunglasses, trying to read, constantly surveying the water to be sure her children had still not drowned. Their screeches of delight and frantic pleasure at jumping, diving, plunging into the water had always been a mystery to Margaret. The water had always seemed painfully cold to her. And the few times that she attempted swimming, it seemed that she had to summon up all her energy to fight against the water, to hit out at it, because it wanted to bury her with its remorseless weight, to close over her, to pull her down.

She still felt that way; she could not relax in the water. Floating took more energy from her, the energy of tension and resistance, than the breaststroke. And she could not get over the feeling that she was still ugly and ridiculous while swimming. She did not like the feeling of herself in a swimming suit, or the fact that others could see her that exposed. It was true that she had lost a great deal of weight, and in street clothes she looked quite trim and lovely. But in a swimming suit certain facts could not be hidden: she had been overweight for too long, and the skin around her upper arms and thighs was, in spite of exercise, hopelessly loose and wrinkled. She would never be firmly rounded, supple and resilient again. The sight of Daisy, almost as fat as Margaret had once been, had thrown Margaret into a silent rage: Daisy's body had been *so beautiful*, so slim and graceful and voluptuously ripe. Margaret could close her eyes and envision her oldest daughter as she perched on the diving board during her teenage years; Daisy in a pink bikini with a flat belly and two dimples on her lower back, her smooth sleek buttocks peeking out enticingly from the suit bottom. No, Daisy, no! she had wanted to cry; don't do this to yourself. Don't pad yourself with extra flesh, you'll regret it, you'll regret it terribly! But Margaret did not want to give advice—and she knew Daisy would only be hurt. Besides, it would not be fair for her to be angry at Daisy's fat; it was her own that she regretted, and no amount of dieting on Daisy's part could bring Margaret's body back to a perfect shape.

But the thought of it, the remorse for both herself and her daughter, made Margaret rise up off the bench, throw her towel off, and dive into the water. On different days she swam with different kinds of energy: hope, delight, exhilaration, or grief, regret, anger. Three times a week she came to the pool and forced herself to do thirty laps. She could still do only one lap across the length of the pool at a time; then she had to grab on to the side of the pool, and hang there, gasping for breath. It took her an hour to swim the thirty laps, and when she finally got out she was usually shuddering with exhaustion. But some days were different from others: some days the water streamed by her freely, as if it liked her, as if it were trying to make her work easy. Other days it fought her, pulled her down, and she lost her timing and swallowed water and choked. If she had been a man, she might have taken up boxing instead of swimming; it seemed a sport that she might have really liked. She might really have found pleasure in putting on heavy padded gloves and hitting repeatedly, with a relentless rhythm, a punching bag or some other hard inhuman object. As it was she could not box, and instead she hit out at the water, as if with each stroke she were knocking away a part of her life that threatened to drag her down: her weight, her past, her wasted years.

Thirty laps. One hour. The repetition of thrashing across the pool, grabbing the side, gasping until her breathing came more easily while her heart clamored in her chest, then pushing off with her feet and thrashing her way back to the other end. It hurt. She sometimes felt like a butterfly pushing her way out of endless cocoons, endless enclosing sacs; she pushed, she flailed, she kicked. There were some things you never got over, so the best you could do was to go through them again each day, and then force them away from you so that for a while you could go free. Guilt. She would endlessly swim through her guilt; would she ever swim free of it?

Daisy had been born ten months after Margaret's marriage to Harry, when Harry was just beginning his residency at a small hospital in Des Moines. Two years later, Margaret had gone to the hospital to deliver her second child—and it had been a boy, and the little boy had died. *Placenta previa* was the medical term for the cause of the baby's death; the placenta had planted itself too low in Margaret's uterus, and had dug into the wall of the womb. The baby was premature; and in addition, there was massive hemorrhaging. The doctors had had to perform a C-section, and the baby had died anyway, and Margaret had almost died, too. Even now it made her stomach cramp with horror to remember it all, the pain and the sorrow; and then she remembered the clear clean lines of her husband, bending over her as she awakened, weak from loss of blood and from medication. "It's all right, darling," he had said. "It's not your fault. Don't feel bad, it's not your fault." Which of course had meant that he and everyone else thought that it *was* her fault, that it was her fault that the little boy had died. Oh, God, the grief, the pain, even now it made Margaret churn through the water to remember it.

Two years later she had gotten pregnant again. It seemed an irony to Margaret that Dale preferred her father to her mother, worshipped her father, was really her father's child, when it had been Margaret who had fought for Dale's life, who had really saved Dale's life when Harry had been willing to kill her.

"You should not have another child," he had said. "You

might die. You should not go through another pregnancy."
By then he had many connections with physicians and hospitals and could have easily arranged a legal abortion for Margaret, even in Iowa in 1954, because of the danger to Margaret's life. But Margaret had fought for the baby, had even threatened to divorce Harry if he did not let her have the child. And so she had had the baby, but again there was massive hemorrhaging, and although the baby was brought out alive this time, Margaret came very close to death. The doctors had decided, while she was unconscious, to perform a hysterectomy, and had done so then and there, after taking out the live baby. When Margaret was twenty-three years old, she had had a hysterectomy. Swim through that, beat at it, it would never change, it would never go away. She had wanted six children. At twenty-three she had carried a void inside her.

But she did have the two daughters, lovely healthy daughters, and so she would not let herself grieve—except occasionally, for the lost little boy. Daisy and Dale. When they had first moved to Liberty, Margaret had overheard a woman discussing the strange names Margaret had given her children: "Mrs. Wallace must be a bit queer," the woman had said. "She's got two fine daughters, and she's given one the name of a cow and the other the name of a boy." At first the remark had hurt Margaret, then infuriated her, then given her a goal: she would not let the women in Liberty mock her; she would be so good, so overwhelmingly correct that before long they would be naming their own daughters Molly and Frances, Bess and Lynn, Daisy and Dale. The naming had been a simple matter, actually; Daisy had been Margaret's grandmother's name, and Dale had been her grandfather's name, and the grandparents had left Margaret a nice sum of money, and she wanted to do something in return, because she had loved them so.

Margaret was on the sixteenth lap. She had established a
routine by now; this was the lap that she did on her back,
with a lazy backstroking of her arms and a casual frogleg-
ging kick of her legs. She stared up at the round lights on
the ceiling, at the cross beams that marked her progress;
now she was halfway across the pool. She would backstroke
for three or four laps before turning over and pushing herself through to the end.

And these laps, of course, were for Harry. Margaret felt
no guilt over Daisy and Dale, no remorse; she had done
for them all that she could. She had done all that she could
for Harry, too, until the past two years, when she realized
she could do nothing more. And so she had left him, but
taken a large weight of guilt with her—and a larger portion
of anger, because he stayed in Liberty, being righteous and
sad, and not ever understanding that perhaps he ought to
feel some guilt on Margaret's account.

At the beginning it had not been Harry's fault. Margaret
had willingly abdicated her own self, because that was
what she had been raised to do. Now, years later, after
reading feminist books and psychology books, she saw what
she had done, and knew that she had done it to herself, it
was her own fault. And for a while she had been happy
doing it: happy taking care of the girls, and decorating
their new home, and taking care of Harry, and becoming a
pillar of the community. But after thirty years of it, when
she had wanted a change, only a slight change, Harry had
not been able to accept it. He wanted Margaret as she had
always been: subservient and worshipful. She saw it now
rationally, it helped to see things rationally, and still she hit
the water as if it were her past.

Harry had been poor, and becoming a physician had
been a victory for him of the largest possible order. And he
had been a good physician; he had truly given himself over
to his community. He had swelled and thrived on his posi-

tion as physician, healer, arbiter, guardian, counselor, god. And Margaret had helped him: she had wiped tears and held hands and given advice and loaned money and babysat children and driven out in snowstorms to fetch stranded patients. Their money had accumulated in the bank; Harry never felt secure enough—or conceited enough—to spend much of it until the girls were in their teens, when he took his family each summer on a trip to Europe or Mexico. But the spending of the money had meant nothing to Harry; the *having* of it mattered. Margaret had never been able to convince him that he would never be poor again, that he could spend money frivolously and still have enough to eat. She could not convince him that there was a complete world out there that existed apart from Liberty, Iowa; from him. When she tried to tell him that the lives of many of the people she had been assisting bored her to tears, that she had been bored to tears for years, he had looked at her as if she were a monster. He had suggested that she was entering her menopause and was not in her right mind.

Oh, it was complicated, complex; the reasons for the fat she had accumulated on her body were as tangled as the reasons she had stayed in Iowa, doing good. First, her upbringing; she had been brought up to do good. She had been brought up to give love. She had been raised to feel that any pleasuring of her own body was vulgar and evil. How tangled, how tangled it was: one fall when Daisy was five and Dale was one and they had not yet moved to Liberty but were living in Des Moines while Harry finished his residency, that fall two things had happened.

First, Margaret had taken Daisy to see Richard Atwater, who was a pediatrician; Daisy needed a medical checkup in order to enter public school. Richard Atwater was a few years older than Harry, but still a young man, and a handsome one, and after examining Daisy he had sent her out of the room with a nurse, and asked Margaret to remain

behind. Margaret's heart had thundered with fear; she was
afraid Dr. Atwater was going to tell her that Daisy had
something horribly wrong with her. Instead, the physician
had made a pass at her. He had said wonderfully complimentary things to her, and crossed the room and taken her
in his arms and embraced her. And Margaret had responded. She was twenty-four years old, and had been married for six years, and had not traveled or even gone to a
decent theater; to her Richard Atwater was romance. He
was also sin to her; and although she agreed to meet him
later that week at a motel, she did not keep her promise.
She could not. She felt that God would have struck her
dead—or, worse, would have killed one of her children. She
had fretted and burned to think that she could love her
husband yet still respond to another man in such a clearly
sexual way as she had responded to Richard Atwater. She
had begun eating—not purposefully, not knowing what she
was doing or why—but she had begun eating then, had
begun gaining weight. Before long she felt fat and safe,
secure; no man would make a pass at her. She would never
feel guilty again; she would never feel the threat of in-
fidelity overcoming her; she would always be faithful to
her husband: she would never have to make a decision. She
accumulated flesh as if it were a bodyguard—which, of
course, it was.

The second thing that happened to her when she
was twenty-four also involved Daisy. When Margaret had
taken Daisy to the public school to sign up, she had met a
pleasant young woman with a meek-looking little boy, and
over the course of their conversation it came about that
Margaret offered to drive the little boy to school for a
while, because she had a car and the woman didn't. Actually it wasn't Margaret's car; it was Harry's, and the only
way Margaret could have it to drive Daisy to and from kin-
dergarten was by getting up very early in the morning and

dressing both little girls and taking them with her out across the city as she drove Harry to work; then repeating the same thing in the evening. It cost her two good hours of driving in order to have the car to drive Daisy to school. It took her an extra fifteen minutes to pick up Chuckie, the meek little boy, and an extra fifteen minutes to take him home, and as the fall turned into winter and the weather grew rainy then snowy and driving became difficult, Margaret began to regret her offer. She wished that at least Chuckie's mother would call her on the phone and thank her, or ask her in for coffee, or offer to babysit some afternoon when there was no school because of conferences in order somehow to pay Margaret back. But Chuckie's mother had almost disappeared after the day of enrollment at the public school. She was represented only by a hand that shoved Chuckie out the door of his small frame house in the morning and was seldom seen at all in the afternoon. Margaret talked it over with Harry, growing more and more indignant: who did the woman think she was, asking Margaret to drive her boy to school, and then not so much as phoning to say thanks after three months?

One early December day, when the roads were icy and the wind was bitter and Dale was whining in the back seat with a bad cold and Margaret had a sinus headache, she decided the hell with it, she would stand it no longer. Instead of letting little Chuckie—who was not an especially endearing child—out at the sidewalk as she always did, she parked the car.

"I'm going in to say hello to your mother," Margaret said cheerfully. She dragged Daisy out of the car and threw Dale over her shoulder and went boldly up the walk. If nothing else, she would get a cup of coffee from Chuckie's mom.

She entered the house behind Chuckie, calling, "Hello! Hello?" She tried to make her voice bright and friendly.

Then she stopped, paralyzed by what she saw. The house was indescribably dark and messy, with plastic curtains pulled across the windows and a dirty linoleum floor littered with more things than Margaret could take into account: there seemed to be cans on the floor, and toys, and food, and clothes, and papers, and clumps of dust; it was startling. Margaret had not been prepared for this filth, this chaos: Chuckie was a meek little boy who often had green mucus streaming from his nose, but his clothes were always neat and clean.

Then she saw Chuckie's mother, who was seated in a torn brown chair in the corner of the room. There was something not right about the woman; her limbs did not come out from her body in the way they should, and her head lolled downward toward her chest like a drunkard's. Yet her expression was alert; she looked worried.

"Is something wrong?" the woman asked.

"No, no," Margaret had gasped, still standing stiffly, holding on to Daisy's hand. "I just thought I'd come in and say hello. I hadn't seen you for so long."

The woman made an effort and her head rolled back so that she was looking up. "Has Chuckie been giving you trouble?" she asked.

"Oh, no," Margaret said. "Oh, no, he's been just *fine*. I just—I just wanted to say hello to you. You look—excuse me for asking, but are you ill?"

The woman laughed, and in doing so her body lost some of its control. When she could finally speak, she said, "I've got M.S., Multiple Sclerosis. I've had it for four years now; I found out I had it when I was twenty. Sometimes I'm better, sometimes I'm worse. Today I just happen to be worse; I've been worse for quite a while."

Tears sprang to Margaret's eyes: the woman, Chuckie's

mother, was exactly her age. "Is there anything I can do to help?"

"You're driving Chuckie to school," the woman said. "That's the biggest help I could have."

"But who takes care of you?" Margaret said. "Who fixes your dinner?"

"Oh, I can do most of it," the woman said, and she sounded impatient. "My ex-husband comes around now and then, and I can take care of myself and Chuckie just fine. I don't need any social workers coming around to snoop. The place isn't so clean right now, but I'll get it cleaned up, and Chuckie wants to stay with me no matter how messy the place is."

"But how do you—" Margaret began.

"Look," the woman interrupted. "I don't mean to be rude or anything. But I just don't like to have strangers see me when I'm this way. I really appreciate you driving Chuckie to school, okay? I really am grateful. But none of the rest of it is any of your business. I wish you would just go on back out the door and pretend you didn't see me."

"But—isn't there some way I could help you?" Margaret asked.

The woman's eyes began to roll back up toward the ceiling. "Please just go away," she said as best she could.

Margaret looked: Chuckie had crawled up on a sofa and was eating saltine crackers out of a box. He seemed to think everything was perfectly normal; he seemed content.

"Well, I'm sorry," Margaret said. "I'm so sorry. Please call me if there's anything I can ever do to help you."

She went out the door then and put Daisy and Dale in the car and drove away, back to her house. By the time she had gotten a block away from Chuckie's home, she was overcome by uncontrollable sobs. The wretchedness of the young woman seemed to be more than anyone should ever have to bear. It occurred to her then, as she drove through

the city with her healthy daughters falling into light afternoon sleeps in the back seat, it occurred to her how monumentally lucky she was. She was lucky; and it was not fair.
And she thought of Harry, who with each passing year at
the hospital became less and less carefree, more and more
weighted down with a heaviness he would not discuss. And
this was the reason, she now knew: that each day he had to
leave his fortunate home and go to the hospital to face
misery and grief and injustice. No wonder that he often
seemed morose, withdrawn. It was a wonder he had sur-
vived at all. How could anyone survive when faced with
such disasters? And *he* was doing something about it; he
was trying to help others, he was trying to make them well.
He was brave; he faced it. He did not back down easily as
Margaret had, he did not turn and nearly run out the door.
Margaret felt distraught with shame: if she had been a decent person, she would have brushed away the woman's
feeble words, she would have said, "Nonsense. You need
help, and I can help you. It won't take me an hour to do a
little cleaning here, and I can go buy you some groceries
and fix you a hot meal. I'll come back once a week to do
that; now don't tell me that wouldn't be nice for you and
Chuckie. I'm a healthy woman and it would give me great
pleasure to help you." That was what she *should* have
done, Margaret thought, no matter what the woman had
said. But she had not done it, and she would never do it
now. She would continue to drive Chuckie to and from
school, and she might occasionally give him a little bag of
cookies or fresh fruit. But she would never set foot in
Chuckie's house again. Unless Chuckie's mother called
her, and Margaret did not think she would call.

Was she a coward? Was she bad? The woman *had* asked
her to go, had not seemed to want anything from Margaret, had seemed to feel totally uninterested in whatever
Margaret had to offer. Had Margaret's face been too reveal-

ingly distressed? Or had she looked curious? Undoubtedly she had looked shocked; had she looked repulsed? What had she done by barging in on that woman that way? And what could she do about it now? There seemed to be nothing she could do to atone for the good fortune of her family and the bad fortune of Chuckie's. Perhaps, it occurred to her, perhaps the one thing she could do would be to help Harry in every possible way; to be patient and understanding and loving and giving, and in that way to help others, through him.

She was now on the twenty-second lap. Her chest heaved as she pulled herself up to the side of the pool to catch her breath before going on. Close by came the slap of someone hitting the water from the diving board, but Margaret did not turn to watch. Her focus was completely on herself now, and the rest of the pool and the large steamy room blurred into insignificance. There was only her lane, marked by a long white underwater line, her lane and the enormous box of water which she had to fight her way through eight more times.

She had gone to Liberty with Harry, and she had devoted herself to him and to the community they lived in. As the girls grew older and spent most of their time in school, Margaret developed one private luxurious vice: reading. She spent every afternoon lying on her bed, lost in the undemanding world of books—reading, and eating. She did not know when this habit of hers—reading, eating, resting away from Harry and the town—became a necessity, an oasis of reality for her in a life which was otherwise unreal. Harry became more rigid and demanding in their private life as he became more important in his public life. Sex became a duty for Margaret: she serviced him, the great god of goodness. Sex became routinized, almost mechanical: there were certain things he liked in certain definite orders, and that was all he wanted, and he never wanted anything different, anything else. He was a good physician: he saved many lives, and went out in the middle of many nights to help a worried mother with a sick child. He gave advice; he healed. With each passing year he became more and more beloved by the people in the community: and he deserved their love. "How lucky you are," they said to Margaret, "to be married to such a wonderful man!" And she was lucky, she knew it, she was lucky to be married to a good man, she was lucky to have two healthy daughters, to have a fine house and plenty of money. She was lucky, she was lucky, and she endlessly tried to discharge her debt to fate by doing what she could for others. She cooked fried chicken and mashed potatoes and creamed vegetables for Harry every Sunday of their marriage; because that was what he wanted, what he liked, he thrived on the security of the routine of food. She spent hours working for the parent-teacher organizations, and for the church board, and for various charities. She knitted sweaters and made phone calls and drove old people into the hospital in Iowa City and gave tea parties and if it struck her that she was almost shriekingly bored by it all, she felt ashamed of herself for that thought.

What had she been trying to do? To bribe fate with her actions so that her daughters would grow up healthy? Partly so—and when they had turned eighteen and gone off to college she had been astounded at the relief she felt, because she was no longer responsible for their lives. It was an incredible realization, an incredible freedom.

She read, she read, she knew: by taking the responsibility for her daughters' lives, and for the health of the community and the happiness of her husband, she had been able to abdicate the largest responsibility of all: that toward herself. But what she wanted seemed so shameful, so terrifying, that it took years for her to admit it: she wanted to live by herself, to think only of herself, to get to know herself, to see who she was and what sort of life she would choose if all constraints were taken away.

She began to lose weight. The day she had her hair dyed and fixed in the gentle, loose flow instead of the tight sausage curls had been a turning point in her life. If she could *look* so different, what might she be able to feel and think and do? If she were free from responsibility for others, what could she do for herself? She was starting late in life, but surely after all those years of being good she could now safely be selfish for a while.

But people in Liberty did not want to let her change. They became miffed and snide when she politely refused to attend the ladies' church auxiliary luncheons which she had attended for twenty years. They became openly hostile and nasty when she refused to listen to any more problems, to offer any more advice. Harry had turned silently away, offended, when she suggested that he touch her in places he had never touched her before, that he try to help her have an orgasm. He told her she seemed obscene to even speak of it.

Margaret struck the water with one shaking arm, and then the other. She inhaled, then blew air out in bubbles into the water, and turned her face to the left and inhaled again. She battered her way across the pool, hitting, flailing, nearly sobbing with exhaustion. She had only two more laps to go.

She had tried to talk to Harry, she had tried to explain to him how she felt. But he did not want to understand. He was so pleased with his position in life, and he did not want it threatened. He had never been unfaithful to her, he said; how could she be selfish enough to be unfaithful to him—for her changing was a form of betrayal. He was a private person, he reminded her, he would never be able to trust another woman sexually, to build up the security he felt with Margaret. She had no reason to change: hadn't he given her everything? Children, financial security, occasional trips to Europe—everything. Her sexual desires were vulgar and demeaning, he told her; after all she was almost fifty years old—she was merely in a menopausal state. She should not ruin both their lives over a hormonal imbalance. How could she leave him after all he had done for her? How could she leave the town she had lived in for twenty years, the town where she was respected and loved?

"But I'm not respected and loved," Margaret said. "Mrs. Harry Wallace is respected and loved. No one even knows who I am."

"You're letting all that feminist stuff you've been reading get to you," Harry replied. "You'll be sorry."

Norma Stevens, who had been the closest thing to a best friend Margaret had in Liberty, had also been unsympathetic. Margaret had taken care of Norma's children more times than she could count, while Norma was in the hospital having various operations. Margaret had spent hours talking with Norma's children when they were going through various crises over drugs or sex or school. She had a sense of humor, and Margaret felt that Norma loved her. But when she tried to explain her feelings to Norma, Norma had said, "Oh, Margaret, you can't save up good works in the bank like money. Goodness has to be a constant thing that starts anew every day. I'm afraid you've let yourself become vain by losing weight and dyeing your hair —dyeing your hair at your age. Just remember: pride goeth before a fall." Margaret had stared at her friend, who was skinny from illnesses, and who wore a shapeless print housedress, who played bridge on Mondays, read to the blind on Tuesdays, worked at the Iowa City hospital gift shop on Wednesdays and Thursdays, drove the volunteer Hot Meals wagon on Fridays and did church work the rest of her spare time, and Margaret saw that her friend could

never understand her change, and would never forgive her
for the change, would never bless her.

The trip to Vancouver, the visit with cool intellectual
Miriam and her humorous husband Gordon, saved Margaret's sanity and life. Things became perfectly clear. It
was as if the outline of Margaret's life and body suddenly
came into a crisp sharp place around her, when before she
had been only a shapeless mass.

"It's like loaning money," Miriam had said during one
of their long talks. "Most people who borrow money eventually hate the person who loaned it to them, especially if
that person wants the money back. People have learned to
count on you for all sorts of things, and they can't help but
hate you if you suddenly stop giving it out. In the mean-
time, you're going bankrupt."

So Margaret had gathered together her courage and done
it: she had divorced Harry and moved to Vancouver. The
amount of hateful, spiteful, evil-wishing mail she received
from former "friends" in Liberty had astounded her. People called her insane, evil, wretched, pitiful, bad; they
wished her bad fortune; they told her she would be sorry.
Harry had gotten terribly sick, so sick that a doctor had to
come out from Iowa City. Harry had cried; he had
pleaded; he had threatened; he had spread Margaret's life
thick with a layer of almost impenetrable guilt. How could
she leave him now, when he was fifty-three years old? How
could she leave him now, after all they had gone through
together? What was the meaning of life if she could suddenly change and leave him? Margaret had been weak with
relief the day that Harry made a nasty scene over money;
she saw that he had strength enough to survive without
her, to be angry at her, and that he had wickedness enough
inside him to wish to deny her any of their money at all.
Still they had a lot of money tucked away in the bank, and
the courts had awarded Margaret enough so that she would

never have to worry about money the rest of her life. She would only have to worry about whether or not she had ruined the life of the man who had given her the money.

She was so tired of being responsible for other people. She was so tired of tears and grief and confessions and confidences. She was not wise; she did not have the answers to people's lives. She wanted to be left alone, to use what energy she had to create her own self. She did not want to give another drop of energy over to another person.

Not even to her daughter. Daisy had been the child she had loved best and been closest to; Daisy had been much like Margaret. But Daisy was twenty-nine years old now; she was not a little girl who did not have the experience to solve her own problems. She had been living away from Margaret for ten years; she should have made close friends by now, she should have developed her own inner strengths. She should be able to stand on her own. Margaret felt as though she were on an unsteady ladder climbing toward her best self, and if she stretched out a hand to help anyone, even her daughter, the ladder would tumble down and she would lose all chance of ever reaching the heights of her life.

Thirty laps. Margaret pulled herself up onto the side of the pool and sat there awhile, heaving and gasping for breath, her eyes burning from the chlorine, her heart racing. She was unable to see or hear or think. For a few minutes she simply sat, letting the water run off her cap and shoulders into a puddle around her buttocks and hands. The world sharpened about her slowly: she could see the vast turquoise pool of water take on a clarity and shape and outline, she could see the masses of color in it become individuals: a man in orange swimming trunks, an old lady with flabby arms, a pregnant woman doing a backstroke, her tummy floating along on top of her like a ball. Her ears lost the blurring roar and she could hear separate sounds:

the slap of feet against the tiles, laughter and voices. She
rose, gathered up her towel, and went into the women's
locker room. She entered a shower stall, stripped off her
cap and suit, and stood sagging under a downpour of hot
water.

Her years in Liberty had not been totally wasted. She
did not regret them. She had loved many of the people she
had helped. She had loved her house, her flowers, the sense
of the goodness of her life. She was not bitter. She was not
full of despair. She would not waste her time in regret.

But she would not go back. She could not go back. She
let the heat of the water soothe her, massage her, as it
poured down over her resting body. The pleasure of being
alone, warm and silent except for the sound of the shower,
was rich and full. It was the best part of her day, standing
there exhausted and triumphant from her swim, being
soothed by the impersonal rush of warmth.

Finally she began to wash. She took up the small expensive soap she carried with her in her blue plastic bag, and
began to scrub her body, harshly, everywhere. Then she
shampooed her hair and dried herself with a rough towel,
rubbing moisturizing lotion into her skin everywhere. She
dressed, she blew her hair dry, she put on makeup. More
women were beginning to come in now for the swimnastics
class, and some of them spoke to her cheerfully. Today she
did not want to stay for the exercise, though: Daisy was at
home waiting for her. Daisy. Her daughter. Could she
make Daisy understand that she had needs that were as important as Daisy's even though they were not so obvious?
Perhaps not; Daisy was in a terrible fix, and Margaret had
to admit that Daisy and her plight pulled at her own
heartstrings fiercely. All the more so now that Daisy was
making such a valiant attempt not to talk about her troubles and fears. Margaret felt proud of Daisy; she admired
her; and she was deeply touched. Still Margaret knew she

could not reach out a hand for Daisy to lean on. Not this time. She was fighting for her own life; she would help Daisy, but only by making her fight for hers.

Every morning for a week Daisy slept till nine. She wanted to sleep till ten, till noon, but the habit of rising early was too strong within her, so she contented herself by simply lying in bed after she awakened, moving her arms and legs luxuriously against the fresh sheets. The first morning she had tried to lounge about in her robe, but Margaret would have none of that: there was too much to do. So Daisy showered and dressed and breakfasted on omelets and fresh fruit, then went off with her indefatigable mother to an amazing variety of places. It seemed they went everywhere. They walked through Queen Elizabeth Park, through the Japanese gardens at UBC, beneath towering evergreens at Lighthouse Park, across the swinging bridge that spanned the violently rushing Lynn Creek. They took the ferry to Vancouver Island and toured the magnificent provincial museum in Victoria; they rode in horse-drawn cabs with red blankets over their legs and lunched at the Empress Hotel. They shopped for dresses and jewelry in downtown Vancouver, they shopped for toys for the children on Robsonstrasse, they saw Skana the killer whale smile and jump at Stanley Park. Every night they ate at a different and marvelous restaurant; but even so Daisy lost two pounds that week from all the walking she was doing, and when she told her mother, Margaret rewarded her with a smug smile. Daisy's head whirled with impressions of colossal evergreens, stupendously towering mountains, rushing water, totem poles. She fell asleep each night with a tiredness in her body that did not pull and drag but instead sparkled: her lungs were so full of fresh air, her body so exhilarated by the exercise, her mind so

stimulated by the realization of how much there was in the
world.

Daisy could not decide how she felt about her mother.
One afternoon in a dress shop in Gastown, Margaret pulled
a bright-blue flowing cotton dress off the rack, and said,
"Here, darling, this will look lovely on you!" Daisy stood in
front of the mirror in the tiny dressing room and stared at
herself, delighted. She looked slim and young and pretty.
She felt rejuvenated. And then she loved her mother. But
at other times she felt she hated her mother: Margaret
seemed so relentless. She made Daisy walk when Daisy
would have taken a cab; she suggested that Daisy have fruit
instead of pie for dessert. And she would not let Daisy
complain. She did listen calmly enough as they sat on
lounge chairs on the ferry staring out at the blue water, the
green and white mountains, while Daisy described her own
wonderful house in detail. But when Daisy explained why
she wanted to keep it, and how much money she would
need in order to do so, Margaret only replied, "Oh, Daisy,
it's not necessary for you to have such a large house. Don't
be so gloomy, look on the bright side. A smaller and newer
house will be much easier to clean and keep in repair." And
that was all she would say on the subject. So it seemed
there was to be no help on that score. The last day Daisy
spent with her mother, they took a long walk along the sea
wall, and part of the time Daisy was charmed by Margaret,
and responded happily when Margaret pointed out a piece
of driftwood shaped like a seahorse or the way the blues of
the ocean changed in intensity with the depth. But much
of the time she was thinking: all this is very well and good,
but *my* life is not here, and winter is coming, and what am
I going to do?

The night before she left for home, Daisy went out to
dinner with Margaret and her friend Miriam, Miriam's
husband, Gordon, and Margaret's lover, Anthony. Daisy

liked Anthony in spite of the fact that he called himself Anthony, which she felt was pretentious. He was a handsome British man in his fifties, very refined, almost courtly —well, Daisy decided, he could hardly be called Tony. He told wonderful stories and asked her questions in such a way that she found herself telling wonderful stories. Yes, she liked him, although sometimes she found it hard to see Anthony hold her mother's hand. Before dinner, the group had drinks at Miriam and Gordon's house, and at first Daisy had enjoyed it all—they were so witty and quick, they discussed art films and galleries and concerts and literary reviews and gossip about people Daisy hadn't heard of. They seemed so carefree, so happy. They did not need ever to worry about diapers or childhood diseases or missing daddies, and it helped Daisy to know that such a world did exist. But toward the middle of the evening, when they were gathering into various cars to go to the restaurant, Daisy grew quiet, and found the talk about her losing its brilliance. Tomorrow, she thought, she would be flying home, leaving this land of Oz and these carefree people. She would have to take care of the children by herself, have a baby, sell a house, raise three children alone—and suddenly the entire week she had spent with her mother seemed like an absurdly imperfect gift. It was as if she were a peasant who had just received a diamond bracelet from the queen, when what she wanted and needed was one simple loaf of bread.

They were having dinner at the restaurant on top of Grouse Mountain, and to get to it they had to ride up the mountain in a gleaming red cable car. Margaret and the others exclaimed over the fantastic view, but the thought that crowded Daisy's mind was that just one thin wire was all that kept the cable car from plunging down the mountain, making Danny and Jenny into motherless children. Daisy envied the people around her; it would be years before her own children were grown and away, years before she would be able to see the beauty in life before the danger.

At last the cable car lurched to a stop and everyone stepped off. They went quickly from the cold night into the warm restaurant and were shown to a table which looked out over Vancouver; it was an awesome sight. The lights of the city and the boats and ships moving in the harbor glittered and shone. The others, thinking they were doing Daisy a kindness, gave her a seat next to the window so that she could have the best view, but suddenly she found herself terrified. She wanted to turn to someone and say, "I'm afraid. This window, this wood, does not provide me enough protection. Safeguards as sturdy as this wall have broken before in my life. I'm terrified that I will fall. Look at me, I'm sitting here alone, hanging out over a dark void."

But Miriam and Gordon and Margaret and Anthony were leaning away from her, discussing the menu and the wine list. They were laughing. They would be puzzled or even irritated by her fear—and probably they could not help her anyway. Daisy studied her mother, who had just placed her hand on Anthony's wrist with casual and graceful possessiveness. Her mother. Margaret. After all, Daisy thought, she was glad she had spent the week with this new woman, her mother; although she realized that it would be a long time before she fully appreciated just what it was she had lost, and what she had gained.

FIVE

❦❧❦❧❦❧❦❧❦❧❦❧❦❧❦❧❦❧❦

A little before midnight two days after Thanksgiving, Daisy and Dale stood in front of the enormous gilt mirror that hung in Daisy's bedroom. They were each holding a glass of champagne, and they were naked, and they were laughing their heads off. They really were a funny sight. These two sisters, who had grown up taking baths together, snuggling in bed together, each as carelessly used to the sight of the other's body as to her own, these two sisters who had been skinny together, all knees and knobby elbows and smooth cleft pubic flesh protruding like two sections of fruit, all the juice and seeds then an uninteresting secret inside, these two sisters had so very much changed. They had seen some of the changes over their adolescent years, when first Daisy and then Dale began to curve and bulge and sprout hair, but then of course they grew more modest, and first Daisy and then Dale hid in bathrooms and dressed with the bedroom door closed, and if neither girl startled or turned her back when the other entered to find her slipping into a bra, still they stopped having casual glimpses of the other's completely bare figure. But now, drunk on champagne and the pleasure of their rediscovered intimacy, they felt that that was too bad; for it was important, the knowledge of the other's total body; it was so very *fine*. To know comfortably, easily, the back and front, the sides, the top and bottom of your sister, all that smooth pretty flesh, the skin, the muscles, the brace of bones, the wings of back; you had to know it all, around and around with innocence and pleasure, like knowing a ride on a merry-go-round, like knowing the post of your bed.

So much is lost with growing up. The intimate holding of a husband or wife is certainly a glorious thing, but how sad that that is *all*: the one other person, husband or wife, the only grown person one gets to see in complete naked loveliness for the rest of your life. What a burden that puts on a marriage. What a shame people couldn't go around naked together—not for sexual and orgasmic purposes, but simply for the pleasure of seeing skin—which has more subtle varieties of color and light than the sky—and rounded spheres or balls or cones of flesh which push outward steadily, resiliently, like the spirit of life itself. There are no words, not enough words, to describe the marvelously diverse forms that different sections of the body will take.

One could say that Daisy's belly was a ball, while Dale's was a flat plane; but the words are dead and insufficient, do not convey the suppleness, the silky rounded slide of Dale's belly, nor the opalescent sheen of Daisy's taut skin over a belly that was not a ball at all, that moved and bulged and rippled with the baby's slightest stir. People really ought to go naked more often with each other, simply for the joy of it, simply for the joy, the pleasure—and even the amusement, because something like Daisy's buttocks was really as witty and delightful as the best New Yorker cartoon. And it is all so interesting, the sags and lumps and stretches of flesh, the turnings more delicate and miracu-

lous than the best Louis XV table leg, oh, you could look
at it forever, another person's body, and all dimensions are
satisfied. People should go naked in front of one another
often, really they should.

Or so Dale and Daisy thought. There they were, quite
drunk, standing in front of the mirror, arms around each
other, laughing. There was Dale, there was Daisy. They
were almost of the same height: Dale was five seven, and
Daisy was five six, but because Dale's arms and legs were so
slim while Daisy's were plump and ample, and because
Daisy had her enormous belly bulging out in all directions,
Daisy looked much shorter, squatter, wider—and wider she
certainly was. They turned and stood back to back as they
had been asked to do so often as children in order to let
their parents measure their heights; but the sight of themselves in the mirror, naked, shoulder to shoulder, buttock
to buttock, made them laugh so hard they couldn't stand
still. Daisy looked as though she had little kittens snuggled
inside her skin, hiding in her buttocks, all curled up at the
top of her thighs, at the bottom of her bottom, making fat
weighty wobbly bulges that pushed out from within her
skin. Except for her large breasts, Dale looked skinny. She
really wasn't, it was just the contrast with fat Daisy. "You
could be a centerfold in *Playboy*," Daisy said, scrutinizing Dale carefully. "Oh, wouldn't Daddy *die*," Dale said,
horrified and delighted at the thought, and they both
laughed even more, imagining the sight of their father in
his leather recliner, idly flipping through *Playboy*—which
he did not take, which some kind person would have
thought to send him—to see his youngest daughter, his darling girl, naked and glossy to the public eye. But Dale did
have that sort of figure, and it wasn't her fault, and as they
stood in front of the mirror she declared that even though
perhaps her body was more esthetically pleasing, Daisy's
body was far more *interesting*. There was so much more

there to consider, and while one might want to stroke Dale, one wanted to squeeze and bite Daisy; her body had the fat and innocent seductiveness of a child's. But she would never get a new husband this way, they both agreed on that, no, she would never get a new husband. She could never wear a bikini—she could never wear a swimming suit, unless it would be one of those one-piece black things with a ruffled skirt on it—and the thought of Daisy who once had lived in bikinis going around in a matronly suit made them cackle till tears came to their eyes.

"Where's your birthmark?" Dale shouted all of a sudden. "My God, your birthmark, what have you done?" She was referring to a small leaf-shaped spot of skin that had been darker than the rest of Daisy's body, that had always been there, just below Daisy's belly button, and which had kept Daisy frantic for a few months, afraid to wear a bikini, afraid that people would laugh. But now it was totally gone. Instead there was a brown line from Daisy's protruding belly button to the top of her curly pubic hair, and blue veins showing beneath the pale skin, but no birthmark.

"I've lost it," Daisy said. "It got lighter and lighter with each pregnancy, and now it's just gone away. I'd forgotten all about it."

"But how can you lose a birthmark?" Dale asked stupidly, drunkenly.

"They fade, they fade," Daisy said, not interested in the question, and she dismissed the topic by a wave of her hand which sent her champagne sloshing over the rim of her glass.

They were happy. They shouldn't have been, neither one had very much to be happy about, but it was precisely that which made their happiness so keen. Dale had flown back to Liberty four days before, to spend Thanksgiving with her father, and it had been—well, almost not bearable, the change in her father, the pitifulness of it all.

Then today she had flown into Milwaukee and had been met at the airport by Daisy, who had told her about the divorce and her uncertain future. They had driven home in a car so full of chaos that Dale was dumbfounded. There were the two children, wallowing in the back seat—sweet, pretty children, but sticky with the lollipops Daisy had given them to keep them quiet so that she and Dale could talk. They were really lovely children, but the result of their existence, as evidenced by the state of the back seat, was so messy Dale could not take it all in. The floor was littered with everything: old lollipop sticks, gum wrappers, pennies, pictures painted at school and abandoned to be shredded by the children's feet as they got in and out of the car, lids off things, dolls' arms, a few books with pictures of three pigs or three kittens on the front, a lonely holey mitten—or was it a sock?—headless paper dolls, unidentifiable chips of bright colored plastic. The back seat itself was dusted with various crumbs of different sizes and colors: cookies, graham crackers, potato chips, even a bit of apple skin. In the rear window shelf of the back seat were more things: a little beaded purse of Jenny's, a small airplane of Danny's, a tiny furry bear with the stuffing leaking out of his bum and one of his eyes flipped onto the floor, more gum wrappers, more lollipop sticks.

"Don't pay any attention to the car," Daisy had said, noticing Dale's dismay. "I haven't cleaned back there since last summer. I've been *meaning* to, but first I was so nauseated with morning sickness, and then all this mess with Paul came up and I just can't put my mind to it, the back seat just doesn't seem important. I just don't have the energy. And sometimes, you know, I feel that *this* is the only home we have, the car, I mean we're going to have to leave our house, and sometimes I put the children in the back seat and give them a picture book and a bag of chips and I just drive around, listening to music, and feeling safe, and enclosed, as if I've got us all securely together here, with walls snug around us, and a window to see out of, and the illusion that we're going somewhere, that together we are on our way." Daisy grinned at Dale. "I know. It sounds silly, doesn't it?"

Daisy's words frightened Dale, but Danny and Jenny in the back seat seemed not to hear. They did not notice the disorder at all. They even seemed happy. They giggled and bumped into each other and spoke nonsense and snorted, and it made Dale smile, she couldn't help it, to see the pretty boy and girl rollicking about in the back seat together.

The house had also been startling: elegant and stately, outwardly solid and secure; but inside a jumble of half-packed cardboard boxes that displayed the good crystal or orange plastic jack-o'-lanterns that the children used to collect their Halloween loot in. Boxes of tiny baby booties and shoes, bibs and blankets—"God, I packed all the baby stuff," Daisy laughed, "then remembered I have a new one coming, and had to dig through it all and open it up again." Daisy made her way through her hodgepodge house with the assuredness of a loony queen. She thumped and thudded about here and there, settling the children in front of the TV, fixing Danny and Jenny peanut-butter sandwiches and carrots, and then surprising Dale by lighting a fire in the living room and opening a bottle of good champagne.

"I'm so glad to see you," Daisy said, and hugged her sister.

They sat in front of the fire and talked, and they agreed to eat later, after the children were in bed, but then somehow they forgot to eat, which accounted for their midnight drunkenness, and Dale asked if she could bathe the children and put them to bed, and she did, and that was a treat for them all. The children in the bathtub were like treasures in the sea: they sparkled and shone like jewels; their wet skin glistened and their laughter sparkled off the walls. Dale rubbed soap on her hands, then rubbed her hands on the children's skin, scrubbing gently their fragile backs with the vulnerable, blameless curve of spine; washing their desperately lovely and defenseless necks, their energetic arms and legs, their joyous fruitlike bums. They were giddy with the novelty of being washed by their aunt; she was giddy with the access to this new source of fleshly delight. After their baths she dressed them in pajamas and held them on her lap, reading them bedtime stories, inhaling the scent of their dampened hair. Nothing was ever so clean as a newly bathed child; nothing fit into a lap as well; holding the children Dale had a flash of insight and knew that all sciences and mythologies were wrong: the world was a globe but not desolately turning in empty space, nor was it supported on the shoulders of some tired muscular masculine Atlas: it was a globe, a living round sphere, nestled into the arms and lap of some glorious invisible woman, its mother, who let it turn and turn in her arms with its inextinguishable optimism and energy; but who never let it fall.

While Dale had been bathing the children, Daisy had been taking her own luxuriously solitary bath in her bathroom, soaking in bubbles and drinking more wine; a rare treat for her, to have someone else bathe and tuck away the children. She had not reflected on anything, she had merely felt the warmth of the water, seen the bubbles, smelled the sweet fragrance of the bath oil. Then she put on her old soft robe and went in to kiss the children good night, and finally went back down the stairs with Dale, to sit in front of the fire. One of the things which Paul had forgotten to take with him was a case of good champagne that had been sitting in a dark cool place in their cellar; Daisy carelessly dumped a jar of peanuts into a silver dish

she had been intending to pack, and brought the peanuts
and another bottle of champagne into the living room by
the fire. The champagne was lovely and cold from being
lost in the cellar, and the fire was lovely and hot. Dale and
Daisy pushed the furniture away and sprawled on the rug
right in front of the fire. Dale had gotten so wet washing the children, the sleeves and front of her shirt all
splashed, that she had changed as soon as the children were
in bed, and she had come down wearing only her robe, too.
So a natural, indolent intimacy sprang up immediately between the two sisters: they pulled up their robes to let the
heat strike their legs, they ate peanuts sloppily, not mind-
ing if they dropped one, not bothering to see where it
rolled. They drank another bottle of champagne. They
were at that stage where one is too tired and tipsy and comfortable to be sad; that stage where the immediate past and
future become only words to be exchanged like markers in
a lazy game, and *now* is all one feels, and now feels blurred
and good. They felt cozy.

"Tell me about Dad," Daisy said, and Dale said, "Oh,
God, you don't want to hear about Dad *now*," and then
they went quiet until Dale said, "Tell me about Mother,"
and Daisy said, "Oh, God, you don't want to hear about
Mother *now*." And they both burst out laughing, and that
was the way the evening went. They ended up gossiping
about people they had known in Liberty, and telling secrets
that had been worth dying over when they were seventeen
but which seemed ludicrously unimportant to them now,
and the whole world was so full of absurd things that
there was nothing to do but to become more and more gay.
Somehow they came to a conversation about their toes:
Dale's were long and knobby and humorous; Daisy's were
short and plump, like a bouquet of thumbs; and they just
couldn't understand how two sisters could have such
different toes. This led them to the contemplation of

Dale's little toe, which was shorter than the others because it had been quickly chopped in half one summer after-noon: Daisy and her mother and Dale had been in the car returning from the swimming pool, wearing only swimsuits and nothing on their feet, and Daisy had wanted to do something, go to a friend's house for overnight perhaps, and Margaret had said gently, no, and Daisy had yelled, "Oh, Mother!" and jumped out of the car, slamming it furiously behind her, right on innocent Dale's bare foot. Dale had screamed with the pain, and then had sat there holding the severed piece of flesh in her hand, saying over and over again in shock: "I'm holding my toe in my hand. I'm holding my toe in my hand." Daisy had been overcome with guilt and had vowed that she would never slam a car door for the rest of her life, she would always be *good*. She had tried to chastise herself by not swimming that summer —Dale hadn't been able to go for a long while, because her toe was done up in an elaborate bandage—and Daisy stayed home too and played paper dolls or Clue with Dale. Dale had loved it—had loved having her five-years-older sister hanging around trying to please her. Actually, Dale had never thought that Daisy should have taken such a burden of guilt on herself, after all it had been stupid of Dale to try to get out of the car when it was so obvious that Daisy was angry, was going to slam the door.

"I never thought you did anything really wrong," Dale confessed. "I idolized you, you know. You were so brave and so pretty and had so many friends."

"But you were so *smart*," Daisy countered. "And you turned out every bit as pretty as I, you know that."

"Oh, that's not true, that's not true," Dale said. "You'll always be prettier than I; you just can't help it."

So they got into a tussle of compliments and ended up going up to Daisy's bedroom and throwing off their robes, to stand naked in front of the enormous mirror, studying their bodies and faces, drinking more champagne, and laughing at the sight.

"I had to learn to walk all over again without putting weight on that little toe," Dale said. "Remember? It's amazing how important one fraction of a toe can be to the whole balance of your body."

So of course Daisy had to try to walk around her bedroom without putting any weight on her little toe, and that set them off laughing again, the sight of naked Daisy lumbering lopsidedly about.

"Still," Dale concluded, "even fat and pregnant, you're still the more beautiful, Daisy." She spoke with complete drunken honesty.

"Do you really think so?" Daisy asked, amazed. "How in the world can you think so? Look how fat I am, and all the veins running about all over my skin, and look how my breasts sag, and after the baby my stomach will sag, too. And then look at you—why, *you're perfect.*"

"Oh, I'm okay," Dale said. "I'm acceptable enough, but something's lacking about me; I'm too—bland. You look voluptuous and successful—that's what you look: successful. You have a successful body."

"I do?" Daisy asked in amazement, and stared at herself again in the mirror, at all her fat appurtenances. "Well," she said at last, "I must admit, I'm *busy.*"

"Oh, Daisy," Dale said, and wrapped her arms around her sister and hugged her.

"Oh, Dale," Daisy said, and hugged her sister back. They stood there, hugging awkwardly around the bulge of Daisy's tummy, and it was lovely, the touch of skin.

"Do you want to know something?" Dale said, withdrawing a bit from Daisy's embrace, holding Daisy at arm's length, one hand on each upper arm, scrutinizing her. "I'm jealous of you. Of that." She nodded at Daisy's belly.

"I can't imagine how it must feel to have a real *baby* inside. I think you must feel very *smug*."

"I do feel smug," Daisy said. "I always have, each time I've been pregnant. There's nothing like it. I feel self-contained, and self-content, and excited and hopeful, and oh, just terribly, terribly pleased. I'd love to have fifteen children. And I can't blame Paul, you know, for going off; he really can't share this pleasure. No matter what, he's still got only his cold hard empty lonely body; he'll never hold any magic—and that's what it is, you know, no matter how many photographs or clinical books are brought out on the subject—that's what it is, making a baby: magic. It's not fair, I know—and I really don't understand it. Why should nature deny half of the human race the joy of being magic? Poor little Danny; it *kills* him because he can't grow up and have a baby in his tummy. You know I think all that stuff about penis envy is absurd, a hoax, or maybe Freud thought it up hoping to make men feel better about themselves, less powerless. Jenny has never said she wanted a penis—although she has pulled Danny's from time to time, I mean it does hang down there, just looking like it should be pulled. But Danny has said over and over again that he wished he could have a baby in his tummy like me, and when I sat down and tried to explain it all to the children, that Jenny would get to when she grew up because she was a girl, but Danny wouldn't because he was a boy, well, Danny was just terribly upset. Heartbroken. No, I think it's good that Paul will have Monica—that she'll tie her tubes and he'll get a vasectomy, and that way neither one of them will be able to make a baby, to make magic, and they'll really be *equals* then, and probably have a very *equal* relationship. As for me, I wouldn't trade one of my children, not even this new unborn one for a lifetime with Paul. My only regret is that I won't be able to have more children. And it's hormonal, a trick of body chemistry, this continual high, this delicious sense of well-being, and self-importance, and superiority, and smug delight; it's a trick of body chemistry—but so is love, and so is recovering after being sick. And of course there's always the other side of it —morning sickness, and stretch marks, and the real exhaustion that wears you down after you have the baby and must tend to it. I'd rather be pregnant for three years, and give birth to a three-year-old—I think I'd be much more energetic!" Daisy smiled, and as if her thoughts suddenly weighed her down, sank onto the carpet awkwardly, catching herself with both hands, and lay on her back on the floor. She stared up at Dale, tall naked Dale, whose skin was firm and flawless, without a mark, like whole fabric, smooth and perfect. Tears began to trickle out of Daisy's eyes and down the side of her face into her hair. Finally she was crying. She had wondered when it would come, when it would hit: and here it was. The champagne had loosened her up, and Dale's presence provided just enough safety; so she let the tears come.

"You know, one really can't go on being pregnant forever. You've got to have the baby, and there it is, and you love it with all your life, and that is what life *is* then—those children, their health and safety and happiness. The joy of holding them. And the work. But once you've had them— oh, Dale, don't envy *me. I* envy *you.* You're *young.* Look at your body. It's so lovely. You're so lovely. You look so young and firm and appealing. And look at me, look at my breasts: those stretch marks won't go away. Oh, when I'm through nursing my breasts will get smaller, but those little silver streaks will always be there, on my breasts, my hips, my belly; even if I lose weight I will never again be able to look like you. Oh, Dale, I'm getting old, old, and no one will ever love me again, no one will ever take care of me, give me presents, help me. I'm so old and fat and tired—"

Daisy closed her eyes and tears trickled out and down her face.

"Daisy," Dale said, alarmed, and knelt beside her sister. "Please don't talk that way. Don't even *think* that way. You are lovely; you will be lovelier; men will want you again—"

Daisy was lying flat on her back on the rug, arms crossed protectively over her belly. Tears kept flowing. "No, no," she said, not opening her eyes. "It's all over. Don't envy me, Dale; it's all over, gone—my youth, my prettiness, my slim body, my hopes. Things change, and that's the truth, and there's no way to get around it. Things change. We age. We get older. We begin to sag. Children are the compensation, the reward, but the truth is we still after a while begin to lose it all—the energy, the body, the shining face. Life really is a series of rooms, and we go from one into the other, but the door goes only one way, and we can never go back. It happens to everyone. Youth—love—children—loss. Not a circle, but a straight inflexible line. Youth—love—children—loss. It's all in front of you. But it's all behind me, and I can't go back. Oh, Dale, I am so tired. And so cold."

Dale knelt next to her sister, staring, frightened, wanting Daisy to open her eyes and wake up and be tipsily happy again. She gently touched Daisy's shoulder. But Daisy was drifting into an alcoholic sleep. Well, if there was nothing else she could do, Dale thought, she could at least keep her sister from being cold; and she crossed to the bed and took the blankets and the afghan off and covered Daisy with them, head to toe. She covered her sister who, like an enormous swollen child, lay naked and vulnerable on the floor, now completely asleep. Dale tucked a blanket about Daisy's feet and ankles so that the covers wouldn't come off in the night, so that she would keep warm all over. Then she went through the house quietly, turning off lights, putting the screen in front of the dying fire, checking the children, sipping the last of her champagne, and finally falling on top of the guest bed, pulling part of the bedspread about her for warmth.

In the morning both sisters were cross with hangovers. Dale sat in the kitchen in her robe, drinking instant coffee and feeling mucky and thinking that Daisy was, after all, disgusting. Daisy did look a fright, all lumpy in her sagging old robe, her hair going this way and that, her face swollen. But what repelled Dale most about Daisy were the bits of hard dried Play-Doh that littered the kitchen floor. All the bright cheerful colors—pink, yellow, blue—had been mixed together by the children into repulsive feculent tones of brown, green-gray, and puce. Daisy had managed to put most of the Play-Doh back into its little cardboard cartons, but much of it still stuck to the sides of the kitchen table or lay hideously about on the floor, with bits of cat hair stuck into it. It seemed much more than anyone should have to bear on awakening. Daisy didn't notice the Play-Doh: she thumped around between sink and stove and refrigerator, heating little precooked sausages for the children and making them waffles from the toaster, and then eating some of the stuff herself—frozen waffles, toasted, slathered with imitation maple syrup and butter. Dale politely refused any of it, it made her stomach turn, she thought—all those *chemicals*, all that junk food. She sipped snobbishly at her instant coffee.

"Oh, God," Daisy said, sinking into a chair at the table, "I'm so tired. I've got such a headache, and I feel like I've been eating onions all night. But we've got to talk, you know."

"I know," Dale said. She had to fly back to Maine that day, in the late afternoon, for her Thanksgiving vacation was over and she had to teach again tomorrow morning.

Hank, Maine, the clean school, brisk Carol, her whole real life, all seemed hopelessly far away.

"Well, let's talk a bit, and then perhaps you can help me pack," Daisy said. "There's so much to do I feel overwhelmed sometimes, sometimes I just don't think I can face it. And Paul wants me to keep the house looking *presentable* for prospective buyers, but I can't do that and pack at the same time. Not to mention the children. Anyway, they're watching 'Captain Kangaroo' now, and that should keep them occupied for an hour, then we'll have to pay them some attention. So let's talk now while we've got the chance. Tell me about Dad."

Dale looked at Daisy; Daisy looked almost exactly like Margaret except for her mouth, her large well-spaced teeth, which were like her father's. "I don't know how to begin," Dale said. "Oh, God, I am *so* hung over. How much champagne did we drink last night? Maybe I'd better have a piece of toast—oh, hell, give me one of those waffles. Anyway—well, I don't suppose we really have to *worry* about him, I mean he's keeping his practice up and is still very busy with that. So that's one good sign, I mean he isn't completely falling apart. But he's lost so much weight, and his skin looks absolutely *gray*, and he looks tired, and he looks sad. He seems defeated. He seems defeated by the smallest things: every morning when he made breakfast for me he burned the eggs and ruined the coffee and spilled the juice. I tried to fix breakfast for him, but he got irritable and said, 'No, no, I can do it myself, I have to do it for myself all the time, you know.' I tried to talk him into getting a maid, even a live-in lady to do his cooking and cleaning—the house is filthy, you wouldn't believe it. But he said he was too private a person to have someone strange in the house; he said he couldn't trust anyone. He insisted that he could take care of himself just fine. And he doesn't go anywhere anymore, he always stays at home, watching TV or sleeping, and when I told him he should get out more often, he said, 'Oh, I hate seeing people. I know they're either feeling sorry for me, thinking I'm a pathetic old fool, or else they're secretly wondering just what kind of monster I am to have driven Margaret off.' So he's all alone there, and the house is getting dirtier and dirtier, and there's nothing in the refrigerator. He seems to subsist on TV dinners. Sometimes he doesn't even go to bed at night, I mean in the bedroom, he says he hates it there all alone. He sleeps on the living-room sofa, with an afghan over him. God, it's pathetic. I told him he should sell the house and get himself something smaller, easier to keep, that that might help him psychologically, but he said, 'Oh, who do you think you are, young lady, talking that way, throwing those words around. Everyone in town knows that this is Dr. Wallace's house, and when I bought it I intended to live in it until I died, and I still do. I've lost everything else, don't ask me to give up my house.' I've asked him if some of the other women—mother's old friends—hadn't been helpful, hadn't wanted him to come to dinner or something, but he said that they were all such a bunch of gossipy old snoops, and he didn't want to have a thing to do with them. Oh, Daisy, it's so awful. He's so pathetic. Are you sure you want to know it all?"

Daisy said yes, emphatically, and sat silent, cradling her coffee cup in her hands, listening.

Their father had cried. Four nights in a row, their father had sat in the living room and put his head in his hands and sobbed shamelessly, out of control. The first night Dale had quickly crossed the room and put her arms around her father and said, "Daddy, don't cry, don't cry, come on." But that hadn't helped, hadn't stopped her father, and then she thought that perhaps he needed to cry. Perhaps he had not been able to cry before, perhaps he needed her, someone he could trust, there to witness his grief. But, dear Lord, it had been painful for Dale, it had made her nearly sick. To see her father, who had been like a king, a sort of god, a strong and powerful man, wise, indomitable—why, he had shaped her entire life, and she had spent her grown-up years wondering if she would ever be able to meet a man her own age who was half as fine as her father—to see her father sobbing, out of control, shameless, pathetic, grief-stricken, afraid: it was perhaps not right for any daughter to see her father in such a way. A daughter can't do what a wife does.

Dale had watched her father sobbing, his back heaving, his nose running, and at first she had been filled with a helpless pity. She had put her arms around him, soothed him; she had babbled frivolously about other, happier things, trying to turn his attention away from himself. But the next night, as they sat down together in the living room, with the large television screen flashing uselessly nearby, her father had cried again, the same way. He had cried and said that he missed Margaret, that he couldn't bear to live without her, that he didn't know what he was going to do. Dale's ministrations were failures, and her grief quickly changed to impatience; her father seemed grotesque. My God, she thought, he is an adult, and it has been several months, he's supposed to be *wise*—he's been handing out advice and wisdom all these years as regularly as he handed out prescriptions and pills—and here he couldn't begin to handle himself. Was he a fraud? Had he always been a fraud? And what in the world did he want of Dale? She couldn't change things for him, bring his wife back to him —*my God*. What did he want of her? She fixed him a strong scotch and water, which he only sipped. She bent over him, saying, "Daddy, Daddy, please. Don't do this." At first she had wanted to console him, to comfort him, but soon enough she wanted only to shake him, to strike him hard across his shaking hands, to shout, "Stop it! You are my *father!* Just stop it right now!" He seemed ludicrous; and Dale could not bear it, she could not stand the sight of her father so shattered, shameless, broken. In the daytime he dressed decently to go out to his office, but at night he changed into a pair of comfortable and shapeless, sagging pants, and an old cotton shirt, and a baggy old sweater which Margaret had knitted for him once long ago. Dale kept sitting on the arm of her father's chair, awkwardly attempting some sort of cheering embrace, and the feel of her father's shoulders and back beneath the loose old sweater repelled her. It was possible, it was almost certain, that she had never held her father before in just such a way. As a daughter she had always sat on his lap, or held his hand as they walked together, and then as she grew older, most of their physical contact stopped, was limited to brief hugs and embarrassed pecks of kisses. She had never in her life had her arms around his shoulders—which were large and loose and soft, not flabby, but not stern and valiant, not invulnerable, as Hank's were, as she thought a man's shoulders should be. She had never in her life been in this physically superior arrangement with her father, perched on the arm of the chair above her father, her head and arms higher than his, the great bald spot at the back of his head exposed, the ridge of wrinkles on the back of his neck exposed, his shoulders bent and drooping, his whole body sinking helplessly into the chair, nothing triumphant left about him at all. Dale felt that it was disastrously wrong, *wrong* for her to be sitting here like that with her father, above him, helplessly patting his shuddering back. And she saw what she had not come to see, what she did not ever want to see: that her father, her daddy, was growing old, was growing close to the edge of death. Her father was vulnerable. Her father could die. As he sat there, crying into his hands, he was dying in front of her, before her eyes, changing shapes like a tired and wicked sorcerer who is playing a nasty trick on a gullible child. It seemed the worst sort of treachery. And she did not know if she could forgive him. She felt she despised him and of course despised herself for the thought.

She did not think her father sensed any of her distaste. Finally he would stop crying, and he would blow his nose and pat her hand and say, "Oh, Dale, it's so good to have you here. I've been so lonely." Then Dale would go into the kitchen and cut a piece of Sara Lee cheesecake or a bakery pie and bring it in to her father with a cup of Ovaltine, and they would sit watching television for a while, anything that was on, as if they were normal people. After a decent interval, Dale would excuse herself to go up to bed, and when she came down in the morning, she would find her father curled on the large sofa like some bizarre child, wrapped in an afghan. The television would still be on; some perky woman with fluffy hair would be reading the news. The worst was over: Dale would awaken her father, and he would go up to shower and dress and come down looking and acting like his old, real self. And they spent the four days of her stay pleasantly enough, walking about Liberty, visiting old friends, eating dinner and lunch with old friends; or Dale visited alone while her father was at his office. Only the evenings were bad, but they were bad enough to change the shape of her entire visit.

And of course the absence of Margaret in the house was noticeable. That is, it changed everything absolutely and completely. Nothing was the same. The very furniture that stood where it had stood for twenty years wore a different mien, was colder, less attractive, less receptive. Dale had to admit it—when she finally figured out what it was that was troubling her—she *hated* the house without her mother in it. She had never thought that much about her mother's presence before; it had been her father whom she thought had given the spirit to the house, who had made the house seem a triumphant and exciting and protective place to live. Her mother had seemed only a sort of ambulatory bit of furniture, constant in function and intent, necessary as, say, a floor is necessary, but then not any more noticeable. But with Margaret gone the house did seem cold and barren, even with her father there. Dale's bedroom did not seem the same. Margaret had made the curtains, had made the bedspread, had crocheted the pink-and-white afghan that was folded over the footboard of the bed. But now these seemed only *things*, material items getting a bit worse for wear, a bit sun-streaked and time-worn, which would bring very little money in a tag sale. Dale finally realized that just being in her old home without her mother in it gave her the creeps. It did not feel good; it felt awful. Something was lacking—a warmth, an energy, an invisible dispensation of affection and acceptance. No wonder her father felt so desolate; she could not blame him for that. But why didn't he *do* something, why didn't he move out, or bring a brand new chirpy wife in to brighten up the place; why didn't he at least get a live-in maid and cook? My God, he could certainly afford it. What was he trying to do to himself? Did he think that by living in this house that so purely reeked of the loss of Margaret he still in some way had Margaret? That he still in a way was attached to her, and that another person or house would for once and for all sever that attachment? Oh, it was too much for Dale, it was disagreeable; she couldn't puzzle it out; she didn't want to: why should she have to! She had never in her life felt such relief as she felt the day she left her father's to fly to Milwaukee to visit Daisy.

"Can you come back for Christmas?" Harry had asked Dale as he drove her to the airport. He had kept his face toward the road, and to his credit had kept his voice firm and unemotional; still Dale felt he was wheedling her.

"I don't know yet, Daddy," Dale had answered nervously.

"If it's a matter of money—"

"No, no, it's not that. I'm just not sure what my plans are yet." She was planning to go skiing in Vermont with Hank. But she could not tell him that; he had not been receptive to any talk about Hank; it had made him irritable. "Perhaps you could have Daisy and her children down, or go up there. I know she would love to see you, and she's having such a tough time these days."

"Um," Harry had said. Daisy was not his favorite daughter; Dale was. And Daisy looked so much like Margaret. And Daisy had flown out to visit Margaret; Dale had told him that much, so Daisy would be on Margaret's side. He was not very interested in seeing Daisy right now, though he did still love her, she *was* his first child.

At the tiny midwestern airport, Dale had embraced her father, and then in a fit of remorse and affection, had taken him by the shoulders and looked him in the eye as if he were someone not her superior and said, "Daddy, please, for my sake, for your sake, try to get out to see people more. Start dating—don't cringe—there are lots of lovely women in Liberty who worship you. I can't stand to think of you going on and on there all alone when there are so many people who would be overjoyed to have your company. You can't grieve for Mother forever—she is never going to come back, never, won't you please accept that? And try to move on? You're young, and handsome, and—and many women would be"—Dale had faltered, embarrassed to be verging on such sexual territory with her father —"many women would love to be a companion to you. Or even to marry you. And I would be so much happier if I knew you had a friend, someone to take care of you a bit. I mean, your breakfasts do leave something to be desired."

She tried to end jokingly, with an affectionate but definite point.

But her father had pulled back. "You don't understand, Dale," he had said, shaking his head, his tired old head. "You are of a different generation. You know how to make and break relationships easily. It's different for me."

"Daddy, *please*," Dale had cried, almost desperate, "don't be this way. I can't bear to think of you living so unhappily from day to day. It's not right. It's not *you*. I want you to be happy and strong like you used to be. Come on!"

But the flight was called and people began moving toward the door, and at last all Dale and her father could do was to hug each other quickly, clumsily.

"I love you, Daddy," Dale said finally. And she would have cried, but her father had beaten her to it. Tears seeped out of his eyes and ran in rivulets down his wrinkled face. Dale had stared at her father one long moment, absolutely sick with despair, with anger, with what she had to admit was disgust. She turned and went out to board the plane.

"Oh, *poor* Daddy," Daisy said, shaking her head. "Oh, what's going to happen to him?"

"He'll be okay," Dale finished lamely. "He'll be fine. I think it would be a great idea if you and the children could go down for Christmas. Or invite him here. It would do wonders for him to see the children, and to be away from the house. Why don't you invite him up?"

"Oh, I don't know, Dale," Daisy said, "I don't know." She sipped her coffee and then put her elbows on the table and leaned her head on her hands, her chin digging into the crosshatch of fingers. "Although maybe it's not a bad idea. I mean I keep worrying about the children having a man around, and if nothing else, Daddy is a man. And he always was good with them; he always held them a lot.

Well, I'll think about it. It might be a good idea. I certainly would like to have someone else around at Christmas, but I wasn't thinking of Dad."

"Now tell me about Mother," Dale said.

"Oh, well, I told you most of it on the way from the airport. She looks terrific, she's all skinny and svelte and chic, all those things she never was before. It really is *shocking*. And her house is so clean and cold. But it's not the change in appearances that upset me; it's the change in her entire personality. I just don't understand how someone could change so completely this way. She always used to be—well, you know—*Mother*. She always used to be so good and kind and loving. Always there whenever we needed a shoulder to cry on, someone to listen to our problems, to cheer us up and tell us what to do. She really used to care about us, to love us. And now—now she doesn't seem interested in people. I mean, she was not interested in *me*. She seemed bored by me. She seemed to think that I was making a fuss over nothing, that Paul's leaving me and my having to move and all was simply a trivial matter that any intelligent adult should be able to handle quietly and quickly, without bothering anyone else. She seemed *cold*. She almost seemed hateful—no, that would be too strong an emotion. She just was distant, and uninterested, and subtly superior. I didn't get any feeling that she cared for me at all, that she cared whether I was happy or not. She kept saying that she had been good for forty-eight years of her life and now she intended to be happy, to stop taking care of other people and to take care of herself. Well." Daisy stopped talking and her eyes glazed over as she sank her chin into her hands, remembering.

"Do you think she's sick?" Dale asked. "I mean mentally sort of bonkers?"

"Well, she doesn't *seem* to be," Daisy said. "I mean if you were anyone else but her daughter, or someone who had known her from Liberty, you would think she was simply a charming and independent woman, a bit brusque and chilly, perhaps, but terribly witty and intelligent. She suddenly seems to know all sorts of things that I never realized she was aware of. I mean about music and books and architecture and so on. It's amazing. It's like Dr. Jekyll and Mr. Hyde. But no, I can't say she's crazy. She's just gone selfish, that's all. And she's gone selfish at the time in my life when I need her most, and I don't know how to handle it."

Dale, afraid that Daisy would become maudlin, jumped up from the breakfast table. "Let me help you do these dishes," she said.

"Thanks, Dale," Daisy said, and lumbered to her feet. For a few moments the sisters were quiet, involved in the movements of clearing the table and rinsing the dishes and organizing the kitchen. Daisy went off to the family room and collected the children's breakfast dishes. When she returned, she leaned against the stove and watched Dale putting the dishes into the dishwasher, and said, "But tell me about Hank. You've never told me much about him. Are you in love with him? What's he like?"

But Dale began running the hot water and furiously scouring out the skillet that Daisy had heated the sausages in. She was suddenly superstitious, afraid to discuss Hank in this house so abundant with problems, as if speaking of him here would make him seem like only another problem —which perhaps he was. For she was in love with him, she continued to be in love with him, her love for him grew so that she knew she would rather die than live a life without him in it. And she felt that he loved her in the same way. And yet—and yet, if this was what love led to . . . She had been nineteen when Daisy had married Paul, and she could remember how glorious it had all seemed, the brilliance of joy that Daisy had worn about her for days and days, for months, before and after the wedding. To believe that

Daisy and Paul had not loved each other as much as Dale and Hank loved each other was surely deceptive and the worst kind of snobbery; she could not set herself apart, above, quite so much. And what about her mother and father, what about Margaret and Harry? Had all her senses misled her? Had her mother never loved her father? Oh, no, that really could not be the case. Dale had to believe that her mother and father had truly loved each other—and look what their love had led to. Look what love led to; was it as Daisy had said the night before, lying naked on her back like a drunken prophet? Pregnant, drunk, exposed, half mad, like an old fat Cassandra; perhaps what she said was true. Perhaps this was the way things went: youth—love—children—loss. And it seemed now from what Dale could see, in the swollen devastation of her sister, in the grieving huddle of her father's bones about himself, that the loss of love was so dreadful, so complete, so painful and ruinous and torturous—so *unbearable*—that if one had any sense at all, one would do all she could to avoid it. To step aside, off the path that led toward love and children and loss, even if that meant standing always and forever alone.

"Dale?" Daisy said. "Dale, I'm talking to you! What in the world are you thinking about?"

Dale turned from the sink and dried her hands on a terry-cloth towel patterned with a red rooster standing in yellow flowers. "Daisy," she asked, "is it worth it? All this"—and she spread her hands to indicate the mess, the physical mess, dried clots of Play-Doh and cardboard boxes and ransacked cupboards—"all this mess and disorder, all your loneliness and sorrow—was marrying Paul worth all this? Are you still glad you loved him—married him?"

"Why, yes, of *course*," Daisy answered instantly, wide-eyed with earnestness. "Because of the children."

Dale went upstairs to shower and dress, then came back

down, determined to help Daisy pack and clean house before they had to leave for the airport. But she went from
room to room, bewildered, not knowing where or how to
start. It was all such a jumble. In fact, it seemed insane.

"Daisy," Dale said, when she discovered Daisy in the
family room, trying to squeeze Jenny into a pair of red cotton coveralls and a striped sweater with a duck on it, "why
is it all such a complete mess? I don't understand."

"You mean the boxes, the house? Well, look, Dale, first
of all I don't know when we're going to move. It could be
anytime after Christmas. I've agreed to move out thirty
days after an offer is accepted, and an offer could be accepted any day now. That means I would have to move out
right after Christmas. So I've got to get fairly well packed,
and get ready for Christmas, too. I don't think you can
imagine what an undertaking it is to make a good Christmas for children. I have to"—she looked down at Jenny—
"get ready for Santa Claus, I have to decorate the house,
bake cookies, put up the crèche; I am determined to give
my children a lovely, serene, rich Christmas this year, because I think it is important. I mean Christmas is one of
those times that accumulates and accumulates through the
years, like a tree growing each year until there is a marvelous forest one can return to and wander back through,
whenever one wants, in our thoughts. Don't you feel that
way? It is so important. And I will not let one year go by
with a stunted tree; I will not let this mess with Paul completely ruin my children's lives. So I have to plan on spending time getting ready for Christmas. And we do have to
live here, stay here, in this house, until we move out. So I
can't pack the everyday things—and there are so many everyday things! And then I pack unnecessary things, like the
crystal, although it seems wrong to have the crystal packed
at Christmas, I'll miss it—I pack the crystal, carefully, and
look, it doesn't quite fill the whole box. So I have to go

around the house, searching for something that will fit in the top of the box, something that is unnecessary, that is not too heavy to put on top of the crystal. And so on. Oh, God, I know it's a horrible mess, don't think I don't know, my God, I live in it, I walk about in it every day. And I hate every minute of it, I hate leaving this house. It means so much to me. It makes me miserable, sick at my stomach every time I pack a box, so then I have to stop and go do something else, lie down awhile, or eat. Oh, God, Dale, it's just the worst thing in the world."

"Well," Dale said, "I really can't see how I can help you pack, but let me clean your house for you. Why don't you go rest and I'll watch the children and tidy up? I'd like to do it, I really would, Daisy; I *need* to do it, it will give me a chance to see what life would be like if I were married and had children."

"Oh, Dale, I don't want you to clean my house," Daisy said halfheartedly. "But I am tired. I mean we drank so awfully much last night, and stayed up so late. I usually fall asleep right after the children do."

"Well, go up and lie down and rest," Dale said. "This is your only chance; I've got to leave at three. Go on, please."

So Daisy waddled up the stairs, pulling her robe up about her so she wouldn't trip, and Dale sat down on the floor of the family room and played for a while with Danny and Jenny. They were such pretty children. They had fat cheeks, rosy and dimpled, and little white squares of teeth, like toy teeth; Dale loved to see the teeth when the children smiled. They were delighted by her interest and affection, and they brought out their favorite toys, and Jenny sat on her lap and cuddled while Dale played garage with Danny. Dale had never had much interest in little children; she preferred young adolescents, kids who could share jokes and knowledge, who could carry on a decent conversation. For that reason she had gone into secondary-school teaching instead of elementary. But now as she sat on the floor with her nephew and niece she became slowly aware of their charm, their real entrancing charm. First of all, of course, there was their size: they were so tiny, such miniature people, and as Dale held them or felt them topple against her, she grew amazed that such small creatures should contain all the necessary human parts: a heart, a spleen, lungs, a stomach, intestines, a brain, tiny veins and capillaries. She thought their organs must be like little trinkets, like baubles, that for them to be of such a frivolous size and yet to work such wonders—pumping blood, digesting food, bringing in air, keeping the small body alive—must be a real kind of miracle. So the two children were both delightful, like toys, and yet enormous in significance, showing how the force of life is not one only of brute power, but also of clever delicacy.

And then they did talk, they did try to carry on a conversation, and they were not jaded or brittle like the students Dale taught in Maine, who came slouching in reeking of the smoke of some kind of cigarette or other, who pretended to feel no excitement at any wonderful thing, not the workings of the human body nor the intricacies of a leaf. Everything was of vast interest to both Danny and Jenny, although Jenny's attention span was not very long. Dale told the children that she taught French and biology, and she spoke a little French for them, and taught them a few words—how easily, with what willing readiness they learned—they were not constrained by fears of appearing foolish; and Dale realized that at their young age it was all the same to them, English or French, those were all new sounds they must learn to shape in their mouths, new sounds they must try to connect a meaning to. They were without embarrassment. That was the important thing. "*Bonjour, chérie,*" Jenny said sweetly, perfectly, as if she had been born French. "*Je m'appelle Danny,*" Danny said.

For one weird moment Dale had a glimpse of what the world must be like to someone two or four, how vast and peculiar the world must seem, full of awesome and arbitrary bits of sounds and objects that must somehow be brought down, like chairs and broomsticks floating haphazardly through the air, into a sort of organized room so that one could walk and sit. It was eerie. And of course the only way to get by was not to be embarrassed; you had to reach out and snatch at a word or idea quickly, before it floated away, and by saying it you possessed it, you made it your own, brought it to earth, and kept it, though sometimes you must stomp on it a bit, to make sure it did not escape. Oh, it was eerie, frightening, wonderful, exciting. Everything was possible to children; so they believed in Santa Claus and goblins and shadows and light. But mostly they believed in adults, in the wisdom and goodness of adults, they believed in them without embarrassment, with total surrender, and with all their complete little lives at stake. Look how easily they believed that the sounds Dale was making—"*Je t'aime, ma petite*"—were real words which had some worth. Look how they trusted her with their minds. My God, they were marvelous, children were, Dale thought, they were so *brave*. It was their courage that impressed her most; it almost moved her to tears.

And then their persistence, and their innocence, their unusual way of seeing the world. Dale told the children that she also taught biology, and she tried to explain to them, on their level, what that meant. She said she taught about the way the body worked, and about animals, and about trees and leaves and grass and flowers.

"Oh, good!" Danny interrupted her, pushing at her, intense. "Then you can tell me why grass is green."

Pleased by the question, Dale began to talk about chlorophyll, and the sun, and carbon dioxide, and water, and

Danny sat listening to her patiently. "Do you see?" she finished.

And Danny said, "No. You've just told me *how* grass is green. I want to know *why*."

And there was nothing she could do but to hug him with great affection, and to laugh, and to cop out: "Because God made it that way, I suppose," she said. "What color would *you* make the grass?"

They would make it orange, they would make it pink, they would make it yellow; it was all the same to them. And they got so silly that Dale decided to take them out for a walk, to use up some of their energy. "Come show me your lake," she said.

She dressed the children warmly—Daisy had told her about Jenny's fall illness—and put on her own coat and a pair of Daisy's rubber boots, and walked out with the children down the sloping back yard to the beach. It was a cold, windy day, but bright with sun and startling with the quick blots of clouds that the wind blew now over the sun, now away. The lake was dancing. Dale watched it, trying to capture its rhythm. Swells began far out and crested and broke, smaller whitecaps rose and fell, and birds swooped. Dale was surprised to see seagulls; she did not realize they lived inland. She walked with her hands shoved deep into the pockets of her coat for warmth, and watched Danny and Jenny as they scurried about on the sand. The far stretch of lake seemed not to interest them at all; several times she tried to call their attention to it—look at the streak of sun on the horizon, see how it glows?—and they would politely agree that it was nice, but then return to their own business, which was scrabbling about in the sand, looking for bright chips of glass or pebbles, or making circles with their fingers or a bit of driftwood in the sand. Why did they so obviously prefer circles and spheres? Dale wondered as she watched. Why was that shape so satisfy-

ing to children? For they made it over and over again. But
she could not come to a conclusion, and soon they were
off, running to try to catch a flock of sandpipers that
pecked at the water's edge.

The children's noses began to grow red, and so did their
cheeks and hands. It was cold; winter was very much
nearby. Dale suggested that they return to the house, but
first they begged to throw some stones in the water, and
Dale acquiesced. She watched them, she threw rocks herself, and felt strangely pleased to see the concentric circles
that spread out in the water each time a rock entered. The
children did not seem to notice or care; it was the plop of
sound they were interested in, and the drama of a splash;
they shrieked with joy if a few drops of water sprang up
onto their faces or clothes. It seemed that they were interested in the water only as much as it was close to them,
that they were unimpressed by its vastness, or at least that
they didn't want to, or couldn't, deal with it. But the water
within their reach was exciting; Dale could feel how the
children longed to walk right into it in spite of the cold,
just for the pleasure of entering it, that fascinating, intriguing stuff that was somehow a solid thing like a box, and
somehow something moving, like a bird, and somehow
something spiritual, like a laugh. Danny and Jenny kept
going closer and closer to the water, getting the toes of
their boots and then all the boots wet, and then the cuffs
of their jeans, and before she knew it they were wet up to
their knees. She knew the water had to be very cold, but
the children didn't seem to care. They wanted to go more
and more into the water, as if they were entranced. She
took them each firmly by a hand and led them away.
"You'd better wait until next summer to go swimming,"
Dale said. "The water is too cold now. You'd get sick." But
they were reluctant to leave, they dragged their feet and
looked back over their shoulders, and Jenny became whiny,

and Dale felt irritated until she realized: oh, why, she's tired and hungry! That's why she's acting this way.

So she got the children into the house and into dry clothes, feeling a sensual satisfaction as she dried their wet pale legs and put them into clean warm dry cotton clothes and sweaters. She put them in front of the TV, as Daisy would have, and brought them plates with peanut-butter sandwiches and apples, and they were quite happy, and Dale felt immensely pleased, almost smug. It pleased her too that Daisy was still asleep upstairs, trusting her children and her house to her sister's care.

Danny did not have school that day because it was Thanksgiving vacation, so Dale told the children they would have to rest in the TV room, and made them snuggle up at opposite ends of the sofa under blankets to watch a TV show. It was a *nice* TV show: two young women were in a flawless stage garden singing songs to their audience, trying to teach them songs. There was a puppet, too, and it all seemed quite pleasant. Dale left the children there and went into the kitchen. She made herself a cup of coffee and ate an apple, and then began to work. She cleaned the Play-Doh off the kitchen table and washed the counters, the outside of the refrigerator and stove, wiping away millions of fingerprints. She swept the kitchen floor and then hurriedly washed it with hot water and scented detergent. She became aware of what a bright, cheerful kitchen it was to work in, how agreeably the sun shone in the windows, how really attractively Daisy had painted and wallpapered the room. Then she went through the rest of the house as if seeing it for the first time, dusting and straightening what she could, realizing how lovely Daisy's house was, how lovely Daisy had made the house. And she suddenly became certain that it was not right for Daisy to have to leave this house, not when it seemed to embrace Daisy and the children so perfectly, not when

each room seemed to have such a perfect, salutary function. Daisy and her children fit the house; the house fit
them. It was right. It was so right that the very walls were
warm with it, so right that even the dust seemed cheerful.

Dale found the cat curled up in a living-room window.
She picked the creature up and held it in her arms, to give
herself comfort. Then she sank down into a large wicker
rocking chair and looked at the room around her. In this
room the woodwork was eggshell white, all the woodwork
—high ornate ceiling moldings, fireplace moldings scal-
loped and curved and ridged, doorframes, doors, and the
beveled panels of wooden and glass bookcases that rose on
either side of the front bay window. And Daisy had
scraped, and then primed, and then painted—twice—all
that complicated woodwork. It was so fine and smooth and
clean-looking, the woodwork, and as Dale studied it she
saw how it all had the look of a sculpture, of a piece of material that had been painstakingly, lovingly adorned with
more than paint, with craft and care and love. The walls
were a bright, almost daffodil yellow, and were hung with a
wonderful variety of pictures: an enormous bright acrylic
in bold fresh greens and pinks and yellows, a dark Chagall
poster framed in chrome; blown-up photographs of Danny
and Jenny and Daisy and Paul down at the water, with the
wind blowing their hair, one with them snuggled all together in the same bed, with toes peeking out of the covers
every which way and everyone laughing. (Who, Dale wondered, had taken *that* picture? For everyone in that photo
looked naked.) There were books in the room, and large
bright pieces of pottery—a large vase holding peacock
feathers, a lamp base with plump naked nymphs floating
about on what must have been clouds of marijuana or
opium, so sly and silly were their smiles, a large flat bowl in
the middle of the coffee table, bright with slashes of blue
and pink and green. Of course the bowl held various

strange things: a pink rubber pacifier, two safety pins, what appeared to be a plastic replica of the head of Captain Kirk of *Star Trek* (where was the body?), a fingernail file. And there were the cardboard boxes standing around half full of books and *things*, large brown cardboard boxes which seemed like mute and tasteless intruders, like nasty deaf secret police who had invaded the house and were standing about immobile, carrying out their duty to ruin everything, to make everyone miserable. It was wrong for the boxes to be here, Dale thought, and she actively hated the boxes. Here the house was, spreading itself about, harmoniously cluttered with children and toys and the paraphernalia of life, and all of it sheltered by these warm, lovely, loving walls. It was not *fair* that Daisy should have to leave, it simply was not fair at all. Daisy should not have to leave this house that was so truly *her* house, and she should not have to leave the access to the lake. Not now.

Dale rose, restless with annoyance, carefully put the sleeping cat down in the chair, and left the room. She checked on Danny and Jenny—both children had fallen asleep on the sofa, so she adjusted their blankets and then quickly left the family room. The *family* room; well, the television was there, and the stereo, and it was not as formal a room as the living room, or as large, and the furniture seemed older and less expensive, but still it was a nice bright room, done in bright blues and yellows; it was a cheerful room. The house was a cheerful house, Dale thought, Daisy had been happy when she had worked on it, and this happiness showed in every doorframe and windowsill, in every curtain and rug. Dale shook her head and went into the kitchen to make a big pot of tea.

Daisy lay in her bedroom staring at the ceiling. She was tired, but she could not sleep. She heard Dale moving through the house and smiled at the sound—oh, it was such a pleasant sound, that of a friendly adult moving capably about the house. She often thought she missed just that, the simple presence of another grown-up human being. It occurred to her that she should go down and help Dale, but she was so tired, and it was so sweet lying still underneath the quilt. Still she could not sleep, and her thoughts drifted away from Dale and focused finally on what Dale had told her.

Her father. Her daddy. He had always been so strong and optimistic, and she almost could not bear the thought of him as Dale had described him, pitiful and pathetic, burrowed in his grief like some surly animal, almost greedily licking at his wounds. He was better than that. Oh, they'd be a fine pair if he came up for Christmas, Daisy thought, smiling to herself: they could sit by the fire together like a pair of invalids and commiserate. Yes, they would be a fine, maudlin, mawkish pair. For Daisy had all too clearly seen herself in Dale's description of their father —how many nights over the past month had she sat in a chair or in bed or in the bath, sniffling and crying and thinking over and over again how lonely she was, how afraid. Now she was as irritated with the thought of herself like that as she was at the thought of her father. She would have to hold on to that irritation, Daisy thought, and use it somehow to force herself into a newer mood, into some sort of positive action. But then it seemed her thoughts went into helpless circles: she was five months pregnant, she had two young children, she was lonely, she was afraid —what could she do?

After a while, she heard Dale climbing the stairs, and she decided that for now she could do at least this much: she could put on a pleasant face. She sat up and smiled.

"Tea—how nice!" she said.

Dale sat on the end of Daisy's bed and together they drank the sweet tea and talked about Daisy's house. Daisy

didn't have to pretend pleasantness as she talked with
Dale; she became almost vivacious as she described all the
work she had done.

"But you haven't seen the attic yet!" she exclaimed.
"Come on, bring your cup up, let me show you!" And she
threw back the quilt and went ahead of Dale, moving up
the back stairs as lightly as her stomach would allow.

The attic was a wonderful place, perhaps the most wonderful place in the entire house, because it had once been
the servants' quarters in the days when people had live-in
servants. So the original oak woodwork was unpainted, and
the walls were papered in lovely old pale flowered paper,
and the windows in each room were leaded and rounded or
triangular or oval in shape, and the ceiling slanted down
differently in each room, giving the rooms strange and
magical shapes, as if they had been cut like diamonds or
emeralds into small jewels of rooms. The water view from
the windows was quite fantastic; one could see far out onto
the horizon. There were four large rooms in the attic, each
with built-in wooden drawers with large ornate brass pulls.
The light fixtures were electric, but looked like candle
sconces. There was a delightful bathroom with a shining
wooden floor and a mammoth white porcelain clawfoot
bathtub, and a huge porcelain sink with porcelain taps that
said hot and cold in an inky blue. The walls in the bathroom were wainscoting; it was one of the most charming
rooms in the house.

"I *love* it!" Dale said, wandering through the wide hallway and in and out of each angled, slanted, cozy, elfish
room. "If I lived in this house, this is where *I'd* live!"

"I know," Daisy said. "It's marvelous. But it's too many
stairs for me and the children to climb. Still, it's a shame to
let it sit here empty— *Oh, Dale!*" Daisy stared at her sister,
then rushed into and out of each of the bedrooms.

"What is it?" Dale asked. "What's the matter?"

"Each room has its own radiator," Daisy said.

"What?"

"And each room has its own window, and its own cupboard. Unfortunately there are no closets, but those could be added, or maybe hooks would be sufficient. Dale. Dale! Why couldn't I rent the attic out as apartments? Or as rooms. Student rooms! Or whatever. Look, a little kitchen could be put in here at the end of the hall, and the bathroom is so large—well, there are four fabulous bedrooms. I could rent them to college students. We're within easy walking distance of the university. It would have to be all boys, or all girls, but then maybe not, not these days. But I could fix it up, and rent the rooms, and I'm sure I'd make enough money to pay the taxes and perhaps some of the mortgage or some of the fuel bills. Then I could stay here! We wouldn't have to move!"

Dale looked at her sister, whose hair was sticking out in frazzled clumps from lying so recently on a pillow, and whose face was pink with excitement. Dale wanted to cry, she found her sister so touchingly hopeful, so vulnerable.

"It might be a good idea," she said cautiously. "You'd have to check the cost of putting in a kitchen. And then you'd have to get some furniture—"

"Yes, yes, of course," Daisy said. "There would be a lot to do. But then I could keep the house—and I'd have *people* in the house. More life. Young people clattering up and down the stairs, thinking of love or their homework. Oh, yes, Dale, yes! Now. Let's go through this attic and make a list."

But two hours later, as Daisy was driving Dale to the airport, Daisy was crying. Her face was red and blotched. Mrs. Wentworth had called shortly after lunch to say that an offer had been made on the house, a good offer; could Daisy please come down to the real-estate office at four

that afternoon so that she could explain it to her and to
Mr. Mitchell at the same time?

Daisy had taken her children to her friend Karen's
house; Karen would keep them while Daisy took Dale to
the airport and then went on to the real-estate office. So
there was nothing cheerful in the car; the back seat seemed
only a filthy back seat, without any sign of energetic joy,
and the front seat was absolutely dismal. Daisy cried; Dale
felt hopeless.

"The bastard," Daisy was saying. "The bastard. Oh, God,
Dale, never trust a man, *never*. Marriage is a pack of
lies. Love is a nasty trick. No wonder mothers cry at wed-
dings; they're thinking of all the misery their daughters will
face in the future. And these damned deceitful songs!
Someone should murder Barry Manilow!"

Daisy hit the radio with her gloved fist so hard that Dale
was afraid she had broken it, but the violins, the tender
masculine voice, the surging of desire continued to flow out
from the radio like a river that Daisy's worst wrath could
not stop.

"These love songs that make women mushy and weak.
Love! Sex! What tricks! What lies! All those times Paul
held me in his arms, telling me how he loved me, how I
possessed his soul, how my slightest touch moved him so
greatly, how he was no longer afraid of death because he
had experienced the best life had to offer—why do people
say such things! We should all have our tongues cut out.
All we can talk is foolishness and lies. What are we anyway, what are people? Fucking machines. That's all it's really about. At least that's all men are about. Oh, Dale, I
married the wrong person, *everyone* marries the wrong person. I wanted a family, I wanted a big house full of children and Sunday picnics—I wanted to be the goddamned
Brady Bunch. Instead I'm just an old wrecked divorced
woman, and I've got to give love to all these little children,

and there's no one around to give love to me. Oh, *damn* Paul, why did he stop loving me? Or what's wrong with nature, why doesn't it involve the man equally in the child-rearing thing, why don't women carry the babies but men nurse them or something? It just does not work out the way it is now, it just does not work. Why couldn't Paul love the children the way I do, and be involved with them the way I am, and have his sexual energies channeled toward them—for just a few years? This way is so lopsided, so unfair. Or I should have been Victorian; then he would have had to stay married to me, I could have kept the house, he could have screwed around on the side, I would have had ten children and been happy. Oh, Dale, Dale, never fall in love, never get married, it's all a farce, it's all a bad joke." Daisy had to stop talking to blow her nose.

"Daisy," Dale said, taking advantage of her sister's momentary silence, "don't be so upset." Although Daisy's words had upset Dale more than she could say, more than Daisy could guess. "Look. Be sensible. That house is enormous, and would be difficult for you to keep up. There are lots of lovely smaller homes in Milwaukee, and homes in neighborhoods where there will be other children for Danny and Jenny to play with. They will probably be happier somewhere else. And you'll be less exhausted; just think of all the energy it takes just to get from your bedroom down through that huge house into the kitchen. You'll find another, smaller house that you like better; you know you will. And then you'll have your lovely new baby, and you can just totally devote yourself to your children and have a lovely gooey time like you have talked about so much. And then in a year or two you can start losing weight, and you'll meet new men, you know you will, you are beautiful, Daisy, really you are. And just because Paul wasn't a good father, a good husband, well, that doesn't mean all men are bad. All men can't be bad; come on,

Daisy, that doesn't make sense. Men are people. Men can be good. And lots of people can have good, fine, solid marriages. Don't be so despairing. You're young, you aren't even thirty yet, and you've got two wonderful wonderful children, oh, Daisy, I love Danny and Jenny so much, you're so lucky to have them! Stop beating at yourself, try to be optimistic, try to be cheerful, it will all work out, it *will*."

On and on Dale went, on and on, so that she was babbling, turned sideways in the seat of the car toward her sister, talking earnestly, rapidly to Daisy, as if the sheer quantity of hopeful words could offset Daisy's dismal ones. Dale continued to talk this way, on and on, until they got to the airport. Daisy had to be on time for the real-estate appointment, and so could not go into the terminal with Dale, but dropped her off at the departure gate. The two sisters kissed clumsily in the car, and Daisy still cried, her eyes swollen and bleary and her face puffy and sad, and Dale stroked her sister's cheek and wiped some tears away, and looked her sister in the eyes and said, "Oh, Daisy, it will be better, it will, *it will*. I'll call you tonight, I promise. Don't be so sad. I love you."

"Thank God you love me," Daisy bawled shamelessly. "You're the only adult who does."

"Oh, Daisy, what nonsense!" Dale laughed, and kissed her sister again, her lips tasting salt. "Now cheer up! I'll call you when I get home." And she crawled out of the car and went off into the airport, carrying her overnight bag and large suitcase and purse with the competent ease of an experienced traveler.

Daisy watched her sister walk off, slim in her jeans, young and slim and carefree and capable; all the things Daisy was not. She wished for one brief moment that she were her sister; then thought of Danny and Jenny and the new child inside her and changed her mind, and was glad, no matter what, to be herself. But as she pulled away from the terminal, looking over her shoulder to check the traffic, she did wish in spite of herself that Dale weren't quite so perfect, that she at least had fat thighs or perhaps less thick and shiny hair. She did not wish ruin on her sister, she was not truly jealous of Dale; and yet she knew that she would honestly be a little happier in her life if Dale had fat thighs instead of such long straight smooth ones. She blew her nose again and tried to compose herself so that she wouldn't be a total mess at the real-estate office. She dug a Snickers candy bar out of the bottom of her purse and began to eat it as she drove. She turned the radio to a news show; two men were droning on about the crisis in the Mideast, and this relaxed Daisy greatly. She was really rather glad to hear about crises elsewhere, because they did not seem to affect her, and yet they made her feel not quite so alone, not quite so *picked on* by God and the Fates. She liked thinking of the two newsmen, wearing pin-striped suits and vests and ties, mumbling away in some smoky room that had never seen the likes of any human under five feet of height. Their drama seemed so elegant and composed, so grown-up, so civilized, so theatrical, so clean compared to hers. Although as she continued to think about it, she knew that she preferred her drama, messy as it was, to theirs, because those men had only words to work with, and she had all the materials of life: flesh, fabrics, foods. There those men were, thought Daisy, juggling entire nations of people, and yet they touched no one, not with their hands: so what sort of satisfaction could they get? Those poor men, Daisy thought, they had to live in such a stilted world, such a distorted world: it was all words for them. While Daisy had words, too: the talk and laughter and confidences of her good women friends, the chatter of her children, the radio, television, magazines and newspapers. But she had so much more than that, she had what

balanced it all out: substance. The bodies of her children
which always filled her senses with a rich heady joy—she
was always greedy to hug or see or smell her children, and
sometimes at night she stood above their beds, looking
down at them enraptured, as if filling up her soul with the
knowledge of their existence before entering the dark night
of sleep. And food, she liked food, liked handling it, and
felt a personal, intimate response to each kind of food.
Sometimes she would stand in her kitchen struck still with
awe, with wonder, at the intricacy of the food she held in
her hand.

   Oh, that was not always so, of course; she often got tired
of handling food. There were days when she threw TV dinners in the oven for her children, there were days when
she halfheartedly chopped away at whatever vegetable was
around and threw it in a pot of boiling water and didn't
give it a thought. Just as there were days when she walked
through her house without appreciating its beauty. Just as
there were days when she felt her children were driving her
mad. But on the whole, she liked what she did and she did
not want to stop doing it, at least not for a while. Her life
gave her pleasure; and Daisy thought that that was after all
what life was about. So she dug yet another Snickers out of
her purse—she kept stashes of chocolate around close at
hand always, as other women might keep alcohol or cigarettes or Valium—and began to eat that. The chocolate
was so sweet, and her friend Karen had invited her and the
children to dinner that night, so there would be laughter
and gossip and wine, and comfort, the comfort of a good
friend. The chocolate was so sweet; and it was all right,
Daisy could get through it, could get through walking into
the real-estate office to talk about the selling of her house.

   On the plane Dale had no chocolates and wouldn't have
eaten one if she had. She did order a drink, but it didn't

help. The plane to Boston was crowded, and she had to sit in a middle seat, between two big men whose elbows kept protruding over the armrest and into her small private space. Dale hated the men and their elbows, and wished she could magically change, like the people on the cartoons that Danny and Jenny watched, into an animal—a dog; then she could bite those pushy elbows and snarl and make the men back away. She was in a foul mood. She told herself that it was just the crowdedness of the plane, the insensitiveness with which the stewardess had slopped the plastic glass of soda and the little bottle of scotch down on Dale's shaky tray, the elbows of the men and the way they kept clearing their throats and rattling their newspapers. She told herself that she was tired; she had not had very much sleep the night before. But of course that was not all of it, that was not it really, and she wasn't even angry, and she knew it: she was sad. She was almost heartbroken. Daisy's words, Daisy's life, rang in her ears and filled her mind with melancholy images. Youth—love—children—loss. In the car on the way to the airport Dale had felt in some vague but guilty way, relieved; as if she were leaving a hospital or a prison, as if she were escaping the presence of someone inescapably less fortunate. Even as Daisy had raised her fist to strike the radio, Dale had felt the power of the love song being sung there. It was a corny song, as bad as sweetened cereal, and Dale knew that—still the words seemed to fit her life so well. The song was about the relentless need of lovers to be with one another; it was about separation; it was about holding one's lover again. It was a song full of clichés, yet Dale knew that the strength of a cliché is in the knot of truth at its core.

Dale had missed Hank so much. She had missed him so much that she had honestly been afraid she would die of it. The thousand miles between them had suddenly been too far, threateningly far, and she had panicked, thinking she could never get back, and her heart had gone wild inside her, thrashing about; she had felt wild, nearly insane, with longing and the need just to *see* him. To hear his laugh. *To touch him.* She had been sick with the need to touch him.

She had almost phoned him, but he was at his parents' home in Boston for the Thanksgiving holiday—they had agreed to go home for Thanksgiving, in hopes that this would lessen their parents' dismay when they did not come home for Christmas—and she did not know the number. Of course she could have gotten the telephone number, but she did not really want to call him there, she did not know if he had told his parents about her, and she did not want to embarrass him. What could he have said to her with a roomful of relatives standing around listening? But she almost called anyway, just to hear the sound of his voice. He was to meet her at the airport in Boston this afternoon, and they would drive back to Maine together. So she knew she would be seeing him again very soon—and it was only five days, after all, that they had been apart. But it seemed the very worst time in her life. She had felt physically sick without him, and not just with lust, although there was that, too, but more with a simple strong need just to be in his presence. For the world had become divided for her: into now and before, into with and without, into joy and misery, into life and death.

But now it had all been tainted. Dale could not shake it off: could not shake off the knowledge of her father's grief, her sister's devastation. She could not forget how Daisy had struck the radio and called love a lie. She could not keep from before her eyes the sight of her father's shoulders as he sagged and sobbed in his old armchair, and the sight of Daisy's constantly tear-streaked and fear-contorted face. Dale felt as though she were a person whom fate had suddenly, freakishly, awarded future sight. "Look," fate was saying to her, "this is life. Let's say that there is a tunnel, one which you are about to enter, one which almost everyone else in the world enters, because it is so alluring. But—and this is the secret only you get to share—it is a tricky tunnel, a curving one, and what lies ahead is so far out of sight that you don't even think of it when you enter. But I will show you: look: you will move through days of love, and then through days of complacency and settledness, and then implacably, through days of loss and despair and devastation and anguish as deep as hell. There is no way out, there is no way back; everyone moves through these days, only the pace differs. Now I've shown you—and you are lucky, you have a chance not to enter, you are standing only at the opening, you can turn and refuse to enter if you choose. What will you choose?"

What would she choose? Dale nearly cried aloud. She twisted wretchedly in her seat. For she felt that she did not want to live without Hank; the world would have no meaning without him by her side. Yet that feeling was trite: trite! Everyone felt it, and everyone was wrong. Love led either to boredom or, worse, to suffering and the fragmenting of bonds which held not just a marriage, but each separate person, into a healthy whole. Look at Daisy! Look at their father! And Daisy said that their mother had gone cold and heartless, which had to be a kind of suicide on her mother's part. Look what happened after giving oneself over to love! Dear God, she did not want such devastation to come to her. And even more she did not ever want to cause such a thing to happen to Hank. She loved Hank, she could not imagine not loving him, and yet it seemed that her loving him could only end with her hurting him, or with his hurting her. Oh, why was the world this way, why was it all this way? She would rather that everyone died at thirty of diseases and plagues, as people used to, than to die this way, through the death of love.

Dale was twenty-four, and it seemed to her now that she

had spent all the grown years of her life resisting this, or thinking in some back hidden part of her mind that it would not happen to her, this thing of falling in love. And now it had happened, and she was overwhelmed by the power of it all, and she was filled with dread. She was afraid. She was so terribly, terribly afraid. She felt that if she were to experience a grief as profound and enormous as the joy she felt with Hank she would die from it, she would purely shatter apart and die. It seemed to her that to give oneself over to love, to enter into love, was to give oneself over to a kind of death. And so as the plane began to descend toward Boston, she felt herself moving backward, backing out, backing away; and closing herself off from any of the tempting sensations which threatened to lure her back in. She felt herself closing off, closing up, turning cold. The plane plummeted through the skies down toward the spot where her lover waited, and she sat rigid in her seat, gripping her arms tightly, feeling all tears sink back down into her depths, back into some cold dark dry place where no one could find them, and the tears left her, the moisture left her, and she went hard and dry. So when she rose to leave the plane, she felt solid and invulnerable: as if she had turned to stone.

SIX

❧❧❧❧❧❧❧❧❧❧❧❧❧❧❧❧❧❧

It was the end of January, and children were roaming Daisy's house like elephants in a jungle. Down in the kitchen, where Daisy and the other three mothers sat, they could hear the thumps and thuds through the ceiling, through the walls, the jarring noises of lots of little children jumping off beds, bumping into each other, careening through the house with shrieks of mad childish glee. Everyone was nuts, the children were simply nuts, they hadn't been outside for a hundred years because of the weather, and Daisy's huge house seemed like an indoor playground to them, a vast jungle of space in which to roam and run. And Daisy and her friends were just drunk enough to still be in charge of the children but not to mind their noise. They were having their own party, they were having their own fun, and the gaiety of their children only reinforced their own.

Oh, God, it was so good to sit and laugh with someone else while the children rumbled about in some other room. The other mothers loved Daisy's house because it was so large that one could get away from the children. Daisy still had packed away in tissues and cardboard boxes all of the breakable, valuable, unnecessary things, and so she didn't worry much about the children's wildness because there was really nothing sitting out for them to break. Even the kitchen had been stripped of nonessential items, of wine-glasses and crystal candy dishes, of heavy ironstone mixing bowls and casseroles. Daisy had kept out a cookie sheet for heating up frozen french fries, and a skillet or two, and the everyday plastic Heller plates and cups, but almost everything glass and breakable had been packed away. And she found that she quite enjoyed the limitations this set on her cooking. She didn't have to worry about making cakes or bread or elaborate dishes. She fed the children hamburgers and raw carrots, or soup and toasted cheese sandwiches, or made a rich beef stew in a large pot and fed everyone off it for days and days—it was amazing how easy the cooking had become with Paul gone. It was amazing how easy life had become. It was amazing how happy she was.

Although that was not always true; she was not always happy. She worried about money, the future, then money again, almost constantly. The house had not sold after all. Daisy had reluctantly abandoned her idea of fixing up the attic to rent and had gone to the trouble of packing almost everything, and had spent hours with real-estate agents looking for a smaller house. Then it had developed that the buyers had been unable to get financing. Another couple had made an offer, but it was far less than Paul thought they should get for the house. Then winter had struck in earnest, and no one was interested in being on the lake. Prospective buyers worried about the price of oil; they worried that it would be colder near the lake, that the damp cold air would seep through the house. Daisy knew that the house was tight and firm, that the damp did not seep in, but she didn't bother to tell anyone, knowing they probably wouldn't believe her. So she could only wait, now really stuck in the house, unable to move out or settle in.

After Christmas she had written a long and carefully rational letter to her mother, asking outright for a loan. She had tried her best to sound mature, but she knew that what she was doing was what she had sometimes done as a child: ruthlessly trying to play her parents against each other in a desperate attempt to get what she wanted. When her father had come to spend Christmas with her, Daisy had explained her situation to him, and he, in his new quiet and burdened manner, had told her not to worry about the money she owed him. The twenty thousand could just be a gift to her, he told her, or a long-term loan with no interest, payable whenever she had the money, which as far as he was concerned could be never. But he could not give her the other ten thousand so that she could pay off Paul. He was getting old, he said, and needed to keep his money; it wouldn't be so long before he would be too old to work. Daisy had had to hide her annoyance at his easy misery behind the real gratitude she felt. She wrote to Margaret: Daddy had more or less given her twenty thousand dollars so she could keep the house. Couldn't Margaret "loan" her ten thousand? But two weeks had gone by, and Margaret had not answered. Daisy was hurt. She was too proud to call her mother and beg. So she tried to stay calm and hopeful. She waited. She began dreaming seriously again of renting out the attic. She waited to see what would be done about her house; would her mother come through with the money before another buyer was found? She waited while her new baby grew in her tummy. She felt suspended in time.

She was trying to be grown-up and optimistic and capable, but it was very hard. She could not seem to get her hands on the reins of her life. After Dale's visit, when Daisy had at last been able to grieve, Daisy had realized that that was a fine and necessary thing to do—to grieve, to complain, to cry—but it was really of little lasting help. The next day the same problems were there. She was eager to rent out the attic so that she could actually be doing something positive in her life, but at the moment that seemed impossible. She was trying to diet and exercise in order to be more attractive, but that just seemed rather silly. She was seven months pregnant now, and the only men she saw were the pharmacist, the mailman, the gynecologist, and the husbands of her good friends.

Christmas had provided bitter news for her: when mutual acquaintances had holiday parties, it was Paul and Monica they invited, rather than Daisy. Of course her closest friends stood by her, and invited her to parties, but the greater social world which Daisy had been part of when she was living with Paul now ignored her. It made a kind of sense; she could understand it: of course the people who worked in Paul's firm would invite him and Monica rather than Daisy; and most of their social acquaintances had been first of all business acquaintances. Then, too, Daisy realized, Monica, sleek and chic, a reporter for a local newspaper, would quite simply be more fun, more interesting to have at a party. Daisy thought that if *she* were the hostess, she would rather invite Monica than a tired pregnant mother. There was no avoiding the cold hard fact that walking into a party now—no matter how well she had combed her hair and dressed—brought about a much different reaction than it had when she was twenty-three and slim.

She was glad when Christmas was over. Her father had come to stay with them over the holidays, but that had had its own difficulties, and she was simply relieved when January rolled around and things settled down, when no one else was going to parties much, either. But January brought yet another cruel surprise: the worst winter in that region's recorded history. There were three blizzards in a row and snow had piled up like barriers, like hostile walls, and for three weeks the temperature had not risen up to 20 degrees. Children could not play outside for more than a few minutes; in fact, they spent more time getting into and out of all their snow clothes than they did playing outside. Grocery stores had trouble stocking fresh items such as milk and eggs, and everyone else had trouble getting to the stores because the roads were so congested with the piles and piles of snow. Twenty-seven inches, and then more. Milwaukee was declared a national disaster area, and snowplows and dump trucks whirred and hummed day and night, but still getting around the city was almost impossible. And the walls of snow which had been pushed back by the plows rose up six or ten feet into the air along the side of the road, blocking the sight of the houses and street, making everyone feel claustrophobic and trapped. Daisy had taken to getting the groceries at a small local store, because it was so frightening to try to drive on the snow-ruined streets; cars were always sliding off and getting stuck, and everywhere she went she saw terrible accidents. So she got out a large flat orange plastic sled and pulled the children on it to the small grocery store that was about five blocks away. Then she put the groceries on the sled and made the children walk as she pulled it all back home. It was immensely difficult, with the fierce cold making their eyes sting and water, and the wind ripping off the lake at their clothes, and little Jenny and Danny only barely able to force their way through the piles and drifts and heaps of snow. At first the children started off cheerfully enough, using up their energy to leap and scream and plop in the snow, making designs with their bodies, giddy with the sight and feel of the world gone so cold and white. But after a block or so they grew tired, the snow pulled and sucked at them like a quicksand, and it made them angry and frustrated because they were so small and it was so strong. They would begin to whine and grouse and cry, and Daisy, who was only barely making it herself, with seven months of baby sticking out in front of her and the sled heavy with groceries jerking along behind, tugging at her wrists, would have to summon up all her courage in order not to simply sink down into the snow and bawl. It ended up that Jenny got to ride in the sled because she was the littlest and because she really did get stuck in the snow, she really did not have the size or power to make it through some of the drifts. So Jenny would finally get to ride in the sled with the groceries, and Daisy would have to walk even more slowly, panting with the exertion of pulling the weight of the groceries and Jenny's little body, and Danny would trail along behind, weeping and complaining because he couldn't ride, Jenny always got to ride, Jenny always got her own way, why did Jenny always get to ride, why couldn't he ride, too, why couldn't he ride just once, Daisy loved Jenny more than she loved him. And sometimes as they were crossing a street a sack of groceries would topple over and something would fall out, an orange would roll dismally off on the hard gray ice, or the eggs would break, and then Daisy would think that she might just as well go ahead and die right there because she couldn't go on with this life. But of course she did go on with it. She would see a car approaching, and she would grab up Danny and hurl him onto the side of the road and yank the sled with Jenny out of the way of the slithering car and wait till it had passed, then pick up the orange or the egg carton, and continue to make their way back to the house.

It was a hard winter for everyone, but an especially hard one for mothers and children. Daisy felt that if she hadn't had a television set she would have gone mad, they all would have gone mad. For she felt so isolated—she *was* so isolated, for so many days when there was no preschool because of the weather, the "snow days" as they were called, when school was canceled because it was not possible to get there—she felt isolated, and the outside world looked so desperately empty and colorless, that she began to love the television set almost as if it were a person. It brought life and laughter and color into her house. It brought people into her house. It entertained her children when she could no longer bear to play another game of Candy Land with them, or read them another story, or pretend to be a witch or a bear one more time. And now that Paul was gone and there were often stretches of days when Daisy went without setting eyes on another grown human being, another real adult, she yearned toward the evenings when the children were asleep and she could settle down on the sofa with a glass of wine and watch grown-up people doing grown-up things—fighting, kissing, walking about, talking on talk shows. The world did exist out there, it really did, and it was such a good and fascinating world that it was worth it, Daisy could survive, she would make it through all this, because she knew that was all still there.

What was also saving Daisy's life was that she had built up a network of women friends who had many of the same problems and who supported her through telephone calls and inexpensive humorous gifts and through get-togethers such as the one in Daisy's home this evening. Or, quite often, at night when the children were asleep, Daisy would sit in her bed sipping a cup of hot tea and talking with a friend on the phone for hours. She and her friends discussed *everything*: they analyzed Paul's personality ruthlessly and concluded that Daisy was better off without him, then went on to discuss men and their flaws in general, and then went on to discuss the lovelier side of men, and all the men with whom they had once had happy relationships. They talked about raising children and decorating houses; they talked about books and movies and politics and religion; they talked about how many calories were in apples or pears; they talked about the boys they had had crushes on in the ninth grade. They laughed a lot. And Daisy felt nourished and enriched. How wealthy life was, Daisy thought, she hadn't realized this before; and she felt almost grateful to Paul for leaving her because it enabled her to discover all this other life. All these other women, going about their lives, with such complexity and valiance and good humor. Before Paul left, she never would have taken the time away from a husband to share with a friend. She would never have been so readily available. With Paul gone, she felt free; she even in some ways felt young again.

Occasionally, about once a week, she managed to get out to a friend's house, or to have a friend in. Then everyone, children and adults alike, was almost manic with laughter, with the sight of other people, with hysteria. It was such a difficult winter. And this evening a sudden party had fallen into place: Karen, Daisy's closest friend, had planned to have Daisy over for dinner, but then Jane, another friend of Daisy's, had called in tears of desperation because her husband was out of town and had called to say that he wouldn't be home tonight after all, and she felt she would end up murdering someone if she didn't get out of the house. So Daisy had told Jane to come over, and she told Karen to come over, and at the last moment Jane had brought a friend of hers, a young pregnant woman named Martha, and they had all brought wine, and there they were. Each woman had two children: that made eight children running about. The women had fed the children first; Daisy had cooked hamburgers and Jane had poured milk and Karen had doled out the potato chips and catsup and Martha had peeled and sliced cucumbers and celery sticks and it had all gone wonderfully well, with the children giggling at the table, and all the spilled milk something the women shared, something they could only laugh at.

"My God, just think," Jane had said, "women used to have eight children. Why, some women *still* have eight children! Eight children. Think of feeding eight children every night, every morning, just think of it!"

And they had all thought of it, and had been astounded, and then felt weak with relief at having only two children apiece; they had felt silly with good luck. They gave the children apple slices and Oreo cookies for dessert, and leaned against the stove or kitchen counter smoking and drinking wine and supervising the fruit intake of their offspring until they were satisfied. They wiped the children's hands and let them run off into the other room then, and were left with a kitchen table thick with unappetizing items: partially chewed apple skin that a child had gagged on and spit out, broken chocolate halves of Oreo cookies of which another child had eaten only the cream filling, hardening bits of hamburger which had fallen off the plate and onto the table or floor, thousands and thousands of potato chip crumbs, green strings of celery.

"Let's just burn it all," Jane suggested.

"We could eat in the dining room," Daisy said. "It's dusty in there, but fairly clean. I haven't eaten in there for ages."

But the women didn't want to eat in the dining room, because the kitchen had gotten warm and bright and friendly with life, with their life, it had become a comfortable and glowing place. So they finished off their wine and whirled into the task: Daisy stacked the dishes in the dishwasher, and the other women brought her the plates and scraped stuff into the garbage and wiped off the table and swept under the table and in a few moments the mess had been fairly well tidied up. Then Daisy brought out their dinner which they had kept warm in the oven: a pizza which Jane and Martha had brought with them from a pizza shop, an enormous thick pizza rich with cheese and

onions and greasy pepperoni and sharp green peppers. The
women sat at the table gobbling the pizza with a greed as
keen as their children's. They drank more wine. After they
had finished, Daisy set apples and oranges on the table and
told her friends to help themselves, and she asked if anyone wanted tea, but no one did, they wanted to keep drinking. In fact it was really time for them to take the children
home to bed, but no one wanted to. It was a Friday night,
there was no school the next day, so they all decided the
hell with schedules, they would stay until the children got
cranky. But the children were having as much fun as their
mothers, they hadn't seen other children for days because
of the weather, because of school cancellations, and they
were loving the feeling of running with a herd. Jane's
daughter Greta was the oldest child there, a tall eight-year-
old with braids, and she easily became the leader and the
arbiter of the group, so that the children didn't even need
to run to their mothers. What they did do was to strip
Danny and Jenny's beds of blankets and sheets and spreads
and each child had one as his house and they all rolled
around on the floor, bumping into each other, snorting and
giggling, pretending to be trolls or snails or some really as
yet unthought-of creature, a small quick creature in a blanket shell that did somersaults and backrolls on the floor. If
Daisy had seen what was going on, it would have occurred
to her to worry about the sheets or blankets getting torn,
but as it was she was in the kitchen drinking and eating
and enjoying her friends, and she didn't really want to
know what was going on, and as it happened nothing
did get torn. So it was a totally successful evening. Daisy
and Jane and Martha and Karen sat in the kitchen and
talked.

They had a lot to talk about. There was Daisy's house:
they knew that Daisy could neither unpack nor pack up
completely and move out, and they knew how she wanted

to keep the house, but wished that if she had to leave she could do so now, while the lake was frozen and white. But her friends could offer little help or solace on this particular point; so they talked about having babies instead. Daisy was nervous about having the new baby. She had not yet been able to arrange for any long-term help, although Karen and Jane were each going to keep Danny and Jenny for a week while Daisy had the baby and was in the hospital and then newly at home. Still Daisy worried about how she would cope in the winter, and it helped her when her friends assured her that she could.

They had their most lively conversations when they talked about Daisy's divorce. Everyone had counseled Daisy to get a certain divorce lawyer known for his competent nastiness, and finally, with a sinking feeling in her stomach, Daisy had gone to see him. She had disliked Milton White intensely, but realized that he would probably do the best for her, do what she could not do for herself: he would manage to force Paul to support his family. Still it made her sick, literally sick, to think of all the things she had to say, all the forms she had to fill out, all the intimate details of her life which she had to reveal to this stranger, in order to get help and protection from him. How very weird the world had become for her, that she had to hire the services of a stranger, an older, unpleasant man, to protect her from Paul, the man she had loved and slept with and had babies with and lived with for years, the man to whom she had once entrusted her life. It was bizarre. Sometimes Daisy awoke from her nap and felt disoriented and dizzy and she would think that the whole divorce was a dream, a nightmare, and it would make her nearly retch to face the truth of it, the fact that it really was happening to her.

Knowing other women helped. Daisy had been amazed at the helpfulness of other women, how other women offered their own lives up to her as bits of comfort, how they revealed their own problems to her in order to sustain her, to make her realize that she was not alone. Daisy was beginning to see that she had lived on the surface of her life for too long; that what she had thought of as being real life was only the glossy superficial surface of things, and that underneath it all there were emotions and actions as turbulent and unquiet as the depths of the sea. She had been looking at life as if it were the sheen and shine of sun on water; now she knew that underneath that, even on the best of days, fears and hates and loves and desires rampaged and plunged and sometimes surfaced with the relentlessness of sharks. All lives were full of this, she now saw, full of wet shining swiftly moving sea creatures sliding pitilessly through half-lit depths; all lives were full of eeriness and beauty, unspeakable fronds of weed and flower waving and tugging inside, down under the surface, past the reach of words, past the reach of normalcy and the constrainable order of everyday life. It was frightening, it was wonderful, it was good to know.

Jane had been divorced once before; her daughter Greta was the child of a man named Tom who was now married to someone else. Jane had married again, and had another child with her new husband, and now she was thirty-three and fighting the knowledge that perhaps she didn't even like being married, that perhaps if she really could have her own way, she would live alone and have occasional lovers, but live alone. Daisy had listened with fascination to Jane's description of how she would live her life if she could; it was so different from what Daisy wanted. Yet Daisy could see the charm of it, the sense of it, and Jane's longing to live her own life unhampered by the desires and limitations set off by a husband made Daisy value her own new husbandless life a little more.

Martha, whom Daisy knew only slightly, was pregnant

with her third child, and was living the life Daisy had once thought of as the perfect life: she and her husband got along well, and lived according to a sort of plan that included family vacations in northern Wisconsin, camping out, carrying the baby in a backpack, cooking hot dogs on branches over a fire ringed with stones. If Daisy could have, she would have chosen Martha's life; it was so sane and ordinary. And yet Martha, who looked bland and blunt but spoke with a surprisingly sharp tongue, who said things in quick short sentences, seemed to think she had sold out somehow, that she had lost out, that what she had was all right, but boring. Not enough. Somehow not enough. She felt she was turning acid with a vague dissatisfaction she could not rid herself of. She sighed, and smoked another cigarette, and said she assumed she would be better after the baby was born, she was just always so tired and grumpy when she was pregnant.

It was Karen who surprised Daisy the most, who introduced an element of what seemed almost insanity into Daisy's thoughts: Karen had a lover! Good solid predictable Karen, who drove her children and Danny to preschool each day; Karen who made her own bread and grew chives in a bowl on her kitchen windowsill; Karen who grunched on the phone for hours about the leaky toilet or the price of snow tires; Karen, who was not even that pretty, who had fat hips and small breasts and hair that looked stringy if she didn't wash it every day—Karen had a lover! She had had a lover for two years. For two years she had secretly been meeting a man who was also married. It was simply a man she had met at a party, and they didn't even have that much in common except sex, and Karen said she went through every hour of her life desiring him and longing for him and wishing she could be with him and knowing that the entire thing was hopeless and impossible. She had come to the point of realizing that this affair, this love affair, this *sex* affair, made her more miserable than it made her happy; she spent more time yearning after him than seeing him; more time wanting more than remembering what she had just had; more time crying about the unfairness of life than being grateful. But she could not get through the day without hearing his voice, she could not get through the week without seeing him, and she did not think she could get through her life without him somehow in it, even if his presence made her miserable. She had tried to break it off a hundred times, and so had he. She had purposely gotten pregnant by him six months ago; then had an abortion. Her life was ravaged; she had seen a psychiatrist, but the psychiatrist told her to give up her lover, and so she had given up the psychiatrist. She was developing an ulcer. But she would not trade her life for anyone's. She spoke of holding her children on her lap, reading them a fairy tale, and at the same time envisioning the arch of her lover's eyebrows, the smug smile on his lips when he held her.

Over the past few weeks Daisy felt she had almost shattered, perhaps really had shattered, under the impact of the knowledge of the lives of her friends. Life. It was so incredibly varied, so incredibly strange, it was never, ever, what it seemed. Everything was possible. And perhaps the only crime, the only sin, was to hide from it, to pretend that it could be only one thing, and nothing else. For what she saw in her friends, in the lives of her friends, did not dismay her. It astounded her, or made her slightly sad or uncomfortable; she had to admit that certain emotions were there, certain acts were taking place: Jane was not happy in her marriage; Karen had a lover; Martha was restless. But those things did not dismay her. It was what she had seen in her father when he stayed with her over Christmas that dismayed her. And perhaps that had been because what she saw in him reminded her so much of herself.

It had not been a totally bad visit. Her father had arrived three days before Christmas and had helped her choose and carry in and decorate the tree. He had loved his two grandchildren and had played with them with real fondness; there had been signs of joy on her father's face when he had been with Danny and Jenny. Oh, he had tried, and she had tried, too, but Daisy had been so depressed, and Harry had been so depressed, that although they tried their best to hide it, they had really been pretty miserable together. Harry missed Margaret. He spoke of the pecan-and-mushroom stuffing she made for Christmas dinner, of her pumpkin and mincemeat pies. He spoke of his ex-wife as if she were some poor dead saint, and that had irritated Daisy beyond all reason. She longed to tell her father about Anthony, about her mother's lover, for heaven's sake, her mother's *lover*, Margaret's *lover*. But she had kept still. Oh, it had been nice to have him there, at least he was a grown-up and a man. And he had pulled himself up and out of his lethargy the day that Paul had come over to take the children out to his apartment to have his Christmas with them. Daisy had been proud of her father then, proud and grateful, because he had pulled himself up to his true arrogant self and had treated Paul with such cold disdainful disaffection that Daisy knew it had to have shriveled Paul's soul a little. But then she hated herself for those thoughts, she could not go on that way, hating Paul and wishing him ill; that did her no good. She did not want to be like her father, lost in life because a spouse had left. His presence grated on her, but in the end had helped her, because it made her see how she must not be; she must not be despondent and hopeless; she must not give up her life.

Christmas day they had spent pleasantly with the children and Christmas dinner and an early-evening church service. The day after Christmas had been cold, but windless enough so that Daisy wanted to take her father for a walk along the lake. She had bundled Danny and Jenny into their layers of sweaters and snowsuits and mittens and boots and mufflers, and wrapped herself up, and dragged her father down to the shore. He had not much wanted to go. He seemed to have lost much of his old energy and vitality; he seemed to spend too much time watching television, and far too much time talking about how he missed Margaret. He had grudgingly gone down to the lake with Daisy and the children and had walked along the shoreline with his shoulders hunched up miserably against the cold.

"It's really quite gorgeous in the spring and summer and fall, Daddy," Daisy had told him. "And even now, you have to admit it's interesting. The way the waves have frozen in great chunks, like triangles, like small icebergs, and the pale aquamarine blue that you can see under the snow —even now, even frozen, I think the lake is fascinating."

But Harry had not thought it was fascinating. He had not liked it at all, not at all. "I'm too cold down here," he had said. "I guess I'm just getting too old to put up with such cold." And he had turned and gone back up to the house.

Daisy had almost stamped her foot with impatience, had almost cried out, "*Daddy!* Would you get with it!" But she had turned away from the sight of his hunched and doleful back and watched her children stepping cautiously on the rim of the lake, and then more bravely walking right out on the ice.

"Look, Mom, we're walking on the lake!" they had cried, startled at their own courage and at the wonder of doing it, of walking on the lake. Daisy had watched them carefully and then in spite of her own common sense, had joined them. It was too fascinating, to be able to walk about on the lake, right out where they had seen ducks swim and toy boats float in the summer. The ice was hard, it held firm. It was so thick it did not crack under their weight. It was as

hard as if it were eternal, and uneven and jagged and grotesque, fantastic, a landscape of frozen incongruities. Finally everyone had gotten cold and Daisy had worried
about frostbite and taken the children in. She had made
them hot chocolate and meant to let them watch television, but her father had already seated himself in front of
it, watching a football game, so she had spent some time
playing with the children, helping them learn how to play
with their new toys.

The next day they had all gone to the Performing Arts
Center to see *The Nutcracker*, and even little Jenny had
been good, had enjoyed the ballet and laughed and clapped
her hands. And her father had taken them all out to a nice
restaurant for dinner, so that day had been okay. Really,
the entire visit had been *okay*—but Daisy had wanted more.
Her father was *her father*; she had wanted him to comfort
her now at this time when Paul was leaving her. But he
would not, he did not seem to even notice her need. He listened to her talk, and gave advice offhandedly: get a good
lawyer, get all the money you can now, if you need a thera-
pist I'll pay for it, don't worry about money, I'll help you
out if you need it. But he was not really there for her, as
her mother had not been. He was not able to break away
from his obsessive misery enough to care much about the
problems Daisy was having. He clung to his grief almost as
if it nurtured him, or shielded him. He was not really concerned about Daisy; and though she was truly grateful to
him for the money, she wanted more from him than that.
She wanted the comfort and wisdom handed from a parent
to a child, and especially now she wanted the grand masculine protection which had always been part of her father's
love for his daughters. But it was not there. She could get
nothing from his spirit. He was behaving selfishly, he was
grudging with his spirit, as if he truly enjoyed his sorrow

and would not let go of it, would not make space in his heart for other emotions.

As the days passed by, Daisy came to a terrible realization: her father bored her; after a while he really irritated her. You've got to have pride in your own self, she wanted to shout at him. You can't go moping around like a damned oversized Raggedy Andy doll, all limp and flopping just because Mother is no longer around to prop you up. Where's your self-respect? Why don't you get yourself in control? Life cannot hang on the love of one other person; you have got to hang your life on yourself. There were many things she wanted to say to him, but in the end she said nothing at all. He was not really seeing her or talking to her; she was not dumb enough to think that if she spoke he would really hear.

So she was relieved when he left. When she returned from the airport she spent the rest of the day just lying about the house, eating peanut butter on crackers or leftover turkey and pie, and letting Danny and Jenny roam the house at large. She didn't even take them outside to play that day, although it was, for late December, fairly mild. She felt absolutely enervated by her father's visit; she felt drained; she just wanted to sleep and sleep.

After that the days began to move of their own accord. There seemed to be so many things she had to work through. And she did not want to lean on anyone else, she did not want to be a drag, she did not want to be dependent, to *bother* anyone; but still the more time she spent with Karen or Jane or one of her other friends, the happier she found herself, the more she was able to come awake. Her friends became curatives for her; they became like healing air. She could go out among them and breathe them in, and become almost immediately better, and each day a little stronger, and yet the best part of it was that this did not diminish them, this did not take from them. They were still there, also like air, they were still there, her friends, being themselves, and her going out and standing among them, breathing them into her life, curing herself by their presence, all this did not bother them, did not alter them, they existed still as freely and constantly as the air of the earth.

And now here they all were in her kitchen, starting the third bottle of wine and rocking in their chairs with laughter. They were talking about men, about sex, and Martha had just stated that she would never be able to have sex with any man except her husband because her body had gotten so bad after the birth of her children. Her stomach was puckered and striped. She wouldn't be able to bear having any other man see her. Daisy laughed at Martha's harshly humorous description of her body, but her ears perked up, perked up, because she felt this way about her body, too, and was glad to know she was not alone.

"Oh, for heaven's sake," Karen said impatiently. "Don't worry about your stomach, or anything for that matter. What do you think men are, what kind of a lover do you think you'd have? Men aren't children, you know—even if they think it, they aren't going to say, 'Oh, gross, look at your stomach! Yuck!' Lovers are wonderful, and if nothing else, they're tactful. You've just been around children too long and children think everything is gross and yucky. Men aren't that way—and remember, men aren't perfect, either. They have stretch marks, too, or fat stomachs, or funny chests. We get too used to the perfect smooth bodies of our kids, but no adult is that way. Men are just as vulnerable as women, they're just as imperfect, and they can be awfully nice."

"I did a mean thing once," Jane announced with a slur in her voice. "Oh, dear, oh, dear," she said, remembering, and laughed. "But he certainly deserved it."

"Well, tell us about it!" Daisy said.

"It was with one of the men I dated after I was divorced from Tom and before I married Phil. I was at some party, and I met this man named Karl. He was a dentist. He seemed nice enough, and to make a long story short, we dated for a while and finally ended up in bed. And the poor man—well, he had the smallest little penis I've ever seen! It was hardly there. I never said anything about it to him, of course, because I didn't want to hurt his feelings. In fact, I tried my best to make him feel good—I told him how much I liked the hair on his chest and stuff like that. Now you would think that having a—problem, let's call it— like his would teach him compassion for other people, but it didn't. I kept on dating him, but the more I saw of him, the less I liked him, and not because of his penis. He was always making cutting remarks, or little innuendoes which showed just how little he thought of other people. Do you know what he gave me for Christmas? A pair of wool slacks two sizes too big for me! As he handed me the box, he said, 'These might be too small for you, but you can always exchange them.' There he was, sometimes telling me he *loved* me, and at the same time giving me slacks two sizes too large, indirectly telling me he thought I was big and fat! I decided he wasn't very good for my ego, and I started dating someone else, and I tried to phase Karl out of my life. But he wouldn't take a hint. He kept pestering me. He started showing up at my house without notice, pressuring me to be with him—I couldn't seem to get rid of him. So one night I agreed to go out for a drink with him, and there we sat at a little table in a nice bar, and I was being as tactful and kind as I could, trying to explain to him that I was in love with someone else. But he wasn't getting the message. He kept rubbing my knee with his knee under the table and stroking my arm and leering at me and I panicked: I thought, 'I'm never going to get rid of this guy!' Then the waiter brought over a breadbasket, and inside were these little breadsticks—about the size of a little candle or a finger. So I just picked up a little breadstick, and looked at it and looked at Karl and said, 'Remind you of anything?'" Jane had to stop talking while everyone laughed.

"But that's *terrible*, Jane," Daisy cried out, still laughing. "That's cruel. How could you do it? What did he do?"

"Oh, he just looked confused for a minute, and then stricken, and then he took his knee away from mine and we finished our drinks and he took me home. Poor man, but I really had tried other ways of getting rid of him. This was the only thing that even got his attention. But that was the meanest thing I've ever done. Still, you'll come to that, Daisy, once you've had your baby and your divorce. You'll arrive at the point where you'll sleep with different men, and some you may even love, but they won't love you, and some will love you frantically, but you won't love them. If you're lucky you'll find a good lover, but you might not get lucky for a while. The point is, don't worry about yourself, or what you look like. The nicest feeling in the world is to accept yourself, all the sags and flab and warts and all, and if someone wants to love you, that's fine, but if someone doesn't love you, then that's okay, too."

"Oh, dear," Daisy sighed. "I don't even *want* a lover. What are we talking about! I want to have this baby. Martha wants the lover. No, she doesn't want a lover, she wants a flat stomach. Who wants the lover? Who started all this talk?"

"I *have* a lover," Karen said. "And I recommend lovers highly. Every woman should have one: a husband, a house, some children, and a lover. There's just nothing like a lover to make you feel good."

"But shouldn't your husband be your lover?" Daisy asked. "I mean it starts out that way. Why can't it end that way? Can it end that way for anyone? Does it ever end

up, after three children and ten years, that your husband
is your lover? Does it? Can it?"

But no one answered. They all fell silent, Jane and
Karen and Martha, they all looked down at their cigarettes or their wineglasses, and went silent with their own
thoughts. They were almost glad when the shrieks from upstairs indicated that the children were getting tired and
fussy and that it was time to take them home. They rose,
all the women, and went up the stairs to sort their children out one from the other, to stuff them into their parkas
and mittens and mufflers and to cajole and carry them out
to the cars.

Daisy turned off the porch light and turned back to her
own children. They were manic and silly from all the activ-
ity, and Daisy smiled at their happiness. In spite of the divorce, her children were happy, she thought, they were normal. She marshaled them up the stairs and made them
pick up the toys that had been scattered around their
rooms while she put the sheets and blankets back on the
beds. She only halfheartedly scolded them about the mess:
they had had such a good time, and Daisy had managed to
have a full evening with her friends. She always felt more
courageous after such an evening.

She went through the nightly routine of supervising the
children while they washed and brushed their teeth and
put on their pajamas. When she tucked Jenny into bed,
Jenny fell asleep almost instantly, thumb in her mouth.
Daisy kissed her daughter, then stood, eager for her own
soft bed. But when she went into Danny's room to kiss
him good night, Danny wanted to talk. Daisy smoothed
the sheet and blankets about her little boy, then sat down
next to him, her hand on his.

"Tell me," she said.

"I hate Megan," Danny said. Megan was Karen's four-
year-old daughter. "I really hate her."

"Why do you hate her, honey?" Daisy asked. "I think Megan is a nice girl."

"She wouldn't play with me all evening," Danny said. "She wouldn't play with me because Eric was here, and he's six and she likes Eric better than me. She went into the bathroom with Eric tonight and showed him her bum. She wouldn't show me her bum."

Daisy looked at her sweet son, whose face was tense with earnest anger and innocent despair. Oh, *God*, Daisy thought, this is how it goes, all up and down the line; trouble about sex, about love, all up and down the line. Her father and her mother, herself and her own husband, and now, at four years of age, Danny and Megan. Love, sex, betrayal, all up and down the line. What could she say? What could she tell her little boy? She could tell him it would get better, and of course now and then it would. Someday some little girl, some very cute little girl, would show Danny her bum. Maybe that was the important thing for him to know right now. Maybe that was what he needed to hold on to: not the whole entire confusing convoluted truth of the constant turnings of love and sex, but just one simple part of it. The good side of it, that was all he needed to know for now, so that he could get a good night's sleep.

"Megan will show you her bum someday," Daisy said. "She was just impressed with Eric because he's so much older than she is. But she won't be able to see Eric as often as she sees you, and I know she loves you best; she told Karen she wants to marry you. Anyway, if she doesn't show you her bum, I'm sure some other pretty girl will. The world is a big place. Lots of girls will love you."

Danny grinned. "Yeah," he said. "Like Jessica." Then he giggled and dug his head into his pillow.

Daisy kissed him and tucked in the blankets and turned off the lights. She wandered from the room stunned. Who was Jessica? She must be the new girl at the preschool. The way Danny had grinned, she must have already shown him her bum, or something!

Daisy continued to think about Danny as she got ready for bed and crawled gratefully beneath the warm covers. She hoped she had said the right thing; she hoped she had helped him. For unwittingly, he had helped her. He had handed her all his ready faith and optimism as easily as if handing her a childish present; he had believed what she had told him. She fell asleep accompanied by his hopefulness, and it was as if that hopefulness existed tangibly in the room with her then, like a stuffed bear or a red balloon. So she drifted off to sleep with the same sort of thought that Danny had gone to sleep with, the very same thought advanced by a few years: in the turnings of love there was the good side, the bright side: someone would love her again.

Dale had a cold. She sat in her empty classroom in the gray late afternoon, grading the French exams she had just given that day. Everyone else had gone home. It was five-thirty, and the school building was empty and still. Dale felt snuffy and achy and miserable. She felt chilled. She was wearing long underwear and heavy wool slacks and a cotton plaid shirt and a thick wool sweater and fur-lined boots and her parka, and the school building was of course heated. But still she felt cold. She felt nasty and irritated because so many of her students had made the same mistake in translations, had written "*Je suis fini,*" instead of "*J'ai fini,*" when the context was that of sitting at a dinner table, being finished with the meal. It hurt to hold the red marking pen in her fingers; it hurt to breathe. She longed for some Vaseline to put on her chapped reddened nose, but that was at home and she didn't want to carry all these papers home with her tonight. She wanted to finish them now. She wanted to finish everything now. She wanted to get into bed and go to sleep and never wake up.

"Terrible weather, isn't it?" Mr. Jersey said. Mr. Jersey was the school janitor and a nice old man, though he tended to talk too much. Now he was entering Dale's classroom, pushing his long-handled enormous dustmop before him, pulling his trash cart behind him, a large metal circle of keys clanking at his belt. "I said to my wife only this morning—"

"Oh, Mr. Jersey," Dale said, "could you please wait and do my room last? I've got a rotten cold and I just have to grade these tests now, and I'd appreciate it so much if you could wait and do my room last."

Mr. Jersey stopped in his tracks, amazed. Usually Dale was the friendliest of teachers, always ready to engage in a little conversation. But looking at her he saw that she truly did have a cold, she really did look puny and pale and awful.

"You poor thing," he said. "You should be home in bed. Sure, I'll go on down the hall and hit your room last. But if I looked the way you look, I sure would be home in bed with a hot toddy. Do you know how to make a good hot toddy? It would be the best thing in the world for you. My wife makes them all the time and they get me through my colds real fast. You mix up hot water with lemon juice and honey and salt. It sounds strange, but it works wonders. If you want me to, I could call my wife and get the exact measurements for you. I—"

"That's all right, Mr. Jersey," Dale said. "Don't go to the trouble, I've got lots of medicine at home. I'll just finish these papers and go home and take the medicine and go to bed."

"Well, now, your new expensive store-bought medicines aren't always as good as you think," Mr. Jersey said. The inferiority of the new, the plastic, the scientific, as opposed to the superiority of the homey and old-time, was one of his pet topics of conversation. "I was just telling my wife—"

"Mr. Jersey," Dale snapped. "I really need to grade these papers. I really need to get back to work." And she glared at him.

"Yes, yes, you go on right ahead, I won't keep you," Mr. Jersey said, and went out the door, pushing and pulling at his broom and his cart with a sudden shrunken, forlorn dignity. She had hurt his feelings.

Dale sat staring at the doorway. Mr. Jersey had not thought to close the classroom door behind him, and she could hear him clanking and shuffling and sweeping down the hall, and the very space of the doorway where he had stood seemed to be alive with reproach. Dale got up in a sudden snit of energy and crossed the room and pulled the door shut against the janitor and his wounded pride and his noise. Then she went back and sat down and tried to concentrate on the tests. She only wanted to put her head down on the desk and sleep. She was so tired. She was so sick. She was so miserable.

It was late January, and this cold had been building up and coming on for at least two weeks now. Dale felt as though her body was doing it on purpose, was making her feel weak and sick on purpose, to get back at her for what she had done to it. That is, she had tried, she was trying, to disengage herself from Hank, from her love for Hank; she had told Hank she didn't want to see him so often, that she needed to get back in control of herself, that she needed to have more time and space just for herself. But that wasn't really what she needed at all. What she really needed, what she really wanted, at least what her *body* wanted, was to be with Hank every possible second of the day.

For Dale it had come to this, it was as simple as this: it was a matter of pain ending and peace reigning. It was as complete and simple as that. When she was with Hank, then she was content within her body, within herself. When she was not with him, she was in real constant physical pain. She twisted and longed. Sometimes she would leave her classroom and go into the faculty washroom and shut herself inside a toilet cubicle and simply lean up against the door. She would press her entire body against the door, the hard cold surface of the door, and press herself, and yearn. She was obsessed. She was in love. It was so powerful. And she wanted to fight it off. She thought of Daisy, she thought of her parents, she worked through it all with her mind, and now her mind, her reason, was fighting with her body and her desires. And she was sick and weak with the battle. Her mind feared the consequences, the future; but her body craved and craved the joy, the present joy.

At Christmas they had spent ten days at a ski resort in Vermont, and in the hot rush of pleasure of those days Dale had forgotten her Thanksgiving resolution to escape the lures of love. It had been too overwhelming, too sweet, she had completely given herself over to the pleasure. It had been such a luxury to fall asleep in the same bed with Hank and to wake up in the same bed with him. The first three days they hadn't even left the room to ski or eat. Time had fallen away. It had been almost frightening, how time had really fallen away. They had not had to worry about time, they had not had to measure out their lives by the clocks. There were no class bells, no alarm clocks, there was no reason to leave in the middle of the night in order to have the car parked respectably in front of one's own house that morning. They had been able to stay awake late into the night, watching wonderful old black-and-white movies on the motel room television, not worrying about waking up for classes or responsibilities, sleeping on into the day, waking up in the afternoon, and even then not getting out of bed. They had been able to touch and touch and touch each other. They had lost themselves in each other's flesh. The sheets and bed had become sticky and moist and aromatic, as if an extension of their desire; they hadn't let the maid in the room for three days. The very motel room, with its piny walls and prints of deer and mountains, seemed to become an extension of them, seemed to become beautiful and sexy and warm. They had hated leaving the room; on the fourth day they had gotten up and showered and dressed, intending to go out and ski because the sun through the window did promise a world outside, and they had gone down to the resort's dining room and eaten a huge hot breakfast, but they had missed their room so much, and its hot familiar indulgent walls, that they had gone back up to the room after breakfast. They had not always made love; sometimes they had just lain together, holding each other, talking or not talking, nestling. The fourth day they had gotten up and gone out and skied, but Dale had been weak from laziness and love and had taken many spills. Hank had had to stop and stop to help her up and kiss her and laugh. Then for the fifth through the eighth days of their stay they had gone out a lot, skiing or just walking about in the day, down to the bar to dance and drink at night. They had loved dancing together, they had just been delighted with dancing together.

The last two days of their stay, though, they had again not left the room. They had been aware that the end of their time together was near. And so they had gone back into the room, back into the bed, and made love and clung to each other, as if they felt they were on a ship that would sink in two days, as if in two days they would die.

Finally they had had to leave, to drive back to Rocheport. Dale had to grade papers and make lesson plans. Hank had to prepare for his classes, too, and to go round the farm to be sure that the young boy he had hired to do the chores for him had not neglected anything. The night before the first new day of classes, Hank and Dale had eaten at Hank's farm, and made love, and then he had had to drive her home. And they had sat in the warm cab of the red pickup truck together, holding each other, and saying over and over again, "Oh, I love you, I love you, I love you." It had been a real tearing for Dale to leave the truck to go up to her apartment. She had gone up, and bathed and gotten ready for bed, but as she moved she had been in pain because she missed him so much. He had called her to say good night, and then she had gotten into bed. She had been exhausted and happy with the memories of his touch, but she had missed his presence, his body next to hers, and so she had lain there, feeling riddled with pain. In the next few days there had been reasons that she could not be with Hank after school: he had meetings, she had meetings, he had extra work on his farm. She had been miserable. And she had hated herself for the misery, and feared it.

Finally she had tried to talk to Carol about it. But Carol had been almost appalled. Here Carol was, engaged, and she had spent a loving holiday with her fiancé, too, but now she was not in pain. She was just going ahead with her life. She listened to Dale talk and then told Dale that it didn't seem right to her. She thought Dale's love bordered on the pathological.

"I would resent it very much indeed if Bob took up so much of my attention and energy and emotional space," Carol had said. "In fact, I think it's almost sick to be so obsessed. You've really got to get yourself in control. It's super to be in love, but it's crazy to be in love this way."

"I know," Dale said. "I know. I do have to get myself in control."

But she loved it, even as she feared it. She loved the marvelous druggedness of it. She loved the pleasurable bodily sensations, the way her body remembered those sensations; the way she would feel a rush, a hot wave of desire pass through her body, making her weak, as she was just driving the car down the street to the school. She loved the high of it, the exhilaration of it; she loved the joy of her body. For although she was in pain when she was not with Hank, she was in such luxurious rich delight when she was with him that it seemed to make it all worthwhile.

And then she would have to leave him, and she would be in the apartment alone, or at school, and she would be gripped by fear. She would be afraid that she would never see him again. Or that when she did, he would have changed. For they had reached a point in their relationship where they took each other for granted and talked to each other every day and made casual plans fitted around their own schedules. So there were days when Dale would enter the school in the morning, facing a day of teaching biology and French to adolescents, and she would not be sure whether she would be seeing Hank that night or not—he had mentioned that he might have a conference with parents, or an animal might be sick—and she would feel the day stretch long and drab in front of her because she was not sure she would be seeing him that night. And she had come to hate the days when she did not see him; and she had come to scorn herself for hating those days, for she thought surely each day must be welcomed for itself, days should not be hated simply because one other person did not enter them.

One weekend Hank had not seen Dale at all because a neighboring farmer, an older man, had come down with influenza, and Hank had done all the chores on his vast farm as well as on his own. He had only been able to call Dale that weekend; he had been busy every minute of the day, and then exhausted. And Dale had hated herself because she had not had anything equally pressing to do, and she had hated Hank because he had not been driven to see her, because he had not said, "Oh, I can't bear not to see you, I'll come see you no matter how tired I am." She felt that no matter what she had to do on any given day, if she had to push hundreds of boulders up a mountain all day long, still she would have found a way to see Hank, to hold him, just for a moment. Dale would chew on her lip as she drove home from school or bite into her yellow lead pencil as she sat marking papers: *damn it,* she would think, *oh, just damn it.* She was so frightened of her love for Hank. It was extreme. She felt that she did not want to live without Hank's love, without Hank in her life, and she knew that was wrong, that was threatening. For he could leave her life at any time.

One especially cold gray evening, when Hank had had a meeting and had said he wouldn't be able to see her that night, he would call her instead, Dale had driven her little VW out to the Rocheport beach and sat there, huddled in her coat, with the engine still running and the car filling with heat. She had sat in her tiny warm car looking out at the ocean. It had been so dangerous-looking, the water, so turbulent and relentless and cold. It did not care what it dragged down within it. It did not care that it overpowered. It did not care whether it gave life or took it; it did not care. Dale sat in the car, suddenly remembering an oil painting by Winslow Homer which hung in the Clark Art Museum in the town where she had gone to college. The painting was entitled "Undertow." It showed two men bringing two women out of such a violent ocean that Dale, standing staring at the painting, had been able to feel the tug and pull of the waves. The four people were moving toward the sunlight, the shore, the bright froth of ocean, but directly behind them the water sank down—Dale could feel the powerful sucking of it—and then rose up in an ominous, dark, huge wave that was about to break down over the people, to pull them all under.

The two women had been perhaps drowned, or almost drowned, it was not clear. It was obvious that the men were rescuers, lifeguards, and one man's shirt was torn, the other's muscles were taut with exertion. One woman's face was hidden as she lay clinging to the other woman's body, limp with fatigue. What had always fascinated Dale so that she had stood staring and staring at "Undertow" was the expression on the face of the other rescued woman. That woman had seemed more than just exhausted by her near-death by drowning. She seemed disappointed, somehow resigned to the rescue from drowning at sea. Why, Dale had thought, staring at the picture, wondering, why does she look so disappointed, so resigned? Had she been trying to commit suicide? Had the other woman rushed out into the water to save her and been pulled down under, too? The woman's expression was unfathomable. A few drops of water clung to the woman's face, under her eye, against her cheek, and Dale had the certainty that those were tears, that the woman was crying, that it was not just the spray from the ocean. Why was the woman so sad to be rescued? What had she wanted from the drowning?

Later Dale had gone to the trouble to gain admittance to the museum's well-guarded library, and she had spent almost an hour on the hushed fourth floor, looking through books about the paintings of Winslow Homer. But the books were of no help. In fact they irritated Dale by their technically artistic tone. Each different write-up described with stark unimaginative detail the action and color of the painting, which had been done in 1886. No one seemed to find any significance in it; they all seemed most impressed with the fact that Homer had used real female models for this work, and that he had made the models lie on the floor in bathing suits with water thrown over their bodies so that he could see exactly how wet skin looked. Dale had put the books away, depressed. The mystery had not been solved; the question had not been answered.

But then on the Rocheport beach, as she sat staring out at the dangerous movements of the relentless gray waves, she remembered "Undertow" as if it had been a message from a passing stranger which only now could be of use to her. She felt strongly the significance that particular painting had for her life; she understood why she had spent so much time in front of it, wondering at it, again and again during the four years she was in that town going to college. The painting had fascinated her; it had frightened her; yet it had drawn her to it, it had held her. *This is true*, she had thought. And what she had meant—she now understood— was that for her, going into love would be a kind of drowning, a surrender to a passion so violent that she would be completely pulled under, overpowered, overcome. And so she had avoided it; she had not fallen in love. Not until now. And now she felt like the exhausted swimmer in the painting, who must somehow find a way to resign herself to the tranquillity of life. For after that relentless pull and tug of passion, after the buffetings of love, after the violent gratifications of desire—gratifications so wild and fierce and powerful that at times they brought her as close to pain as to pleasure, that at times Dale thought she truly would die, so that she lost control of herself and felt her blood pound in her throat—after all that, the rest of life did not matter.

"But that's absurd, that's *wrong!*" Dale had shouted out suddenly to herself, her words startling the hot silent air of her gently reverberating car. The rest of life *had* to matter; life had to matter whether Hank was there or not. "Oh, you're so stupid!" she had said to herself, and had put the car into gear and driven away from the ocean, driven home and forced herself into a frenzy of work. High school students had probably never had a teacher devote so much time and energy to their courses before—and they had probably never had a teacher who worked so hard at simply keeping her mind on them as she stood in front of them in the classroom, holding up a live and twitching frog, or writing verb conjugations on the board.

Now she sat at her gray metal desk, trying not to sneeze on her students' papers, dismally making small red checks and totaling up scores. She would not see Hank tonight; she had told him that she felt too sick, that she would just go straight home and to bed. This would be the third night in a row, the third long day in a row, that she would have gone without seeing Hank. He did not seem disturbed by it, he did not seem upset. Yet Dale felt like a raving maniac. She wanted to run to find him, and shake him, and dig her teeth into his flesh. She felt angry with him: how could he be so calm? How could he say so casually, "Okay, I understand," after she had given him her little speech about needing to stay apart from him a little, to get her own life back in control. He had seemed to think that what she was saying was normal and reasonable, and yet by his very reasonableness he seemed to imply that it would not touch him, it would not hurt him, it would not bother him all that much if she was with him less. Oh, love was so unbalanced, it was such a goddamned *seesaw*. She felt that she loved him more than he loved her, that he was still sensible, in control, while she hung helpless and vulnerable, suspended at his mercy.

She wanted to marry him.

She wanted to marry him so that she could live in the same house with him and be with him every day for the rest of her life. She wanted to travel with him. She wanted the security, the restful blessed security of marriage, of being really connected to him. But they had not even once discussed marriage. And she knew with the rational side of her being that marriage could be a farce: look at her father and mother, look at her sister. She had never been so confused.

So she sat in her classroom, grading the papers, sneezing and aching, with her confusions and her desires running through her constantly like a current, like an undertow. So she did not hear Mr. Jersey's shouts at first; or she heard them, but they did not register on her consciousness immediately. When she did realize that it was shouting that she heard, and that it was Mr. Jersey shouting, she thought that the old man must have somehow electrocuted himself, or caught himself in some sort of machine, so frantic and brutal were his words. She hurried from her desk and out and down the hall toward the noise. She found Mr. Jersey's cart and broom just outside the door to the faculty and staff lounge, and Mr. Jersey just inside the door, waving his arms and yelling.

"Mr. Jersey?" she said. "Mr. Jersey? What's wrong?"

Then she entered the lounge and saw what was wrong. Mr. Jersey had caught two high school students making love on the nubby orange lounge sofa. Dale recognized them both: the boy, Jeff Benton, was a senior who had done well in Dale's French class the year before and was doing well in her biology class this year. The girl, Sally Martin, was also a senior, and in Dale's second-year French class. Both students were *good* kids—responsible, pleasant, intelligent, leaders in school activities. Both were well liked and attractive. Dale had actually never thought much about Sally, who had seemed just another nice pretty girl, but Jeff was good-looking enough to draw comments from some of the younger teachers. Now he stood red-faced and awkward in the presence of Mr. Jersey's almost inarticulate wrath, his face clenched with embarrassment and fear. Yet Dale admired him; even as he stood there, he had placed himself in front of Sally, protectively, to ward Mr. Jersey's words off of her, and to keep her from Mr. Jersey's sight.

Jeff had already managed to get his pants up, although his belt was undone and his fly was unzipped. But Sally, who still sat on the sofa behind him, was all disheveled, her jeans down around her knees and her blouse all undone; she was frantically attempting to button it, but she was shaking so hard that it was taking her a long time. She would not look up; her long hair hung down around her face, curtaining off her expression.

It took Dale a few moments to realize that Mr. Jersey, for all his truly honest shock and horror, was relishing the drama of the situation. In fact, he was stretching it for all it was worth.

"Now what do you think, Miss Wallace," he said. "Just look at this. I came down the hall to clean up the lounge, and here it was locked, and I got my keys out and opened it, and look what I found! These two young people having sexual intercourse in the faculty lounge! Why, it's outrageous! It's indecent! They should be expelled. We've got to call their parents, we've got to call Mr. Hansen, we've got to *do* something about this! Why, it's probably even *illegal*, we should probably call the police—"

"Mr. Jersey," Dale began, speaking in what she hoped was a clear sensible tone, even though she had begun to shake with fear for the students, "Mr. Jersey, calm down. It's all right."

"What do you *mean* it's all right?" Mr. Jersey yelled. "Students having sex in the faculty lounge in broad daylight is *all right?*"

"Well," Dale said, and she grinned in spite of herself, "it certainly wasn't very smart. But on the other hand, it didn't hurt anybody."

"Well, well, suppose someone walked in!" Mr. Jersey sputtered.

"Someone did," Dale said.

"I mean suppose a young person walked in, an innocent young person—"

"The door was locked, Mr. Jersey," Dale said. "An innocent young person couldn't have walked in. Only you and Mr. Hansen could have walked in. You are the only people who have the key to the lounge. And both you and Mr. Hansen have had some experience with sexual intercourse, I'm sure; I mean it won't hurt your emotional growth. Mr. Jersey, come out in the hall for a moment and let Sally get her clothes on. This is embarrassing her."

"Well, she deserves to be embarrassed!" Mr. Jersey said.

"Mr. Jersey, please come out in the hall," Dale said, and very reluctantly, the old man left the room. "Now look, Mr. Jersey," Dale said, "I don't want you to be so upset about this. I realize that I'm younger than you are, and you are much wiser about many things than I am, but you've got to stop a minute and think about those kids. They weren't really doing anything *wrong*; they weren't damaging the property—"

"They might have stained the sofa," Mr. Jersey muttered.

"Oh, come on, that sofa's so old and grungy no one would notice if a horse slept there," Dale said. "The point is, Jeff and Sally shouldn't have been in the faculty lounge at all. That is the only really wrong thing they did. They are both good students. I have them both in my classes, and they are good smart kids. I don't see what would be gained by calling in a bunch of other people. I'm sure this scare has been enough to keep them from ever trying anything like this again."

"Yes, but someone should tell their parents what they were *doing*," Mr. Jersey said.

"Mr. Jersey," Dale said, "everyone does what they were doing. Times have changed since you and I were young"—she included herself in his age group, hoping to influence him by their union—"and people just don't think that's *wrong* anymore."

"Well, I think it's wrong, and I am going to call Mr. Hansen and those kids' parents and the police!"

"Mr. Jersey, *don't*. Let's talk about this first, please. I know you are a kind man, and you love all the students here, and they all love you. Just remember how they all ask you to sit with them at the basketball games. Remember the cards they sent you last fall when you were in the hospital with your hernia. The students at this school really like you, and they trust you, and they think you like them. You can't turn around and do something mean to Jeff and Sally; why, none of the students would ever trust you again." Dale stopped speaking long enough to sneeze. "Mr. Jersey," she went on, "I just couldn't bear it if you reported those kids. All the students in this school would be heartbroken; they think you are their *friend*. Listen, why don't you just let me handle this. Let me take the responsibility. I'll talk to them and make sure that they never do anything like this again. Oh, I'm sure they won't. I'm sure they've learned their lesson. That's the important thing. Oh, they are so *young*, Mr. Jersey, and something like this could ruin their lives forever. Surely you made a mistake when you were young; surely someone was generous and charitable to you at one time." Dale sneezed again, and coughed. "Oh, Mr. Jersey, I would be *so grateful* if you would call your wife and get that hot toddy recipe for me. I feel just awful."

"Well," Mr. Jersey said, and wiggled the handle of his mop. He looked as though he was not too sure he was not being had.

"Mr. Jersey, you're like a *father* to these students—or at least an *uncle*," Dale said. She coughed.

"All right," Mr. Jersey said. "All right. I'll let you take care of it. You're a teacher, I'm just the custodian; you've been to college and you have faculty regulation books and code books; you should know what's right. Okay. But if I ever catch them again—"

"You won't, I promise," Dale said.

"All right," Mr. Jersey said. He looked at the closed door of the staff room with resignation. "I guess the kids would hate me if I got any of them in trouble," he said. "And I'm too old to work at a place where the kids hate me. So you do whatever you think is right, and it's all on your head. If anyone finds out about this, though, all the blame goes to you."

"Thank you," Dale said. "Thank you very much, Mr. Jersey. I think you are terribly kind, and I'll tell Jeff and Sally that, too. And I really would like the hot toddy recipe."

Mr. Jersey left his cart and brooms on one side of the hall and went rather reluctantly off to phone his wife from the office phone. Dale went into the staff room to confront Jeff and Sally. By now they were completely dressed and smoothed out, and sitting in chairs far apart from each other. They looked absolutely sick. Dale was afraid on entering the room that Sally was going to throw up. For one brief moment she felt a flash of memory of those horrible adolescent years when she had felt like an adult but been treated like a child; when she had had to abide by everyone else's rules and judgments.

"Relax," she said, and smiled and sat down in a chair. "It's okay. I've talked with Mr. Jersey, and he's not going to call anyone; he's not going to tell anyone. He's left it all up to me, and I'm not going to tell anyone. You're both going to get off easy this time. All you have to do is listen to a lecture from me. I'm not going to tell the police or Mr. Hansen or even your parents. You are both old enough to know what you're doing. On the other hand, I'm not so sure of that. This was a stupid place to pick. I mean the faculty lounge of the school? What on earth got into you?"

"But we don't have anyplace else to go," Sally said, tears springing into her eyes. "There's always someone at my house and his house, and we aren't allowed to go out on school nights, and Jeff's car is so *little*—"

"We didn't mean to be disrespectful," Jeff said. "We didn't think anyone would be here. We thought—"

He left his sentence half finished, but Dale felt she could sense what he meant. They had thought, surely, of the luxury of lying together, fully unfolded and pressed against each other, on the comfort of the wide lounge sofa. Perhaps they had never had such a luxury before; their lovemaking had probably been confined to the impossible interiors of small cars and to the uneasy darkness of porches. And now it was cold. They could not even lie on the ground, on the beach, at the park.

"Still," Dale said, "you should have realized it could have gotten you into trouble. It *did* get you in trouble. It was a dumb thing to do. And"—she interrupted herself and looked seriously at Jeff and Sally in turn—"what are you doing about contraception?"

Sally looked down at her hands. "Well, nothing," she mumbled. "I mean we don't—do it—that much. We don't get to be together very often."

"It only takes one time," Dale said. "Look, you're both good kids. You're good students. You're smart. I don't want to ruin your lives, and neither does Mr. Jersey. But you've got to make some promises to me—you owe me something. Do you understand that? If I keep quiet, and I'm going to, you have to promise me three things. You have to promise me that you will go to a clinic—there's a good one in Portland—and get some sort of birth control. If you end up getting pregnant at seventeen, Sally, I'll hate myself for not telling your parents now. So you get some sort of birth control, both of you, and tell me about it next week, or I'll call your parents and let them take charge. Number two: Never get caught here or anywhere again. I know it's hard, but you'll just have to work something else out. Not everyone is going to be as kind and understanding as Mr. Jersey was. And you'd better keep that in mind and be super nice to Mr. Jersey. And three: Don't you dare tell any of your friends about this episode. I could get into as much trouble as you for keeping this secret. I could lose my job. So don't go around like a pair of smart-asses telling all your friends this funny story. It's not a funny story. If you tell anyone, believe me I'll tell someone, and you'll be sorrier than I will. Is that all clear? Do you understand?"

Sally burst into tears. "Oh, Miss Wallace," she said. "Thank you so much. My parents would just *kill* me if they knew about this. I know it was stupid—but we're *in love*." And she raised up her sweet, still childish face and looked at Dale with desperation. Her face was shining with tears.

"Try to talk to your parents, Sally," Dale said. "You'd be surprised at how understanding parents can be. Or go see your minister. That is the best thing to do. Go see a minister, or even see our school counselor, Mr. Robertson. That's what he's here for. You'll find that most old people like us really are sympathetic. We really will try to help. We really do have some advice to give. But use common sense. Don't let being in love ruin your lives." Dale sneezed. "Let's go," she said. "I'm exhausted."

"Thank you, Miss Wallace," Jeff said awkwardly, rising from his chair. He was so gangly and intense and grateful and such a nice boy that Dale nearly cried with the pity of it all. "We're really grateful," he said. "And we'll keep your three conditions. We'll never get caught again, and we won't tell anyone, and we'll get some birth control."

"*You* get some birth control," Dale said, taking Sally by the shoulders and looking at her. "I know Jeff loves you, but it's your body, and you are in charge of your life. You have to be responsible. You have to take care of yourself."

"Okay," Sally said. "Okay. I promise. I'll do something. Maybe I'll even talk to my mother. Or—oh, I don't know. But I'll tell you what I've done next week."

"All right, then," Dale said. "You'd both better go home now. And good luck. And if you let your grades drop, remember you'll be in big trouble with me." She smiled at the two students and opened the door for them.

Jeff walked out first, muttering as he did, "Thank you, Miss Wallace." But to Dale's amazement, Sally stopped at the door and threw herself on Dale and wrapped her arms around her and put her head on Dale's shoulder.

"You're so kind," she said, crying. "This is so nice of you. How can I ever thank you? I was so scared."

Dale hugged Sally hard and felt tears come to her eyes at the feeling of the young girl's grateful, beseeching embrace. She realized in a flash that now she would always care about this girl and the boy she loved; she would want to know what happened to them; she was now involved in their lives. She cared about their happiness, their futures.

"Don't be scared," Dale said. "It's okay. Love is okay. Just keep yourself in control. And I'm glad I could help." She pushed the girl back slightly, and wiped the tears from Sally's young face, and smiled at her. "Take care," she said.

The two students walked off down the hall out to the dark evening, and Dale returned to her classroom to finish the grading. She sat at her desk in a trance of competence, almost speeding through the remaining tests. When she had finished grading and was totaling up the scores and noting them in the gradebook, she was suddenly struck with what seemed to her to be an almost overwhelming observation. Most of the students had done well on the tests: she had taught them some of the basic rudiments of the French language. They would be able to use the language when they traveled; they would be able to perform well in college. She was teaching young people French. She was a teacher.

A chill passed through Dale which had nothing to do with her cold. She looked up from her desk out at her empty classroom and was filled with a great warmth that she recognized as a mixture of hope and love and pride. She was a teacher, and this was her classroom, and she would have an influence on the world. She could teach young people, she could open up the world to them a bit, she could bring the world to them; she could help them. And all this meant something, all this *mattered*. All this was worth something in the world. All this was worth something to her.

Suddenly restless with the force of her emotions, she rose from her desk and began to walk around her room, running her hands along the desks and chairs and windowsills as if those objects could receive and return her love. She had never felt this before in her life: that she was a competent person who could influence the world, who could matter, who could care. Always before it had seemed to her that teaching was merely a kind of employment, a respectable way to pass the time and make money. But now she knew that she had been seized by the importance of her profession, by the significance of her work. She was a teacher. She was a good teacher. And she would be a good teacher all of her life—even when she had a cold, even when her own private life was uncertain—and that would sustain her. That would always sustain her.

Dale hugged herself and laughed out loud. "My God," she spoke aloud into the empty classroom, "this is like some kind of religious conversion." She felt slightly embarrassed, and even as she walked about the classroom she knew that this high would wear off, that there would be days and weeks and months when she would feel cynical and depressed or simply just tired, but that still something had come over her, or something had entered into her, and she was changed.

She went back to her desk and sorted tests and books and papers into their appropriate piles, then put on her hat and mittens—she was already wearing her parka—and gathered up her purse. As she flicked off the classroom lights she felt amused at the drama of her thoughts: but she would always remember this day, the tests, the cold, the boy and girl she had helped, and this empty classroom where she had learned how to experience a new and very rich sort of joy.

Mr. Jersey was waiting for her at the end of the hall with the hot toddy recipe written down on a yellow lined sheet of tablet paper. She thanked him, and stood talking to him for a while, complimenting him for his kindness toward Jeff and Sally. Then she drove home, full of thoughts, full of energetic new plans for French and biology lessons. She almost ran up the stairs, and eagerly told Carol of all that had happened, hyper, high, reliving it as she told of it. And when the phone rang and it was Hank, she almost could not speak to him, she almost for a long moment could not speak, she was so filled with the wonder of the sudden knowledge that she had gone so long without needing him, without even having him in her thoughts. She stood by the phone, talking to him, loving him, smiling—and loving herself at the same time.

SEVEN

❖❖❖❖❖❖❖❖❖❖❖❖❖❖❖❖❖❖

A cat appeared at Margaret's door this morning; she was awakened by its mewing. She rose from bed and wrapped herself in a thick warm wine-colored robe and walked through her quiet house to the front door. When she opened the door she was first struck by the force of the weather: a chill wet wind assailed her and made her nearly slam the door in self defense. Instead she looked down to see, sitting on the sill, a wet and most miserable-looking cat. The cat was of an indiscriminate gray, and was so wet that its fur was stuck dismally along its bones, giving it an unpleasant ratlike look. Vancouver doors and windows do not need screens because there are so few flying bugs in the area; Margaret was still amazed by this each time she opened the door. It seemed an incredibly arbitrary luxury to her after living so long in the buggy Midwest. So now the absence of the screen made it possible for the wet cat to huddle up against the wooden door where it was partially protected from the rain by the overhang. Still the wind blew and gusted and sprayed the poor cat with constant cold wet blasts, and the cat shivered and mewed. It was not a kitten, but it had the vulnerability of a kitten. When Margaret stared down at it, it stared her right in the eye and mewed at her so directly, so demandingly, that she knew she would have to take it in. What else could she do? Leave it to die there huddled in the rain on her doorstep?

She bent to pick the sopping cat up and although her first thought was to hold the cat away from her, her first instinct was to cuddle it against her to warm it. The front of her robe was immediately soaked. She carried the cat into the kitchen, becoming slightly alarmed as she felt the cat's wild trembling. Poor cat; would it die? She grabbed up a terry-cloth hand towel and began to dry the cat. Then she set it on the floor, still wrapped in the towel, and heated up some milk just until it was warm to her little finger. She placed the warm milk in a saucer and dished out some of the moist canned cat food she kept for Pandora and set it on the floor for the cat. It ate and drank ravenously, and for a moment Margaret stayed to watch, pleased by the satisfaction of the cat. Then she went into the living room and built and lighted a large fire. Soon the room was glowing with warmth. The stray cat came in of its own accord and settled itself in front of the fire, very close to the hearth. It tucked its paws under it and looked up at Margaret with approval. Margaret went into the kitchen, made herself some tea, and returned. The cat had fallen asleep.

It was only seven-thirty. Margaret felt slightly annoyed. She had been out late the night before and had intended to sleep late into the morning. There was so little else to do on late-January mornings like this, when the rain and wind were constant. She sank down onto the sofa and sipped at her tea and looked out her large glass windows toward the ocean. But she could not see the ocean for the rain. All she could see was sheets of rain, and dark dense clouds, and the rain blowing up against the windows in such waves and patterns that she felt she could see the wind. But this did not keep her interest; she had seen all that often enough these days. So she looked down at the cat, which was still sleeping, and then at the coffee table, which was laden with the new hardbound books she had bought the day before. She thought she might take the books back to bed with her, to browse over until she fell asleep again. But she did not feel the ordinary surge of desire and anticipation that she usually felt when looking at new books, and instead she felt annoyed by them, because they had lost their charm, because they could not lure her. She knew it could not be the books' fault; they had intrigued her enough yesterday when she had bought them in the downtown bookstore. And she had bought so many various types: a mystery, a romantic novel, a serious novel, a book full of photographs by a famous American photographer of a famous American woman painter. No, they were all good new books. But they did not lure her. They seemed dead and cold. They irritated her. Margaret felt, like the slight trickle of irritation that comes at the back of the throat just before a cold arrives, a tricky and unpleasant chill, a chill about her soul. She was frightened.

She said aloud—she had taken to talking to herself aloud, and why not, it was her house—"Oh, no. Not another morning like *this*." For in the past few weeks she had come to experience black mornings, brown mornings, gray mornings, when she was filled with an irrational grief and remorse and, worse, with self-loathing. Usually she fought off the mood with action; but what could she do at seven-thirty in the morning? She gave the stray cat a bitter look, but the cat did not wake up.

She had been quite happy through the holiday season. She had had a party of friends in to her home just before Christmas to watch the carol ships make their gay bright tour of the harbor, all the masts and decks decked out in lights, looking like floating, wandering Christmas trees.

That had been lovely. There had been children on the ships singing carols, and their sweet young voices had been projected toward shore by loudspeakers. And there had been a man on one of the ships who had called out: "All you in West Vancouver who can hear us, who are watching, blink your lights! Switch your house lights on and off so we know you are there!" It had been wonderful, oh wonderful, the way the whole shore of lights flickered on and off, in answer to the carol ships. Lights in the darkness, candles in the night, stars, people answering people with flashing lights all up and down the mountain. Margaret had stood at her light switch, flicking it up and down, feeling quite satisfied with her life, thinking that this was just exactly the right amount of contact she wanted with the outside world. Just this: to respond when asked, but at a distance, and without consequences, without responsibility. She had turned most happily back to her guests, to be their gay and temporary hostess.

Christmas Eve she had spent with Anthony, and Christmas Day they had gone to a dinner party at Miriam and Gordon's. It had been just at the beginning of this year that Miriam, who had been Margaret's friend for over thirty years, had invited Margaret to fly up from Liberty for a visit. Margaret had immediately fallen in love with Vancouver and had spent hours talking to Miriam about her life and her desires. Miriam had given Margaret excellent, unobtrusive, disinterested advice—and then a great hearty welcome when Margaret made the move. Margaret had even lived with Miriam and Gordon while she looked for and then negotiated the buying of her house. So it seemed fitting that she should spend the holidays with this, her oldest and somehow newest of friends, and with Gordon, Miriam's husband. And the holidays had passed quickly, full of laughter and good food and wine, and with a sense of elegant, unimploring companionship.

But now it was late January, and the holidays were over, and certain things had happened in Margaret's life that she wished had not happened. The world was beginning to encroach; demands were beginning to be made, and she did not like this. She did not want to dwell on this even now.

She sipped at her tea, and then picked up a cigarette from the silver case on the coffee table, and smoked awhile, gazing at the cat and feeling rather nasty. She was quite awake. She was slightly bored. She was annoyed. She had things to face.

It was seven-thirty in the morning—seven-forty now. Both the new stray cat and Pandora in on her bedroom chair were asleep and oblivious to her plight. It was completely quiet in the house except for the sound of the wind and rain against the windows. No one would call at this early hour. Margaret stared at the books on the coffee table, then at her bare foot, which she was swinging in abrupt little flips. She followed the line of her leg up from her foot to her robe-covered calf and then to her lap where her hands lay resting, one hand holding a cigarette from which she had just flicked the ashes. She sat on her sofa, and in an attempt to avoid other thoughts, she studied her hands.

They were the hands of a woman who was almost fifty years old: they were beginning to wrinkle, and the veins showed, but still they were quite attractive hands. In fact Margaret was vain of her hands. She wore three rings: a large diamond that had been her mother's engagement ring; a thick silver band which Anthony had given her; and an elaborate jade and silver ring which Miriam had given her. Margaret kept her nails painted now; she had never painted her nails while in Iowa, but she found she enjoyed doing this now, enjoyed the process of brushing on the sleek oily polish, enjoyed seeing the slick bright sheen of color at her fingertips as she went about her daily tasks. She thought she enjoyed most of all that rather helpless period of time that had to pass while her nails dried; that time when she could do nothing but sit so that the polish would not be smeared or marred. Yes, it was a pleasure to be able to indulge oneself in something as frivolous and time-consuming as painting one's nails, it was a pleasure to go about with painted nails. For of course when she had been at home, taking care of her family, doing dishes, cooking, baking brownies or chicken casseroles for some luncheon or charity or bake sale, she had not even dreamed of having painted nails, because the paint chipped off so easily. In her former life, painted nails would have been a bother, a source of constant worry. Now they were a source of constant pleasure. She felt like a Chinese emperor in pictures she had seen who grew his nails very long to indicate his life of luxury and ease; just so she painted her fingernails, to say to herself: it's okay now, it's yourself you have to please, you can indulge yourself. It was a trivial, frivolous indulgence, yet crucial all the same. And so Margaret stared at her hands, sliding the thick silver band up and down, enjoying the clean polished sight of her indolent hands. She thought she would like to live out the rest of her days in a life as sleek and cool as her hands were now. And then her hands trembled, and she put the cigarette in the ashtray and pressed her hands together in front of her, as if she were praying, and up against her lips. It was no good; her hands continued to tremble: she would have to face it, sooner or later. There were things she had to work through.

For one, there was Daisy. She could not keep up the pretense of not caring about Daisy. She worried about Daisy a great deal, in spite of herself. This fretting made her angry. She really resented this intrusion of worry and concern into her life. And yet what could she do? Daisy was her daughter. And besides, she loved Daisy, she liked Daisy, and could not help but sympathize with Daisy's plight. She

would have been terrified to be alone at twenty-nine with
two or three small children, facing the world without security, without the protection of a man. It was all very well
for Margaret now to feel smug about her new inde-
pendence, but Daisy was not forty-eight, Daisy's children
were not grown, Daisy was young and in distress. There
were periods in people's lives when they needed help. And
Daisy needed help now. Oh, but what could Margaret do?
She did not know how to answer Daisy's letter asking for a
loan of ten thousand dollars. She knew that Daisy would
never be able to repay that loan, and Margaret could see no
way to just give Daisy the money and still live her own life.
But more than money was involved here, Margaret knew,
more was at stake. How did any parent ever draw the line
and say: from now on you are totally on your own? How
could Margaret say: I do love you, but I won't help you?
Daisy's needs were so engulfing, and Margaret did not
want to be engulfed. She wanted to be solitary and free.
But Daisy was her child. Her first sweet child. She could
not think what to do; and it angered her that so much of
her time was given over to this worry.

And there was the problem with Anthony. When Margaret had met him eight months ago at Miriam and Gordon's home, she had been first intrigued and then delighted
by the man. He was so tall, so lean, so knowledgeable, and
above all, so contained. He had held himself with such
perfect reserve. He was so unlike the men Margaret had
known in Iowa, all those men like Harry who had seemed
somehow expansive in a manner that was at once vulnerable and domineering. They had imposed themselves on her
and by their very buttery congeniality had somehow set
more limitations on Margaret than Anthony and his almost disdainful aloofness could ever have. Or so she had
thought.

At first she had been intrigued by him, and for a while

really terrified at the consequences of his affection for her.
This tall cool man liked her: then what kind of woman
was she? What kind of woman could she be? It was all so
new to her: the city, her house, her new acquaintances, and
this new and utterly composed man. For months she had
been in a real state, awakening each day to the sight of cold
blue water, then going through the day at the edge of that
water. She would sit by the window reading her day's mail,
which at that time still consisted of long pleading emotional letters from Harry or one of their mutual Iowa
friends, letters addressed to the old Margaret, the caretaker, the nurturer. Then the phone would ring, and it
would be Anthony, suggesting that they attend an opera or
a poetry reading or a lecture and cocktail party at UBC.
She had for a while visualized herself as a woman made of
layers, who left a thin transparent Margaret sitting by the
window with a letter in her hands as another thin, transparent Margaret stood by the phone. Anthony had wanted
to buy a new car, and had enticed Margaret into buying his
slightly used Mercedes convertible, and that had added another layer to her image: that car. It would have been daft
to have a convertible in Liberty, where it was always too
cold or hot or windy to drive exposed, and Margaret would
have felt pretentious and just plain silly driving to the ladies' auxiliary meeting at someone's farm in such a thing.
Yet here in Vancouver the weather was so different, so
clement, that she could drive with the top down for most
of the months of the year. And it suited her, this low luxurious car; it pleased her enormously, and it was the sort of
thing one could drive to the downtown shops or the univer-
sities or the sleek lovely houses set back on the mountain
roads overlooking the city. Margaret had become more and
more at ease with her new self. Each day, in fact, she had
liked herself more. Each day she had smiled at herself in
the rearview mirror of the Mercedes, saying: why, *look*,

look how I can be! She had luxuriated in being herself, alone.

But she had enjoyed going out to exciting places with Anthony and had been complimented by his repeated invitations. She had slept with him almost at once, simply because when the occasion presented itself she knew that she had to do it then or forever refrain out of sheer terror. She had slept with only one man all her life; her daughters had been with more men than she. Anthony had brought champagne to celebrate the signing over of the papers of the car, and she had gotten very drunk and taken him into her darkened bedroom. It had been amazingly exciting. After all those celibate months, the stretch of Anthony's long naked torso against her own bare skin had been immensely satisfying. And Anthony had been almost efficient in his sexual expertise, so very courteous and capable and aware of just what needed to be done to bring Margaret to a point of gasping pleasure, and yet at the same time somehow still so aloof. How grown-up Margaret had felt. Sex became for her—to her real delight—almost merely another kind of possible, luxurious comfort. How grown-up she was: when she wanted to, she could smoke a cigarette, or have a drink, or have a bath, or have an orgasm. She felt quite smug. She felt that really this was the way people should live.

But now Anthony had asked Margaret to marry him. Three nights before, as they were sitting in his apartment drinking brandy after making love, he had suggested to her, in much the same tone of voice that he might suggest seeing a film that weekend, that they should marry. He had at first spoken of this possible marriage as a rational sort of exercise that would permit them to live the same sorts of lives they were living, except with each other. And then he would have a sabbatical from UBC the coming year and planned to do a lot of traveling throughout Canada, collecting information for a book he was doing on Canadian history. What fun it would be, he said, to take Margaret with him, to show her how enormous and varied Canada was, from the dark interior of British Columbia to the urbanity of Montreal. Oh, marriage would make their relationship so much easier; Anthony's home was in Vancouver proper, a good hour's drive across the Lion's Gate Bridge and through the city. They could live in Margaret's house or in his; how nice it would be, he said, to waken in the morning and share coffee and a newspaper in bed.

Margaret's first reaction to Anthony's proposal had been one of conceited gaiety, as if she were a child who had just been given a candy or a present simply for being cute. She took his proposal as a compliment, and not much more than that. Actually she had sat in Anthony's living room, listening to him talk, and wishing there were someone she could tell. She wanted to preen, to show off, to say: look what I've done! I'm barely divorced, and already this highly eligible man has asked me to marry him! I'm really quite marvelous, aren't I! She had felt herself suddenly deliciously young, brought back to those adolescent years in Iowa when a marriage proposal was the sign of ultimate worth.

It had been a horrible shock when she had realized that she had to give Anthony some kind of answer. He was not just complimenting her; he was asking for a commitment. He was expressing a desire, a demand. And she could see by the way his long lean hands held his brandy snifter that her answer mattered to him. Oh, God, she had thought, under his reserved and splendid façade he was buttery and vulnerable, too. She had been filled with fear.

"Do you love me?" she had asked, because she had to know. She felt that if he had said no, she might have married him.

But Anthony said, "Yes. I do. I love you, Margaret. I'm

sorry I haven't said so before. It must be rather amusing to have a man propose marriage without telling you he loves you first. But I find that sort of thing very difficult to say. I always have been too reticent. But it's true. I do love you. I love you. You have touched my soul."

Margaret had cried out, helplessly, "Oh!" and hidden her face in her hands. She had become almost faint. She had covered her face with her hands and sat that way for a long time, staring down at her dress until she felt herself calmed by the way her mind began to study the intricate pattern of blue-and-violet paisley meandering about the cloth. When she finally looked up, she had gone blank, she had almost forgotten the crisis at hand. She had to look at Anthony's serious face for a long moment before speaking.

"Anthony," she said, "I'm sorry. I wasn't prepared for this. I need to think about it. I'm immensely complimented, but I don't know how to respond. In fact, I'm just stunned."

Anthony had drawn her to him and kissed her on the mouth, her face, her neck. "Take your time," he said. "I can understand your surprise. I know how I am, how I act, but I find it so hard to express my feelings. I don't expect you to answer right away. Please take your time. But please say yes. I did not ask you to marry me frivolously. I love you. I want to marry you. I think we could spend the rest of our lives happily together. And I don't want to share you with anyone."

For there were other men. To Margaret's amazement, there were other men. Anthony was by far the most handsome, but the two other men she had begun to see with some regularity had other points to commend them. For one, they both had a sense of humor which far excelled Anthony's, and since Harry had never had much of a sense of humor, this quality had been almost the most attractive one she could find in a man. It gave her pleasure, as much pleasure as sex, to double over with laughter at what John Mallinson said, or to appreciate some witty intellectual remark of Roger Whitehall's. She found that these men called up new layers of herself just as surely as Anthony did, and she valued these new parts of herself very much indeed. It seemed to her that intelligent lightheartedness was a real gift of God. She wondered why she had somehow never come across it in Liberty: was it that the humor there was always rather heavy and obvious or simply that no one would have thought to be airily lighthearted with her old self? At any rate, she had never dreamed she could have such easy, pleasurable and almost impersonal relationships with men like these, and it appalled her to think of sacrificing the acquaintance and company of these other men in order to limit herself to Anthony.

He had finally driven her home, and left her at her door with a kiss that left no doubt as to the seriousness of his intentions. He did love her; she had touched his soul. That was the worst thing of all. She was almost certain that she did not want to touch anyone else's soul, certainly not now, not for a long while. And assuredly she did not want her own soul touched or meddled with; my God, she was only in the process of discovering her soul, at the age of forty-eight—she wasn't about to give it over right away to someone else's keeping. She wasn't even sure what it was like. For the past three days she had rather barricaded herself in her house, leaving the phone off the hook, or going out all afternoon and evening by herself, to the library, to bookstores, to clever shops which occupied her mind. She had walked and walked inside shopping malls and art galleries, trying to tire herself out so that she would simply not have the energy to deal with the problem. Yesterday afternoon she had sat alone in a small café, drinking cinnamon-flavored coffee and enjoying a cigarette, and she had begun to watch two women of her own age who were

having lunch together at a table near hers. The two women
had been so involved in each other, heads bent toward
each other, talking earnestly, drawing back to eat or laugh,
and Margaret felt a glow of satisfaction come over her at
the sight. It occurred to her then that the person she liked
best in her life at that moment was her own woman friend
Miriam, because Miriam gave and needed just the right
amount—and she imposed no conditions whatsoever on
Margaret's life. Miriam was tremendously busy with her
own life, with her teaching at the university, and with her
pleasant marriage with Gordon, and so she had some time
for Margaret, and would help her if that was needed, or ask
for help, but that sort of request was rare. Margaret spoke
to Miriam on the phone almost daily, and they saw each
other at least once a week; they shared occasional meals
and books and laughter. And that was all. There was a
real elegance about the friendship Margaret shared with
Miriam; there was a fastidious grace. It was unlike any relationship Margaret had ever had, and she felt she valued it
above all others. So Margaret sat impolitely watching the
other lunching women, and wondering about the nature of
friendships and love, until they finished their meal and rose
and left. Then she left, herself, not any the less confused.

And now here she was, on a rainy morning, alone with
herself and her familiar old cat and the sleeping new one.
It fascinated her that the stray cat could sleep so soundly
in a strange house, that it could be so self-possessed as to
enter a new space and give itself over to sleep. Now that it
was dry, Margaret could see that it was a large and graceful
cat, a really quite beautiful cat, and she even found herself
thinking that she would like to keep it. Would she become
a cliché of a woman, an old lonely woman living with only
cats as company? Why did people deride such women so?
She would find it, she thought, a most superior way to live.
She could envision a quite lovely life shared only with

these quiet, undemanding animals who by their own insolent aloofness would allow her an elegant, companionable privacy.

But what to do about the people in her life, these people who reached out, and touched her soul, in spite of her attempted withdrawal, and tried to draw her back into a world where people healed and wounded each other? In the past few weeks, Margaret had become unable to watch the television news or to read the front page of the newspaper. It seemed that the world was just too full of tragedy, of need, of sorrow; and that somehow it was all her fault. Children were starving in India and Africa; families in South America had lost their homes to earthquakes and landslides; adolescents were maimed in totally unnecessary car accidents; baby seals and whales were being killed; old people were freezing and living on cat food. The last evening she had watched the news she had finally slammed off the television set in a fury, and paced about her house waving her hands and shouting to herself while Pandora, her old familiar cat, sat cynically watching her from a comfortable nest on the sofa.

"Well, what am I supposed to do?" she had asked the cat, the pure white, silky, well-fed, and luxurious cat. "What should I do? Should I buy food and mail it to India? Adopt a whale? Adopt an old person? Fly down to Peru with a hammer and some nails and try to build one homeless family a new house? What am I supposed to do? Shall I stand at a curve on Upper Levels Highway with a sign telling drivers to slow down, to drive more carefully? Or station myself at an airport waiting for a crash so I can pull victims from the plane? Give all my money to medical research? Arrive at a hospital and tell them to cut out my eyes to give to some blind child? What shall I do? What would it help the world if I tried?"

In other words, did she have to fly back and help Daisy with her children?

Did she have to marry Anthony and be a helpful faculty wife, ministering to students and young professors' families?

But what else was she good for? She was intelligent and well read, but she had no degrees. She could do several things very well, but she had developed no marketable skills or talents, and she wasn't interested, really, in a career. She simply wanted to live out her life by enjoying each day as she chose. The question was, how could she buy her way? Or had she somehow already bought it?

Margaret let another cigarette, then put it out because it gave her mouth an unpleasant taste. She looked at her watch: it was eight o'clock. She decided to fix herself some breakfast. She went into her kitchen and became involved for a while in the pleasure of making herself a tray with eggs scrambled with cheese and chives, and an English muffin slathered with butter and honey, and fresh pressed orange juice. She carried the tray back to the living room, intending to eat and read, and as she set the tray on the coffee table, she saw Pandora stroll out of the bedroom to come to a dramatic standstill at the sight of the stray cat sleeping on the hearth. Pandora's white fur stood on end and a low nasty growl came roiling out of her throat. This immediately woke the stray cat, who sprang to its feet at once and arched its back. Both cats hissed, then began to do a tense scuttling dance about each other, snarling and hissing as they did. Pandora suddenly reached out one sharp paw to swipe at the stray cat, and the cat leaped back and yowled.

"Pandora, *stop it!*" Margaret yelled. She walked over to her cat and stood above her, frowning down. "You stop that right now. This poor cat was freezing out in the rain and I had to take him in. He's just a temporary guest; he's not going to give you any trouble. Now you mind your manners and settle down or I'll put *you* out in the rain."

Pandora eyed Margaret with an almost sneering distaste, then turned her back and slunk off under a chair, to lie and stare out steadily and nastily at the stray cat. The stray cat settled back down on the hearth but this time with an air of wary unease, keeping his eyes open and facing toward Pandora.

"All right, cats, that's better," Margaret said. "You can both just calm down and be civilized." She sat down and took a bite of her eggs. The food brought her a sense of pleasure and calm and as she looked at the books on the coffee table, she thought she would now like to read them; she would finish her breakfast and take the books back to bed. She took a bite of the crisp English muffin, and then the phone rang. She had to put her food back down in order to go into the kitchen to pick up the phone.

"Mother?" It was Dale speaking. "Good morning. How are you? Did I wake you?"

"Why, no, actually," Margaret said. "A stray cat awoke me about thirty minutes ago and I've been watching him spat with Pandora. And I'm fine. But how are you? Why on earth are you calling at this time of day? What time is it in Maine now? Eleven o'clock? Shouldn't you be teaching? Oh, what's wrong?"

Dale laughed. "Don't worry, nothing's wrong. I've been trying to reach you all week, but either your line's been busy or you've been out. I thought if I called now you surely wouldn't be gone. Everything's fine. I just wanted to ask if it would be all right if I flew out to see you this weekend. I have a cold; I can take sick leave and come out on Friday and stay the weekend."

"Well . . . well . . . well, of *course*," Margaret stuttered. "But *why*? I mean, I would be delighted to see you, darling, but—"

"Stop worrying, Mother," Dale said. "I just want to see you and talk with you about some things. Don't worry. Nothing's wrong. Listen, I'm in the school office right now and I've got to get back to my class. But I've got a reservation on a United flight that gets into Vancouver at noon. Flight two-nine-six. Okay?"

"Yes, yes, of course. I'll meet you at the airport. Oh, this is exciting, Dale."

"Good. I'll see you Friday. Take care, Mom."

Margaret hung up the phone and stood still, staring out the kitchen window at the rain, staring hard, as if she could see the answer to her thoughts if she only watched closely enough. Why was Dale coming out? What in the world was going on? And what kind of mother was she to feel so *suspicious?* Finally she went back out to the living room and sat down. She tasted her eggs again, but they had grown cold, and the honey had seeped into the muffins, giving them a damp and soggy appearance. Across the room, Pandora sat stiffly, watching first the new cat and then Margaret with sulky and accusing eyes.

"Damn," Margaret said, then: "Oh, well." And she picked up three of the new books and went off to her bedroom with them, leaving the muffins and the cats, knowing she would be unable to concentrate on the books or to fall into the oblivion of sleep.

Friday morning Margaret found herself in front of her mirror in tears. She had put on her loveliest clothes and spent a long time with her makeup, and still she looked wretched. Or thought she did. She supposed that she actually didn't look much different from the day before, it was just her mood that was making her look this way, just her damned *mood* that was making her *think* she looked wretched. Oh, the flesh, the sappy flesh, she was thinking. This morning she hated all her flesh, all its pockets and creases and wrinkles and sags, all its flaws. She felt there was so much unsavoriness about her body. It had been so much easier when she hadn't had any pretensions to beauty, when she had been able to hide behind her fat and her tiny-curled hair and her shapeless dresses. Now she felt she had proclaimed herself a person who found herself attractive, and therefore she was subject to criticism. She felt *old*. She placed her hands at the sides of her face and pulled the skin back toward her ears, wondering if she should have her face lifted. So many women were doing it, and they seemed to look and feel better because of it. And she certainly could afford it. She could afford to have everything lifted, everything done. But eventually time would tell, age would show, she would be fifty, and not twenty-four as Dale was. She would be fifty, and then sixty, and then seventy, there was no going back, no evading it: she was going to get old. She didn't want to look old, she wanted to look young and sexy and admirable. But oh the vanity of it all, the damned vanity.

She went back into her bedroom and lay down on her bed and shut her eyes. Growing old was not fair. It was not fair that now when she was just discovering herself she was starting to fall apart. Now and then, in rare moments of despair, she sometimes thought she would have done better to stay in Liberty, where she could have grown old and ugly in comfort, eating and eating, growing fatter and fatter, with no one, most of all herself, placing any demands on her appearance. In Liberty she could have easily stayed Mrs. Santa Claus, jolly, plump, and sexless. As it was she had to fight with herself every day not to eat too much food, or any of the wrong foods which would cause her to gain weight, not to drink too much alcohol, which also added weight but, even worse, made her look bloated and saggy the next day; she had to fight to make herself swim and exercise. Most of the time it was worth it—but just now it was not. Just now it all seemed so trivial, so foolish, so almost shameful. Oh, what was it that one person loved about another person? The spirit of course, above all, the spirit of a person was the most important. But there was no getting around the fact that it was the flesh which first attracted people to each other. There was no getting around the fact that Anthony would never have loved Margaret if he had seen her in her Liberty body. And yet—hadn't that body been a true reflection of her spirit? Hadn't her spirit changed as much as her body? All right, then, but how was she to face the dilemma of the future, when she felt her spirit would grow more and more attractive, but her body could only age? Or even now, now was the problem, *now*: how to face Dale at the airport.

Dale had always been her father's daughter; Daisy had always been her mother's daughter. The spring Dale had graduated from college, Margaret and Harry had driven back to Massachusetts for the ceremony, and had stayed for a week in a pleasant hotel near the heart of the small New England town where the college was. And at each social function, at each expensive gay restaurant meal, even as they had walked about the town, looking at the charming pottery and clothing shops, Margaret had been well aware that Dale wouldn't have cared all that much if Margaret had not been there. In fact Margaret had felt it very clearly that Dale would have liked to be alone with her father. Harry did look so distinguished, did look so much like the sort of person he was: a distinguished, well-respected, handsomely aging, prosperous man, the real man at that time in Dale's life. Margaret had gone into a beauty shop on the main street of the town one morning to have her hair done, and had felt horribly shy and fat and tasteless as she sat in her polyester print dress having her little curls of hair combed out while all about her, sleek slim women, young and old, had sauntered, bright with fashion. She had come out of the shop, stunned by the daylight, and seen Dale and Harry strolling down the street arm in arm, stopping to chat with friends of Dale's. How happy Dale had looked standing there with her father, leaning up against him, proudly displaying him; Margaret had wanted to run away. She had felt like a misfit, a damper on Dale's days.

And then, two years later, just last year, when Dale had returned from her European stay, oh, what a distance had been between the two of them. Margaret had fixed Dale an enormous breakfast that morning, and sat down at the kitchen table across from her with a companionable cup of coffee, trying to talk with Dale, trying to get from Dale some real feeling for who she had become, what she had done, how those two years away had changed her. For once she had been totally interested in Dale, her younger daughter, totally interested and without anyone else in the way. The night before, Dale's first night home, Dale had spent most of the time talking with Harry, telling him about castles or museums, and asking about all his patients and his work. Margaret had know what Dale had wanted— that private time with her father—and had kept as unobtrusively out of the way as possible, doing the dishes, refusing Dale's offer to help, then making a lemon meringue pie for the next day. She had wished it had been Daisy who had been home, because then Daisy and Harry would have sat in the kitchen with her, and Danny and Jenny would have played on the floor with measuring spoons and cups and plastic bowls, and it would have been so comfortable. But Daisy was at her own home then, in Milwaukee, with her husband and children, and Margaret had wanted to turn her full attention toward Dale. She had wanted to get to know Dale, this second daughter of hers. She knew she had always favored Daisy, as Harry had favored Dale; she could call up times in her memory when she had probably unjustly sided with Daisy. There had been a time, a time like many, but this particularly was clear in Margaret's thoughts, when Margaret had at least in her own feelings and actions been unfair to Dale. It was a summer afternoon when she was bringing the girls home from swimming, and Daisy, in a passion about something or other, had slammed the car door shut on Dale's foot and severed part of her little toe. Dale had screamed with pain; she had been in pain and frightened, but Margaret's sympathy had gone out first to Daisy, who had stood stricken and sickly pale by the car, too horrified even to cry at what she had just done. "It's okay, it's okay, Daisy, you didn't mean to, we can fix it, Dale will be okay," Margaret had said to her oldest daughter, and had rushed from the car to wrap Daisy in a consoling hug first, before taking care of Dale. That whole day she had been more worried about Daisy than Dale, because Dale had gone to her father and had the toe sewed back on and treated and bandaged and then had lounged about on the porch or in front of the television while Daisy brought her sister penitential gifts of fruit or candy or comic books. Harry and all the neighbors and all the girls' friends had made such a fuss over Dale; Harry had soundly scolded Daisy for her carelessness; and for days Daisy had been pale with contrition. But that had not been fair, Margaret had felt: Daisy hadn't *meant* to hurt Dale, it had been simply a stupid accident, simply a matter of Dale sticking her foot out at the wrong moment. Her heart had gone out to Daisy. Well, and perhaps not enough to Dale. Perhaps even then Margaret had been growing tired of nurturing and tending and sympathizing with victims. And perhaps her heart had never gone out enough to Dale: but then Dale had always had Harry.

Last year—it had been just last year, in May when Dale had returned from France—Margaret had been really intrigued by her second daughter and had wanted to reach out to her, to get to know her. She had wanted both to call

Dale back into her own world, the world of churches and kitchens and secure family life where Margaret felt she still had a place, and to have Dale pull her out into the rest of the world; because at that time Margaret knew she wanted to change, knew she wanted to leave, but didn't know how. She had already lost a lot of weight, and was proud of the fact, but she had not yet grown her hair out and dyed it, she had not yet changed her style of dress.

"You look good, Mom," Dale had said casually, sitting on a kitchen chair in her own Levi's and blue work shirt.

"Do you think so?" Margaret asked, pleased. "I've lost a lot of weight. And I swim a lot. I feel much better."

"You'll probably live longer," Dale said, and sipped her coffee. That was all the weight loss had meant to Dale, that her dowdy mother would not have as much strain on her heart. Oh, it's not *fair*, Margaret had wanted to cry out: look at you! For Dale had not put on any lipstick or eye liner, but still her face shone with the health and beauty of youth. It was not even blotched yet with the fatigue and blots of motherhood as Daisy's had become; Dale was as perfect as a ripe peach. And she was wearing, she wore constantly, lovely hoop earrings and lots of silver or gold rings and bracelets which she had bought on the sidewalks of Paris or been given by her lovers. Margaret wanted to know about that, she wanted to sit down with Dale and hear all about those sidewalks, those lovers; she had seen enough of the museums and castles, which were after all only another sort of confining home. She had wanted Dale to give her a picture of the world as only a free, beautiful, intelligent, well-educated young woman could have it. She had wanted Dale to lure her away from her safe clean kitchen with tales of a complicated, messy, exciting other world.

But Dale had not been interested in this; she had not sensed Margaret's needs. She kept asking questions about

Margaret's friends, Margaret's charities, in a manner that was heartbreaking to Margaret because Dale was so obviously covering her condescension and lack of interest. Margaret saw clearly how little Dale thought of her and her life, how bored she was with it all, how she was working at being attentive and nice. Margaret knew she was not fascinating to Dale; it was Harry who fascinated Dale. Margaret was only comfortable, well used, well worn, like an old coat, an old dog, an old blanket. And Dale had grown past the need for old comforts. She had gone far past Margaret, and had no thought of trying to bring Margaret with her. She did not even very much want to tell Margaret about her new world.

Dale had talked about the new job she would have in Maine, about her interviews with the school board and principal, about Carol, the woman who would share an apartment with her. She did talk a bit about Rocheport, the ocean, and so on, but she didn't say—as Margaret had overheard her saying to her father—"Oh, you should *see* it; you should come back for a visit before winter comes, it's so beautiful there." Margaret had been reduced to discussing pots and pans and dishes and towels: was there anything from home Dale needed? So they had gone through the house, scavenging up the necessary homely, homey items Dale might need to set up housekeeping, to make the rudimentary backdrop for her new life.

"Don't you want to take your stuffed animals?" Margaret had asked, as she stood with her daughter in Dale's girlish pink bedroom. "Or any of these pictures?"

Dale had shrugged her shoulders at all of it. "Oh, I don't think so, Mom," she said. "I don't really—God, I can't even remember half the stuff. And I've got so much junk with me that I picked up in Europe. I don't want to clutter up the apartment too much. No, no, I don't see anything here that I want. Why don't you give it all to Goodwill or one of the church bazaars?"

"Oh, no," Margaret had said. "You don't want me to give these things away, really, do you? Why don't I just keep them here, just keep the room as it is, so you'll feel at home when you come back to visit." (Later, in Vancouver, after she had herself so easily left that home and most of the possessions gathered from her twenty-five years in it, Margaret was amazed to think of how upsetting this conversation was.)

Dale had smiled at her mother with what seemed to be a fond disdain. "You're sweet, Mom," she said. "You're really the sweetest thing. But all these butterflies and flowers and kittens and posters—even the ones of Santana and Mick Jagger—well, they just make me want to laugh. Listen, I have some nude prints I'm going to hang that would make these things blush. Let's give this stuff to Danny and Jenny. At least let's give them the stuffed animals; the kids would love the stuffed animals." And she had laughed, shaking her head at her adolescent follies, and dismissed her room, the room which held her past life in Margaret's house, with an indifferent ease that made Margaret want to cry. But that huge stuffed giraffe, Margaret wanted to call out, I bought you that when you were sick in bed with a flu that almost killed you your sophomore year in high school! And she could see Dale clearly as she had been then, curled under a blanket, delirious with fever, while Margaret sat at her side touching her forehead with a cool wet blue washcloth.

"I think I'll walk down to Dad's office and say hello to old Trudy," Dale had said. But Margaret knew that Dale was not that interested in chatting with Harry's secretary. Dale just wanted to go be with her father. And Margaret had had to let her go.

So now why on earth was Dale spending the time and

money to fly out to visit her? Margaret wondered. She looked at her watch, saw that she had to leave now to meet the plane, and rose from her bed. She smoothed out her dress, looked at herself in the mirror, and tentatively said, "*Damn.*" She picked up her car keys with shaking hands. She did not want to see Dale; she did not want to subject her old body to Dale's young sharp scrutiny. She thought of changing her clothes—perhaps Dale would find Margaret too colorful and ridiculous; Margaret could almost hear Dale's clever amused voice: "Oh, Mother, look at you! What a gas!"

"Oh, well," Margaret said, and went to the phone.

Dale's plane was early, and Dale walked in the large waiting room at the airport, trying to collect her thoughts. She had so much to say, and it was so important; she felt as though she were rehearsing for a play or a performance or even a trial; she had a cause to plead. She decided that she would get the business about Daddy and his new wife over with first; she and Daisy had discussed this for hours on the phone. Dale had thought that their mother would take Daddy's new marriage with delight and gratitude, but Daisy had been worried.

"Mother's been able to be an independent woman just because Daddy was still in love with her," Daisy had said. "But now that he's marrying Trudy, it will be a real severing of their ties, she will realize that she's really alone. It's so *hard* to be alone," Daisy had said. "It's the hardest thing in the world. I really think someone should be with Mother when she hears the news. I think you should fly out to be with her. I'd do it, but I've got to get these attic rooms ready to rent before the baby comes."

"All right," Dale had said finally, "I'll go. I suppose I should *see* Mother anyway; check her out and see if she's stable." For she and Daisy believed that Margaret might somehow be headed for a mental institution. Dale was afraid that she would find her mother wild-haired and over-rouged, trying suddenly to look young and sexy. Her letters were so bright and chipper, all about plays and lectures and ballets. Dale was afraid that her mother had changed so much so suddenly that she might really be about to flip over the edge. After all, what did her mother know about lectures and plays and ballet? And she couldn't let Daisy handle it, she couldn't let Daisy even continue to worry, because Daisy had enough going on in her own life now.

Poor Daisy: she wasn't going to be able to get nearly so much money from Paul as she wanted, and their enormous house was not selling, no one was even looking at it, and while Daisy was doing her best to work hard and optimistically, she was frantically worried about money. Dale had encouraged her to fix up the attic to rent out, and in a fit of inspiration suggested that Daisy take all the furniture from their old bedrooms in Liberty to help set up the rooms. When their father had called with the amazing news that he was going to marry Trudy, his former nurse-secretary, Dale had tried to talk him into giving Daisy the money so she could keep her house, but Harry, who also seemed to have undergone some sort of psychological transformation, had said, no, he needed all his money for his new life. After all, he pointed out, he had already given Daisy twenty thousand dollars. Margaret had most of the money, he had said, and he wanted to spend what he had left on his new life: he and Trudy were going to shut the practice down to part time and let most of their patients go into Iowa City. He and Trudy wanted to buy a little vacation house in Arizona where they could spend most of the winters. *Arizona?* Dale had thought, Jesus Christ. Mother in Vancouver, Daddy in *Arizona!* But Dale had called Daisy, and Daisy had called their father, and Dale had called their father, too, and it was finally decided that as soon as there was a break in the weather Harry and Trudy would pay a moving company to bring a vanload of furniture up to Daisy.

"Don't forget the cedar chest full of blankets," Dale had said. "Don't forget the boxes of old dishes down in the basement. And send *everything* from Daisy's room and mine, and send *everything* from the basement rec room, the chairs, that old sofa, the end tables, the lamps, everything. Daddy, it's the least you can do for Daisy. She doesn't have the money to buy new stuff for the rooms. Do you want me to fly out to help with the packing?"

But Harry had said with great alacrity that no, no, Dale was not to fly out, he would send everything.

"Trudy won't want all of Mom's old stuff hanging around to remind her of her place in that house," Dale had insisted, pulling every punch she could. She had grown to feel so protective of her older sister, and she had determined that if Daisy wanted so badly to keep her house, then she *should* keep it. It didn't seem too much to want, and it wasn't as if Daisy weren't working for it herself, for she was. She had cleaned the attic of what junk was in it, and scrubbed and refinished and waxed the floors all by herself. She had spent days driving to different plumbing firms, talking with different contractors, in order to get the cheapest bid on having a small kitchen put in. Dale called Daisy at least twice a week to hear how things were progressing, and sometimes she was caught up in Daisy's enthusiasm and longed to be there herself, nailing large bright brass hooks in the wall.

"I can rent each of the four bedrooms at one hundred and twenty-five dollars a month, at least, and that makes five hundred dollars," Daisy had explained. "Daddy said he would send up the refrigerator we used to have in the basement rec room, so all I need to buy is a little stove. The yellow armchair from your old bedroom will go in the far bedroom under the slanted roof. Did I tell you Daddy said he'd send up the fold-out bed from the back porch? That's pretty ratty, so I'll keep my eye out for a twin bed on sale, but I'll put the wicker chair from my old bedroom in the room that has that fold-out bed, and my old white chest and bookcase."

Daisy would go on and on about the attic apartment, and although Dale's phone bill for the month of January was colossal, Dale didn't care. She was so proud of Daisy for her efforts, and she could see how important all this was to her: it was as if Daisy had watched the complicated edifice of her marriage crumble about her, then had set out to rebuild and reinforce at least the house she lived in, in order to have some shelter and structure in her life. Dale wanted to help. She wanted to help because she loved her sister, and because she was now on the side of optimism and enterprise: she wanted things to turn out well for others so that she could believe they could turn out well for her.

But just this past week, Daisy had called in tears to say that they had to forget the whole thing. Corinne Wentworth had showed up with some serious buyers, a manager for one of the largest firms in Milwaukee, and his wife. The realtor was showing the couple other houses, but was sure that they liked Daisy's house best. "It's no good, it's no use, I'll have to sell the house," Daisy had said. "There's nothing else I can do. Paul wants his money, and I don't have it, and I haven't heard from Mother and doubt that I ever will."

Dale did not think she could bear to have Daisy lose her house. Her father had told her that her mother had all the money; the only solution was for Margaret to give Daisy the money, and that was all there was to it. And if she didn't, or wouldn't, or couldn't, well then her mother would have to help *somehow*. At least, Dale thought, Margaret could fly out to Milwaukee to help Daisy with her

new baby and her house-hunting. After all, Daisy really
needed help. Dale couldn't go; she had to teach. Mother
couldn't expect to just lie about in loony luxury while her
daughter faced the crisis of her life.

Hank had driven Dale to the airport in Boston on Friday; he had arranged to take the day off and planned to
spend the weekend with his parents and then to pick Dale
up on Sunday night to drive her back to Maine.

"God, I'm going to miss you so much," he had said to
her as they stood holding each other loosely while waiting
for Dale's plane to be announced.

"I know," Dale said. "I'll miss you. But I really have to
do this. I really want to do this." Leaning up against his
long strong body, looking at his beautiful green eyes, she
had almost lost her impetus, she had almost said: oh, let's
forget this, let's just spend the weekend in some motel. For
now that she had worked a small way past the need of her
love for him, she was caught up in the beauty of it. How she
enjoyed him, how she enjoyed just the sight of him, and the
way the sound of his voice moved her. There were times
when they would both be tired and slightly bored with
their days, cranky because of the cold gray weather, and still
she would want to hear him speak, just to speak, so that
she could feel the tenor of his voice move through her,
causing her great physical pleasure, no matter what he was
saying. One night when they had not seen each other all
day and had exhausted all topics after an hour's phone conversation, Dale had asked Hank to simply read to her from
the day's newspaper; and, laughing, he had done it. How
his voice pleased her. What beauty there was in it, and
what pleasure she took from that beauty. And how intelligent he was, how sensible, how helpful he was to her. How
much it seemed they had in common! His suggestions for
running the film series were almost always so perfect that
they seemed what she would have thought of in the next

moment, or if she had only had the sense. When she had told him of her revelation about teaching, about her sudden realization of love for her work, he had understood, and had agreed with her, had admitted that he felt very much the same sort of thing. Even her feelings about her family, which she was only now coming to examine, were strengthened by the long talks she shared with him, when he discussed his feelings toward his own family. Hank had adored his parents as a child, but came to disapprove of them, to want to really separate himself from them as a young man, when he realized that he could not stay married to the woman they had chosen or pursue the sort of life they thought he ought to lead. So he had for a time even hated his family; but now he was trying—even though it was often awkward, often uncomfortable—to get to know them again, to say to them: this is who I am, and I am still your son, and let's be friendly toward one another. Just so Dale was realizing that for a while now she had to be the real adult, the responsible one, while her father went through this hasty marriage and Daisy went through her divorce and her mother went through—what?—Lord knew what, Dale thought. A mental breakdown? But it was okay that it was all happening now, Dale thought, for she was beginning to feel like a grown-up, she was beginning to put on the responsibilities of a grown-up as one puts on appropriate clothes for a job interview: she was taking care of her courses, and running the high school film series, and still finding the time and energy within herself to attend to these unsettled people who were related to her by blood. It even seemed logical, *suitable*, that all this should be happening to her parents and sister at this fairly stable and truly happy time in her own life. And the best of it this weekend was that she felt that she could leave Hank and come back to him, and he would not die, she would not die, he would be waiting for her in Boston, and he would still love her, he would not stop loving her while she was gone. All the magic was still there, but the good sturdy settledness of it was beginning to be there, too, buoying her up.

Still, as Dale sat on the plane flying toward Vancouver, she found herself thinking less and less of Hank and more and more about her mother. Dale felt a sort of doting sympathy for her father, who had been in such misery but now was in a state of childish, self-centered happiness; she felt great compassion and protectiveness for Daisy, who was in such a terribly difficult situation in life right now; and she felt really nothing but irritation and anger toward her mother, who had been the cause of her father's grief and was refusing to be the source of any strength or consolation or assistance toward Daisy. Dale went over and over it all on the plane, and when she hit the Vancouver airport she felt as adamant and forceful as shot from a cannon. And as she waited and waited for her tardy mother, she grew more and more energetic with anger. She was almost boiling over with words, words she wanted to shout at Margaret. If her mother had gone nuts, Dale would just have to shock her back to her senses. Silly old Mother, she thought, and wished she didn't have to spend any more time with her than would be necessary to get her to do what was needed. Their mother had always championed Daisy; it was inconsiderate, it was simply *immoral* for her to be unsupportive at this point in Daisy's life. Oh, Dale had her words ready like bullets, like arrows, like cannon shot. She paced about the airport, her canvas knapsack over her shoulder, grinding her teeth, nearly muttering to herself, wishing her mother would hurry up and arrive.

And twelve hours later, Dale knelt in front of the fire in her mother's house, almost drunk with happiness. She was sitting on the beautifully woven rug in front of the

fireplace in her warm winter robe, kneeling behind her
mother, brushing her mother's hair while it dried. Her
mother had such beautiful hair. It was thick and lustrous
and as it dried in the firelight it began to glimmer with
rich reddish-brown tones as warm and alive as the fire itself. Dale could not remember ever having touched her
mother's hair before; she could not remember ever even
wanting to. But then of course she had never known her
mother with hair like this; she had never known her
mother as *beautiful*; she had never wanted to touch and
stroke and caress her mother, as one wants to touch any
beautiful creature, before now. She *loved* her mother. She
loved bringing the brush down through her mother's
slightly damp hair, and watching it rise up bristling with its
electricity, and then smoothing it with her other hand, and
then bringing the brush down again. Margaret sat with her
back toward Dale, her arms wrapped around her knees, her
head tilted back.

At the last moment at noon that day, Margaret had lost
courage, had called Anthony and asked him to come with
her to meet Dale and to take her to lunch. So Dale had
had to swallow all her fury and force in order to be civil to
the two people who met her at the airport, the two handsome strangers who collected her and took her to lunch. It
had been a queer afternoon. Dale had been amazed at the
bright, sunlit city with its dramatic backdrop of snow-
covered mountains; and just as amazed at the enchantment
which grew on her as she went through the day with her
two companions. She had not been able to take her eyes off
her mother. She had not been able to resist feeling smugly
proud to walk into the French restaurant with two such obviously intelligent and elegant people, and she had kept
saying to herself as she listened to her mother speak, as
she watched her mother draw a cigarette from a charming
silver-and-blue case: This is my mother! Why, this is my

mother! And listening had been as entrancing as watching Margaret and Anthony; Margaret was actually clever, and witty, and well read, and perceptive. Dale had exclaimed several times: "Why, Mother, I didn't know you knew *that!*" And then her mother had looked at her so fondly, a look passing over her face that brought back to Dale memories of the same look which Margaret had given to Dale almost as a gift in her childhood when she had done or said something especially amusing. Oh, her *lovely* mother, how she was the same, and how she had changed!

The three of them had all gotten on so well, and the day had been so pleasant, just chilly enough to make walking a brisk pleasure, that they had walked all about the city, and then through various parts of Stanley Park, looking at the ocean and its freighters or the Indian totem poles, and talking, and talking. Anthony knew so much about British Columbia; he was an historian, but then he wasn't at all stuffy, and he spoke in such an entertaining way. They had been too happy a group to want to separate, and so had gone back to Margaret's house for a late casual dinner of pâté and cheese and breads and cold crab meat and fruit— and more wine, of course, much more wine. Anthony had finally left about ten-thirty, and as the two women walked him out to the car they had been taken with the way the full moon was shining in the sky, and as he drove away they decided to take a walk along the beach to watch the moon shining on the water. They had walked and walked together, laughing and talking. Dale had told her mother about her father's marriage plans and had been able to see clearly by the moonlight how her mother's face had brightened with delight at the news.

"Really?" Margaret had asked, turning toward Dale and clapping her hands together like a child. "Oh, *really?*" She seemed almost unable to believe such good fortune. "Oh, Dale, how wonderful!" Impulsively Margaret had hugged

Dale to her, as if Dale had been somehow responsible for this event. "Isn't it just perfect! Trudy is just what he needs, oh, they'll get on so well together. Oh, think of it, just think of it, how *nice*."

So they had walked on down the beach, farther and farther, stepping over bits of driftwood and large stones, talking about Dale's father and his prospective new wife. Then Dale was able to talk to Margaret about Daisy in a different spirit from the one she had intended, from the one she had arrived with, and Margaret had been silent, listening, and finally had said, "I see what you're saying. I understand what you want of me. Let me think about it. Give me a while to think this through. I *will* do something. Just give me time to think a bit." And Dale had found it easy to accept this, to let the matter rest, to trust her mother.

Then a sudden wind had come up and blown clouds over the moon and in a matter of seconds a cold full rain had begun to come down on them. They were drenched immediately, but had turned and run back toward Margaret's house anyway, as if by running they could keep themselves from getting any the more wet. In minutes they were totally soaked, with their hair and clothes sticking against them, and in running Dale had hit her foot against a log, but still it had turned out to be gay and crazy, running along beside the ocean in the rain, with Margaret going ahead of Dale and calling back to her over her shoulder, and both of them suddenly laughing with the gaiety of it all. Lights from the houses they passed and from across the harbor streaked and glittered as they ran, and Margaret and Dale were strangely caught up in a festive, even celebratory mood, so that by the time they arrived at Margaret's house they did not go right in but stood looking up at the pouring sky and out at the waltzing ocean, with their arms held out to receive the rain and their heads thrown back. It was as if they had accomplished something, simply by running back to Margaret's house together in the rain; it was as if something astonishing had been achieved. Of course they were a bit drunk from all the day's wine, but it was more than that. Though they could not have said this to themselves in just so many words, it was as if the cold bright rain coming so unexpectedly made them aware of how full of good surprises the world was, of how one can sometimes turn the most casual corner in one's life and come upon a miracle.

Finally their teeth had begun to chatter and they had gone into the house. They didn't want to ruin the rugs, so they had stripped off most of their clothes just inside the kitchen door and let them fall down in puddly globs of fabric.

"God, you look good, Mother!" Dale had exclaimed, seeing her mother there before her in underpants and bra. "You look marvelous!"

"Thank you," Margaret had said, almost shyly. "So do you. Let's go get something warm on before we catch pneumonia, and I'll throw more wood on the fire."

Margaret had put on her robe and stoked the fire, and Dale had put on her robe and made a pot of herb tea, and then they had sat in front of the fire quietly, getting warmed.

"I can't get over your hair, Mother," Dale said. "It's so wonderful now. I wish you had worn it that way all your life. May I brush it?"

"Oh, yes, please," Margaret said. She got up and found her brush and sat on the rug with her back to Dale. "Daisy used to brush my hair when she was very little, when you were a baby," Margaret said. "You never did that, you never were much interested in that sort of thing. But Daisy used to love to brush my hair, as if I were one of her dolls. She would get out all her little barrettes and ribbons and stick them in my hair. Oh, I can remember one day when Daisy was five and you were just an infant, and I was so tired, so tired. I finally got you down for a nap, but Daisy was too old to nap, and it was winter and there was no school for some reason, and I just didn't have the energy to entertain Daisy. So I lay on the sofa in the living room and asked her to brush my hair. Well, she did, and put in every barrette and ribbon she owned, and it felt so good to just lie there having her tend to me with her sweet tiny hands, and I was so *tired*. Well, when she got bored with doing my hair, I told her that she could get my lipstick and put it on me and fix my face up. I was desperate for some rest, Dale, I just needed to lie there and not move. So Daisy got my lipstick and put it on my lips, and then my cheeks, and then began to draw all over my face with it. I was simply too tired to object and I couldn't see any harm in it anyway. Actually, it felt quite good, like having a facial massage, I can remember even now. The delicate pressure of that soft creamy lipstick being spread everywhere across my face. And of course you can guess what happened: one of the neighbors came to the door to bring me a cake and a present for you, since you were newborn, and when I heard the doorbell ring I thought, Lord, no, what shall I do! But before I could stop her, Daisy had gone out and opened the door and let her in. Old Mrs. Schultz; did I ever give her a shock. I managed to sit up by the time she got into the living room, but there was nothing I could do about my red face and wild hair. I tried to explain it to her, and she was fairly understanding, she had children herself, but all the same, I was chagrined." Margaret and Dale laughed and laughed.

"I had something like that happen to me," Dale said. "I mean not that, but the same sort of thing. It was—well, I suppose I can tell you, even if you are my mother. It was this November. I had been in an enormous variety store up

in Portland, getting some stationery and deodorant and all
that sort of thing, and I came across—oh, yes, it was in the
toy department, I was looking at the toys, trying to decide
what to send Danny and Jenny for Christmas. Well, I
came across this wonderful booklet full of tiny fluorescent
stars. It was a small booklet full of yellowish paper, and a
thin liner could be peeled off the back, exposing a sticky
side, so that all these little things could stick. There were
small stars and moons and planets and comets that were
outlined by perforations so that children could punch
them out easily. I actually sent some to Danny. They're
wonderful. You put them about the room, on the ceiling
and the walls, and inside the closets, and while the light is
on, the paper absorbs the light, and then when you turn off
the light and it's all dark, these moons and stars glow.
They give off a marvelous eerie greenish glow. Well, here's
what I did—you mustn't be shocked now, Mother, you're
old enough to know—I bought several booklets for myself.
And that night when I went to Hank's I made him wait in
the darkened bedroom by himself; I told him I had a
surprise. I undressed in the bathroom, with all the lights
on, and put those stars and moons and planets and comets
all over my body. Stars on my breasts, a comet coming out
of my belly button, a sun on each eyelid. Well, it was
amazing! It was really fabulous. I came out into the dark of
Hank's bedroom and it was uncanny and absolutely wild. I
mean I made him turn off all the lights, and so it was too
dark to see any of my body, and all there was, all he could
see, was all these tiny stars and planets dancing around toward him. I saw them in the mirror and couldn't get over
it, it was so wild! Well, I couldn't help it, I danced and
waved my arms about, it was a bit like being a firework, a
sparkler or something, and—and, anyway, the next day I
had to teach. I was showing a film in my biology class, and
I set up the projector and pulled the shades and turned off

the lights and walked back through the classroom to sit at the back. And the students began to whisper and titter— and they're good students, usually well-mannered. So I finally said, 'Okay, you guys, what's going on?' Well, I thought I had taken off all those stars, and I had even showered that morning, but the glue really sticks, and somehow I had missed a few. I had a star on the back of one arm and a comet on the back of the other and a planet at the side of my neck, and there I was walking along with these things glowing in my biology class. Well, I was cool. I just said, 'Oh, thanks for telling me. Now be quiet and watch this film. You'll be tested on it.' But of course for a few moments I wanted to die."

"Didn't they ask you why you were wearing those things?" Margaret asked, laughing.

"No," Dale said. "They could tell by my tone of voice I wouldn't have told them. There, Mother, your hair's all dry. And it's gorgeous. It's incredible."

"Well, it's dyed," Margaret said. "But it used to be this color. I suppose I'll keep dyeing it until—when, I don't know, whenever it seems too obviously phony. Someday I'll have to have the grace to live with white hair."

"Mother," Dale said, "you've got the grace to live with orange hair, or green or purple! I can't believe how you've changed." And she put her arm around her mother's shoulders and they sat there in front of the fire awhile, side by side.

"Yes," Margaret said after a bit, her voice becoming slow as if she were sleepy, "but you've changed, too, you know. You've changed a lot."

"Well, I'm older," Dale said. "And I've discovered a lot about myself. I really love my work. And then, of course, there's Hank. I love him. He loves me. It's—it's really incredible how love can change your life."

"Oh, yes," Margaret said, and her voice grew slower, as

if she were withdrawing into sleep, into a solitary region where Dale could not follow. "Oh, yes, of course, *Love*. Oh, well." She leaned over and gave Dale an affectionate peck on her cheek. "You can tell me about Hank tomorrow," she said. "I really do want to hear all about him. But I've got to get into bed now, I'm really fading away." And she rose with sleepy grace and went into her bedroom, shutting the door behind her,

Dale sat in front of the fire for a while, trying to think about the day and all that had so subtly happened. It had not been quite spoiled by the tone of Margaret's voice when she said, "Oh, yes, of course, *Love*. Oh, well." Yet that had added a touch of sharpness, or perhaps only reality, to an otherwise joyfully blurred twelve hours. But after all, Dale thought, Mother is Mother, and I am myself. She has to live her life, and I get to live my own. And with that seemingly profound thought, Dale stretched out on the rug in front of the fire and fell asleep, with her head flat on the rug next to the pretty brass tray that held the teapot and cups. When she awoke in the morning Pandora the cat was asleep next to her left shoulder, and the new cat, the beautiful large gray one, was curled up with all the heavy warmth of his body right on the small of Dale's back. Dale lay awake for a long time, watching the sun on the water, not wanting to move to disturb the sleep of the cat or the pleasure of her own body in feeling his warm vital weight.

EIGHT

❊❈❊❈❊❈❊❈❊❈❊❈❊❈❊❈❊❈❊❈❊❈❊❈❊

The last Friday in March, it snowed heavily in Rocheport. Dale and Hank and Carol sat in Hank's living room by the warmth of the wood stove, trying to play Scrabble. They were waiting for Carol's fiancé, Bob, who was driving up from Massachusetts to spend the weekend with Carol. Dale and Carol had made a delicious bouillabaisse, which now simmered on the stove, and the salad was waiting in the refrigerator for the dressing. There was even a large loaf of oatmeal bread which Carol had made specially that day, but now she had taken it out of the oven so it would not get too browned. Bob was almost two hours late, and Dale and Hank and Carol were all pretending not to worry. But the snow continued to fall heavily, and from time to time the trees just outside the windows would creak under the weight of the damp snow, and it was impossible not to think of how bad the roads were. Dale was stumped; it was her turn to make a word. She had the letters *deat* on her small wooden holder, and there was a free *h* waiting on the board. She could have made the word *death* and gotten a triple word score, but felt too superstitious to make the word while Bob was so noticeably absent. They had turned the stereo off and the radio on in order to keep up with each new weather and news report, and whenever the announcer's voice broke the pattern of music, the three sitting around the Scrabble board would freeze in order to concentrate on listening. Carol kept getting up to stir the stew, or get more wine, or use the bathroom, and Dale and Hank noticed how she looked out the windows each time she rose, as if by the intensity of her vision she could draw Bob's car safely into the driveway.

"He's got a front-wheel-drive car," Hank said. "He'll be fine. This snow is bound to slow him down."

But they were all afraid that the snow might do more—a patch of ice, a skid, an accident . . . They were all very polite and quiet, like good children trying to charm the universe into kindness.

"He'll call if he gets in trouble," Dale said. It was the third or fourth time she had said it.

"I know," Carol said. "He's a careful driver. He's driven in this kind of weather all his life." But still her face was tense. And no other topic of conversation could hold her interest.

Dale settled on the word *tie*, which gave her only three points, and waited for Carol to make her word. She thought: at least we're here with her, in case anything bad does happen.

"Oh, I can't think of a single word to make," Carol said, exasperated. "I'm usually so good at this game."

"Let me see your letters," Hank said. "Maybe I can help."

Carol turned her letters toward Hank. "Do you know what I'd really like to do?" she said. "I'd like to scrub the toilet. Or the kitchen floor."

"Whatever for?" Hank asked. "Don't you think my house is sanitary?"

"Oh, it's not that at all," Carol said. She rose and went to look out a window. "It's just that at times like this I like to be doing something that I hate. In order to earn a reward from Fate. You know." She gestured vaguely and gave Dale a look that said quite clearly: don't make me be too precise on this point. Don't make me say that if I scrub a toilet, which I hate doing, I will in that way save Bob from being killed on an icy road. "It's an old habit," she went on. "From school. If you study hard, you are rewarded with good grades. Also, I think the time will pass more quickly if I'm active."

Dale rose. "The kitchen floor can always use a scrubbing," she said. "Come on, I'll show you where the soap is." But in the kitchen she encountered her own problem: kneeling down below the sink, where *she* would have kept the floor detergent, she found only a trash sack. This was not her house; it was Hank's; and she felt strangely slighted. She had to call Hank in from the living room to show her where he kept his mop and cleansers.

The three of them were all gathered about the broom closet in an inordinately serious group when they heard the car come into the driveway. Carol was out the door in an instant, not even stopping to put on her coat. After a few moments she came back in, her arm around Bob, her hair sparkling with snowflakes, her face glowing. They all made a great fuss over Bob, who was exhausted from the drive and delighted to be safe inside a warm house. They talked a bit, then Hank took Bob off to fix him a drink, and Carol and Dale went into the living room to put away the Scrabble game and clear up the wineglasses.

"Carol," Dale said, as the two women knelt on the floor, putting little wooden squares of letters into the box, "your hands are shaking."

"I'm so glad he's alive," Carol said. "I was so worried. You know how I've picked on you about how strongly you feel about Hank, and yet I suppose I'm not so different after all. It's a surprise—how love can get to you sometimes."

Dale leaned across the Scrabble board and gave Carol a hug.

"Can we eat right away?" Hank called from the kitchen.

"Of course," Carol called back, and rose, suddenly her usual efficient self.

Dale stayed on the floor for a moment, holding the folded Scrabble board to her chest as if it were a tangible piece of good luck. What a good night it would be now, she thought, all four of them together, safe in the midst of a snowstorm, safe in the midst of love.

The last Friday in March, Margaret sat in the concert hall with her hands resting loosely in her lap. The orchestra was performing Beethoven's *Pastoral*, and Margaret was thinking how literature and music called forth different reactions in her. When she read fiction, she lost herself in the lives of other people; but when she listened to music, it seemed that she lost herself in her own life. Her thoughts drifted back and forth through the past events and years of her life without reason, and a surge of music would as often remind her of a fantasy she had once had as of an event that actually happened. Perhaps she was experiencing early senility. A passage of music brought to mind a dress she had wanted when she was twenty, but had never actually even seen: it was a pink dress with ruffles and black velvet bows on the cuffs, neck, and hem. The sort of dress she had never worn and would never wear. But she had wanted that dress when she was twenty, and had even thought of designing it and making it herself. She never had; and she could not imagine why certain musical notes would conjure it up in her thoughts now. Yes, the music acted on her like some sort of drug: she floated free, like

Alice falling down the rabbit hole, and encountered all sorts of bizarre objects from her real and imagined life.

Now she thought of Daisy; it was the alarm of timpani and brass, no doubt, that brought Daisy to mind. Daisy's baby was due any day now, and in spite of herself, Margaret continually thought about Daisy with emotions as turbulent and complex as the music now being performed. The birth of a baby was always a dramatic event, and there were always so many possible problems. In spite of modern medicine, women did still die in childbirth. Or the baby could die. Or something could be wrong with the baby. Or everything could be fine. Still the labor and birth were events of certain magnitude. Yet Margaret was fixed in her mind that she would not go back to help Daisy. She did not want to be in charge of a large household and take care of her grandchildren, not now, not anymore. The one thing she would have done for Daisy was impossible: she would have actually *had* the baby for Daisy. She would have loved the experience of giving birth, of holding a vulnerable and always somehow magical newborn in her arms; she would have loved lying in the hospital with her needs tended to as she tended to those of the baby. But that was not possible, and as much as Margaret worried about Daisy, she realized that she also slightly envied her this ultimate female experience.

She had sent Daisy a check, with a note that more would follow as soon as possible, and now that that decision had been made, Margaret was glad. She felt she had done the right thing. Surely now she could be free to consider her own needs, her own life. Perhaps, she thought, after she received the crucial phone call from Daisy and knew that all was well with her and the baby, perhaps then she would be able to relax and concentrate on herself. She hoped so. Although it was beginning to seem that the tension between her desire for isolation and the necessity of somehow nurturing the world around her would always be present. Even now, as she sat in the concert hall listening to the symphony, she was aware of Anthony's hand on her arm. As the music built to its climax, Anthony's hand tightened. He might have been totally unaware of his pressure, but Margaret felt put upon, she felt that Anthony was asking her to be aware of his intense reaction to the music. And when it ended, she would be called upon to discuss it with Anthony and his friends, and to hear in detail just what sensations and memories the music called up in them. She did not especially want to know any of this. She did not want to have to comment on the orchestra's brilliance or the conductor's grace. She did not want to have to turn her experience of this music into a structure of words that would be criticized and rearranged by others. She wanted merely to sit listening to the music, appreciating it for itself. For a moment she had a vision of herself as some sort of trapped creature who must continually produce from the world about it food for others' consumption. Yet she knew that was a slightly mad thought: oh, she knew it was not as bad as all that. She did still enjoy the company of others. She was looking forward to the dinner they would have afterward, and to the conversation. A discussion of the concert would be good for her, Margaret decided; it would keep her mind off Daisy, off her own petty problems. So she sat with her hands in her lap, intently listening, and it seemed her emotions rose and fell with the rhythm of the music.

The last Friday in March, Daisy had a date. The baby was five days overdue and Daisy lurched around through life like a whale out of water. She felt enormous, she *was* enormous, and inside her vast stomach things sloshed and tugged and pulled when she walked. All she wanted to do was to sit with her feet up; her feet ached and ached. She really could not breathe easily, especially after eating, but she was so bored and frustrated that she ate almost constantly anyway. She couldn't sleep at night because she was so uncomfortable, and because she kept thinking she was feeling the beginnings of labor, and so she went through the days feeling cranky and tired and falling asleep at odd moments whenever she could sit down. During the days she would fall instantly into a sleep as deep as a black hole, and she would awake with a start, not knowing where or who she was. She had taken to keeping the phone receiver off the hook during much of the day because so many people kept calling her to ask, "Are you *still* home? What's going on?" Jane and Karen and her other friends called her constantly to see if anything was happening with the baby yet. So Daisy was totally shocked to answer the phone one day and hear a man speaking to her.

The man was Jerry Reynolds, an accountant who worked in the same Milwaukee firm as Paul. She had met him many times at company parties, and she supposed that if she had ever thought of him at all she had simply thought, when talking to him, that he was just a pleasant man who was polite enough never to appear bored when talking with her. Well, he was separated from his wife now, and had heard that Daisy and Paul were getting divorced, and had called to ask her for a dinner date.

"But I'm pregnant," she had replied, amazed and rather alarmed.

"Well, that's all right," Jerry had said.

"But I mean I'm really *pregnant*," Daisy said. "I'm nine months along. The baby should come any day now." What she meant to imply was that not only would she be incapable of sleeping with him, but that she would look unattractive and bulgy, that he wouldn't even want to be seen with her in public.

"You can still eat and talk, can't you?" Jerry had said.

And then, disarmingly, "I really would like it so much if I could take you out to dinner. I'm feeling rather awkward since this divorce thing, and I've always felt comfortable around you, and to tell the truth it would be a relief to me just to be able to go out with a woman who would obviously be just a companion and friend."

Daisy was touched by his honesty. "Oh, you mean I could be a sort of trial date for you."

Jerry laughed. "Well, let's hope it won't be too much of a trial," he said. "Really, Daisy, it is partly that—I've forgotten everything about 'dating'—I hate that word—and it's been years since I've so much as sat alone with a woman other than my wife for any period of time. It's—I'm—well, what it comes down to is a sort of situation like getting thrown from a horse. I mean it's necessary to get right back on. I mean I don't want to become afraid of women simply because I've forgotten how to deal with them. But I do like *you*, I always have liked you, and I think we could have a good time together."

Daisy had been moved by his candor. And, hungry all the time as she was these days, the idea of a good meal at a nice restaurant appealed to her. Jerry seemed so unthreatening on the phone, so almost pitiable. And she remembered that while he was not ugly, he was not uncomfortably handsome, either; he was just pleasant-looking enough so that she would feel good with him in public, but not so handsome that she would feel embarrassed by her own bulbous physical state. She agreed to go.

Sara, one of the girls who had moved into the attic apartment, agreed to babysit for Danny and Jenny. Daisy would of course pay her the regular babysitting fee—they had discussed all this at the time the girls took the apartment, and it was agreed that they would pay the full amount of rent and Daisy would pay them regular babysitting fees, instead of trying to work out some other more complicated arrangement. But Daisy was discovering that all four girls, but especially Sara and Ruth Anne, would be of more help to her than she had ever dreamed. In almost no time at all she had come to think affectionately of her four renters as the "upstairs girls." They were lonely young women from farms or small towns in the middle of Wisconsin who had come straight from high school to Milwaukee to get good-paying secretarial or department store jobs and to meet professional men; they missed their homes and families and liked hanging around Daisy's house in the evenings or on weekends, idly playing with Danny and Jenny. They thought Daisy's children were just so *cute* and they were forever asking Daisy if they could take the children with them down for a walk on the lakeshore or for a ride with them to do errands and buy ice cream. In return Daisy found herself spending long evening hours sitting at the kitchen table with them, listening to their life stories, offering them sensible advice, doling out sympathy when they complained of problems with their jobs or boy friends or lack of boy friends. She had already given Sara, who was her size, three of her old blouses, blouses she would never wear again because they were too frilly and young for her, and twice when two of the other girls had had an especially snazzy date she had lent them her long dresses for the evening. She felt that she had somehow accumulated an extended family about her, and she liked it. She liked it very much. All through the month of March she had seldom found herself alone in the evenings—because even on the weekends it never happened that all four girls had dates —and whoever didn't have a date ended up coming down from the attic to share a bowl of popcorn and a television movie with Daisy. One Saturday night she had given Melissa a permanent to make her straight hair frizzy; another night she had sat up late with Ruth Anne and Allison, discussing sex and men and contraception. Oh, she liked it all, the companionship, the laughter, the stories which reminded her of her own unmarried youth, even the pleasant, busy sound of footsteps going up and down the back stairs, the hum of blow dryers and the rush of hot water as the girls got ready for dates or the noise of doors opening and closing at all hours of the day and night. It felt good to go to sleep in a house so full of life, with all the prettiness and optimism of the four young girls filling what had once been empty rooms above her, billowing above her like palpable clouds of hope between her and the cold night air. She liked the girls and thought herself quite lucky. And their first month's rent had paid the largest part of the expense of having the little kitchen installed. April's rent money would finish off that bill, and there would be some left over for babysitting and gas and food; she was eventually even going to be able to start a small savings account.

She felt lucky. In February she had received a check from her mother large enough to pay Paul most of his share of the equity; Margaret had promised another check soon, which would pay Paul the rest of his equity and reduce the monthly mortgage payments slightly. She felt so supported by her family, her mother, father, sister; she felt so supported by all her friends and now these new friendly upstairs girls. And Danny and Jenny were as happy as clams suddenly to have in the house strong, lithe bodies they could climb on or be swung by, sound healthy enthusiastic girls who would roll on the floor with them or bring them sticks of chewing gum or lollipops. Now from time to time she could afford to go out to dinner or a movie with her own grown-up friends, Karen or Martha or Jane, or to pay a babysitter so she could spend a snowy Saturday afternoon strolling through a warm bright mall without little children tugging on her arms, distracting her from the shop windows. The month of March had been happy for Daisy, and she felt inside her the pain of Paul's leaving easing off a bit, fading away.

But by the end of March, when the baby still had not come, she began to feel more and more restless and irritable, and then, irrationally, bitter thoughts would start stirring in her mind. And when Jerry Reynolds called again, to tell her what time he would be arriving to pick her up, she realized that the very low, deep tenor of his voice startled her, even annoyed her a bit. She supposed she had been living too long among only women; and as the day for her date approached, she felt herself growing anxious. What did she have in common with this man, after all, what on earth would they talk about?

He arrived at her house on Saturday night at seven o'clock. Daisy opened the door and, with a casual cheerful manner which she had been planning toward all day, asked him in for a drink. At first she was put off by him, by his maleness. He was tall and a little stout, and so very different from the women and girls and children she had spent so much time with that he seemed instantly threatening. Yet as they moved through the house to the kitchen where Daisy mixed them both scotch and waters, Daisy noticed how his hair was already receding, and how his ears stuck out in such a way that he would never grow into them, and somehow this endeared him to her. At any rate she felt less nervous. Even if her body was so cumbersome, her face was still pretty, she thought: she was as a woman prettier than he was handsome as a man. This comforted her, and by the time they reached the living room and settled into their chairs by the fire, she felt less and less like snapping at him, like telling him to just go away.

"This is a fabulous house," Jerry said, looking about.

"Yes," Daisy answered. "I love it." She looked about it, too, at the bright yellow room she had so recently unpacked and put back together. She told him a bit of the history of the house, and about the work she had done on it, and said that sometime she would show him through it.

"I'm living in a two-room rented apartment in a new complex," Jerry told her. It was apparent that he was trying to be jolly about it, but his tone was mournful. "It's quite a change, after living in my own house for so many years, to have two small cardboard boxes to come home to. I even miss shoveling the snow. I miss standing in my own yard with a shovel in my hand, looking at my house and garage, thinking: this is *my* property, *my place*. I miss taking care of a home. I miss that feeling of satisfaction that comes from shoveling the snow. That feeling that I have just, through my own hard labor, made it possible for me and my wife to be safely connected to the rest of the world. I don't think I'm explaining it very well. It must sound silly."

"No, no, not at all!" Daisy reassured him. As he talked, she had been sneakily evaluating him, checking out her reactions to him, and she decided that he was not sexually attractive to her at all, even if she hadn't been nine months pregnant. It was not just that he had accumulated a bit of a belly, and a sort of flabbiness about his jaw—she didn't remember him as flabby, was it possible that he had put on this weight since his divorce, was it possible that like her he sometimes ate for the sake of consolation? But he was so obviously earnest and nervous and sad that she found him touching. "I can understand how hard it must be to give up a house. I was miserable when I thought I had to move from here. But fortunately my parents helped me out financially, otherwise I'd be living in an apartment, too."

"Well, I'll be able to get my own house again someday," Jerry said. "Scotty—my wife, or ex-wife, or whatever she is now—I hate the word 'estranged,' it has a mad sound about it to me—Scotty is planning to get married again as soon as our divorce is final, and then of course she'll have to sell the house she's living in now, the house *we* lived in, and I'll be able to get something for myself. But that's a few months away. It's like suddenly living on the moon. Our house wasn't as big or magnificent as this by a long way, but it was cozy, and it was familiar. In the new apartment complex the walls are all white, and can't be painted, and the rugs are all dark-brown nylon, and everything seems so thin and transient. I really hate going down to the basement to do my laundry in the coin-operated machines. There are these weird flickering fluorescent lights down there making the place seem spacy, and there's always something like a man's lost gray sock lying about, making the place look so lonely— Well, God, I didn't come here to depress you. It's not *that* bad. I'm usually out at work, anyway." Jerry smiled. "I've taken to working at night in my office and I'm doing some personal tax work for people. At least I'm making a bit of extra money. My office seems more like home to me than my apartment now. But I miss the birds. I know this must sound strange, but one of the things I miss most of all, even more than my wife"—he interrupted himself to laugh—"is the birds. I mean I had built several feeders and put them out in the back yard, and I had built a large wooden tray right outside our kitchen windows, and we kept them full of birdseed, and every day there were so many birds around our house. I could eat breakfast and watch the cardinals or sparrows land on the tray and peck at the seed—they were so bright and fluffed out against the cold—" Jerry stopped and looked down at his drink, and Daisy could not tell from his expression whether he suddenly felt embarrassed or sad.

"You don't have any children," she said.

"No." Jerry still did not look up from his drink. "I wanted to have children, but Scotty didn't."

"*You* wanted children?" Daisy asked, surprised. "And Scotty didn't?" She had always thought that all women wanted children and that all men, like Paul, could either take them or leave them, according to their careers or moods or financial situations.

"Well," Jerry said, "Scotty gets bored easily. And she likes nice things, nice clothes, winter vacations, and so on. And then her own family was a bit strange. . . ."

Jerry went on talking, telling Daisy about Scotty and Scotty's parents, about his marriage to Scotty, and Daisy sat and sipped her drink and listened only half attentively. She was busy thinking. She was busy thinking: why is this strange man telling me all this? How can he so easily tell me these intimate details of his life? Part of it, she knew, had to be that he simply needed to talk, he had to talk about all of this to someone. But why to her? Why was he talking so openly to her? He was going on and on, telling her private details of his life which all touched her as sadly as his description of the birds fluffed out against the cold on the feeder he had built. Why was he telling her all this? Was it because he thought she was wise? Perhaps it was just that he felt sure she was kind. And she did feel kindly toward him, kindly and generous and even slightly affectionate, because by his very vulnerability he was opening up to her a new way of viewing men. There were men out there in the world, then, who would want a home with children, who would want the stable, ordinary, mundane pleasures, who might want Daisy with all the homey opulence of her body and her life. Jerry was not going to be the new man in her life, she could tell that. Or rather, he was not going to be the new love in her life. It was quite possible that he would become a friend, a good friend, just as much a friend to her as Karen or Jane or Martha or the upstairs girls. It would be nice to have a man for a friend, Daisy thought, and then with a flash thought how very nice it would have been to have had him as a friend a few days ago, when she had to hang the heavy gilt-framed mirror back in the hall.

Daisy had been in tears trying to hang it, she had stood in the hallway panting from her efforts to lift the mirror back onto the hook, she had complained to Jenny and Danny, who stood watching her with open mouths: "It doesn't matter how independent, how self-sufficient I am, I just am not strong enough to lift this goddamned mirror back up there, and I never will be!" That afternoon she had been exhausted and aching and bitter, wishing the baby would hurry up and *come*, wishing life were not so physically difficult. Her body had felt wretched and pressured in its every part. It seemed that the new baby weighed at least fifteen pounds and was standing upright with the full force of its body pushing against her bladder, so that she had to run to the bathroom constantly; if she coughed or sneezed or laughed, she wet her pants. The baby's head was lodged into her lungs so that it took real effort simply to breathe. And she had incredible stomach pains and indigestion, because the selfish baby had shoved and bulged all her intestines into the corners of her stomach. She couldn't imagine how her digestive system was still managing to function. She was tired. A brown blotch had shown up between her eyebrows, giving her a heavily moronic sort of look. It was not fair, she had thought, that all Paul had to do, all a *man* had to do, was to expel a bit of viscous fluid from his body and then walk away, all his organs and substance completely unchanged by the growth of a new life, while she, the woman, was stuck with a bulging heavy physical growth that caused her legs to cramp with pain every time she stood.

"What lamebrain half-assed idiot thought up this system?" Daisy asked Danny and Jenny, who of course did not understand what she was talking about or why she was yelling at them.

Daisy had finally gotten a chair, and climbed up on it, and eased the mirror up to the chair and then finally into its place on the wall. It had seemed absolutely essential to have the house back in order before she returned to it with a new baby. When she lifted the mirror onto its hook, she had felt as though tissues just under her skin were ripping. She had climbed back down and collapsed onto the chair, rubbing her painfully stretched stomach with shaking hands.

"This baby is not going to come out through my legs like ordinary kids," Daisy informed Danny and Jenny with clenched teeth. "It's going to pop right out through my belly. And I'm going to end up looking just like your beanbag chair with stuffing spilling out all over."

"Really?" Danny asked, fascinated, staring at her belly, obviously hoping the baby would burst out then and there.

But Jenny began to cry. "You took the beanbag chair to the dump," she said. "Will they take you to the dump?"

"They should, it's where I belong," Daisy said. "Right out there with all the other overused, torn-up rubbish." But then she begrudged herself her bitterness, and pulled Jenny against her leg and fondled her. "The baby is not going to come out that way," she said truthfully, wearily. "I'm not going to break apart, and I'm not going to the dump. I'm just very tired and very grumpy, but I'll be fine in a few days. Don't worry, honey, don't cry. Don't worry. Come on and smile for me, honeypot. Let's go in the kitchen and find something yummy to eat."

"I'm not hungry," Jenny sniffled, and Danny echoed her.

"Well, I am," Daisy said, and hefted herself from the chair and lumbered into the kitchen to find something sweet. But even sweet food had not changed her sour disposition that day.

Paul had called early in the morning to say that something had come up—friends had given him and Monica tickets to a concert—and so he would not be taking the children to spend the night with him that night after all, but would take them the next day. Daisy had longed to say: "Well, you *have* to take them. I was planning to get into bed the minute they left and stay there till the minute you returned them; if I don't get some rest I'll go batty." But she had been too weary to try to argue. Perhaps Sara or one of the other girls would take the children for a walk, she thought, then she could lie down and rest for a while. Still it chewed at her heart that Paul, who had helped create these children, could so easily slough off responsibility for them. She knew she could not rely on him for help; he would be moving to California in a matter of weeks, and she was aware that his connection with the children would quickly grow less and less strong. She realized that before long all she would receive from him would be the child-support checks he was legally bound to send. She hated Paul that day, purely and cleanly, she hated him. She thought perhaps she hated all men, all men with their inviolable bodies.

But she had not really wanted to hate men, and it was not in her character to nurture bitterness, and so tonight she was glad to have Jerry sitting across from her, distraught and vulnerable, as vulnerable as any other human being. And because she had had a nap that day, and was looking forward to a good dinner, she had flipped out to the other extreme of mood, where she found herself perched on her pregnancy like a bird at the top of a marvelous tree. If she had the burden and the weight, she also had the richness and the joy. She was more complex than the man sitting there before her, she thought, she was truly a more complicated being. All he had was his lone body, which could never change as dramatically as hers. While she could change shapes like a sorceress, she could sit looking perfectly still, and have extraordinary and elaborate

magic bubbling away inside her. *She* could grow and carry
secrets, the ultimate secret. And it occurred to her to wonder as she sat there what Jerry would think if she suddenly
acted on impulse and interrupted his monologue to say,
"Nyaa, nyaa, nyaa! You can't do what I do, you can't do
what I do!"

Oh, it was clear that the fluids from the unborn baby
were pressing on her brain and making her feel and think
strangely. For as Daisy sat smiling politely at Jerry, nod-
ding and commenting at appropriate times, all the queerest
thoughts were running through her head. She wanted to
taunt him like a child with a new toy, a better toy. She
wanted to interrupt him to ask, "Tell me. You're a man.
Do you think I'm sexy? Do you think any man will want to
marry me? I mean after I've gotten back in shape. Do you
think anyone would want to marry a woman with three
children? What do you think of my legs, look at my legs,
they're still good." What would poor Jerry do if she pulled
up her skirt and showed him her legs? Daisy wiggled on the
sofa. She felt restless, crazy. She wanted suddenly to turn
on the radio or a record and dance, she really felt like dancing—although she knew that if she did she would probably
pass right out on the floor, because she could scarcely walk
anymore without struggling for breath. But Jerry did not
sense her itchiness; he talked on.

Finally the children came thundering into the living
room with Sara behind them.

"Are you still here?" they asked, and Jenny attempted to
jump on Daisy's lap while Danny stood openly scrutinizing
Jerry with the same suspicious look Daisy's father had worn
on his face when she had started dating at fifteen.

"We're just leaving," Jerry said, to Daisy's relief. "Good
Lord, look how long I've been talking. We'll be late; I
made reservations."

Daisy struggled up from the sofa, kissed the children

goodbye, and awkwardly fit as much of her body as she could into her coat. Last week she had tried to button the coat and the strain of her enormous belly against the fabric had made two of the buttons pop right off, so now she had to be satisfied with having her arms and back covered while her stomach sailed ahead of her into the cold, covered only by the bright blue wool of her dress. Jerry was a gentleman; he took her arm and steadied her as they went out the door and down the steps to the car. He was quiet in the car for a while until they were headed in the direction of the restaurant, and when he finally spoke he said, "I should apologize. I can't believe I talked so much. I hope I didn't bore you."

"No, no, not at all," Daisy answered, smiling. But, in fact, her mind was wandering even then, so that she had to almost physically force herself to pay attention to him. She was foolishly staring at the lights of cars and houses and shops they drove past, she was letting herself get lost in the patterns of light. She found it difficult to concentrate on the man sitting next to her.

"I don't usually talk so much about myself," Jerry said. "But you are so sympathetic. You're so nice."

"I'm so *pregnant,*" Daisy said. And as she spoke, she felt a most surprising warm gush of fluids between her legs. It startled her. Her first thought was that she had wet her pants, but then she realized that she hadn't sneezed or coughed or laughed and that in fact this fluid felt different. It was so warm, so sticky—there was so much of it— "Oh, my God, Jerry," Daisy said. "My water just broke!"

"What does *that* mean?" Jerry asked, looking sideways at Daisy with apprehension.

"It means I'll owe you some money to get your upholstery cleaned," Daisy said. Even as she spoke she could feel the fluid seeping through the material of her dress and coat and into his car seat. But she felt strangely apathetic about it all; the fluid was warm, and the car heater was warm, and she was both comfortable and uncomfortable; most of her body had gone relaxed and somnolent, but her belly was drawing into itself with a deep pulling cramp. She put her hands on her belly to check; it was as if she had become schizophrenic and had to feel with her hands and see with her eyes if that strange foreign country, her stomach, was doing what she thought it was. It was. Her belly was as hard as the shell of a walnut, but it was a vulnerable, living hardness, an animate hardness, and as she moved her hands over her stomach she felt the hardness relax of its own accord.

Daisy sat very quietly for a few minutes, intent on herself, on the workings of her body, listening with her hands: and there it was again, that deep and irresistible pull. So it was starting. The baby was finally coming. In a few hours she would hold her new living child in her arms, in a few hours her life would be once more completely changed. She was ready for it, she was more than ready, she was eager. She welcomed the labor, the entire wracking process of giving birth: *giving* birth, giving life to a new person through her own efforts. This time she knew she would not be afraid of the pain, for she had been through it all before. The first time, with Danny, she had been frightened. She had lain in the high labor-room bed for hours, trying to breathe, trying to be brave, and staring at the chart on the wall that showed how the cervix dilates from two centimeters to something the size of a grapefruit. And she had tormented herself with crazy, uncontrollable fears: that might be what happened to other women, but it could never happen to her. Her body couldn't possibly change that much. It would be impossible for something as large as a baby's head and body to push its way through her muscles and bones without breaking her apart in the process. And with both Danny and Jenny, as the pain had grown stronger, she had really been convinced that she would die, with the next contraction, of a broken back. She had thought the pain truly unendurable.

But she had endured it. She had endured it twice, and her back had not broken after all, and she knew now that it would not break with this new baby. She knew now how babies came, she knew that on the other side of the mountain of pain which she was beginning to climb was a really glorious valley of hormonal delights, a sensual paradise of relief, relaxation, rest, and love. With Danny she had felt, at a certain point, when the labor pains grew severe, that she had somehow gotten on a roller coaster: it was just as it had been when she was a child, and had willingly sat down on a roller coaster, and then realizing the inescapability of her act, had screamed and screamed as the rickety cars went clanking up and up and up the steep incline, "I didn't mean this at all! I don't want this! I'm scared! Let me off, let me *off!*" It had been terrifying to realize that there was no way off that particular mad ride, that she was locked into it, and had to go through with it, even if it resulted in her death or in pain past describing.

But this time it was different, this time it was better. She felt so much more supported than before, she felt supported by the memories of the births of Danny and Jenny, she felt supported by the love and concern of her family and friends, and she felt really strengthened within herself by what she had gone through in the past few months. If she could go through all of that—the pain of the divorce, the pain of the loss of Paul and her marriage, which in its own way had been as intensely agonizing as the pain of labor—if she could go through all of that, and come out on the other side intact and smiling at life, then she could certainly go through the birth of this new and already loved child. This time she was not on a dry dreadful roller coaster whipping up and down toward a fate she could not foresee. This time, she could feel already, was more fluid, more graceful; as if she were riding the surge of a wave. Yes, it was like that, as if she were a raft, a liferaft, being borne forward by a great and billowing wave, and the wave supported her, held her up, carried her forward with no effort on her part, and she in turn supported the baby, she was the vessel that would carry it safely to the shore. And so she was not frightened; she was glad.

Her stomach continued to tighten and release rhythmically. It was all coming on very fast this time. The contractions were less than four minutes apart, and were rapidly growing fierce.

"Jerry," Daisy said, "I don't think we're going to make it to dinner tonight. I think you're going to have to drive me to the hospital instead."

"Really?" Jerry asked, turning to her with a face bright with surprise. "Are you okay?"

"I'm fine. But the contractions have started, and they are serious ones. God, I'm sorry. I didn't intend for this to happen at all."

"Oh, it's okay, it's okay. My God, it's wonderful! It's exciting!" Jerry stopped at a red light and frankly studied Daisy's body as if by looking he could tell what was going on.

"Yes, well, just don't let it worry you if I should all of a sudden stop being a good companion," Daisy said. "You see, usually the pains start at four minutes apart, and then gradually come quicker and quicker, but now it seems to be hitting me hard all at once. I'm going to have to do some breathing exercises, and I'm going to have to— Just a minute—" And she ignored Jerry and began the quick shallow panting that she remembered from her earlier labors. There it was, for sure, just like the other times, the enormous hand that grasped her body and squeezed. She knew she would have to give in to it, she knew she would have to not fight, but surrender. She pulled her coat about her as tightly as she could, wanting not to look too horribly disheveled and out of control in front of the poor man she had so inadvertently trapped into sharing this particular trip. The next contraction was so hard that she scrunched down in the seat and pressed her knees up against the dashboard of the car, and grabbed onto the door handle. "Ouch," she said. "Oh, my God. Jerry, you'd better drive fast."

"I will, I will," Jerry said, and pressed down on the accelerator. He drove studiously, rapidly, for a few minutes, then suddenly said, "But where are we going? Which hospital?"

This made Daisy laugh, causing her to lose control of her cadenced deep breaths. "St. Mary's," she said. "And hurry. And Jerry—thank you. I'm—I'm not going to be able to talk to you anymore—"

"Do you think we should stop and call the police? Or an ambulance?" Jerry asked.

But Daisy this time could not speak to answer him, she could only shake her head in reply, and moan. How hard the contractions were hitting, how the pain was pulling her down and down. She had to give in to it, she had to submerge, she had to let go. She turned her face away from Jerry so he would not be frightened by how she looked, all contorted and lost and inhuman, and she braced herself as well as she could in the car, and she concentrated on the breathing, and she let her body be taken over. She rose and fell with the pain, she billowed and plunged, she let herself be pulled under, and she heard herself sob when she was lifted for a few seconds up free from the pain.

"God," she said to no one in particular, "it feels so good when it stops."

By the time they got to the hospital she had to push.

"Jerry," she said, "you'll have to go in and have someone

come out for me with a wheelchair or a stretcher. I can't possibly walk."

Jerry burst from the car and ran toward the emergency room. As soon as he was gone, Daisy let herself indulge a bit in sounds that she had been holding in, afraid that she would scare him. "Oh damn, oh shit, oh hell," she yelled into the dark night, "oh, I don't like this, oh, baby, I hope you're quick." Her back was arching in spite of herself and she was immensely uncomfortable in the car. She was extremely hot inside her coat and wool dress and tried her best to take the coat off, she felt so mussed and wretched, but all she could manage to get off was one sleeve. And then the attendants were there with a wheelchair, and as Jerry stood helplessly watching with eyes as large as Danny's, they managed to get her from the car and into the chair with a gentle clumsiness that came from the fact that she could no longer control her body to help them. She could scarcely stay in the chair, her back was arching so furiously.

"Are you okay, are you okay?" Jerry kept asking, running along beside her into the bright clean emergency room, his eyes vivid with worry.

Oh, poor man, poor man, Daisy thought, he doesn't know. "I'm fine," she told him.

"But you're crying!" Jerry said.

"Well, I *hurt*," Daisy shouted at him. "I hurt a lot. But it's okay, Jerry, don't worry. It's fine—" Then she was talking to a nurse, babbling almost incoherently her name, her doctor's name, her telephone number, her address, her insurance number, her social security number, and the nurse wrote frantically on a set of forms until Daisy screamed, "If you don't get me into the delivery room, I'm going to have this baby right here!" The last thing she saw before they wheeled her away was Jerry standing helplessly wringing his hands, and her last civilized thought was: why, he's actually wringing his hands! I've never seen anyone wring his hands before!

And then they were in the delivery room and were half carrying her, half throwing her onto the table. A young doctor she had never seen before came rushing in, pulling on his white jacket and gloves, strings flapping about him. Almost before anyone could move to help her, Daisy had arranged herself: now she was better, now she was in a place she could remember, now she knew what to do. She gripped the armholds on either side and pushed against the stirrups and let her head fall back. She stopped holding in, she stopped puffing, she let her body remember the fearful rhythm of the past, and she took an enormous breath and pushed. When she looked up, she saw that the doctor had taken scissors and simply cut her pantyhose and underpants away from her body. "Hahahaha!" she laughed, suddenly overtaken with a lunatic glee. She was in such pain she was almost demented: perhaps this time her back *would* break. When she pushed again, the doctor said, "The head is crowning." So she pushed again, moaning deep in her throat, knowing she sounded like nothing so much as a mad dog, and hoping with one clear part of her mind that poor Jerry was not standing outside the door listening to her, listening to her lose all control of her civilized, human self. For one excruciating minute the baby seemed to be stuck inside her; it seemed lodged tightly, it seemed stuck; it seemed suddenly far too large to be able to leave; it hurt like hell; it hurt, it hurt, the round fluorescent light above her went square and blurred with her pain—and then the baby was out.

Her baby was born. Her new child. She heard its pitiful wail.

The doctor said, "It's a girl."

Daisy raised her head, but could see only the white-robed backs of the doctor and nurses as they gathered around to wash and tend the baby.

"Give her to me," Daisy said.

"We can't," the doctor told her. "You're wearing street clothes. You would contaminate it."

"Give me my baby," Daisy said, raising herself up on her elbows in spite of the contractions that continued to tug at the lower half of her body. "I'm not secured in here, you don't have me tied down, and if you don't give her to me now, I'm going to jump up off this table and bleed all over your floor and knock you all down and take my baby from you."

The doctor stared at Daisy for one moment and Daisy stared at him. They had never seen each other before in their lives. Yet something flashed between them, perhaps a mutual admiration, or a recognition of some kind, and then the doctor smiled.

"You're really a tiger, aren't you?" he said.

"No, I'm a mother," Daisy told him. "A tiger, Jesus Christ, what decade are you in? No one talks that way anymore. Give me my baby."

And he did. He handed her the wriggling blotchy child and Daisy held her against her breasts for a long moment, suddenly lifted out of the delivery room and away from the whole earth with the wonder of this new creature, this new child, this creature she had borne, her daughter. The baby looked like a wet rat.

"She won't look like any of the rest of us," Daisy said aloud, more or less to herself. "She's going to look like— why, I think she's going to look like Dale! I think she'll have brown hair. My other two were so blond." The baby pushed and nuzzled against her, stretching tiny wrinkled legs and arms, squalling and squeaking with her wild general wrath. "Oh!" Daisy said. "Oh! Please, help me take my things off. I want to nurse her." She saw the attendants exchange looks with the doctor.

"Go ahead," the doctor told them. "Let her nurse."

"These modern mothers," the old nurse sighed, but she helped Daisy off with her clothes with gentle hands.

The baby took Daisy's nipple immediately, and immediately went calm. And Daisy found herself entering that old lovely world where only she and the nursing infant mattered, and everything else blurred and fell away. She loved the sexual tug that moved through her from breast to crotch, and while she was vaguely aware that down below, far far away, the doctor was taking out the placenta, her feelings were focused on her new daughter and the almost irritating pleasure of her tiny nuzzling mouth. How small the baby was, how perfect, how vulnerable she was, and how remarkable. Her skin was almost iridescent, gleaming with subtle pastel colors that nearly shimmered like the lights of an opal; and her nails looked like mother-of-pearl, like small translucent stones; she was indeed like a jewel washed up from the sea, all fresh and gleaming in the warmth of her mother's warm dry arms. Daisy stared at and studied her new child, ran her hands over the tiny sculpted body, over the small cranky-looking limbs. And she was lost again; she was in love. The baby nestled against her, softly sucking, tugging open in Daisy's body a whole vast new space of love.

Finally a nurse came and officiously took the baby away to do the routine things that needed to be done. Daisy fell back down against the hospital bed, relaxing into her own body and suddenly realizing how she ached in every part. She was grateful for the competent hands that worked so efficiently about her body. She closed her eyes.

"We can let your husband in now to see you and the child, if you'd like."

Daisy looked up to see the young doctor who had delivered her daughter standing next to her, smiling down.

"My husband?" she asked, surprised. "I don't have a husband."

"You don't have a husband?" the doctor said, puzzled.

"No. I'm divorced, or almost," Daisy told him. She was too tired, it was all too complicated, to explain.

"But there's a man out there—the man who brought you in—"

"Oh," Daisy laughed feebly, "he's just my date." And she had to laugh again, thinking of it. "I missed my dinner," she said.

"Well, you certainly must lead an interesting life," the doctor said.

"Oh, I do, I do," Daisy told him, laughing even more at this. "But I get hungry a lot. God, I'd give my soul for a cheeseburger with onions and a Coke."

"I'll take care of it," the doctor said lightly, and moved off.

Daisy closed her eyes again and drifted off, only vaguely aware that she was being moved onto another cart and carried out of the delivery room and down to a private hospital room. Nurses tightened her white gown and tucked her in bed and took her temperature again and checked her pads and murmured, and Daisy let it all happen to her as if she were in a dream. She asked for some aspirin and someone gave her some pain pills and another kind of pill that she was too lazy to ask about, and then she drifted again, smugly indolent. It was all over. Her new child was here, the work had been done, the pleasures of the flesh were ahead. She could rest.

"Are you still hungry?"

Again it was the young doctor. He had in his hand a big white paper sack, and he carried with him the most delicious smells that had nothing to do with a hospital, smells of meat and onions.

"Do you have a *cheeseburger* in there?" Daisy asked, all at once awake and ravenous.

"Yes," the doctor said. "I had someone run across the street, I'm hungry, too; do you mind if I join you?"

"Of course not," Daisy said. She let the doctor crank her bed up and pull the table around in front of her. He sat down on her bed and spread the food out on the table: cheeseburgers and french fries in cardboard cartons, Cokes in cardboard cups.

"This is so much better than the hospital food," the doctor said. "And I felt we really should share this meal. If I could get champagne in here, I would. You were my first delivery."

"Really?" Daisy said. "How exciting. Well, you did a marvelous job."

"Thank you. But you did all the work. I just got to be there. It was wonderful."

Daisy ate and ate—he had had the sense to bring two cheeseburgers for her—and listened to the doctor talk. He was a homely young man, and yet endearing, and Daisy felt her affections flowing out toward him doubly, because he had been her physician and yet seemed such a child. It seemed extraordinary, a special treat, a unique prize, to be able to sit in the pale-yellow hospital room eating cheeseburgers with her obstetrician. It never could have happened with her regular physician, a capable but dour older man who had delivered so many babies he practically sighed with boredom at having to go through it all again. With Dr. Leston she had always felt a bit like a child who had willfully gotten herself into a scrape and needed help. With this young man she felt like a grown-up, a contemporary, and if he was a god because he was a doctor, then she was a goddess because she had carried and given birth to a child. She felt comfortable with him, his equal. In fact, she felt almost euphoric in his presence, but that was, she knew, because of the pain pill, and the food, and the physical aftermath of the birth.

"What happened to Jerry?" Daisy asked, struggling to be sensible now that her stomach was full and sleep was overtaking her again.

"I told him he should go home," the doctor said. "He said he'd be back to see you tomorrow. And he's going to stop by your house on the way home to tell your sitter what happened."

"Oh, good," Daisy said. "Well, Sara knows what to do. I'll call her in the morning. Oh—I have to call Mother, and Daddy. I have to call Dale!"

"I'll leave you, then," the doctor said. "I'll stop in and see you tomorrow. You need your rest. Don't stay up talking too long."

Daisy smiled. "I couldn't if I wanted to," she said. "I'm fading away fast. Thank you so much for the cheeseburgers; that seemed like the best food I've ever eaten."

Daisy waited until she was sure the doctor was gone, then reached for the phone. No one answered at her father's house; she would have to call him the next day. She called her mother next, and gave her a long and detailed report.

"Oh, thank heaven. I'm so pleased, I'm so glad," Margaret said. "I'm so glad you're both fine. I've been wondering about you constantly. And darling, what a wonderful story this will make—you going into labor on a date. I'm glad you're dating, you know."

"I am, too," Daisy said. "I'm glad about *everything*. In fact, right now I'm absolutely high. And it's not just the drugs. How are you?"

"Oh, I'm well," Margaret said. "You know, when Danny was born, I went around for a week saying to myself:

you're a grandmother now. A *grandmother*. I felt so old. I guess the first grandchild is always the shocking one. This new baby doesn't make me feel any older at all."

Daisy smiled to herself to think that her mother would turn even this event into a reflection on herself, but she ended her conversation with Margaret amiably enough, and thanked her again profusely for the money, and said she would send pictures as soon as possible. Then she said goodbye, and called Dale, who responded with whole-hearted enthusiasm and concern.

"I'm so sorry I can't fly back and help you out," Dale said. "Are you going to be okay?"

"Oh, I'll be great," Daisy said. "I've got Karen and Jane helping me for the next two weeks; they'll have Danny and Jenny with them. And I've got the rooms rented out to girls I really like, and I've got enough money, and I've even got a nice doctor who brought me cheeseburgers!"

"You've got the sun in the mornin' and the moon at night," Dale said. "What kind of happy pills do they have you on?"

"Oh, Dale." Daisy laughed, but even as she spoke she felt the effect of the pain-killers take a turn; she was suddenly so sleepy she wanted to simply drop the phone on the floor and pass out. "Dale, I've got to go. I'm all woozy. I'll call you tomorrow."

"No, you save your nickels and dimes. I'll call you."

"Okay. Thanks. I love you. And guess what—I've done my bit with babies, now—it's your turn. The next babies in this family will be yours."

"Well," Dale said. "There's a thought. Well."

Daisy said goodbye to her sister and hung up the phone, then slid down into the comfort of the warm blankets. She felt as though she had just gotten in from a most unusual, serendipitous, and strangely erotic party. How lucky she was, she thought to herself, and instantly fell asleep.

NINE

❖❘❖❘❖❘❖❘❖❘❖❘❖❘❖❘❖❘❖❘❖❘❖❘❖❘❖

O h, the color of the trees: such vibrancy! Margaret's gaze kept catching on the trees, the flowering apple and crab and dogwood, the cut-leaf maple, and the myriad gentle greens of the spruce and low shrubs. She was looking out the window of her new home, or rather trying not to look out; she had so much unpacking to do. And it was only nine-thirty this Sunday morning, and she had vowed to herself that she would have her new house in order by that night, so that the next day, when she came home from work, she could have some sort of order to return to. But the flowering trees, the ebullience of all the flowers, lured her, lured her, and finally she took up her cup of tea and went out the door and sat down on her back porch step simply to stare.

It was late April, and the sun warmed everything, made everything glimmer with a golden light. There was nothing more pleasant than this, to sit warmed and private in the sunlight of her own back yard, surrounded by the pinks and whites and greens and golds of spring. Pandora, the white cat, was sprawled luxuriously near a rich green bush of peonies which were almost ready to bloom. Ulysses, the gray cat which had adopted Margaret, was further out in the garden, creeping around under the azalea bushes, trying to find something to capture his attention. He had turned out to be such a whimsical, frivolous sort of cat, so unlike Pandora, who spent most of her life lolling about, that Margaret had become really fond of him; he entertained her, he was past her imagining. He chased his tail, something Pandora would never be naïve or energetic enough to do, and he talked incessantly to Margaret. He was a bit of a ham. Now, seeing that Margaret had come out of the house and was watching him, he executed a clever graceful dance among the bushes and ended by leaping up into a low branch of the apple tree. Then he mewed questioningly at Margaret.

"Yes, I see you, Ulysses, I see you. You're marvelous," Margaret said.

This seemed to satisfy the cat. He turned his back on her and began to groom and preen himself with such brisk concentration that Margaret smiled, sure that sooner or later he would fall out of the tree. Some things you choose for yourself, and some things fate brings you, Margaret thought, and perhaps you can never know, even at the end of your life, at the summing-up, just which sort was better. For she needed the aloof and luxurious Pandora, just as she needed an aloof and luxurious life; but now she knew that she also needed, still needed, in her life, the unexpected, the enchanting, the lively things. How full life could be, Margaret thought. Life could be full and long, and now she knew that the choice of one way of life over another did not mean placing any sort of limitations—or if limitations were placed, then so were new possibilities opened up. It was a matter of making the best of both.

She sipped her tea. She was content. And yet underneath it all ran the tension that came from knowing that even as she arranged and rearranged her chosen life, fate was working its devious ways to unsettle her. That is, she had come to realize how brief life could be: she was aware of her own mortality.

After Dale's visit in late January, Margaret had spent hours sitting at her desk, pondering, poring over her checkbook and savings account, thinking about her life. The question was how to best help Daisy without totally removing from her own life all financial comforts. There was so much that Margaret wanted to do. She wanted to take trips: short vacations to Hawaii when the rains hit Vancouver, and longer trips to Europe or the Orient. She wanted to feel she could attend the ballet and concerts and theater, to give gifts to her friends, to continue to buy pretty clothes and books, to live her life *well*. Then, too, there was the darker side of it, which Miriam's problem had all too sharply brought home these past few weeks: there was the possibility of illness in her future, and at least the certainty of old age, and she wanted to be able to take care of herself during those times. All that took money. And if she planned on all that, then there was not enough money to go around, not enough money so that she could give Daisy what she needed.

The only solution was for Margaret to sell her house by the sea. It was a terribly costly house because it was on the oceanfront, and the taxes were so high. Why, Margaret suddenly asked herself, why did she have to live by the ocean after all? She had enjoyed it, but as often as she found it lovely, she also now ignored it, or found it tiresome. Once she had sat gazing out her window at the harbor, watching a massive steel Norwegian freighter slowly make its way from Point Grey to the Second Narrows, and she was strangely exasperated by the sight of that ship carrying the goods of the world and the men who handled those goods. That afternoon she had driven around West

Vancouver with a realtor, looking at houses farther up the mountain, and had found one house—this house she was now moving into—which provided her with an antidote to that early oceanside dissatisfaction. It was small, rather cottage-like in appearance, with a lovely little garden behind. The garden was totally private, walled on all sides with high cedar boards and shrubs and trees, and on seeing it, even in its rather dismal February state, Margaret had thought: oh, this would be perfect, *this* is what I want. So she had sold her waterfront home, and bought the little cottage with the private garden, and the difference in the price of the two properties was so great that she was able to send Daisy the money to keep *her* house and to have some left over to add to Margaret's own savings. It had all worked out well. Margaret felt she had dispensed with her obligations: Harry had married Trudy, Dale would never need her in the way that Daisy did, and Daisy would now be forever supported, each and every day, by Margaret, because she would be living in the house which Margaret had helped make possible for Daisy to have. Oh, Dale and Daisy were young, and undoubtedly during the course of their lives they would come to Margaret with troubles again; but the important thing was that Margaret now felt that she had done all she could for her daughters. She had done enough. She could feel free.

She had set herself free of Anthony, too, but that had not been done as well. It could not be done by sending a piece of paper in the mail, it was not a task so distantly dispatched. Yet when Margaret had told Anthony she would not ever marry him, she would not ever marry anyone, he had carried it off with the ease and insouciance she expected of him, and they were still friends. In fact, they still saw each other, still slept with each other, though not as often. She knew from Miriam that Anthony had begun to see another woman regularly, and she knew instinctively that before long Anthony would probably marry that other woman, and that made her slightly sad. But not sad enough to do anything about it. She would miss Anthony's elegance and charm, but there were other men. There were enough other men to dine and sleep with, and if there weren't any particular men around, then there were her women friends, and she had herself, her own solitary desires and pleasures, which she preferred above all. And she could talk to her women friends and her daughters.

She had discovered, gradually, with a growing sense of delight, that she had a mind. She knew this was not the same thing as having a talent or a career, but still it satisfied her immensely. It was a real surprise and pleasure to realize that she had a mind, that her mind had a life, that it wanted to expand itself and grow, and that it could do that, within the solitary confines of her own head, just as life expanded and grew amid the jumbled complexity of people and things.

She had decided to put herself to the study of three things: religion, the music of Beethoven, and botany. She wanted to come to understand before she died the structure and systems of plants and flowers and trees, especially those which were self-regenerating. She wanted to comprehend the mysteries of scales and movements and measures of music. And she wanted to compare and examine the anatomies of all religions, not just the western ones, because although they were man-made, as music was, still they reached past the human in ways that were awesomely complex while still rigorously bound. There were whole realms of experience and knowledge which Margaret had never really been aware of, and now she wanted to enter into those realms as one might enter new and gracious rooms, she wanted to wander about, exploring at her own pace. She saw how she could live quite happily among the complicated edifices of religion, music, botany; she was eager to fill her life and her mind with words such as morphology and genus, transfiguration and Nirvana, cadenza and clef. *Obbligato, oblanceolate, oblation:* Margaret chanted these words to herself through the months of February, March, and April, as if they could work a sort of charm. There were so many ways to live a life.

To live a life: for that was it, that was the key, that was everything. For a time just before and after Dale's visit, Margaret had been—she now realized—indulging herself with the seductive charms of a sense of belatedness. She had felt old; she had felt sorry for herself, for the way she had lived out her life. She had pitied herself for her sagging flesh and her lack of marketable talents. She had envied her daughters, who were young and pretty, with all of life and its physical enjoyments ahead of them. She had become almost obsessed with thoughts of her past, with profound and despairing regrets for the way she had lived her past. She found herself sobbing as she read certain strongly feminist books, and once she had had to run from a drugstore because the simple, cheerful, brightly printed words on the cover of a women's magazine brought home to her just how successfully younger women were managing to combine a family life with the life of the self. Bitterness and remorse began to taint her days so completely that she found herself turning away from even Miriam, her closest friend; she could not keep herself from thinking jealously just how much more of a life Miriam had led.

Then one day in early April Miriam had insisted that Margaret come to her house for lunch. Margaret had been so turned in upon herself that she expected that Miriam would lecture or chastise her for her recent growing gloom; she had been taken aback to find Miriam vague and preoccupied as they ate: they both just picked at the lovely crab salad Miriam had made. They took their coffee out to the sunporch of Miriam's house and settled into the gay striped cushions of the wicker chairs, and Margaret thought: now she's going to say it, now she's going to comment on just how unpleasant I've become.

Instead Miriam said to Margaret: "There's something I have to tell you. I'm going into the hospital next week. I may have to have a mastectomy."

"Oh, no," Margaret had said. "Oh, *no*."

As she went through the next few weeks with her friend, she had tried to express to Miriam not only her sympathy but also her sense of gratitude and irony: that it had taken this sudden terrible turn in Miriam's life to bring to Margaret an awareness of the importance of the present, of the life that Margaret had left. In fact Margaret had felt guilty, as if her own spiritual malaise had brought about her dearest friend's physical illness.

"But that's absurd!" Miriam had laughed. She then had been sitting cross-legged on the hospital bed, wearing a white nightgown and a plastic bracelet with her name on it: the operation was to be the next day. Still she had laughed. "Don't be so egotistical, Margaret," Miriam had said. "You're not responsible for my illness, or for anyone else's. The only thing you're responsible for now is your own happiness—and while I'll be sorry if you continue to make yourself miserable, you'll be the only one who will really suffer. You've always been responsible for yourself. You've just never realized that until recently. And it's natural that you should feel a certain amount of real regret at what you've lost. But it would be foolish to lose what you have now, and what you can have in the future, by endearing those regrets so strongly to yourself. Oh, Margaret, we *all* have regrets. Look: I'm forty-nine years old, and I've been reasonably happy all my life. And this surgery does not really upset me all that much, except that now, for the first time ever, I regret that I never had any children, that I never had a baby nurse from my breast. I suppose it is

the possibility of losing the breast that makes me feel this; ·
though I've never felt it before, and I'm long past the age
when I could have a baby or nurse a child. Yet it's only a
small sorrow, and God knows everyone has her share of
small sorrows. I've really had so much from life, Margaret
—and so have you. It's true, you know. So have you."

Margaret had left the hospital when visiting hours were
over and returned to her oceanfront house in an almost
trancelike state. Above all she felt the tension of Miriam's
operation, she felt that she could not eat or sleep or feel
until she knew just how serious Miriam's illness was. Toward evening she debated with herself whether or not to
have the comfort of a fire: would her temporary discomfort
somehow balance out some scale so that Miriam's cancer
would be small and insignificant? But she remembered
Miriam's words, and knew at last that her most seriously
superstitious acts would in the end affect only herself. She
could hear how Miriam would laugh: "Oh, Margaret, how
dumb of you to sit in the cold. If you are thinking of me,
for heaven's sake, sit by a fire. If you're thinking of me,
think of the happiness of life: sit and be warmed, let your
evening be warm and bright."

Margaret gathered up the kindling and wood from her
back porch, and knelt at the hearth to build up an imperfect pyramid of sticks and logs. She rolled up newspapers
into cylinders and placed them under the grate and struck
a match. Then, seeing the fire successfully started, she
went into the kitchen to fix herself some herb tea. She
would not eat: she was not hungry, she could not eat, no
matter what Miriam might say. But she sank onto her sofa
by the fire with a steaming cup of tea warming her hands,
and sat there a long time, simply watching the dancing
flames. And this, too, she decided, was a superstitious act.
Although she had never thought of it before in this way,
she now realized that being happy, giving joy to oneself,

could be as much a superstitious act as being miserable and deprived. For it was happiness and optimistic endeavor and a life well lived that sustained others, after all; joy and contentment could circle out into the world just as surely as gloom, and just as Miriam's laughter in the hospital room had lifted Margaret's spirits, so it was the knowledge of the happiness of others that made people go on to strive for happiness for themselves. Otherwise everyone would simply end up in despair. Margaret sensed that for the first time in her life she had been verging on real sin—one of the Seven Deadly Sins, the sin of *accidie*, of sloth, of the refusal to movement and joy.

She rose when the fire burned low and put more logs on, large heavy chunks of wood that sent out billows of glowing warmth. She took her teacup into the kitchen and poured herself a snifter of good brandy. Then she settled back down on the sofa, and noticed with satisfaction that both Pandora and Ulysses had come into the living room to join her by the fire, and gave herself over to such thoughts as the brandy and the fire and her love of Miriam could cause.

Miriam. Miriam, who had not had children, who had traveled and taught, had listened to Margaret talk and talk about her past, her present, her desires, and never once had she disparaged the life that Margaret had led. In fact, she had told Margaret that she thought that had been a good and valuable life; then she went on quietly to point out the possibilities ahead. She had had an uncanny power and wisdom: she had lent Margaret enough strength to help her cross that particular great chasm in her life, but not so much that Margaret became dependent or obligated. She needed nothing from Margaret's life to satisfy her own; she would have been equally approving if Margaret had married Anthony or gone back to Harry. It was Margaret she loved, no matter what Margaret might do, and Miriam knew that Margaret loved her with the same steadfast elegance.

Oh, it was really something to be thankful for, Margaret thought as she sat in the light of the fire, this friendship with Miriam, this lasting and complex connection. Margaret slid down on the sofa, stretched out comfortably, and covered herself with a beige afghan which had been folded over the back of the sofa. And she thought how this night, this eve of Miriam's fearful operation, had two sides to it, two textures, like the pillow she was resting her cheek against; she could really choose whether to feel the rough or the smooth. For the sorrow and fear had to be dealt with, it could not be denied. Ever since Miriam had told Margaret of the probable need for a mastectomy, Margaret had been more and more aware of the brevity of her own life as well as that of her friend's. The statistics were awesome: each year 106,000 women had breast cancer, and although many recovered from it, the threat of its return, the awful threat of death, was always there. For weeks Margaret had been having nightmares, and worse, had lain awake in the night with vivid visions that were too cruel to go by the softer name of dreams. She had had what Dale had once called "the death willies," she had imagined herself dead and cold and shut away in a hard box, away from the warming company of people, she imagined her body losing its cover of flesh, her rings lying against bone. These visions had made her stomach cramp, and for once she had wished that someone were in the bed with her so that she could touch them and say, "Please hold me." Instead she had risen at three or four or five in the morning, and made tea and tried to read; once she had even dressed and gone out to drive around the darkened rainy city, listening to the insipid conversation of a disc jockey who played rock music to night workers and other insomniacs such as herself, until the sun had come out and she was able to go back to her house, to fall asleep.

"Don't you ever worry about death?" Margaret had finally asked Miriam, hating to bring up such a terrible subject, yet needing to know just how Miriam felt. "Don't you ever wake up in the night and worry, or find it difficult to go to sleep?"

"Not really," Miriam had said, then seeing the expression on Margaret's face, had laughed. "When I feel like that, I take a Valium. Gordon does, too."

"Oh, Miriam," Margaret had said, and gently touched her friend's arm. But later she had called her own physician and explained the situation and gotten a prescription for the same calming drug.

But the night before Miriam's operation, when it all seemed to hang in the balance, Margaret did not feel she should trick her mind and body of its honest emotions. She could not take a Valium; somehow that would betray Miriam and their friendship and in fact the whole significance of what was hanging in balance: life, the life of a friend. Margaret rose from the sofa to throw more wood on the fire, then snuggled back under the afghan, with a large glass ashtray resting on her stomach. She smoked— knowing it was stupid to have a friend in the hospital with cancer, and still to fill her lungs with smoke—and looked at the fire, and talked with Pandora when she came to settle warmly on top of Margaret's feet. No, she would not take a Valium, she would not cheat herself of the fear and awe-some worry which still made her stomach cramp. But then, she knew, there was still the other side of it all: she could not dishonor Miriam's friendship or the value of her life by indulging in the bleak stringy luxury of grief. Miriam's friendship had brought Margaret joy and pleasure and comfort—and Miriam was still alive, the operation was not until the next day—and the only decent way to honor the life of her friend was with thoughts of comfort and pleasure and joy.

Margaret really didn't take a drug of any sort that night, and the amount of brandy she drank was insignificant, yet later when she looked back on that night, she realized that if someone had looked in the window and seen her there, lounging on the sofa, smoking cigarettes, sipping brandy and then negligently setting the snifter somewhere back down on the carpet so that she always had to search for it when she wanted it again, the observant person would have thought she was either high on drugs or crazy. She had been talking aloud. At first she had addressed the cats; their presence did provide some sort of audience. But as the night had deepened, Margaret had grown strangely exhilarated, so lifted up and high with memories that she almost seemed to leave the earth and enter a drifting sphere of reverie where Dale as an infant and Daisy as a clumsy adolescent floated past each other like giddy grinning fish in a psychedelic sea. The joys, the pleasures, the comforts of her life—for in remembering Miriam, in honoring her friendship with this one particular individual, Margaret had to admit to the importance of all the joys she had had in life. She nearly babbled with excitement at her memories; she held out her hands as if she could literally touch those objects which had once given her such pleasure. The skin of her children. Almost above all, the complex clarity of a Black Watch plaid cotton she had sewn into a dress for Daisy and trimmed with black ribbon; remembering that material filled her with a real sensual satisfaction, for the sight of it, so complicated yet so neat, had been as palpably pleasant as the taste of food. Food itself—so much food, so varied, prepared with care over all those years, ritualized food: the first hot homemade chili of the fall, the pies and turkeys at Christmas, the elaborately decorated birthday cakes, celebratory feasts for friends with anniversaries, served in the dining room with all the lace and crystal and candles in the tall old silver candlesticks. Oh, she had taken pleasure from all the objects in her life. How long ago it was when she and Harry first bought the house and began to furnish it. She had always taken pleasure in the solid and well-wrought objects in her home. Coloring Easter eggs with the girls: those pastels, so pure; and then Dale and Daisy in white robes, singing down the aisles of the church with the youth choir, waving palm branches: Hosanna, hosanna, hosanna in the highest; the secure cordiality of her friends at a large ladies' auxiliary meeting, sipping coffee, eating coffee cake, discussing just which way to raise money for some particular charity; rubbing the frail freckled flesh of strangers in their white hospital beds, chatting with those people, bringing them the ordinary news of the world outside, the weather, the local town events, and the gratitude those poor ill people gave her: "Oh, thank you, my dear, that felt so good. You are so kind." She had been glad to be kind, and in the warmth and light of her private fire and her long memories, she saw that she did not have to completely disavow her past in order to have the future.

Now she saw that she could think of Harry with affection and even gratitude. He had been a good husband, a good father, a good provider; there had been years when she had gone through each day simply and unthinkingly happy to be his wife. He had kept her warm and secure for many years, and he was, she had to admit to herself, not an evil man. He had not meant to enclose her in a life she did not care for, and the truth of it was that for years she *had* cared for her life. That she had changed, that she now wanted something different and new—that she had *changed*, and he had not changed and had not wanted to recognize or approve of her changes—was not a bad thing, but then it was wrong in the light of her future to look with a bitter eye at her past. With a bit of sappy wisdom that came from the fire and the strong brandy, Margaret realized that in the past year she had been going through the sort of crisis an adolescent goes through when she leaves home: she had had to negate and furiously criticize the past in order to strike out on her own. But now she was here, really here in her own new life, and that time of ferocious, almost desperate movement was over. She was safe in a new place. And now she felt she could look at her past in a clearer, more generous, and undoubtedly more honest light. She felt she could now place her past in her mind as if it were the mist from a genie's bottle which she could summon up at will, or leave at rest. It would threaten her no longer. In fact, it was valuable to her, again and at last.

So she arranged her past; and in the next few days after her nostalgic night by the fire she continued to arrange her future. She went out in search of a job, and found three available to her, one that pleased her immensely. She could have been a saleswoman in a gift shop, but she found that the objects for sale bored her; she also did not take a job as a receptionist at a plush advertising agency in downtown Vancouver because there was something about the garrulity of the other people who worked there that put her off. The job she took seemed so perfect that at first she could not believe her luck: it was a position as an assistant in a bookstore in West Vancouver. Margaret sold books, stocked books on the shelves, returned books, sent out notices telling people that books they had ordered had arrived, kept records. After only a few days there, Margaret knew that this was a job she would want to do for years and years. For she knew that she would always like people, she would always be interested in them, she would always want to know how they worked through their joys and troubles, how they went through their lives. And with books she would be able to do this, but at a distance. She could read a book, and put it down when she chose, she could watch the lives of other people, she could be part of the world, and yet have no responsibility for it. And her contact with the real people who frequented the shop was a limited and cordial one; when she closed the door of the shop at the end of the day, she carried no one's problems home with her. She was dispensable. She again served a purpose in the world, but it was a rather nonchalant one. How different it was, for example, from being a mother and wife, from feeling responsible for the happiness and health of a family. How different it was even from the volunteer work she had done at the hospital, when she came home daily driven with a need to do more for those poor people who lay stricken in their beds with various life-and-death problems. Books were such a nonessential commodity; or if they were a product that some people at times in their lives felt they really needed, as Margaret always needed books, still they were never needed with the urgency that food or medication was, and the customers who entered the store seldom did so with desperation. Books nourished the mind and soul, but in the sense of absolute survival those were luxuries; Margaret felt that her job was luxurious. She could spend time chatting with the customers about books, but she was able to keep busy, for there was always something needing to be done around the shop. Andrea, the energetic young woman who ran the shop, had told Margaret that she was a real plum, and Margaret had been pleased by this. In fact, she could envision the day when Andrea would grow bored with such a rather plodding enterprise as the bookstore and would move on to something bigger and more challenging. Then perhaps Margaret could buy the bookstore from her, and hire someone to do the work she was now doing. She could envision working in the shop for years and years. She liked it so much: the size of it, so small and cozy, and the tiny cluttered back room full of cardboard boxes and papers and the electric burner for heating water for coffee or tea. She liked having a key to the shop, and being able to open the glass door with the ringing silver bells on the inside handle in the morning, or to close it at night. The keys made her responsible. Yet nothing really horrible would happen even if she failed at her responsibility; only books or money could be lost, not lives.

For the knowledge of the vulnerability of people would always be with her; it was an issue she would never resolve —who could resolve it? There was no solution. She felt such great pity for people, such compassion. And she had to admit such a large defeat. Miriam had lost her breast completely, and would have to take unpleasant chemotherapy treatments for the next year, and there was absolutely nothing anyone could do about it. Still Miriam managed to laugh and talk, to dress beautifully, and attend concerts, to cook meals for herself and Gordon, to read her students' papers with concern, to teach them as if the knowledge of the theme of a river in a book by Mark Twain really mattered. If Miriam could do that, then Margaret knew she was bound to live her own life cheerfully and well. If she had one duty left, one obligation left with which to attend to the rest of her life, it was that of living her own life with all the good humor and good will she could summon up. If it in the end came down simply to the fact that the only person she could really affect in this life was herself, then she determined to do that as well as she could: she would live her life well.

And it was not that difficult a task, perhaps, or so she thought as she sat alone in the sun on the back steps of her new home. The rich waxy reds and yellows of the tulips were as real and amazing a gift as always; the fluffy unconcerned cats entertaining her vision were real, too; the dark loam feeding the flowers and bushes and trees surrounding

her new home was real. She moved off the porch to sit by a
bed of irises which were just beginning to bud. The flowers
were still curled together in a tight cone as complicated
and intriguing as a shell; the pale sheath about the bud
hinted of the brilliant color hidden inside. Margaret felt a
surge of affection for this glorious, ordinary flower, which
had bloomed in her grandmother's gardens, and in the gardens of her Liberty home, and which now had come up of
its own bulbous volition in this new garden of hers, in this
her very own and private garden. She remembered a quote
from a gardening book which had always pleased her:
"Bearded irises are just plain durable." Casually, almost
aimlessly, Margaret began to pull out the green weeds that
sprouted at the base of the flowers. It crossed her mind
that she felt much more content here in this garden, surrounded by the sturdy walls of green trees and shrubs, than
she ever had by the ocean: all that spread of turbulent
water had somehow made her troubled. She preferred this,
after all: the steadfast earth, the restful protective greens,
the hopeful variety of perennial plants. She shook the earth
off the roots of a cluster of weeds and watched the brown
soil fall like an infinitely small, satisfying rain, back to the
ground. She told herself that in a few more minutes she
would go back into her house to finish the unpacking. She
would set up her stereo and put on some Beethoven. But
for a while more, she let herself sit in the sun, enjoying the
warmth of this spring day, feeling somehow protected by
all the green spears of stems and trunks which so fragilely,
so optimistically, enclosed her in her new and private
world.

It was early May, and Rocheport was burgeoning with
the fragile optimism of spring. Inside her apartment, Dale
leaned against the window; she could have seen the spring
sun lingering into the evening, shining onto the trees and

houses with a pastel warmth. She could have seen all this, but she didn't; her eyes were glazed over and she was so nervous and tense and furious that she couldn't see farther than her own nose. Nevertheless she spoke calmly: "All right, love, have a good time. Goodbye." And she calmly put the receiver into place and stood with her hands together on top of it, as if forcibly holding it down.

"Are you okay?" Carol asked, coming to stand beside her.

"Yes, I'm fine," Dale said. Then she burst into tears. "No, I'm not. I'm not fine at all. Oh, Carol, I'm so jealous and angry and *frightened* I could just die. I'd like to yank this phone from the wall and throw it through the window!"

"Yeah, well, that'd really show him," Carol said. She took Dale by her shoulders and pushed her toward a chair. "Sit down. I'll make you a drink. And for heaven's sake, don't be so upset. It's just *dinner*."

"It's just dinner in a *hotel* with an old girl friend," Dale wailed.

She sat down in the chair, then jumped up again, jammed her hands in the back pockets of her jeans and began to pace about the apartment. "*Leland*," she said aloud, more to herself than to Carol. "Jesus Christ, what a name. You know what she looks like—Leland—she's another one of those tall cool Boston blondes that his parents love. Her family is close to his family. They'll be so *cozy*. Of course it will be more than dinner; he'll kiss her, you know he'll *kiss* her. And then dinner with her bedroom so conveniently just up the stairs. Oh, it's too much, it's too much. I feel like driving down there and standing outside the window and watching them."

"That would be real cute," Carol said. "Clever. Sophisticated."

"But I'm *not* clever or sophisticated. I'm anxious and

jealous and miserable. I don't want Hank to have dinner with an old girl friend. I don't want him to have any old girl friends. Oh, this isn't fair. All my old boy friends are either in Massachusetts or Europe. God, God, he knows that while he's all dressed up, looking good, sharing an intimate evening with an old love, I'm stuck at home in my jeans with *you*."

"Thanks a lot," Carol said, handing Dale her scotch. "Drink this before you spill it all over yourself. Look, nothing is going to happen. Hank loves you. You know he loves you. Besides, you're both still free agents—that's what you want, isn't it? You've got to accept things like this. Now look, I've got work to do, and I know you've got papers to grade. Be a big girl and sit down with your drink and get into your work. That's the only cure."

"Oh, Christ," Dale said. She sat down on the sofa and grabbed up a pile of tests from the coffee table and plopped them onto her lap. But the tests might have been written in Swahili for all the sense she could make of them. "Carol," she said, throwing the tests back on the table and springing to her feet, "I'm going to call Lloyd Peterson. He's been wanting to take me out for weeks. I'll call him, go have a drink with him, dammit."

"But you don't even like the man," Carol said. "Oh, Dale, don't be so ridiculous. Think how awful it would be for you. Think how rotten you'd feel in the morning. And you don't know that Hank's going to like Leland. And if you do even go have a drink with Lloyd, you'll have him calling you constantly—he's a nice man, too, and you really shouldn't just use him. Oh, Dale, be sensible. Hank loves you. Why can't you trust him?"

"I don't know," Dale said. "I don't know! Why *can't* I trust him? Why do I feel so insanely jealous? Carol, I can't stand it. Oh, God, I just want to *break things*." Dale looked wildly about the apartment.

"I think you should go out for a walk," Carol said. "I mean it. It's a nice evening. Go out for a walk. Go out for a run. Run it off."

"All right," Dale said. "I will. I'll go run until I drop. But if Hank does sleep with her—then I'll, well, I will sleep with Lloyd and with any other man in Maine." She grabbed her sweater from the chair, slammed out the door, and clattered down the stairs.

Outside it was cool and bright, a fresh breezy early-May evening. Trees were greening up, and all the world about her held that particularly hopeful prettiness that spring brings. Daffodils. Tulips. Tender grass. Bikes and trikes and roller skates were scattered on driveways and porches. Birds twittered in trees; mothers called children in to bed. Dale stalked down the sidewalk, looking at it all with a jaundiced, nasty eye. Her breasts were too big, she thought, and her hair needed a good shaping, and her turtleneck was too warm and shabby. She felt just so god-damned furious that she wanted to kick a blossoming apple tree until the petals flew off and the tree fell over. "Oh, God, oh, God, oh, God," she muttered to herself, and kept on walking. Down the street, around the corner, over to the church, down toward the center of town.

So here it was again, the other side of love, the dark side: the pain, the doubt, the fear, the anger, the incredible and absolutely maddening vulnerability. Last week, when they had been eating comfortably together in Hank's kitchen, he had said, ever so casually, "Oh, I've been meaning to tell you. An old friend called today, Leland Hunter. She's coming up to Cotsworth-by-the-Sea next week for a three-day conference for art teachers. I'm going to go down next Thursday to have dinner with her."

"Oh, how nice," Dale had said. What else could she say? And truly then, even though jealousy was stinging at her heart like a wasp, she had said to herself, be calm, you can handle this. But of course Hank had been sitting there with her then, he had been with *her*, not with his old girl friend. It had taken all of her self-control not to ask, "Just how close an old friend is she? Is she prettier than I am? Have you slept with her? Will you sleep with her?"

Oh, she could not understand it, she could not. She was a reasonable person: why did she feel that she wouldn't be satisfied until she had Hank locked away forever in some room in her house where no one else could touch him? Why did she feel so possessive? And how would she ever manage to be satisfied? She had been in love with Hank for almost eight months now, and the force of it continued to grow rather than diminish or even stabilize. Dale slowed in her walking and began to study the houses she passed by, thinking: had all the men and women now living such apparently placid lives in these attractive houses at one time been as insane with love as she? She stopped at a corner and leaned against a tree and looked up and down the blocks around her. All those houses, full of families: now she knew why marriage was such an enormously popular institution. It was the only alternative to unbearable madness. Undoubtedly some of the married people inside those houses were awfully bored by now—but how glad Dale would be, how delighted, to be sitting watching some TV show with Hank, bored and casual in his presence. Boredom seemed suddenly such an enviable state. Oh, how hard life was. She wasn't sure she could really believe in *God*, Dale thought, but she could easily believe in Love: personified, Love would be as artlessly attractive as Don Hepplewhite, the lanky blond senior who played quarterback at the high school; he would look just as sweet and innocent and adorable—and he would play the same mischievous, hurtful, unnecessary tricks.

Dale looked at her watch: forty minutes had passed since Hank's call. He would be with Leland now. Had they

embraced? Had his heart jumped to see her? Whenever
Dale saw Hank, as he entered her apartment and said a
pleasant hello to Carol, or came walking up the sidewalk to
the school, Dale always felt that someone had just slugged
her behind her knees with a baseball bat; she nearly fell
over with love every time. Would he feel that way on seeing Leland? My God, what if he did? And what if Leland
felt that way, too? And what if she invited him up to her
room for an intimate drink before dinner?

Dale started walking again. Hank had not said that he
would call her when he got back from the dinner, and she
had had too much pride to ask him. Every night for
months now they had talked with each other on the phone
the last thing before going to sleep. If they didn't talk tonight, it would break some kind of spell, some kind of
chain—oh, if he slept with Leland, Dale would just die.
She would *hit* him if he slept with Leland, she would grab
a skillet from the rack and whack him on the head with it,
then shove him from her apartment and tell him never to
bother her again. And then she'd sleep around and sleep
around, just to show Hank—to show him what? For she
did not want to sleep with any other man. She did not
want to shove Hank from her life. But how could he be so
insensitive? How could he not know how terribly he was
hurting her? But what could she have done? She had too
much pride to say: Please don't go see her. Please don't
sleep with her. Please at least promise me you won't sleep
with her. How goddamned nonchalant he was. Was it possible that he did not realize that she would be jealous if he
had dinner with an old girl friend? Was it possible that he
would not be jealous if she had dinner with an old boy
friend?

Dale crossed the square and began to walk down the
main street. She slowed her pace, hoping the objects in the
shopwindows would distract her. Kites, books, medicine,

crazy T-shirts, leather boots, toys, scarves: these objects and the glass and bricks and wood that surrounded them seemed less physically real and less spiritually necessary than merely the word that named her lover: *Hank*. Other people fell in love and lived through nights of jealousy, but how? How did one fight it off? With walking, or alcohol, or sleep? How did one make the time pass? How could she make the time pass until tomorrow, when she would talk to Hank, to find out if he had slept with Leland? How would she make this evening pass, when she was here, alone on an empty street in the spring, and he was there, in a hotel with another woman? Jealousy dogged her steps. She wanted to lean up against a storefront and sob against the cold reflective glass.

"Hello, Miss Wallace, how ya doin'?"

A kid on a bike—for a moment she could not think of his name—slammed to a stop in the street beside her.

"Hi," she said, smiling. It was Benny, a dull sweet boy from one of her biology classes. He had terrible acne and crooked teeth; she felt suddenly sorry: who would ever fall in love with him? "Isn't it lovely that spring's here at last?" she asked, and at the same time thought: look at me, I can still speak normally, he has no idea just what kind of raging maniac I am at this moment.

"Yeah," Benny said. "I can't wait till it gets warm and we can go in the ocean. And I really can't wait till school's out. No offense."

"Oh, there you are!" someone called.

Dale turned: a pretty girl with her blond hair braided and tied with striped ribbons wheeled up on her bike and came to a grinning stop facing Benny. "Mom said just an hour," she said to Benny. "I've got homework."

"Okay," Benny said to the girl, and to Dale, "See ya." He turned his bike around and went riding off next to the girl, casually showing off by taking his hands off the handlebar and sticking them in his windbreaker.

Dale watched the two kids disappear around the corner, and when she turned back to the storefront she saw in the reflection of the glass that she was smiling. So even pimply little Benny had a girl friend; oh, it was the way of the world. Something in her heart went out to them, and came back pleased.

Love was magic. It tracked her steps like a jealous beast, and then suddenly changed forms and came grinning along easily: two young kids riding on bikes. Perhaps the reason that Benny was so dull in class was that he was daydreaming about that girl, who had taken the trouble to tie pretty striped ribbons in her hair. "Save me, Benny," Dale whispered, and nodded her head and began to walk back down the street toward home. She felt for a moment slightly lifted up out of herself, as if she were not for a moment quite human, as if she could see it all, the patterns of life. And they would save her, Benny and all the other students who came into her classroom and confronted her on the streets of the town where she lived. They expected her to be someone: Miss Wallace, a grown-up and teacher, competent and all of a piece, strolling down the street enjoying the fresh spring air. Dale had signed up for courses at the university in Portland for that summer and the next fall. She wanted to get her master's in education. It had been suggested to her by Mr. Hansen, the school principal, and some of the other teachers that she should become a counselor because she worked so well with the students, because they liked her so much, and she so obviously liked them. She had been asked to chaperone all the dances and major school activities, and she had been pleased and complimented by their favoritism. Oh, she did like the students, they refreshed her so. They *would* save her.

No. She would save herself.

Dale walked quickly back to her apartment, jealousy still chasing at her heels, biting at her heart, but she kept ahead of it, determined. She went up the stairs as hurriedly as she had come down them, and once inside the apartment went immediately to the coffee table to pick up the tests she had to grade.

"Hi," Carol said, "I made some popcorn. Want a bowl?"

"Sure," Dale said. She took off her jacket, hung it up, gathered together her necessary papers and pens and grade-books and settled down on the sofa to work. She read: "The two functions of the root of a plant are: 1. to anchor the plant to the ground. 2. to provide the intake of nutrients for the plant." The student had given the right answers. So. She had taught him something, even if it was only how to study for a test. Jealousy danced about, waving enticing colors, just at the periphery of Dale's vision, but she focused on the tests, on the clarity of the white paper, the strength of the black or blue ink, the solemnity of the answers. From time to time, as she stopped to eat some popcorn or record a grade, she felt jealousy teasing at her gnatlike, pulling her attentions away. Yes, jealousy was gnatlike, a pest, a carrier of pestilence, and although it stung at the edges of her mind, it flew in her soul. It originated in her very depths, in her stomach and heart; it bred right at the side of hope and love. It was the most destructive passion she had ever come across, for even now, as she held herself tightly together, forcing herself to work, forcing herself *not* to think of just what Hank was doing at this moment with Leland at the oceanside hotel, it stung at her with such force that tears came to her eyes. She bit at her lips, at her fingernails, at her hands. She chewed the erasers of the top of two marking pencils.

But she did a week's worth of work in one night. She graded all the tests, recorded all the grades, and prepared lesson plans for the next week. By ten o'clock she felt both totally exhausted, from all the work and from fighting back the allurements of jealousy, and strangely exhilarated. She could not keep from looking at her watch, wondering if Hank were on his way home now, or if he had gone up to the hotel room with Leland. That worry, that fear, filled her with an unpleasant energy. Yet she also felt triumphant. She stood in the bathroom in her blue nightgown and robe, brushing her teeth, glaring at herself in the mirror.

"Congratulations, Dale," she said to herself, grinning phonily through the toothpaste foam. "You made it through the evening. I'm proud of you. You deserve a great big scotch. Or maybe you'd better ask Carol for one of her magic pills. Or maybe she'd just better go on and knock you in the head and put you out of your misery. God, how will I get through the night? Shut up, Dale, you're a big girl now, you're going to go have a stiff scotch and crawl in bed and fall sound asleep instantly. No pills. Now shape up."

"Dale?" Carol asked from the other side of the bathroom door. "I hate to bother you when it sounds like you're having such a good conversation in there, but I thought you might like to know that Hank's here."

Dale was able to see in the mirror just how her expression changed at Carol's words. Her face broke into the most stupid and delighted smile she had ever seen on anyone. Her knees went weak. For a moment she thought she wouldn't be able to leave the bathroom. For a moment she thought: let me die right now while I'm so overcome with pleasure.

But she opened the door and went out into the living room. Hank was sitting on the sofa where she had spent her long grueling evening, and he smiled to see her come into the room.

"Hi," he said, casually, "want to come out to the farm and spend the night?"

Dale still grinned, dizzy with relief at the sight of him, but she spoke casually, "I don't know. Do I?" What she meant to say, but could not, was: Did you sleep with her? Did you kiss her? Do you love me? Can I trust you?

"You do," Hank said, and crossed the room and pulled Dale against him. They stood there a moment, simply holding each other. Carol cleared her throat and said loudly, "Well, good night, everyone, I'm going to bed."

"I'm in my nightgown," Dale muttered into Hank's coat.

"That's all right, we'll just be in the car and then the house, no one will see you. I'll bring you home in the morning in time to get ready for school."

"All right, then," Dale said. "Let's go."

In the car on the way to the farm she managed finally to say it, as nonchalantly as she could: "Did you have a good time tonight?"

"Oh, it was all right," Hank answered. "Leland's a nice girl, though a little screwed up, and to tell the truth I don't think she's all that bright. But she's pretty, and she's very nice. We had a good talk. I told her all about you."

"You did? What did you tell her?"

"Oh, what you look like, and what you do, and how you make me laugh, and how you've made me feel whole again, and how I love you, and that I want to marry you."

"And what did Leland have to say about all that?" Dale asked. She had to turn her face toward the window.

"She thought it was a wonderful idea. She thinks you sound perfect for me. She thinks I should ask you to marry me."

"I think I'd like to meet this woman." Dale laughed. "We could be the best of friends. How could you possibly think she's not bright? *I* think she sounds absolutely brilliant."

"Is that a yes?" Hank asked. He pulled the truck into the farm driveway and shut off the engine and turned to Dale.

"A yes?" Dale asked. "What do you mean?" Although of course she knew what he meant, and went cold all over with an emotion that was not quite just fear. She had been so giddy with relief at the sight of Hank, so childishly pleased that he had spoken about her to another woman, that she had let herself chatter away senselessly—and now what did she want to do?

"I mean to the question of marriage," Hank said, and took both her gloved hands in his, so that she could not turn away.

"Oh," Dale said. "Wow. Well."

"Look," Hank said, "we've got to talk about this sometime. I know how you feel about marriage. I know what you've been going through with your mother and sister. I don't want to frighten you or make you back off. But I do want to marry you. The first time I got married was to please my family; and it was a mistake. Now I want to please myself, and the only way I can do that is to plan to spend all my life with you. I really can't imagine ever being happy again without you in my life. I want to live with you, always."

"Oh, Hank," Dale said. "Never, ever, always. I'm so scared."

Hank pulled Dale into his arms and held her to him for a long time. The bright outside farm light shone against the window of the truck's cab in such a way that the glass acted as an imperfect mirror; Dale could see her reflection, her own solemn face. And it occurred to her that she would always have this: this gaze into her own eyes, this private vision, this single yet infinite certainty of self; she had come to attain that surety. Yet that knowledge gleamed back at her coldly—and how warm it was in Hank's arms, how deeply satisfying it felt to be held so dearly. Perhaps she could do it, she thought: paradoxes did exist. She could give herself; she could keep herself. There were no guarantees in life, but surely there was the chance that each marriage could be as different as each set of people. *Marriage.* Suddenly Dale shivered.

"You're cold," Hank said. "Let's go inside."

They went through the farmhouse silently, doing the routine chores they did every night when Dale was with Hank: checking to be sure the water bowl was filled for the dog and cats, pulling down the window shades against the night, turning down the furnace, shutting off the lights. If I marry Hank, Dale thought, this will be my home, I will live in this house with this man. She moved her hand against the doorframe of the bedroom and was pleased at the warm solidity of the wood, at the security of the definite, lasting structure. It all pleased her, this strong old house, the large capable presence of the man she loved moving through the dark and light rooms at her side: this is how it will be, Dale thought. She would help Hank clean house, she would eat meals with him, she would lie down again and again in this bedroom, and awaken to routine tasks. They would have their separate work and their mutual cares and pleasures, they would go out into the world together. They would push a grocery cart down brightly lighted aisles, seriously considering bread and mushrooms. Oh, it was lovely, that the world held such mundane, minute, trivial things by which to anchor down something as awesome and uncontrollable as love. People were clever, to surround themselves with such homely plain objects and habits that would keep them from floating off the earth with dread and joy.

They began to undress in the bedroom, still without

speaking, and Dale suddenly saw how straight and tense Hank was holding himself as he moved. Oh, he *cares*, Dale thought, he is concerned, he wants to know my answer, he wants to marry me. He loves me. He does love me.

"Hank," she said, but could not go on.

As if he knew her thoughts, Hank dropped his clothes on the bed and came to Dale; he took her in his arms and held her close against him. They stood together for a long moment then, body pressed against body, naked and trembling, warm breasts against chest, strong torsos touching all up and down, and Hank's generous giving genitals pushing out against Dale. Then Hank took Dale's head in his hands and pressed his mouth against hers and kissed and kissed her, as if he could not stop. All that he was, was coming toward her now, and searching against her, asking. Her face and Hank's were suddenly wet with tears; she did not know when she had started crying. She did not know precisely why. *Oh, Mother, oh, Daisy,* she thought, *oh, Hank, oh, love.*

She moved away from Hank. "Just a minute," she said. "I need to go to the bathroom." And she crossed the room and went into the safety of the bright common room and shut the door and leaned against it. What did she want? Earlier in the evening she had been driven with love for Hank, certain that she did love him, yearning for the security of marriage. But there, on the same breadth of land which held this house where they both now stood, across the miles of earth, there stood her mother and her sister, proof that love does not always work. And so what was she to do? How was she to decide? What was real?

She felt something moist against her thigh; she put her hand down and brought it back up, shining and wet with liquid from her body. She stared at her hand, glistening with the fluid of desire, and she thought, with a slow rush of understanding: *this is real.* God help me, this is real.

This is what is real in life, past words, past arranging, past all conscious intentions, past control. And she knew then, because of that real rich moisture, which flowed inside her in spite of the intricate troublings of her mind, because of that, simply that, she could change her life, surrender her life, give herself over to love, and let come what may. She loved Hank. Whatever the price she might have to pay in the future, it was worth it, it was all worth it. She loved Hank. She would believe what her body told her; she would marry him.

She went back into the bedroom where Hank sat waiting for her on the broad double bed. He rose when he saw her, but he did not speak.

"Well," she said, and her voice held solid though her body trembled, "well, then, let's do get married. Let's do get married, at least for a while." And she crossed the room, and went into his arms, and they embraced. And as they stood together she felt good from head to toe, she felt glad and strong, in her body and in her mind, she felt altogether good, and glad, and at peace, and right.

The last weekend in May was so warm that the beaches around Rocheport were busy with people of all ages and sizes, who had come out to soak up this first rich sun. Some of the bravest were going into the water even though it was still cold. Dale and Hank had come prepared for the day: they had brought blankets and beer, cold cuts and chips, books and towels. Dale lay on her stomach, feeling the heat of the sand rise up through the towel, feeling Hank's gentle hands as he spread lotion on her back. She was so happy. She had not realized that it was possible for real human beings to go on for so long being happy. She and Hank would be married in two weeks; they had told their various friends and families, and were making rather casual plans. They would be married in Rocheport, and would drive to Bar Harbor to take a ferry across to Newfoundland to spend two weeks vacationing there before they returned to begin their busy summer. Dale would take courses at the university; Hank would work on the farm, and begin renovating the farmhouse. They were buzzing with plans; it seemed that all the days of eternity could not give them enough time to do all that they wanted to do together. And they felt so *smug*, so smug about marriage, that society sanctioned such an institution that would enable them to greedily fulfill their lust for each other every day.

Margaret had written; she would fly back for the wedding and for a short visit; she was happy, she wrote, loving the bookstore and her own full life. Daisy could not come because of all the children, but she was happy, too, and during their phone conversations Dale had been amazed at the complete, unreserved delight with which Daisy had greeted Dale's plans for marriage.

"I'll probably get married again myself someday," Daisy had said. "You know, marriage is really so nice."

"Oh, Daisy," Dale had laughed, "*you* are so nice."

How they pleased her, her mother and her sister, how their optimism and the simple continuation of their lives pleased her; it made the whole world and all the actions in it seem possible. So one could go into good times and then into bad; but then one could go into bad times and out again into good. It was all possible, if one was brave.

"Do you want a beer?" Hank asked, breaking into Dale's thoughts. "I'm getting hungry."

"Umm," Dale said. She twisted around and sat up. "Yes, I'd love a beer. Where's the opener?" She rooted around in the basket she'd brought. "Sorry," she said, "I think I left it in the car."

"I'll get it," Hank said. He jumped up and raced off toward the car, and Dale smiled, filled with a silly vain pleasure to think that that tall lean lovely man would be her husband. How happy she was. She could not believe her happiness. Yet she accepted it, as one must accept what seems clearly a gift from God. She accepted it, she reveled in it; she let her love for Hank be the controlling force of her life—for how could she do otherwise?

Yet someone was crying. Dale glanced around, suddenly filled with dismay: how could anyone be crying on this sunny, fine day?

She saw a small child, a little boy of around five in red swimming trunks, standing a few feet from her, staring out at the ocean and rubbing his eyes and crying. She looked all about, but could see no parent in sight. She rose and padded across the soft sand and knelt down next to the little boy.

"What's wrong?" she asked. "Are you lost?"

"No," the little boy cried. "My mommy's back there, with my brother."

"Then why are you crying?" Dale asked. "What's wrong?"

"It's my plastic raft," the little boy said. He pointed to a bright yellow object that bobbed up and down on the waves of the ocean about twenty yards out. "Mommy told me not to let it go, but I did, and now it's gone out so far I've lost it. I can't get it back."

"Well, stop crying," Dale said. "I'll swim out and get it for you. Okay?" She rose, eager to do the deed, grinning with pleasure at a problem so easily solved.

The boy looked at her in amazement. "But you can't swim out that far," he said. "That's way out. That's dangerous."

Dale laughed. "No," she said. "It's not so far for a big person. And I'm a good strong swimmer. I won't drown."

And she walked to the edge of the water, and boldly plunged into the cold. She began to swim with even, strong, completely sure strokes, to rescue the toy for the child.

TEN

One Saturday in late May the sun came out strong and full and the entire day was golden and fresh and warm. Since it was a Saturday, all the girls on the third floor were free from work. Daisy heard them giggling up and down the back stairs, but paid little attention to them: she had so much to do. She had settled Danny and Jenny in front of the Saturday-morning cartoons on television and carried baby Susan with her in a backpack as she moved around the house tidying up. She was in the laundry room off the kitchen, folding diapers, when Sara and Ruth Anne burst in on her.

"You've got to come outside," they shouted at her. "It's just heaven. It's so warm!" They were both wearing startlingly bright bikinis, and their tight bellies shone with the whiteness of winter.

"Umm," Daisy said, "all right. In a while. I've got to fold this laundry."

"Well, *hurry!*" they told her, and turned away.

Daisy stood dumbly, a rectangle of white cotton cloth in her hands, and watched the two young women rush back out through the kitchen to the sun. Ruth Anne needs to lose a few pounds before she hits the public beaches in her bikini, Daisy thought to herself, then shrugged. Who was she to cast a critical eye? She wouldn't dare show up in a swimming suit, let alone a bikini. Oh, it wasn't fair. Those girls looked so fine, even with their bits of plumpness here and there, they looked so young and healthy and all of a piece that they fairly glowed with it. Even the way they moved, almost bouncing off the balls of their feet with their energy and enthusiasm for life—while Daisy still collapsed into a chair whenever she could. Daisy wanted to sink down into the pile of dirty laundry and cry. Susan had been born two months ago and after the euphoria of birth had worn off, the exhaustion remained. Susan still awoke at two in the morning for her feeding, and for the past week both Danny and Jenny had had colds and coughs. *They* managed to sleep through their coughing, but Daisy couldn't; she would lie in her bed, listening, so tired she felt she was drugged to the bone, saying to herself that if Jenny coughed again, she would get up and give her some more cough medicine. But she knew that if she woke Jenny to give her the medicine, she would have to rock her for a long while to get her back to sleep, and she felt simply too tired to deal with that. So she lay in her bed, waiting for one more cough, and then one more before she finally fell back to sleep. Susan liked to wake at six in the morning, and so Daisy began her days in a state of queasy dizziness, and not even the richest, creamiest coffee could get rid of her headache. Oh, it was hard, it was *so hard,* to be alone in the house, the sole protector and caretaker of three small children. The first month had been a little easier, because first Jane and then Karen had taken Danny and Jenny in their homes, and the four upstairs girls, entranced with the novel presence of a tiny baby, had volunteered to take care of Susan now and then during the day so that

Daisy could sleep. But now the novelty had worn off a bit, and although the girls still dropped in spontaneously to peek at the infant, they were more interested in their own lives, their clothes, boy friends, jobs, amusements. Daisy had to keep talking herself out of begrudging them their freedom, their irresponsibility. They're only eighteen and nineteen, she kept telling herself. I was free at that age, too, I didn't have to take care of children. But still she found herself making a bitter mouth from time to time as she compared her present state to that of the girls.

They were all giddy now about buying new spring clothes and rushed in to show Daisy clever little slips of dresses or a new shirt which they wore braless and tucked into their jeans. And Daisy would admire them appropriately—and she really did admire them, they did look so pretty, but she had to keep swallowing back her envy. She wanted those pretty, skimpy clothes, she wanted a pretty, skimpy body. Instead she was still wearing her loose old maternity clothes, because whenever she nursed she had enormous breasts and was unable to lose much weight. And she was far too tired to even think of exercising, although this time, as with the last two times, she had promised herself she would start immediately doing leg raises and waist bends. Now her own body seemed to her a loose collection of sagging sacks which she unceremoniously stuffed into yet another shapeless set of sacks so that she could go through her days. At least her hair looked good. She had left the children with a sitter one day and gone out to The Clip Joint where for two luxurious hours other people tended to her needs. They washed her hair and massaged her scalp and cut her hair into short crisp layers that she could wash easily in the shower and brush dry. She was pleased with the haircut, because it made her eyes look larger and her face look thinner, and even more so because it gave her such hope. Whenever she ran a brush through her hair, she released the fragrance of the perfumed shampoo she had chosen for herself, and she felt this fragrance fall around her briefly like a mist of hope: the pleasures of self-indulgence and vanity were all slowly coming back to her. Because of this new haircut, she had been brave enough to try to look really pretty, like the old Daisy she had been, for the meeting she had had yesterday with Paul.

Paul. Now he was out in California with Monica—with Monica, his new love, and his new job. He had called yesterday before he left town for good, to tell Daisy he would like to come over to say goodbye to Danny and Jenny and to see Susan. Daisy had washed and set her hair and put on makeup and then tried for over an hour to find some combination of clothes that would make her look attractive; she had ended up throwing almost everything she owned on the floor in despair. But she had vowed to herself that she would not let Paul see her again in her old baggy robe, and finally she had gotten into a pair of jeans which she could not zip and her favorite maternity smock which hung down over the gap where her stretch-marked belly protruded from the open zipper. Each time she bent or sat, the zipper bit into her belly, and the seam of the jeans pressed into her crotch, but she could tell by the mirror that at least she didn't look pregnant anymore, and perhaps she looked almost slim again. And she had been gratified by Paul's first words: "Why, Daisy, you're looking wonderful!"

"Thank you," she said shyly, as they stood in the front hall. "You look wonderful, too."

And he did: there he was, her husband—now her ex-husband—just as tall and handsome and lean as he had been the day he had walked out of her life. It was hard for her to look at him without loving him, in spite of everything. Whatever it had been that had caused her to love him at first was still at least partly there for her, and she had to turn her face away to hide the way she felt. "Would you like to see the baby? She's in the playpen in the kitchen."

She led Paul back through the house to the kitchen and together they stood and looked down at tiny, wriggly Susan, who was lying on her back, wearing one of Jenny's little old pink terry-cloth pajamas. She was cooing rapturously at her fist and trying to get it up to her face and into her mouth. Daisy leaned on the playpen, looking down, instantly amazed all over again at how healthy, how well formed, how really adorable her baby was. Who could resist falling in love with such a lovely child, she thought— and then looked up at Paul and saw, with a plunge in her heart, that he could, *he* could.

"Would you like to hold her?" Daisy asked.

Paul looked uncomfortable, but "Sure," he said.

Daisy bent over and took the baby out of the playpen, carefully supporting the wobbly head. Paul took his daughter into his arms with a conscious awkwardness. He studied her for a while. "She's pretty," he admitted at last. "And she doesn't look at all like Danny or Jenny."

"I know," Daisy said. "I think she's going to look like Dale. Although I'm not sure yet that her eyes will be brown; they seem to be getting lighter."

Paul, obviously aware that he should do something, gently bounced the infant against him for a minute and said with forced heartiness, "Well, she's certainly all there. But she's so light. I'd forgotten how small babies are."

Susan began to root around against his chest, searching with her mouth for a milky breast, nuzzling at him with her whole face, pushing at him with tight demanding fists. This always made Daisy go weak in the knees with love, but Paul brought Susan away from him, held her out to Daisy and said, "Could you put her back now? I'd do it, but I'm afraid I might drop her."

So Daisy took the baby and settled her in the playpen,

and busied herself awhile adjusting the pads and giving the baby a pacifier and a pink rattle in the shape of a flower. So this was the contact that her third child would have with its father, she thought grimly, and struggled to hold back tears. Poor baby, she thought, poor little father-less girl—and poor, lonely, pitiful me. For a moment she felt almost overcome with self-pity.

"Where are Danny and Jenny?" Paul asked. "I brought them a little present."

"They're on the third floor with the girls," Daisy said. "I'll call them." She went to the back stairs and called up to her children that their father was there, then turned back to find Paul staring at her with an expression she could not fathom. In the clear afternoon light it seemed almost that he was looking at her with love.

"You look tired, Daisy," Paul said. "I mean you look awfully pretty, but you look tired, too."

"I *am* tired," Daisy said. "It isn't easy."

"I know. I know." Paul sank down into a kitchen chair and put his head in his hands a moment, then looked back up at Daisy. "I'm sorry about all this, you know. Or maybe you don't know. Maybe you can't know how sorry I am. I feel I've fucked up so badly. I mean the children— I wish people could somehow keep from making mistakes. Or I wish at least we could erase them."

"Mistakes?" Daisy asked. She had to lean against the doorway for support; she was unnerved by Paul's sudden willingness to talk, and by the way he was looking at her. "Do you think of the children as mistakes? Would you erase them if you could?"

"Oh, I know it sounds heartless to you, and I don't mean it that way. But yes, I suppose I do think of the children as mistakes. We were so happy before the children came, Daisy; I keep remembering our first two years together, I keep thinking of those years over and over again.

We had such good times. I felt we were on our way somewhere together. And then the children came and stopped
everything, threw everything off track. We never got to go
to Europe together, we never got to enjoy having money
together, we hardly even got to know each other. I love
Monica now, but I can't say I love her any more than I
loved you at first, and I hate it that my life is so messed up
and fragmented this way. God, Daisy, before the children
you were so happy, so lighthearted, so full of laughter and
good ideas, I loved being with you. There's no one like you
in the world, you know. Monica's wonderful, but she's so—
serious, often. You were just such a pleasure in my life. I
loved knowing someone like you."

"Oh, *Paul*," Daisy said, "I'm still that person. Or I can
be that person again. I still have fun, I still laugh—" For
one wild instant a great hope sprang up within her, a silly
false television commercial sort of vision of herself and her
three children and Paul all walking along the edge of the
lake, frolicking, loving each other, being a family. In her
eagerness she found herself crossing the room to stand at
the table next to Paul's chair. She put her hand on his
shoulder. How solid he was, how hard, how big. A man.
She felt the old sexual desire move through her like a current from her hand on his strong firm arm down through
her body.

"I know, Daisy, I know," Paul said. "But it's too late. It
really is. I just don't like children. I don't like living with
them, I don't like having to focus my life around their
needs. I've thought about this a lot, and I know I'm being
selfish, I'm horribly selfish, but I had so little chance when
I was growing up to do what *I* wanted, and I want to be in
control of my own life now. I have to have my life. I want
to enjoy my pleasures."

At his words Daisy took her hand away and started to

move off, but to her surprise Paul grasped her hand in both of his and sat staring up at her.

"But I'll always love you, Daisy," he said. "*You*. In my own way. I'll always be sorry that it worked out this way, that you needed to have children, that you weren't satisfied with just me, and that I'm not capable of having children in my life. I've been wanting to tell you this for a long time —that I'll always love you. In my way. I— Well, I've brought you a present. You mustn't laugh. It's a sort of goodbye present. I got it on impulse yesterday. I was driving the car and I heard this song on the radio, and it seemed to say just what I feel. So I stopped at the first record store I came to and bought it for you. It's in the sack with the presents for the children. It only cost about two dollars, it's not much, but—I just wanted you to have it."

"What does it say? How does it go?"

"I can't remember it all. You'll have to hear it yourself. But the refrain is—oh, God, I'm sorry to be so corny—the refrain is—" And Paul rose awkwardly and stood just a small distance from Daisy, looking shy and endearingly embarrassed. "It goes—'when you remember me, if you remember me, try to see it's not the way I want it to be. For I'd be with you now, but wherever you go, my love goes with you.'"

"*Paul*—" Daisy said, and tears of real anguish came into her eyes. She longed to go to Paul, to embrace him, and damn it, damn it, not to let him go.

"Hi, Daddy!"

"DADDY! DADDY DADDY DADDY!"

And Danny and Jenny were suddenly there, stampeding down the back stairs and into the kitchen with all their childish wild energy unleashed. They rushed at Paul, meaning to attack him in their love, and Jenny fell over a chair leg and began to cry, angry at falling down, angry at not being able to reach her father as Danny had.

Paul and Daisy looked at each other; they exchanged the last strong look they would ever share, a look full of love and regret and—inescapably—of irony. "See?" Paul seemed to say. "See?" Then he and Daisy released each other from this shared gaze and Paul bent to pick up his son.

"Come here, Jenny, don't cry, sit on Daddy's lap and let me kiss your knee where you hurt it," he said.

Daisy turned away and walked into the other room for a moment. She simply leaned against the wall, struggling to regain her breath and her sense of composure. When she went back to the kitchen, Paul was standing.

"I have to go now, kids," he said. "But I've brought you a present. I left it in the front hall."

Like some kind of roiling mob, Paul and Danny and Jenny and Daisy made their way back through the house to the front door where Paul had left a plastic sack sitting on the floor. He took out two presents: a fat baby doll for Jenny and a circus train set for Danny. The children squealed at their presents and immediately thumped down on the floor to inspect them.

"And this is for you, Daisy," Paul said, and handed her one thin 45-rpm record in its paper jacket. Then he kissed her lightly on her cheek and put on the coat he had flung across a hall chair and went hurriedly out the door.

Daisy stared at the closed door for a moment—the last, the final door which Paul would close against her—then said absentmindedly to the children, "What wonderful presents Daddy brought you," and walked past them to the living room to put the record on the stereo. The music swelled out at her, melodramatic and sweeping, and Daisy stood next to the stereo and cried and cried and cried, until Susan's fierce wails called her away from her own misery and made her go tend to her child. She picked her baby up and laid her on the kitchen table and put a clean diaper on her and put the soiled one in the diaper pail. She got a can of beer out of the refrigerator and poured it into a glass, speaking to Susan in a lulling voice all the while, "There, there, I'll feed you in a moment." She went into the family room and sank onto the sofa and began to nurse the baby. After a while Danny and Jenny came into the family room, complaining: Jenny wanted to see Danny's new train set, but Danny didn't want to share it right now, he had just gotten it, he didn't have a chance to even look at it himself, Jenny was selfish and greedy, she had a new doll and he didn't want to see her doll, and so on, and so on, until Daisy found herself nearly screaming:

"Jenny, you can look at the train set later. Leave Danny alone now and play with your doll. It's a lovely new doll. And be quiet, you're scaring the baby with your noise."

"Dumb old baby," Jenny said, and shot Susan a resentful glare. She took her new doll off to hide behind a big stuffed chair, and Daisy could hear her crying quietly to herself. If it hadn't been for the nursing baby, Daisy would have gone over and taken her elder daughter in her arms, but Susan was really engaged now in the business of getting her food, and would have been enraged to be disturbed. So Daisy had to sit and listen to Jenny sniffling behind the chair, and to Danny making his new toy clack and whistle, and she worried that once again she wasn't doing the perfect thing. It was so hard to keep three children happy at the same time. And Daisy was actually worried about Jenny. Danny was okay, he was not going to have the same problem with jealousy, but then of course he had the preschool. He was able to leave the house every day, to leave the baby's presence, and to enter a world of his own where people had never even seen the baby, where people knew and loved and played with him. He had all of that to sustain him. But Jenny was just two, too young yet for preschool, and used to being the baby. Now here was this new baby, this baby *girl* who always seemed to have the dominant spot in the household. That morning, while fixing breakfast, before Paul arrived, Daisy had turned just in time to stop Jenny from dropping a heavy skillet in the playpen on top of the baby.

"JENNY!" she had screamed, and rushed toward her daughter and yanked the skillet away. "Shame on you! You must never do anything like that again! Why, you could kill your little sister, or hurt her very badly!"

Jenny had glared at her mother for one long moment, her eyes full of anger and frustration, then she had run from the kitchen into the family room, where she collapsed in tears.

Daisy's scream had startled Susan, who burst into her piercing cry, and the eggs were sizzling in their pan, needing turning, and the toast was drying in the toaster, and the phone rang.

"Oh, my God," Daisy said, not knowing which way to turn first. Then she grabbed up baby Susan and tried to comfort her against her body with one hand, while with the other she attempted to turn the eggs, which was almost impossible because the skillet kept wobbling around on the burner. The phone rang and rang.

"The phone's ringing, Mommy," Danny said.

"Well, it will just have to ring!" Daisy had said frantically. She took the burned toast out of the toaster and threw it in the sink and stuck two more slices of bread in, and cuddled the baby, saying rapidly, "There, there, there, there, you're okay now." Then she put the baby back in the playpen and hurried back to the stove to finish the eggs. The phone stopped ringing. Daisy buttered the toast, fixed everyone's plate, and hurried into the family room. She knelt down beside her daughter, nearly falling over in her awkwardness, and tried to gather Jenny into her arms. Jenny's face was tear-streaked and blotchy, a sign that she was truly upset.

"I'm sorry I yelled at you, Jenny," she said. "Please don't cry anymore. Oh, Jenny, let Mommy cuddle you a moment. I love you so much, I love you as much as I love the baby, and she will grow up to be a wonderful little friend for you, you just have to give her some time. Come on, don't let your breakfast get cold. I'll let you put honey on your toast from the honey bear."

But Jenny resisted Daisy's advances; she pulled away and shrugged up into herself.

"Jenny, please," Daisy said. She heard the phone begin to ring again. Who could be calling? she wondered, everyone knew better than to call at this time of day. "Jenny, come on," she said in a firmer voice. "Your breakfast is ready, and if you don't eat it you'll be cranky all morning, and I'm not going to fix you anything else to eat. Come on, sweetie, come on with Mommy."

"The baby's choking!" Danny yelled.

"Oh, *shit*," Daisy said, and left her surly daughter to sulk alone behind the chair. She pushed her weary body back up off the floor and rushed into the kitchen to pick up Susan who was trying to cry with the pacifier in her mouth. "There, there, damn it," Daisy said, picking the baby up once again. She took the pacifier out of Susan's mouth and cuddled her against her, and Susan peed through her diaper and pajamas right down the front of Daisy's robe, soaking through the thick material into her nightgown and onto her skin. How could one small baby have so much urine inside her? Then she smelled the horrid smell and realized it was not just urine; she looked down at her robe and the baby's pajamas and her hands, and saw everything stained with a mustardy-brown goo.

"I'm thirsty, Mommy, where's my juice?" Danny asked. He had already seated himself at the table and had finished his breakfast.

"You'll just have to *wait*," Daisy told him. "I've got to

go change everything, this baby just pooped all over me."

Danny thought that that was hysterically funny, and Daisy trudged out of the kitchen and through the hall and up the stairs to the sounds of his silly laughter, and Jenny's persistent sobbing, and the shrill ringing of the telephone, and over it all, the baby's angry yells. She changed Susan and deposited her in her crib, then went into her bedroom to strip off her murky clothes. When she got back downstairs, she found Jenny still crying, her own breakfast turned cold and congealed on the plate, and Danny standing in a puddle of orange juice because he had tried unsuccessfully to pour himself his own drink. His pajamas were soaked with orange juice and he was crying. And it was only eight o'clock in the morning.

That very afternoon, there Daisy was again, listening to Jenny cry as she hid behind the chair. Paul's presence had been only a momentary fluke in the pattern of the day; he had not changed a thing. Daisy took Susan off her right breast and held her over her shoulder to burp her, and the baby expelled such a quantity of milk that Daisy felt her blouse totally soaked; she had forgotten to put a diaper on her shoulder. She glanced behind her to find that some of the fluid had hit the sofa, too, and was sinking in fast. Oh, the mess of it all, the *mess*, she thought. She had forgotten the mess of it all. Each morning she awoke with aching breasts and her nursing bra and nightgown and sheets dried to a starchy stiffness from the milk she had leaked in her sleep. "I should wear paper clothes and sleep in the bathtub," she said to no one in particular. Susan started to fuss again, so Daisy fastened her onto her left breast and just sat there, letting the milk dry on her blouse and on the sofa, listening to her other daughter cry.

Now Daisy stood in the laundry room with a diaper in her hand, remembering yesterday, which with the exception of Paul's visit seemed like all the other days, which were scrambled together in one jumbled blur. And she thought that Paul was a fink, that he had cheated, that he had encroached on her emotions with a cheap and maudlin trick by bringing her that tacky sentimental record, by telling her he loved her. If he loved her, he could show it with actions instead of words. She had let him get away with a trashy trick, she had let him go off with a soothed conscience, and here she was left in the ruins. "My love goes with you" were the last words of the song, and Daisy had tried to comfort herself since Paul's visit with those words, had tried to support herself by thinking that Paul's love was with her. But it was not, not in any way. It did not make one minute of her life any easier. It was not in any real way there. And what she needed from life at that moment was not that particular lie. Daisy dropped the diaper on top of the dryer and went into the living room. She picked the record up off the stereo, carried it into the kitchen, and swiftly snapped it in half, then dropped it in the trash. For some reason that deed gave her immense satisfaction.

Movement out the window caught her eye, and she saw that all four upstairs girls were settling themselves on the back lawn in different poses of hedonism. They had brought out blankets and towels and were lying on the ground, letting their bodies soak up the new spring sun. They had a portable radio, and cheerfully chatted above the sound of the music; they had glasses of Coke and a tray of cheese and crackers and apples nearby. Oh, it looked so nice, it looked so pleasurable. But Daisy turned away with resentment: it was *her* lawn, and yet she would have to stay away from it today; it wouldn't be fair to spoil the girls' day off by bursting into their luxurious afternoon with three noisy rambunctious children. The girls were really such nice girls, and she was so glad to have their company—and their rent money—that she didn't want to strain their relationship in any way. She decided to put Susan in the carriage and take all the children for a walk. But first she really did have to finish folding the laundry so that she could put the clothes from the washer into the dryer. She still had a pile of wet smelly sheets to launder: Danny had started wetting the bed at night, and in addition to the extra work this caused, having to carry the soggy sheets and mattress pad down the stairs and back up again, she had the burden of worry: perhaps Danny was in his own way jealous of the baby, too, and this was his way of expressing it. She turned back wearily to the diapers. After a while Danny and Jenny clamored into the laundry room, screeching at her about a toy they were fighting over, and Daisy really could not get too angry with them, for they had played very nicely together all morning while she did the necessary housework.

"I'll take you outside in a minute, kids," she said. "It's nice and warm out. I'll take you for a walk. Danny, you can ride your bike. You've been wanting to all winter and it's finally nice enough out."

"Yay! Yay! Can we go now, can we go now?" Danny yelled.

"In a minute, I have a few more things to do," Daisy said. "Go play in the family room just a few more minutes."

"Will you pull me in the wagon, Mommy?" Jenny asked, tugging on Daisy's robe.

Daisy stared down at her blue-eyed daughter, her elder girl, and wanted to cry. Jenny was too young to manage a trike, and last summer Daisy had pulled her everywhere in a wagon. But now she had to push Susan in the carriage; she wouldn't be able to manage the wagon, too. But that wouldn't be fair to Jenny; what could she do? It seemed she was continually shorting this second child of hers, this little child, because of the new baby.

"Sure," Daisy said finally. "Sure I will, sweetie. But we'll have to put baby Susan in, too. She won't take up much room." She could pad the wagon bottom and sides with blankets, Daisy thought, and there wouldn't be too many bumps on the sidewalk, and Jenny could sit with her feet scrunched up—

The phone rang. Daisy halfheartedly plodded into the kitchen to answer it, the two children trailing along beside her. Both children seemed more than ever jealous of her when she talked on the telephone; the phone ringing acted like a radar on them, drawing them to her, causing them to cling and pull at her arms and legs.

"Daisy? This is Jim Duncan," a man said. "How are you?"

Jim Duncan, Daisy thought, Jim Duncan; who in the world is he? "I'm sorry," Daisy said, trying to keep the long phone cord from strangling Jenny, who was tugging on it and managing to get it wound around her neck.

The man laughed. "*Dr.* Duncan," he said. "I sort of delivered your baby."

"Oh!" Daisy said, amazed. She had often thought of the man after she left the hospital, smiling at herself to remember how nice he had been, how special he had made her first night in the hospital with his present of hot cheeseburgers. And when she had gone to the enormous doctor's clinic for her recent checkup, she had asked her old obstetrician if he knew the young doctor. But he hadn't, and Daisy had let the idea of the man fall away, thinking she would never see him again. She couldn't imagine why he was calling her now. Danny and Jenny began to squabble loudly right at her feet, and Daisy made hideous faces and gestures at them, trying to get them to be quiet and back off so that she could hear and think and carry on an intelligent conversation. She was glad Jim Duncan couldn't see her now; he would think she was mad, but she could think of no other way to suggest silently to her children that they let her talk. So she spoke pleasantly to Jim Duncan, and simultaneously grimaced and lunged at her children, who fortunately went completely still with wonder at this strange sight.

Jim Duncan was calling to invite her out to dinner! Something a little better than cheeseburgers this time, he said. And perhaps a movie if she thought she could leave her infant for that long a time.

A bottle, Daisy thought, Susan can have a bottle for just one time, and if she doesn't like it, tough, she'll survive, let the babysitter handle her, she decided with a quick giddy surge of rationality. She had never missed nursing her first two children until they were three months old; but things were different now. The thought of an evening out, a long evening spent entirely with a pleasant adult male, was too enticing. They made plans for the following Friday evening.

Hanging up the phone, Daisy felt that the world had changed entirely. She sank down onto a kitchen chair and absentmindedly pulled both her son and her daughter onto her lap and kissed them on their necks.

"Mommy has a date, Mommy has a date," she sang to her children.

"What's a date?" Danny asked.

"It's like a fig," Daisy said, and laughed hysterically at her dumb joke. Something had snapped, or popped, inside her, something had changed. She had been wallowing in her martyred motherhood long enough, she realized, and now she would stop, she would change just a little bit. Now she would be brave and call Jerry; he had called twice after Susan's birth to say that as soon as she felt like going out or having company in, he would like to see her. So she would see him, and she would see Jim Duncan, and she would let herself add this new dimension to her world, she would force herself to do it. For she knew that in spite of the difficulties of the isolated world she had shared with her three children over the past two months she had still felt safe and comfortable, secure. Now she was ready, perhaps, to feel something else, something a bit more challenging. Perhaps, she thought, perhaps she would even start doing exercises today. But then she looked through the kitchen at the laundry room, and her heart sank.

Lord, it was still all there, waiting to be done, the stinky sheets, the mountains of diapers waiting to be folded, the whole bit. By the time she finished that, and finished pulling Jenny and Susan in the wagon and watching to see that Danny didn't ride his bike into the street, she wouldn't have the energy to do exercises; if she lay down on the floor to try, she would probably fall asleep. Oh, it was hopeless. Hopeless and seemingly endless.

"Aren't you ever coming out?"

Daisy looked up to see Sara and Allison standing in the back doorway, staring at her.

"I still haven't finished the laundry," Daisy told them. "Besides, I don't want to bother you girls. You look so peaceful out there."

"Oh, *God*," Sara said, entering the kitchen. "You sound just like my mother. 'You girls just go on and enjoy yourselves, have a good time, and don't worry about me in here suffering away in the cold.' Geez, Daisy, I thought you were better than that. It's a good thing you have us around to shape you up before you start doing that number on Danny and Jenny."

"I'll fold the laundry," Allison said. "It'll take me five minutes."

"No, no," Daisy said, "I've got to wash the sheets, too."

"Well, I can probably handle that," Allison said. "I've been known to be capable of such things. A little soap,

stuff them in the machine, press a button; I don't think it
will wear me down too much."

"And I'll take Danny and Jenny on outside with me,"
Sara said. "You go take off that horrible robe and get into
some shorts. You're beginning to look about as healthy as a
slug."

"Thanks a lot," Daisy said, but she had to fight back
tears: how nice these girls were, how nice.

"The kids have some sand pails and shovels in the garage, don't they?" Sara asked, already heading back out the
door, holding each child by the hand.

"Yes," Daisy said, "way at the back, by the garden hose.
Well, they might be hidden by some boxes, I'll come help
you find them—"

"Daisy," Sara said, turning and fixing Daisy with a look,
"cool it. Go change your clothes. You don't have to do everything. Finding sand pails is not a major operation." And
she walked away, leading Danny and Jenny with her.

Daisy walked up the stairs, smiling to herself, and
slipped into an old pair of maternity shorts and a short-
sleeved cotton shirt. She peeked in the baby's room and
saw that Susan was still soundly sleeping, so she went on
down the stairs. Allison was still in the laundry room, singing a rock song to herself and folding the diapers with a
flippancy that came from knowing it wasn't the thou-
sandth time that week she had done such a thing. "Go on
out," she told Daisy. "I'll be through here in a minute."

The sun almost blinded Daisy as she walked out into it,
and the warmth made her stop still. She felt like an animal, she just wanted to stay there, absorbing the soothing
heat.

"Come on, old lady," Ruth Anne called. "We've got
you all set up."

And they had. They had dragged out a folding plastic
lounge chair from the garage and set it down near the

water. Danny and Jenny were already on the sand, building
sand castles with the help of Sara and Melissa. Daisy sank
into the chair and put her feet up, almost stunned by her
sudden good fortune.

"Here," Ruth Anne said. "Have a Coke." She handed
Daisy a tall glass filled with icy cola, and a pile of magazines with pictures of gorgeous women in brilliant summer
clothes grinning on the covers.

"This is so nice of you all," Daisy said.

"Oh, I know, I know," Ruth Anne said. "We're just piling up points in heaven like crazy." Then she went back
and stretched out on her towel.

Daisy sat for a long moment staring at the magazines
before she realized she didn't want to read them. Later,
maybe, but not now. Now she wanted simply to sit, letting
herself take in the delicious warmth of the sun. This was a
rare day, she knew, for it would be cool and rainy again before it got really warm and bright, but change was in the
air: spring was here. Spring was here, and summer was
close, and when fall came Danny and Jenny would both be
going to preschool. By the time the weary winter rolled
around again, she would be able to have some time free to
herself while her baby napped and her children were off in
the afternoons. She had come out of the winter, she had
come out of the worst time in her life, and all sorts of
warm and pleasurable things lay ahead. Why, her life was
manageable after all; after all, her life was even happy.

Jenny and Danny jumped up from their sand castles and
began to gather sticks and rocks and shells to decorate
them; Danny had taken off his shirt and his pale skin
gleamed in the sunlight. Daisy watched her children,
pleased at the sight of their small bodies. Just past them,
the bright blue of the lake stretched out endlessly, the
waves peaking up and down gently, flashing sparks of light
when the sun hit just the right way. How beautiful the

water was, Daisy thought, and how fortunate she was to be able to live near it. How fortunate she was to be able to sit out here on this luminous day, basking in the warmth of the sun, looking at the expanse of dancing blue. Yet it was the presence of her son and daughter, running back and forth by the water that pleased her most, she realized. She found them by far the most beautiful; they were so compact, so complete, so delineated and defined. She could gather them up in her arms and squeeze their solid responsive flesh; she could gather them against her in a way she could never hold the water. And it was that that she loved, she realized, it was the flesh. She loved the flesh, the sight, the textures, the smells, she loved the flesh best.

She stared at her children, marveling at them, stroking them in her thoughts, running her hands over their firm miraculous heads, down over their vulnerable necks, their delicately framed rib cages, their busy energetic arms. Their stomachs, she loved their fat full comical protruding stomachs, and she loved, oh, she *loved* their thighs, thighs so stuffed with life that they seemed full to bursting. Oh, the fat sweet goodness of the flesh, Daisy thought, it was so substantial, so receptive, so real. Now even the fatigue that mellowed her very bones seemed sweet, seemed pleasurable; she felt her body flowing with the pleasure of life.

So she did not have regrets. She did not regret her marriage to Paul, because it had brought her all this: her children, her house by the water. She did not regret the divorce, because it had brought her herself. She had learned to manage, she had learned to cope. So far she had made her life come out as she wanted it, she had arranged life more or less to her satisfaction. Someday she would come to love a man again, because someday the flesh of her children would not suffice and she would desire something larger and different—and if she was attractive to Jim Duncan and Jerry Reynolds now, now when she looked worse than she ever had in her life, then surely as the months went by and she was able to manage such monumental activities as losing some weight and doing exercises, surely she would find men who would want to touch her and love her and someday even share her life. What was not possible? Everything was possible. Daisy felt strong and immensely vital. She felt happy.

She heard Allison come out the kitchen door and looked over her shoulder to see the young girl walking out into the sun, carrying baby Susan in her arms.

"Don't worry," Allison said. "I heard her cry and thought she might like to join us out here. I've changed her and everything. She can hang around with us on the blanket for a while. We haven't had a good chat for several days. I've got to tell her about my date last night. She's two months old; it's about time she started learning about men."

Daisy watched as Allison and Ruth Anne settled the baby on the blanket. She listened for a moment as the two girls chattered to each other about the men they had been with the night before. Susan hunched about on the blanket, cooing and drooling, perfectly content. Daisy turned back to the sight of the water, thinking how nice these girls were, how nice. How nice life could be, she thought; I must remember this. I must save the memory of this afternoon to carry me through some rainy night.

And so she sat, relaxed and warm, buffeted by the sounds of her laughing moving children and her friends, and watched the sun sparkle on the water with a radiance that almost equaled the radiance of life.

1

(9,5/21)